D0129297

THE JAMAICA STATION

The Third Carlisle & Holbrooke Naval Adventure

Chris Durbin

Chris Durbin

To

The Royal Navy's

Principal Warfare Officer's Course

Number 184

HMS Collingwood

October 2017 to October 2018

The Jamaica Station

Editor: L.M. Durbin

Cover designed by Book Beaver.

ISBN: 9781720266334

Chris Durbin
Visit my website at www.chris-durbin.com

First Edition: 2018

Chris Durbin

CONTENTS

Chris Durbin

LIST OF CHARTS

THE SEVEN YEARS WAR

Pitt's Maritime Strategy Starts to Bite

The Seven Years War is known to Americans as the French and Indian War, but that name doesn't do justice to the scale of the conflict, even though the spark that ignited the powder keg was indeed lit on the frontier lands of the American continent. The British colonies along the American eastern seaboard and the French colonies that flanked them to the north and south both wanted access to the heartland of the continent. The French in Canada and Louisiana planned to link up along the line of the Ohio and Mississippi rivers and started building a series of outposts along those two waterways. To the English-speaking people of America, those forts threatened to confine them to the narrow strip of land between the Atlantic and the Appalachians, condemned eventually to fall under the influence of the encircling French.

That is how the war started, but it quickly spread, and by its end in 1763 it was being fought in North and Central America, the West Indies, West Africa, India, the Pacific Ocean and throughout Europe. It drew in all the great empires and kingdoms of the Old World, and it was sustained by the traditional dynastic jealousies and suspicions of the ruling houses of the continent.

In 1755, Britain staggered towards its third major conflict in the century with only a small professional army and a navy that, as an economy measure, was mostly laid up in the harbours of the south coast and the rivers and creeks of the Thames estuary. The predictable result was a series of disasters in 1755 and 1756. At sea, Britain lost its principal Mediterranean stronghold at Minorca, and with it the ability to keep a watch on the French fleet at Toulon.

Amidst the outcry that followed, Admiral Byng achieved notoriety as the only British admiral ever to have been judicially executed, throwing the country into turmoil and causing the collapse of the government.

By the end of 1756, the government was being led by William Pitt as the de facto Prime Minister. Pitt understood that so long as Britain used its financial power to build an overwhelming navy to support its colonies and its merchant fleet, then in the long run, whatever France may do on the continent, she could neither gain new territories nor hold those she already owned. Pitt kept the French in check in 1756 while he oversaw a massive increase in the British fleet. He used his new maritime power first to ensure the security of the kingdom; then, in 1757, he went on the offensive.

This is the fictitious story of Captain Edward Carlisle, a native of Williamsburg, Virginia and his first lieutenant, George Holbrooke, of Wickham in Hampshire. In early 1757 their frigate *Medina* is ordered to the Jamaica Station to carry out Anson's strategy of waging commerce warfare against the French in their West Indian possessions.

If any of Carlisle or Holbrooke's exploits – either ashore or afloat – seem a little unlikely, then I recommend that you read Augustus Hervey's Journal which was published in 2002 by Chatham Publishing. Hervey spent much of the Seven Years War at sea in command and was present at several battles and other operations, including the disastrous battle of Minorca. When you read his startlingly frank account of those times, you'll agree that a novelist has no need of overstatement when writing of the Royal Navy of the mid-eighteenth century.

PRINCIPAL CHARACTERS

Fictional

Captain Edward Carlisle: Commanding Officer, *Medina*.

Lieutenant George Holbrooke: First Lieutenant, *Medina*.

John Hosking: Sailing Master, *Medina*.

Reverend John (David) Chalmers: Chaplain, *Medina*.

Able Seaman Jackson: Captain's Coxswain, *Medina*.

Able Seaman Whittle: A follower of Captain Carlisle's from his home in Virginia.

Lady Chiara Angelini: Captain Carlisle's wife.

Enrico Angelini: Cousin to Lady Chiara.

Black Rod: Chief-of-Household of the Angelini family, real name unknown.

Jacques Serviteur: Freed French slave.

Historical

The Duke of Newcastle: Prime Minister of Great Britain from 1754-1756 and 1757-1762.

The Duke of Devonshire: Prime Minister of Great Britain from 1756-1757.

William Pitt: Leader of the House of Commons from 1756-1761.

George Haldane: Governor of Jamaica, 1756-1759.

Lord George Anson: First Lord of the Admiralty from 1751-1756 and 1757-1762.

Chris Durbin

Vice Admiral George Townshend: Commander-in-Chief Jamaica Station until July 1757.

Rear Admiral Thomas Cotes: Commander-in-Chief, Jamaica Station from July 1757.

Rear Admiral Thomas Frankland: Commander-in-Chief, Leeward Islands Station.

Captain Robert Faulknor: Commanding Officer *Marlborough*, Flag Captain to Admiral Cotes.

Captain (Commodore) Arthur Forrest: Commanding Officer, *Augusta*.

Captain Maurice Suckling: Commanding Officer, Dreadnought.

Captain William Langdon: Commanding Officer, *Edinburgh*.

Don Alonso Fernández de Heredia: Governor of Florida 1755-1758.

Countess San Clemente Elena Marin de Villanueva e Hijar: Don Alonso's wife.

Maria Magdalena Fernandez de Heredia y Marin de Villanueva: Don Alonso's daughter.

Capitaine de Vaisseau Guy François de Coëtnempren, Comte de Kersaint: Commander of the French squadron at Cape François.

4

THE CARIBBEAN & GULF OF MEXICO
1757

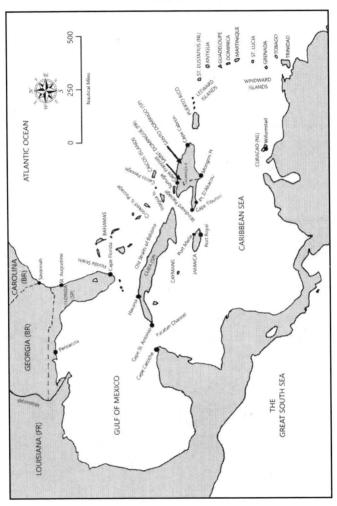

Chris Durbin

THE WINDWARD PASSAGE 1757

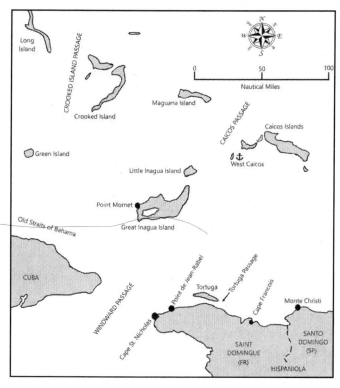

CAPE FRANÇOIS 1757

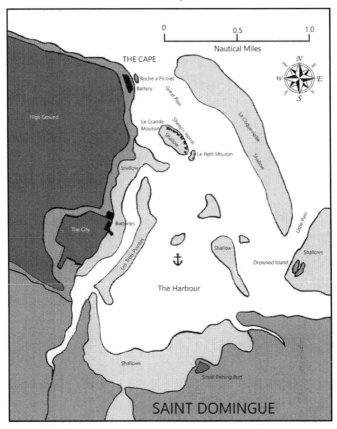

Chris Durbin

PROLOGUE

Nuestra Señora del Rosario

Wednesday, eighth of June 1757
Nuestra Señora Del Rosario, at Sea. Tobago west-northwest 40
leagues

D on Alonso Fernández de Heredia watched as the two sleek, predatory ships manoeuvred to windward. He was confident of their identity – they were Dutch privateers from St. Eustatius – and he was almost sure of their intentions, for Don Alonso wasn't a great believer in coincidences. However, Spain wasn't at war with the Dutch Republic. In fact, Spain was in the unusual state of not being at war with anyone, so those two ships were operating beyond the laws of nations. Perhaps they considered themselves privateers, but with Spain at peace with the world, a better description would be pirates. St. Eustatius was five hundred miles to the northwest, at the far end of the Antilles. That tiny island had a reputation for free-trading, and in Don Alonso's opinion, and in the opinion of Spain, free-trading in the Caribbean was only a short step away from piracy.

The governor of Florida wasn't a man to let a few cannon balls ruin his day; after all, in his time he'd been at war with all the major nations of Europe, on land and at sea. He'd fought the Dutch before, sometimes winning and sometimes losing. However, today he had his family to consider, and he'd already sent his wife, Elena, and his daughter, Maria, below, out of harm's way. He thought for a moment, but it didn't take long. If there was a fight, the slow but comfortable merchant ship that was conveying the family of the governor could contribute nothing and would merely constrain her escort's action.

No peace beyond the line, the English, the French and the

9

Dutch were fond of saying. That old axiom may have been overtaken by treaties a century ago, but if these Dutchmen wanted to fight, he was confident that *Argonauta* could teach them a lesson. He snapped his telescope closed and with a gesture that was part anger and part frustration he walked over to the starboard quarterdeck rail and waved to the man-of-war that hung close on his beam.

The captain of the Spanish naval frigate, *Argonauta*, was watching the two predators warily and keeping himself between them and the defenceless merchant ship that he was escorting. It had been an uneventful passage so far, and with luck, they'd reach Pensacola in Spanish Florida in something over two weeks. They anticipated a pleasant time in the sheltered anchorage while the governor reviewed the rebuilding of the new city after the destruction of the hurricane five years ago. Then it would be a gentle two-week passage to St. Augustine on the Atlantic coast, following the well-trodden path of the Spanish treasure fleets. There they'd deliver Don Alonso and his family to his seat of governance and return home to Cadiz.

'Captain,' shouted Don Alonso, 'We will go ahead, you are to prevent those two pirates following us. If you need to fight them, then you may do so, but don't let either of them get past you into the Caribbean.'

'Yes, Your Excellency,' replied the captain, barely able to suppress his delight at being let loose from the slow *Nuestra Señora Del Rosario*. He would deal with these two Dutchmen in short order and by the grace of God may even take a prize or two. He remembered with pleasure that the governor of a colony held the presidency of the Vice-Admiralty court and could condemn prizes out of hand, war or no war. Acting under the orders of the governor himself, there would be little doubt of the findings of the court. 'I will overtake you before you enter the Caribbean Sea,' the captain shouted back, speaking pedantically to avoid misunderstanding, 'but in case we are delayed, please ensure that the master doesn't deviate from the navigation plan.' He gestured with his hands, ahead and slightly to starboard. 'South of Jamaica, then take a departure from Grand Cayman for the Yucatan Channel. The current will be with you on the west side of the channel.'

'Go with God, Captain,' Don Alonso replied with a wave.

With that, the captain of *Argonauta* turned to his sailing master and delivered a rapid volley of orders. A trumpet blared, and the frigate burst into life. The port-lids were thrown open, the guns were run out, the sheets hardened in and the helm put to leeward. The sleek fighting machine turned to confront its impudent pursuers.

On board the *Nuestra Señora Del Rosario*, there was barely a ruffle in the calm ordering of the day. The merchant ship didn't deviate from her course, her few guns weren't cleared away, and she continued her peaceful voyage, leaving the hard business of war to the professionals of the navy. An hour or so later, Don Alonso and his family heard some gunfire to windward, but even through the telescope, it was too far to see any details of the fight. That was the last that the governor of Florida saw or heard of *Argonauta*, apart from some sailors' tales that filtered through many months later. Tales of a wild fight and wilder weather; pirates, shipwreck and survival and the last days of one of King Ferdinand's newest and best frigates.

Chris Durbin

CHAPTER ONE

Weather Warnings

Thursday, sixteenth of June 1757
Medina, at Sea. Point d'Abacou, Hispaniola north 15 leagues

The sailing master shook his head warily. 'I don't know, sir,' he said, 'I don't like the look of this swell, not one little bit.' Hosking leaned down the slope of the deck, tightly gripping the hammock cranes until he could almost reach the solid, oak-built binnacle. Then he let go his hold and launched himself the final few feet. That a man with the sailing master's years at sea should need to perform these manoeuvres merely to move around his own quarterdeck was an eloquent testimony to the unsteadiness of the ship. The quartermaster turned and winked covertly at the two steersmen who somehow managed to keep their expressions wooden. In truth, they were concentrating mentally and physically on keeping their course and had little time for old Eli's games.

'Southeast-by-east, sir,' Hosking announced after studying the steering compass and staring over the larboard beam. The regular, modest and predictable series of waves from the east-northeast was being overlaid by a long, low swell from the direction of the Windward Islands. *Medina* was steering southwest-by-south with the wind two points on her larboard quarter. The steersmen were wrestling with an interesting three-dimensional dynamic puzzle. The frigate's stern rose comfortably to the first two waves created by the trade wind, but then the sequence was lost as the third was interrupted by this new swell approaching from further around on the beam. It had the effect of pushing the stern back into the wind, but the force with which it did so was unpredictable, being dependent upon the exact point that the swell intersected

12

the wave.

'Could we be in for a hurricane, Mister Hosking?' asked Captain Carlisle, cupping his hands around his mouth, 'it seems a little early in the season.'

'But not unheard of, sir, oh dear me no. The season starts in May, although they're rare in the first two months and generally not as dangerous as later in the year, around August and September.' He looked at the dog-vanes mounted on the hammock cranes, then up at the commissioning pennant streaming away on the starboard bow. 'The wind hasn't changed yet, so we should have twelve hours before it hits us, if indeed it does.'

Carlisle looked around at the sparkling sea and the towering ranks of canvas ascending to the blue sky, broken here and there by pure white clouds. The weather looked perfect, the central Caribbean at its best. It was hard to believe that they could really be in for a hurricane in less than a day. 'Well, it's best to be prepared. What do you think of our course?'

'Until we see the wind changing, we won't know how to avoid the eye, if it is a hurricane,' Hosking said touching the binnacle for luck. 'If the wind veers or stays steady from the northeast, then we're on the dangerous side and need to beat up to the northwest. If it backs, then we're safer, but in that case, we should head south, as we're doing. South also gives us more sea-room; I recommend that we maintain our heading until we see how it develops.'

Carlisle took another look around the horizon and let his eyes rest on the eastern skyline. He didn't want to be known as a captain who was spooked by every change in the weather, but on the other hand, a hurricane wasn't to be taken lightly. He felt another exaggerated lift and twist as *Medina* responded to the confused sea and, momentarily losing his grip on the railing, skidded across the deck to be brought up against the broad shoulders of old Eli, the quartermaster.

'Thank you, Eli, much obliged,' he said.

'That's nothing, sir,' replied the quartermaster. 'You wait until that old hurricane catches us, then we'll all be dancing around the deck. I'll have to take a turn around the binnacle with my pigtail,' he said, shaking the half-yard of tightly-plaited grey hair that hung down his back.

Carlisle smiled. If Eli thought a hurricane was coming, then it probably was. His mind was made up by that insignificant incident. If he was wrong, then at least he was in good company. Carlisle looked over his shoulder at the midshipman of the watch.

'Pass the word for the bosun, the gunner and the carpenter, Mister Smith. I'll see them in my cabin. And my respects to Mister Holbrooke. If he's at leisure, I'd welcome his attendance.' He heard the midshipman moving nimbly towards the quarterdeck ladder, apparently unconcerned by the ship's motion.

'Mister Hosking, would you join us?'

Carlisle was aware of the absurdity of the conventional phrases that he used to gather his command team. The warrant officers could be politely summoned, but his first lieutenant and the sailing master must be requested to join him *if they were at leisure*. The summons and the requests were equally binding on all his officers, whether they held a commission or a warrant, whether they messed in the wardroom or the gunroom. The difference between the familiar phrases was an acknowledgement of a more fundamental split in the quality of the person being addressed: was he a gentleman or not? This gentlemanly status coloured all relations on board, as it did in all of society, and it was a foundation of the times in which he lived.

It was curious to be thinking about precautions for a storm when, apart from the unusual swell, the weather was delightful. The trade wind was favouring them with a steady topsail breeze, and the regular series of white clouds was uninterrupted by any black or grey. However, Carlisle knew that the advice of the sailing master wasn't to be lightly disregarded. Not only had he experienced – and survived – a few hurricanes, but also, in this modern scientific age, the masters of King's ships regularly exchanged their experiences by correspondence and when they met in person. They also routinely submitted reports to Trinity House, the Admiralty and the Navy Board. Hosking's opinion on the swell and what it foretold was based on a systematically gathered body of information.

When Carlisle returned to the quarterdeck, the ship was a hive of urgent activity. Three bells in the first dogwatch was usually a peaceful time in King's ships. If the weather, the enemy and the first lieutenant permitted, those of the ship's company who weren't on watch would be sleeping or yarning, whiling away the time before the second spirits issue at eight bells. But today the deck was swarming with people. The bosun was directing the hands to send preventer stays aloft, to chain the yards, to turn out the storm canvas and to rig lifelines along the deck. The gunner had a smaller but more specialist team who were lashing the guns fore-and-aft against the ship's side, which was a more secure arrangement than the usual housed position or even the double-breeching that was used when normal heavy weather was anticipated. The carpenter and his crew were reinforcing the steering gear and rigging relieving tackles; with that done they'd move on to the hatches, then the stowage of the boats on the spars, the securing of the anchors and the all-important mast wedges. Hosking, of course, was explicitly responsible for preparing his ship for heavy weather, while Holbrooke, as second-in-command to Carlisle, had a more general, unbounded responsibility for the safety and security of *Medina*.

Hosking spent the night on deck with occasional visits to his chart room behind the wheel. There was little change in the wind until midnight, when it freshened but stayed resolutely in the northeast, looking for all the world like the trade wind that blew for nine days out of ten in these latitudes. The swell, however, increased hour-by-hour. It was still coming from a little east of southeast, but now it overpowered the natural northeast sea so that *Medina's* motion became more predictable. It made the steersmen's task more manageable, but the regular lift and slide of the ship's stern, the bow digging into the backside of the swell and the seats of ease in the heads being out of bounds were clear signs to those of the ship's company that had sailed these waters before. When Eli came back on deck for the morning watch, the wind had increased to a half-gale. The starboard watch, already exhausted from four hours of bracing themselves against the motion of the ship, were obliged to spend another hour on deck when Carlisle ordered all hands to strike the t'gallant masts, to double-reef the topsails and to ready the trysails for the lower masts.

Hosking was now convinced that they were in the path of a hurricane. He didn't yet know its intensity, its present position, its future track or its speed of progress. If he'd possessed the power to soar above the Caribbean Sea, above the clouds in the lower stratosphere, and to look down, he'd have been appalled at what he saw. The great storm had its origin at ten degrees of north latitude, thousands of miles away across the Atlantic towards the West African coast. It had started as a mere thunderstorm, an everyday occurrence in the tropics. But this thunderstorm had coincided with a calm spell, and there was no wind to disperse its heat. That heat had grown, feeding upon itself and producing an intense low-pressure system that had dragged in the surrounding air in a rapidly increasing spiral. The motion of the earth had started the storm moving, easterly but gradually more northerly, gathering heat and power as it raced across the warm water. It burst upon the southerly of the Windward Islands – Trinidad, Grenada and St. Kitts – whipping away the roofs of the houses, sinking ships at their moorings and devastating the sugar crop. It narrowly missed Barbados and St. Lucia and continued west northwesterly across the Caribbean Sea towards Jamaica.

As *Medina* completed reefing her topsails and sent the starboard watch to their hammocks, the hurricane was north of Curaçao and heading directly towards the frigate. Hosking could see no change in the wind direction because, as fate would have it, *Medina* lay somewhat to the north of the storm's track and the winds that it generated at this distance from its centre came from the same direction as the trade winds. Only as it moved closer could Hosking detect the change in wind direction that would confirm his worst fears.

The wind started to veer as the forenoon watch came on deck. From the northeast, it had moved a whole point in a clockwise direction and was now blowing from northeast-by-east.

'We should get the topsails off her sir.' Hosking looked at the gathering clouds in the southeast. 'I do believe we're in the dangerous sector, the eye will pass close to the south of us. We should be heading away to the north.'

'Very well, Mister Hosking.' Carlisle also studied the gathering clouds. 'You'll want to veer I guess,' he said.

The sailing master nodded. He was studying the swell, now grown to monstrous proportions. Tacking would be difficult in the extreme, and they had plenty of sea-room. 'Aye, sir. We'll need to brail the mizzen, but she'll come around easily enough. We should keep the fore and main when we're heading northwest and try to make some northing to get out of the path of the eye. When it gets worse, we should strip down to trysails.'

As it happened, Carlisle had never experienced a full-blown hurricane at sea. That wasn't unusual; the navy always tried to keep its ships safely in harbour during the worst of the hurricane season, and in any case, each location in the West Indies was only struck by a severe hurricane every few years. However, he didn't care to let Hosking know that, but he was reassured by the master's apparent confidence.

'All hands!' bellowed the master, 'all hands to veer ship.' There was a momentary rushing of bare feet around the deck, then silence as each man stood by his sheet or halyard. The crew had been together in *Medina* for nine months, and many of them had sailed with Carlisle in his previous ship, the old *Fury*. With only a very few exceptions, they knew their business and went to their stations willingly. There was no need for the bosun's cane to get them moving.

Hosking waited until everyone was in place. 'Brail the mizzen!'

The quartermaster stood clear of the wheel where he could observe the moment when the great lateen sail stopped exerting its pressure on the stern.

'Helm to windward,' called the master. The quartermaster motioned to the steersman who spun the wheel to starboard. The tiller on the deck below swung across to larboard and under the twin influences of the rudder and the lack of canvas aft, *Medina* turned swiftly across the wind. They were now sailing as close to the wind as their restricted canvas would allow, northwest with an occasional luff of a point higher. With no topsails, and nothing more than a regular gale blowing, they weren't being pressed over very hard, and it was still possible to move freely around the deck.

'Mister Holbrooke. Would you personally check the lifelines, the hatches, the boats and the anchors? You'll need your oilskins I fancy,' said Carlisle feeling the tension on the bar-taut backstays as he spoke.

Holbrooke looked around and caught the eye of Jackson, the captain's coxswain. 'Your oilskins, Jackson. Let's check everything before this tempest hits us.'

Slowly the two men made their way around the upper

deck. Every lashing, every wedge and every relieving tackle was checked. The boats were the most vulnerable. They couldn't be towed behind in this weather – they'd be swamped in two minutes. Instead, they were perched atop the spars that covered the waist, exposed to every wave that swept the ship. Few ships survived a hurricane with their boats intact, but Holbrooke and Jackson were determined that *Medina* should be one of those few. They bowsed down on the lashings, tightened the tarpaulins and blocked every gap that could give entry to the wind and waves. It took half an hour of physical exertion, but eventually, the task was completed. *Medina* was as ready as any ship could be for the trauma that was about to overtake them.

'I expect the wind to continue veering, sir,' said Hosking. 'We should follow it around, keeping as close as we can. But it'll get stronger, and we'll need to furl the main and foresail before it gets too bad.'

CHAPTER TWO

The Tempest

Friday, seventeenth of June 1757
Medina, at Sea. Point d'Abacou, Hispaniola north 12 leagues

The forenoon passed in anxious watching. At eight bells the last of the square sails were furled tightly against their yards, with extra gaskets to ensure that there was no gap that the wind could work its way into. The storm jib was set, and a small, heavy trysail was bent to the mizzen. With the hatches battened down, the lifelines rigged, and every kind of precaution taken, the crew of *Medina* could only await the coming hurricane and pray that they may slip past its northern edge. Being a Friday – a banyan day – there was no beef or pork to be boiled, so the cook had already extinguished the galley fires, and the crew sat down to their cold biscuits, pease pudding, butter and cheese.

By four bells in the afternoon watch, the wind had hardly shifted at all. Hosking had swallowed his pride and consulted the quartermaster. Old Eli had been at sea for over forty years and claimed to have sailed through half a dozen hurricanes – it may even have been true. What the master heard had him shaking his head as he walked over to the captain.

The wind had increased to the point where conversation was impossible on the exposed deck. A strong tarpaulin had been stretched across the weather mizzen shrouds to give some protection to the men at the wheel, and it was there that Carlisle and Hosking spoke.

'If the wind doesn't back, and it hardly veers, then the eye will pass close to the south of us. But often these hurricanes swing to the north so it could pass right over us,' said Hosking, offering little comfort to his captain.

'Is there anything more that we can do?' asked Carlisle.

'No, sir,' the master replied positively. 'I wouldn't want to strip to bare poles, not while we can still make a little way to the north.'

The afternoon was succeeded by the first dog watch. From the quarterdeck, the ship seemed eerily deserted. The watch-on-deck were all crouching in the lee of the gunwales, the lookouts had been recalled from the mastheads, and there was none of the usual dogwatch skylarking. The wind was screaming in the rigging, pulling at the canvas and cordage with relentless fury. It was now blowing a full gale, but more intense than any storm that had ever struck the shores of Britain. Green waves were breaking clear over the fo'c'sle and the waist, but so far, everything was holding fast. They'd lost no spars, the boats hadn't shifted, the storm canvas was still holding, and the steering hadn't been affected. And yet, there was some movement on the deck. Three figures were making their way carefully along the gangway. With bowlines around their waists, Holbrooke, the bosun and Jackson were painstakingly moving along the lifelines, securing themselves to a new position before casting off from the last. They were checking that all was secure, tightening a lashing here, hammering a wedge into place there.

Surely the wind could get no stronger. Carlisle wasn't concerned for the safety of the ship – not yet. *Medina* had all the sea-room he could desire, he'd anticipated the hurricane, and his crew had secured the ship as well as could be. But he was interested in the phenomenon of the tropical storm. Without an experienced master to tell him otherwise, Carlisle would have assumed that this rising wind was merely another of those Caribbean storms that were so common. He'd have thought little of the contrary swell, imagining that it was the result of another blast far to the southwest. Without Hosking's advice, Carlisle would have furled his t'gallants and reefed his topsails, but no more. He now saw the danger of a hurricane and the folly of being unprepared. By the time it revealed itself for what it really was, the wind and the sea had risen to such strength and height that it was dangerous to go aloft. Furling square sails and striking masts in this breath-stopping wind was questionable for a well-manned King's ship, and impossible for a lean-manned merchant ship. That was how even well-found vessels were lost without a trace in these waters.

The wind was now hitting the small group of men on the exposed quarterdeck with unimaginable force. It carried a lacerating spray, and the decks were constantly awash as wave after wave broke over the gunwales. The sky was black to windward and astern, only to the northwest could a scrap of clear blue be seen. With a deafening crash, the first lightning lit up the clouds, leaving an even deeper blackness behind it.

It only lasted two or three hours, but they were hellish hours of straining at the wheel and staring at the sails. The climax came with a deluge of rain blown horizontally by the force of the wind. There were no oilskins that could defend against it, and everyone on the upper deck was soaked, their clothes clinging to their bodies. Then, with a suddenness that took them all by surprise, the wind started to diminish, the rain ceased abruptly, and the waves receded. Unbelievably, the sky cleared, and the sun shone through a high haze. Without the pressure of the wind and her upper sails to keep her from rolling, *Medina* wallowed in the massive and disordered swell. They had survived so far, with nothing more than a few parted lines and some work for the carpenter where the cutter had shifted on the booms and stove in one of her planks.

'The eye of the storm,' said Hosking ominously. 'This is just how it's described. If you didn't know better, you'd be shaking out your reefs now and looking forward to a steady passage. We've perhaps an hour, maybe two before all hell breaks loose again.'

Holbrooke was paying careful attention. Like his captain, he hadn't experienced a hurricane, nor anything like it. His King's commission, at least in principle, trumped Hosking's Navy Board warrant, but he had nothing like the sailing master's experience at sea, and he wasn't too proud to learn.

'Where will the wind come from?' asked Holbrooke looking to the southeast, where he could see a bank of cloud on the far horizon.

'South, or anywhere between south and east. It'll hit us like a sledgehammer and with precious little notice.'

'I'll walk through the ship and make sure the hands know sir,' said Holbrooke to Carlisle. 'There'll always be a few fools who will be easing the lashings otherwise.'

'Please do so, Mister Holbrooke. Make sure they know what we're in for.'

Carlisle thought for a moment then he turned to the sailing master. 'If this wind is going to hit us from the south or east, what should our heading be?'

'Well, now we're in the eye, it'd be best to try to get out of it on the safe side, so we should head southwest, as best we can,' replied Hosking looking dubiously at the sails hanging slack as the frigate rolled heavily. 'We can't tow her head around, we'd never get the boats secured in time, and we shouldn't spread more canvas.'

'Then set the quartermaster the task of having our head to the south as quickly as possible. He can use every scrap of wind, from whatever direction, to help him turn the ship.'

The master shrugged and walked carefully back to the wheel to consult with Eli. They both knew the importance of getting the ship heading southwest before the wall of the eye hit them.

There was hardly a breath of wind to relieve the sultry heat. The sun, barely obscured by a high haze, beat down upon the frigate that looked curiously bereft below its stripped-down poles.

The group on the quarterdeck were all staring to the south and east. A towering mass of clouds, soaring to an unimaginable height, was gathering on the horizon. It looked far-off, no immediate threat, but they all knew that the distance was deceptive.

'Send the watch-on-deck below,' said Carlisle to Holbrooke, 'all but a few of the petty officers. We can call them on deck if they're needed.'

The quartermaster and the steersmen had, by exploiting every odd breath of wind, turned the frigate so that she was heading southwest. *Medina*, however, had no way on in these critical last few minutes, she was dead in the water, her rudder was ineffective, and already her head was starting to swing around to the south. Carlisle could see that there was no value in trying to back the storm jib to get her head back to the southwest; what little wind there was came fitfully from all points of the compass. All they could do was to hope that the wall of the eye – and they could now see what that term meant as the seemingly solid curtain of cloud advanced upon them – would be preceded by a few minutes of more moderate wind so that they could achieve steering way.

The final few minutes before the wall reached them was a blur of rapidly changing conditions. There was no helpful breeze in front of the cloud – it hit them in all its rage, from dead calm to a howling tempest in less than a minute. They were subjected to a deadly blast from the southwest that caught *Medina* on her starboard bow so that, with her jib backed, her head lurched around to larboard. No hempen rope could stand the pressure that the jib sheet was under. It parted noiselessly, or at least with no sound that could be heard above the stupendous roar of the hurricane. The storm jib survived a few seconds, flogging wildly with no steadying sheet, but the wind took it, and in an instant, it disappeared, ripped from its luff-line and carried away to leeward.

'Before the wind,' shouted Carlisle into the master's ear, 'Brail the mizzen and put her before the wind,' backing up the order with a pointed hand. The wind was far, far worse than Carlisle had imagined. They had sufficient sea-room – just – but Carlisle was acutely aware of Hispaniola only thirty miles to the north. The only certainty was that the wind would back as the eye moved away from them, so they had to pray that the wind would shift far enough to give them an offing before they fetched up on the rocks to the west of Mongon Point.

The first of the orders was easy to perform as the brail lines were all handled from the quarterdeck, where the lifelines allowed the crew to work with a degree of safety. Nevertheless, it took courage or blind faith for men to leave the sanctuary of the bulkheads and scamper to the mizzen bitts where the brail-lines were belayed. It was slow, but eventually the job was done, the mizzen brailed tight against the yard, and the bowlines were centred. But neither Carlisle nor Hosking were confident that she'd lie before the wind with both the fore and main spread, even close-reefed as they were. Both men looked doubtfully at the mainsail. Was it providing too much leverage to allow *Medina* to run downwind?

'Helm hard over,' shouted Hosking to the quartermaster. *Medina* started to swing again to larboard as the tempest caught the foresail and pulled the bow around until they were heading northeast with the wind directly astern.

'How's she steering?' asked Hosking.

The steersman could spare no words as he wrestled with the wheel. Even backed up by three mates, it was clear that the weather was taking charge and the rudder, for all the brute strength that was required to manage it, was ineffective. Carlisle watched in horror as the stern yawed wildly, showing each quarter to the wind in turn.

'It's no good, sir,' shouted Hosking, 'we'll have to furl

the main.'

Carlisle looked up at the ponderous yard. He could see that the force of the wind was bending it forward and straining at the preventer chains. There was no question of lowering the yard, no human could get the chains off in this weather. But he could see the master's point. If the mainsail weren't providing that enormous drive from the ship's centre-of-gravity, then the foresail would keep the head off the wind, and they wouldn't suffer those dangerous yaws.

The bosun had joined the small group on the quarterdeck. Carlisle would have liked to go below where they could have a rational discussion, but he knew that the master and bosun couldn't leave the deck in these conditions.

Carlisle nodded at the master who unceremoniously hauled the bosun's face close to his own and shouted his instructions. The bosun had been long in the service. His accounting was flawed, probably deliberately so that his embezzlement of government property was less visible, and his ideas on the rigging were old-fashioned, to say the least, but he lived for occasions such as this and went forward to the quarterdeck rail to bellow his orders.

A dozen men were climbing laboriously up the shrouds. From the quarterdeck, they could only be seen indistinctly through the blowing spray and rain. They looked inhuman, their bodies pressed hard against the ratlines and tensed against the wind that threatened to blow them forward at any moment. Their hands moving laboriously up the shrouds, inch-by-inch, their bare soles fighting for grip on the slippery ratlines. With the wind right astern there was no windward and leeward side, so they climbed up both sides.

Hosking cupped his mouth to the quartermaster's ear. 'Steer small,' and he pointed to the men on the shrouds. No other words were needed. If *Medina* should yaw, then the men on the leeward side would be hanging over the raging sea, grasping ratlines that would be beyond the vertical with the worst wind they had ever experienced trying to rip them away to their deaths. Even the men working in the waist were performing superhuman feats. With water surging around their thighs and fresh waves breaking every few seconds, they hauled on the braces, the sheets, the tacks and the clewlines.

The hunched figures crept along the yard. Now the hurricane was favouring them as it thrust their stomachs against the main yard. It was still perilous; the yard was swaying wildly with the motion of the ship, and it was being flexed by the extraordinary power of the hurricane. With their bodies pressed against the yard, their feet and shoulders were bent to leeward. A parted horse would result in the inevitable death of all on that side of the yard.

Slowly, the job was done. The sail, already reefed, was handed and the gaskets were passed and secured. Carlisle wondered as he saw the bulky figure of the bosun climb up the shrouds with a canvas bag over his shoulder. His purpose became evident when, with one hand firmly clasping the railing around the maintop, he passed additional gaskets along the yard. It was important that no opening was left for the wind to get into the bunt of the sail. Any weakness would result in the mainsail being blown into tatters and perhaps causing *Medina* to yaw, with potentially fatal results. The bosun handed out three additional gaskets for each one that was typically used. With the mainsail furled, steering became noticeably more manageable. The reefed foresail was all the canvas showing, and it kept *Medina's* head off the wind. It also had the effect of lifting the bow, which prevented it from burrowing into the confused waves.

Medina settled down to ride out the hurricane. The watch-on-deck lashed themselves into shelter below the gunwales, the steersmen were already roped into place, and the weather-cloths around the quarterdeck were holding.

With only one lieutenant and a sailing master, Carlisle's options for an officer of the watch were limited – this was no time for inexperienced master's mates and the specialist warrant officers all had their own concerns with the fabric and the rigging of the frigate. Holbrooke needed to be available to provide the direction for recovery from any disaster, so it was Carlisle and Hosking who kept the quarterdeck all through that fearful night.

CHAPTER THREE

Salvage

Saturday, eighteenth of June 1757
Medina, at Sea. South of Point d'Abacou, Hispaniola

The hail was barely audible against the roar of the wind. 'Sail ho! Sail on the larboard bow.' There was no masthead lookout. Even though the worst of the hurricane had blown through, the wind was still blowing a strong gale from the southeast. If anything, the swell had risen overnight, and now the wind was blowing the crests downwind in long white streamers. But with the coming of dawn a lookout had been stationed on the fo'c'sle, wedged against the cathead beam with a turn of one-inch hemp around a knighthead.

Carlisle retrieved his telescope from the binnacle and wiped the salt-encrusted lenses. It was a merchant ship with a high poop, it wasn't an island vessel. This ship had come from Europe – Spain or possibly Portugal by its looks. To describe it as a *sail* required a leap of imagination, because the vessel in Carlisle's telescope had not a stitch of canvas showing, and never a mast or spar to hang a sail. She was rolling horribly in the huge swell and monstrous wind. How she'd survived the wrath of the hurricane was a mystery, but at some point, she'd been dismasted. Looking carefully, a few figures could be seen, all clinging tightly to whatever structure remained on the deck. *Medina* had evidently been seen because one man was waving something white – a shirt perhaps.

'What do you think, Mister Hosking?' Speech was at least possible now, but only by standing very close together.

'She's Spanish, a guinea on it, sir. It looks like she was a respectable ship before she lost her masts.' Hosking looked warily at Carlisle. 'She'll be ashore in a few hours.' Hosking knew very well that Carlisle wouldn't want to leave those souls to their fate, however dangerous it was to attempt a rescue.

Carlisle opened his mouth. Hosking was aware that he was about to ask how much sea-room they had, but in all honesty, he didn't have an answer. Hispaniola could be thirty miles to leeward, or it could be five, it all depended upon a host of variables, and who knew where the hurricane had pushed them overnight? In any case, the captain was interrupted before he could ask the question.

'Land Ho! Land on the bow, right ahead, sir.'

'That'll be Point d'Abacou, sir,' said the master. Now that it was pointed out, the men on the quarterdeck could just about see the outline of the land. Hosking studied the cliffs ahead of them, 'you can just see Cow Island to the east. Five miles away I reckon. We must have been pushed further north overnight. I'll call all hands and get some sail on her. If we can put the wind on our larboard beam, we'll be safe enough,' he added without any real hope that Carlisle would abandon the dismasted ship to its fate.

'Very well, Mister Hosking,' replied Carlisle with a thoughtful, distracted look, 'and pass the word for Mister Holbrooke and the bosun.'

Hosking shrugged. It was madness to attempt to save that ship; she was doomed with this gale pushing them towards the rocks. *Medina* barely had the sea-room to preserve herself, never mind some unknown vessel from God-knows-what country. But it was the captain's decision.

With a storm jib, fore and main coarses and topsails, all heavily reefed, *Medina* regained her manoeuvrability. Despite the master's pessimism, they quickly passed a tow to the much smaller vessel and hauled her clear of the cliffs and out to the open water beyond. By the afternoon watch, the hurricane was just an ugly memory, and the wind – still a strong gale – had backed to the east-southeast. Cape Tiburon was on their beam, and Port Royal was seventy leagues on their starboard bow. For Port Royal was their destination. Their cruise was cut short by the hurricane that had opened their seams so that the pumps were working for two hours each watch, just to keep the water below the bungs on the barrels stowed in the hold. The carpenter had brought the caulker to the quarterdeck, a place where he'd never been seen before. In his anguish, this obscure specialist so far forgot his diffidence as to give Carlisle a lengthy and graphic account of the way that the sea spurted through the seams below the waterline every time the ship rolled.

Carlisle still wasn't sure of the nationality of their salvage. She looked Spanish, but in the free-and-easy ways of the Caribbean, she could have changed hands and nationality half a dozen times. It was entirely possible that they had rescued an enemy ship from being wrecked; they could be harbouring a viper to their bosom. Or they could have saved a British ship from the rocks.

Sunday morning came, the weather had moderated, and now the wind was coming clear from the east. It had been a nerve-wracking night, towing a ship nearly as large as themselves, that apparently had no steering and not a stick to hang a pocket-handkerchief on. With no knowledge of the state of her hull and no means of communication, it was impossible to know whether the ship would stay afloat through the hours of darkness. However, dawn found the salvage still there, wallowing heavily and pumping hard. A lone figure on the fo'c'sle was waving urgently at them. Carlisle studied him through his telescope; he was a man of medium height with a beard that a few days ago would have been neatly trimmed, and what was left of his clothes marked him out as a man of wealth, of fashion even. His words were lost in the wind although it was clear from his actions that he wanted *Medina* to send a boat.

Carlisle was reluctant. For one thing, the carpenter was still working to repair the cutter, the only one of the frigate's boats that was even remotely suitable for these conditions. For another, his men were exhausted, and those that could stand were needed for the pumps because *Medina* was making six feet of water an hour and badly needed to be careened so that the caulkers could get at her seams. But the most important consideration was that the weather was marginal at best for boat-work, and Carlisle was reluctant to endanger his men without good reason.

Holbrooke was also studying the figure through his telescope. 'Chips says the cutter will be tight in ten minutes, sir. I could take Jackson and a good crew and be back in thirty minutes. At least we'd know who we're taking into Port Royal.'

Carlisle looked carefully at his first lieutenant. They had been together now for two years and knew each other as well as any two men could, but Holbrooke's apparent insouciance still took Carlisle by surprise. The lieutenant knew very well the danger of taking a boat to a disabled ship in these conditions. Every step in the mission was fraught with peril, from the swinging out of the cutter on the lower yards, to manning it as it lay alongside in this monstrous swell, to climbing up the side of a ship that couldn't even turn to give them a lee. And yet, Holbrooke had unwittingly shaken Carlisle out of the furrow that his thoughts were ploughing. He was finding too many reasons for inaction. There really was no question, they must board the salvage. There could be injured people on board, the ship may be on the verge of sinking, and they still didn't know its nationality – it may even be a lawful prize. At the least it was lawful salvage.

'Very well, Mister Holbrooke, but no heroics. If you can't safely board her, you must return at once.'

Hosking rose to the occasion. He brought *Medina* into the wind on the starboard tack, keeping just enough way on her so that the drag of the salvage could slow her down. Then with the last of the ship's momentum, he brought her to on the larboard tack. Now the stricken vessel was safe to leeward of the frigate with the towing hawser kept taut by the wind that was both keeping *Medina* lying-to and pushing the towed vessel away to leeward. The bosun had reefed the main and foresails and was now hauling the yards around. Stay tackles and yardarm tackles were rigged, and to the accompaniment of his silver call, the ponderous weight of the cutter was eased over the side and into the sea. Despite Carlisle's concern, the manning of the boat was easy for such seasoned sailors as the coxswain Jackson and his crew; they were over the side and seated on their thwarts in seconds. But they knew the correct procedure for a first lieutenant, and half a dozen hands steadied the cutter while Jackson offered his massive fist for Holbrooke to steady himself as he stepped into the stern-sheets.

If Carlisle had overestimated the difficulty of manning the boat, he hadn't committed the same error when it came to boarding the salvage. The ship was waterlogged and half a fathom below her marks, and with no sails to steady her, she was rolling like a pig in a wallow. Two man-ropes snaked down from the waist that was only six feet higher than the cutter's gunwales, but those were six of the most dangerous feet that Holbrooke or Jackson had ever seen. Both vessels, the ship and the cutter, were rolling in independent cycles. At one moment all that could be seen from the cutter was an expanse of ship's planking towering above them, then the next moment, the whole of the ship's side rolled towards them with furious speed and with a thousand tons of momentum behind it. Then for a brief instant, the crew of the cutter would be looking down at the waist. Holbrooke came close to despair; how could he ever get on board?

'Jump for the mizzen chains as she's on the way up,' Jackson shouted. 'There's a bit of the gunwale left above them. Swing yourself inboard before she rolls back. Me and Davis will steady you,' he continued, pointing at the heroic frame of the number five oar.

Holbrooke nodded and rose to his feet. He could hear the people on the deck and realised that they were speaking Spanish, so at least he wasn't stepping onto an enemy deck. He held onto the shoulders of his two supporters and timed his jump to perfection, catching the broken gunwale with his upstretched hands and wedging his left foot into the iron chains three feet below the gunwale. After that, it all went wrong. He couldn't get his balance quickly enough, and he was still outboard, clinging tightly, as the ship rolled back towards the cutter. For a moment it looked like he'd be crushed between the two, but the sturdy shoulders of Jackson and Davis were ready, and they heaved him over the gunwale as the ship was on its downward roll. Just at the point where Holbrooke's body was in balance, not being committed to either going forward or backwards, a hand grasped the front of his shirt and dragged him inboard before he could be pitched unceremoniously back into the boat. In other circumstances, Holbrooke would have cut a comic figure as was pulled clear of the wrecked gunwale to land with precious little dignity in the waist of the ship. His legs couldn't find a grip at first, and he collapsed onto the deck. For a few moments he was unable to regain his breath, but other unknown hands steadied him and brought him to his feet.

Holbrooke was prepared for a scene of devastation on the deck of the ship, but what he saw when he was able to look around shocked him. All three masts had gone by the board, snapped off clean a few feet above the partners. There was nothing else standing above deck level, no structures of any kind except the remains of the gunwales. He could see the fresh scars in the waist where a deck-house had been and the remains of the pedestal that had once mounted the ship's wheel. The bulkheads to the spaces below the poop deck, quarterdeck and fo'c'sle had all been stove in, and he could see right through the stern, where all the windows and their frames had been destroyed by the force of the wind and sea.

Holbrooke had never been on board a ship being built, so he'd never seen a deck so bare. Even when laid up in ordinary, King's ships generally kept their lower masts, and there was all sorts of other gear on the deck: capstans, knightheads, bitts, pin-rails, crates and barrels. This uninterrupted flat space, this clean sweep of the weather decks left the lieutenant disoriented. It was also horribly dangerous, with each unpredictable lurch threatening to pitch the band of men over the side. There were no lifelines rigged. It would be easy to criticise the crew for lack of this basic safety precaution, but Holbrooke had no idea what else had demanded their attention. Pumping, for sure. They were lucky that their chain-pump could be operated from the deck below, the evidence for which was a steady discharge of water through canvas hoses that snaked up from the main hatch. There were half a dozen men on deck, all standing wide-legged, braced against the ship's sickening roll. Holbrooke didn't trust himself to let go of the two that were holding him while he looked around for someone in command.

'Good morning Lieutenant,' shouted a voice behind him in heavily accented, but correct, English. Holbrooke turned carefully and saw, standing beside the ruined gunwale, a man in the ripped and degraded remnants of a suit in the high Spanish style. This was evidently the man who had hauled Holbrooke inboard, and he looked very much like the man who had been signalling to them since dawn.

'Good morning, sir,' replied Holbrooke feeling faintly foolish, using these conventional greetings in such circumstances, while shouting against the roar of the wind that swept across the naked deck. 'Whom do I have the pleasure of addressing?'

With the best bow that he could make while braced against the wild gyrations of the ship, the Spaniard replied, 'I have the honour to be Don Alonso Fernández de Heredia, governor of the Spanish territory of Florida. I will spare you the ranks, titles and honorifics. And you sir?'

'George Holbrooke, sir – Your Excellency. Lieutenant in His Majesty's frigate *Medina*,' he stammered and gestured stupidly to windward. This wasn't going the way he'd anticipated. He expected to be dealing with a Spanish merchant captain with little or no English and was confused to be confronted by a grandee of Old Spain with a better grasp of the language than Holbrooke had of Spanish. He should now be ordering the Spanish master to show his papers and state the damage to his ship, but instead, he was in danger of a gross breach of etiquette by staring stupidly at this illustrious but ragged personage.

'Will you follow me below?' the governor shouted, pointing to the main hatch where a corner of a crudely-rigged canvas tarpaulin showed the way to the shelter below decks.

'One moment,' replied Holbrooke. He watched while the ship took one further roll, then timed his slide to the gunwale. He made the signal to Jackson to lie off to windward, then with another sickening lurch, he staggered towards the hatch. He realised that making his way around the ship was possible when he became accustomed to the motion, which was like no other that he'd experienced.

There was no artificial light below decks, and the scene was illuminated by thin slivers of daylight infiltrating through the alarmingly wide gaps in the ship's side and the planking above their heads. There were no seats, and as Holbrooke's eyes became accustomed to the chequerboard of light and dark, he saw that they were in the wreckage of a suite of apartments, presumably fitted for the accommodation of the governor and his retinue. The motion of the ship was no more comfortable down below, but now they didn't have to contend with the howling wind, and there were more solid objects to hold onto. Now that his mind wasn't wholly occupied with staying on his feet, he could look around. His first impression was of a host of ragged and sullen figures watching him from the shadows. This would be the crew, battened below decks for their own safety, but their bearing was anything but encouraging. Looking aft, or in the direction that he believed, in his disorientation, to be aft, he saw a curtained space, and as the curtain swayed with the roll and pitch of the ship, he saw two men behind the curtain. Two armed men – with pistols and swords and with matching looks of grim determination on their faces.

The governor started to move in that direction and clearly expected Holbrooke to follow him, but the sight of those pistols had brought Holbrooke back to earth – and to a sense of his duty – with a bump. With a faintly theatrical gesture, he rested his right hand on the pommel of his sword – how it had survived the boarding he couldn't tell – and he halted the governor with an edge to his voice.

'Now, sir. I must ask you some questions before we go any further.' The governor beckoned him on with a trace of irritation showing. 'No, sir. I will not follow you until I'm satisfied with a few points.'

The governor spoke rapidly in English. 'Don't be alarmed by my guards, Lieutenant. They are necessary,' he cast a sweeping glance around the ragged crew. 'It is important that I speak to you in confidence, will you follow me?'

The last thing that Holbrooke wanted to do was to follow this man who claimed to be the Governor of Florida into a closed compartment guarded by armed Spaniards. There was peace between England and Spain, but it wasn't at all uncommon to find that the treaties of everlasting friendship weren't honoured outside European waters. He was on the verge of refusing when he realised how that would appear; it would display Holbrooke's trepidation like no other action could. It was the fear of being considered cowardly that made him square his shoulders and follow Don Alonso, behind the curtain where the gloom was even more profound.

They entered a smaller space that looked like it may have been a separate cabin before the hurricane had wrenched all the bulkheads away from their frames. There were about ten men in the compartment, all apparently in the last stages of exhaustion: unshaven, dirty and wearing the wreckage of gentlemanly clothing. In the corner was a curtain that looked as though it may be screening a bed, and from behind the curtain came the glow of a ship's lantern, a curiously civilised sign amongst this howling desolation.

Only the two guards had shown any signs of alertness. They were similar in appearance to the governor, dressed in the same tattered remnants of expensive clothing. They each held a pistol, and to Holbrooke's wonder, he saw that they were half-cocked. They must have real cause for concern if they were prepared to handle weapons that may discharge by merely being dropped to the deck – in such weather as this! He looked again and saw that each man also had a pair of pistols in his belt and a sword or long dagger at his side.

'You see my situation Lieutenant. This rabble of a useless crew is only being held back by my loyal household,' he waved his arm around the room. 'I hope we will be at leisure to meet in better circumstances, they are not always such a ragged company.'

'I see,' replied Holbrooke. 'Where were you bound?'

'Pensacola in Western Florida, you know it perhaps? But it is of no consequence. Will you tow me to a safe harbour? I regret that I must ask for the facilities of a commercial or naval port. An isolated anchorage will not do.'

'Why is that, sir, if I may ask? There are many sheltered coves on the coast of Hispaniola.' Holbrooke knew that his captain firmly intended to take this ship into Port Royal, there to claim his rights of salvage, but he didn't need to reveal that to the governor.

Don Alonso looked uneasy. His cultured face had been trained from an early age to hide its emotions, but some extreme passion was taking control. There was something that Holbrooke wasn't being told. Was this one of the fabled treasure ships that carried the wealth of New Spain back to Europe? Was Pensacola a lie? But the vessel didn't look quite right for the task and Holbrooke had always understood that the Spanish Navy reserved that role for itself.

'Then it seems I must show you,' replied Don Alonso with a strange look. He stepped to the curtained corner, beckoning Holbrooke to follow him. 'You will forgive my informality, I'm sure.' He carefully moved the curtain aside. 'The Countess San Clemente Elena Marin de Villanueva e Hijar, my wife, and Maria Magdalena, my daughter. As you can see we are quite defenceless and utterly without the means to secure our own salvation. If we cannot be taken to a civilised port, we are lost.'

Holbrooke stared in astonishment at the two figures on the bed. The older woman looked more dead than alive; she was covered in blankets, and her grey face lolled from side to side as the ship swooped and rolled in this tail-end of a hurricane. The younger woman was seated on the edge of the bed holding her mother's hand. She looked up sharply with an angry word on her lips as the gust of air came through the opening in the curtain, but she bit back the reproach when she saw the tall, trim, uniformed figure of Holbrooke, looking like a phantom from a former life of orderliness, clean clothes, washed hands and regular meals.

Don Alonso said something rapid in Spanish that

Holbrooke didn't understand, but before the curtain was replaced he heard the words *Inglés teniente*, presumably referring to himself.

'Perhaps you see my problem, Lieutenant. The men are barely under control, and my wife is very, very sick. Do you have a doctor who could attend her?' For the first time, he looked like a man who was soliciting a favour. The mask of haughty autocracy had slipped, and Don Alonso didn't look as though he enjoyed its loss.

Holbrooke had been struggling to gain the initiative since he'd been unceremoniously pushed and pulled onto the deck of the ship. He'd been unprepared to meet a Spanish governor, even one temporarily bereft of his glory, and the situation of the ship was far worse than he'd imagined. Holbrooke thought rapidly. *Medina's* surgeon wasn't a man for a boat transfer in this weather and in any case, he could hardly be useful with the ship leaping and lurching like a runaway carthorse. The important thing now was to regain control of the situation and to put the countess into competent medical hands.

'Your Excellency. I can set your mind at ease regarding our destination. We will tow you into Port Royal in Jamaica where I am sure the governor will be delighted to entertain you until you can repair your ship or obtain a passage.'

Don Alonso inclined his head in acceptance.

'Meanwhile, the countess must be treated. The wind is diminishing. In an hour I believe it will have moderated sufficiently to take the countess to my ship, where we have a doctor,' The governor opened his lips to argue, the weather seemed to make a transfer impossible.

'You must trust me, Your Excellency. My people are quite capable of this. Now, if your daughter could prepare the countess, I'll make the arrangements. And meanwhile, I'll stay with you. Do you have paper and a pen that I could use?'

By noon it was done. The hastily scribbled note had brought the bosun and six of his best men to the ship, escorted by two files of marines and the indomitable Sergeant Wilson. The rebellious crew had been mastered in an instant. Wilson's grim face and the disciplined force that he brought with him restored a sense of discipline in a way that no orders from a governor could ever achieve.

They had set up a sheerleg on the deck, securing the heels to the remaining ringbolts and the guys to the more substantial parts of the wrecked gunwales. The wind was indeed moderating and with infinite care, and Jackson's skilled manoeuvring of the cutter, they lowered the countess from the deck, tightly strapped into a chair. The poor lady knew nothing of this, her lassitude had been enhanced by a hefty dose of laudanum that the surgeon had sent over, and Holbrooke had administered. The governor and his daughter followed, leaving his nervous household in the stricken ship.

It was late on Monday when they reached Port Royal with their salvage tugging and straining at the frigate's stern, still rudderless and without any scrap of canvas. They coasted along the Palisades and entered the East Channel between Plumb Point and the Middle Ground, keeping the corner of Fort Charles lined up with the peak of Salt Pond Hill. *Medina* had settled at least a foot below her marks, and the water was still entering her hull through the seams that had been opened by the hurricane. Hosking was careful to avoid the two sixteen-foot shallow patches to the northwest of Gun Kay and Rackham Kay – named for the infamous pirate whose body had been hung in irons on the island. They hardened up on the sheets to round Fort Charles and anchored off the navy yard in ten fathoms of water.

CHAPTER FOUR

Port Royal

Wednesday, twenty-second of June 1757
Kingston, Jamaica

Holbrooke, Chalmers and Hosking strolled along the waterfront of Kingston. The early morning sun wasn't yet making the broadcloth uniforms of the sea-officers uncomfortable, and the chaplain could dress in any fashion he chose, but out of deference to his companions, he was wearing a respectable black coat. They were at leisure, but still feeling their way in this strange new world, without any immediate responsibilities and no bells or messengers to summon them at a moment's notice.

The master attendant of the king's yard in Port Royal was the cause of their enforced, but welcome leisure. He'd watched *Medina* come to her anchor, noted that she was swimming deep and had been rowed across before the frigate had stretched her cable. One look at *Medina's* planking had been enough. He ordered the careening wharf to be cleared, Carlisle's exhausted crew were put to weighing the anchor that they had so recently dropped, and *Medina* was warped alongside, to be secured with enough hawsers for a first-rate ship-of-the-line. It had taken a frantic day to remove all the stores and guns, but now *Medina* was in the capable hands of the navy yard, and her officers were free to find what diversions they could. For this was to be no routine breaming and scraping. The hurricane had opened the frigate's seams from forefoot to stern-post, and the oakum and pitch had spewed out, letting in the sea in such torrents that it looked like a hundred hoses were directing their jets into the hold. The officers of the yard had estimated three weeks to complete the work: to burn and scrape all the weed from her bottom, then to remove all the remaining caulking and finally to re-caulk the whole hull and apply a coat of white stuff – a toxic mixture of tar, sulphur, fish-oil and tallow – to keep the boring worms at bay. From what Holbrooke and Hosking had seen, three weeks was likely to be an underestimate.

The three men had seen *Medina* an hour ago as they were rowed across the harbour from Port Royal in their own longboat. She'd been hauled right over against a floating pontoon and a large gang of carpenters, caulkers and less-skilled labourers were swarming over her larboard side. When that was complete, she'd have to wait for the meagre tidal rise to refloat her so that they could turn her around to get at the starboard side. *Medina's* crew had moved into the barracks ashore, and her officers had found lodgings around the town. For the next few weeks, *Medina* was the responsibility of the master attendant.

'There's a fine lot of shipping in the harbour, Mister Hosking,' the first lieutenant said idly. 'You wouldn't know that we're at war, with swarms of French privateers just looking for the opportunity to snap up a fat West Indiaman.'

'Aye, that'll be the last convoy before the hurricane season really gets into its stride, and insurance rates are doubled. They'll hope to be through the Yucatan Channel and riding the Florida Stream before the French know what's happening. That's the advantage that Jamaica has if we're fighting France. There's a useful back door to the Atlantic, which the Spanish in Cuba and Florida generously hold open for us,' he said smiling at his own sarcasm. 'Port Royal will at least be quiet for a while; it'll take half the Jamaica squadron to see them safely on their way,' Hosking tugged at his whiskers, 'and the same thing will be happening off Antigua. Mister Frankland will be worrying himself sick about scraping together enough escorts. He'll be missing *Medina*, that's for sure, and he has the French in Martinique to worry about. There'll be over two million pounds in each of those convoys,' he paused for effect, looking covertly at his audience. 'The treasury will be in a fine pickle if they don't make it back to England.'

'Two million, you say.' Chalmers affected surprise, to Hosking's gratification. 'Two million pounds? That's enough money to buy half the kingdoms in Europe. What a tremendous responsibility to lay on a man, even on the broad shoulders of an admiral.'

'If I understand the grand strategy correctly, that's exactly what it's intended for,' said Holbrooke. 'Prussia has the men, and we have the money. With that combination, the French can perhaps be prevented from overrunning Hanover.'

'Meanwhile, Mister Townshend must scrape together enough ships to see this lot out into the Atlantic,' said Hosking, airily waving his arm to indicate the forest of masts.

'Well, *Medina* won't be of any help,' remarked Holbrooke. 'They should be long gone before our standing rigging is set up again.' They both knew that the caulking was only the first of the essential tasks. The hurricane had stretched all the shrouds and stays, and it would be a good week's work to set them up afresh.

'And will the French be sending home a similar value of cargo?' asked Chalmers.

'That they will,' replied Hosking, 'but their convoys depart from Cape François in Saint Domingue on the northwest coast of Hispaniola, and from the Windward Islands, from Martinique or Guadeloupe, not unlike our own arrangement.'

'And our job,' said Holbrooke, 'is, on the one hand, to see our trade safely on its way and on the other hand to take, sink, burn or destroy theirs. With the emphasis on *taking*. There's no prize money for sinking, burning or destroying.'

'It gladdens my heart to be sailing with a King's officer of the right and proper attitude, Mister Holbrooke,' said Hosking, with sincerity.

They walked on along Harbour Street, searching for the road leading up into the hills and the house that was their destination. It should have been easy. Apparently, there was a street sign that they couldn't miss. However, the heightened level of activity that accompanied the imminent departure of the convoy meant that every step of the way was strewn with obstacles: barrels and bales, carts and mules, coils of cordage and parcels of canvas, each guarded by a sharp-tongued youth with precious little respect for the King's uniform. Not only was progress difficult, but if there was a sign, it was impossible to see through the litter of cargo and stores that impeded their field of view. They had already walked up two streets that proved to be wrong, either ending in cul-de-sacs or petering away into inconsequential, squalid lanes. Their destination certainly wouldn't be found in a grimy alley, for they were to pay a morning call on Lady Chiara Carlisle.

It was strange to think of Chiara in those terms, but a lot had happened since she arrived unexpectedly at English Harbour in February. Captain Carlisle had immediately found lodgings in St. John's for Chiara and the faintly mysterious chief of household, known to Carlisle's followers only by the nickname that they had given him – Black Rod – the same title that was enjoyed by the usher for the House of Lords. It was a fitting testament to this enigmatic man's formidable dignity and bearing. Chiara's cousin, Enrico, had been taken into *Medina's* gunroom as a midshipman. His status, as a mass-attending Catholic in a service that still required an anti-papal oath from its commission officers, wasn't at all clear. Almost by definition, midshipmen aspired to a commission – the French equivalent was even called an *aspirant* – but apparently, that didn't hold true for Enrico. Yet, he'd been absorbed without comment into the cosmopolitan band that formed the non-commissioned, un-warranted petty officers who could claim gentlemanly status. He walked the quarterdeck, he ran out on the upper yards in stormy weather, ate the substantial if unimaginative food that fuelled His Britannic Majesty's navy, and he appeared content. In fact, his life was infinitely more exciting than it had been as an ensign in His Sicilian Majesty's army. King Charles Emanuel had at last found a way of avoiding the annihilation of his territorial possessions that lay uncomfortably on the eastern border of France. To the dismay of his army and navy, he'd declared his country to be neutral in this great war that was engulfing all of Europe and had reserved his seat on the diplomatic fence, from where it seemed that nothing would move him.

The romance between Carlisle and Lady Chiara had blossomed rapidly in the heated atmosphere of Antigua. When *Medina* was ordered to join the Jamaica Squadron at the urgent request of Rear Admiral Townshend, they agreed to be married immediately so that Chiara could take passage in *Medina* for the short run across the Caribbean to Port Royal. It was a quiet occasion in the brick-built Anglican church of St. John; no member of the Angelini family had been married with so little ceremony for generations. Chalmers had officiated, and Admiral Frankland had stood witness, while Enrico, as the only member of Chiara's family present, had given away the bride. This remote outpost of empire, with its informal atmosphere, had found no difficulty in marrying a Protestant post-captain from Virginia to a titled Catholic from Sardinia with a scant few days' notice. The church register hardly acknowledged any irregularity, merely mentioning in a non-judgmental tone that the bride appeared to be a Roman Catholic. The small steeple and the twin bronze guardians of St. John the Divine and St. John the Baptist – loot from a captured French prize –

looked on without interest, comment or censure.

The difficulties that the three men were experiencing in finding their captain's house were a direct result of the pace of activity on the Jamaica Station in these last few months before the real hurricane season. A bare few days after their first arrival in Port Royal, *Medina* was sent out to patrol the waters to the east of the island. Chiara had been left waving from the quay-side, with Black Rod standing a few paces behind. It was then that the presence of the Angelini family's chief-of household started to make sense. Viscountess Angelini had foreseen the difficulties that could be faced by her niece and had insisted on her being accompanied, at least until her marital and residential status was resolved. Black Rod found the house in Kingston, a short boat trip across the bay from Port Royal. He negotiated the lease, engaged the cook and the maid and arranged Chiara's move from her temporary quarters in the admiral's residence. Carlisle knew nothing of this, his entire attention at that time being taken up with surviving the early and thankfully moderate hurricane that had ripped in from the east, and was the cause of their present, unscheduled holiday in each other's company.

'Edward, what can have become of George and David and Mister Hosking?' asked Chiara. She was sitting beside her husband watching the same bustle and hurry of the convoy's preparations that was impeding their guests, albeit from the somewhat higher ground with a grand view of the harbour. By craning their necks, they could see Port Royal in the far distance and could just identify *Medina's* stern, pitched over at an improbable angle. Immediately across the harbour and much closer than *Medina*, they could see the *Nuestra Señora del Rosario*, beached to prevent its sinking, but still mastless and looking more fit for the breaker's yard than the high seas. They were sitting very close to each other. In true naval fashion, they had been permitted little time to get used to being married before the needs of the service had pulled them apart, and the simple act of holding hands as a married couple was still a delicious novelty. 'If they aren't here soon I'll have no opportunity to speak to George before the Spanish gentleman arrives, and you know, I'll be obliged to speak Spanish to him. It will be most inconvenient.'

Before Carlisle could reply, there was a sharp rap at the door and a few moments later a flustered Holbrooke, a tranquil Chalmers and Hosking, wearing the same imperturbable expression that he wore on all occasions, were shown in by Black Rod. Their demeanours reflected their different relationships with their captain. While Holbrooke relied entirely on Carlisle's goodwill for his present place and his future promotion, the chaplain was, as always, unconcerned with his own fate, while the older sailing master was secure in his warranted position. The Navy Board could always find a place for an experienced master mariner like himself regardless of the opinion of a junior post-captain.

'George, how wonderful to see you,' cried Chiara, riding straight over the greeting that was forming on her husband's lips while holding out her hands to the younger man and gazing in delight at his face. From the side, apparently forgotten, Chalmers watched the play of emotions on the faces of the two sea-officers. Happiness and mild embarrassment for Holbrooke but a brief flash of what looked like jealousy and annoyance, swiftly replaced by a mask of welcome on the part of Carlisle. No man cared to see his new bride so frankly happy to see a colleague.

Chiara had known George Holbrooke as long as she'd known her husband. They'd met in the Angelini villa overlooking Nice when Carlisle's previous frigate, *Fury*, had visited in the fevered months before the war had started. For that matter, she'd known David Chalmers just as long; she'd even become used to calling him *David*, when in private, and Reverend John Chalmers when in company. He'd once given her an explanation for his chosen name. The characters of all the new testament Johns were, he felt, too close to that of a typical clergyman for comfort, and he favoured the straightforward robustness of the old testament King David as a counterpoint. Not that he thought his own character was in any way heroic. Nevertheless, he preferred that his real Christian name should be used in formal situations. During the short passage across the sparkling Caribbean Sea in the close confines of a frigate, they had all become very easy in each other's company; Mrs Carlisle, George and David.

'Your Ladyship,' said Holbrooke, 'it's a great pleasure to meet you again.' They had long ago mutually agreed that Holbrooke was allowed one use of the title *Your Ladyship* on first meeting to satisfy his sense of propriety, but from there it must be *Mrs Carlisle*.

Chiara was nothing if not well-bred, and with an acknowledgement to Holbrooke, she turned and greeted the chaplain and the sailing master, with equal ceremony if perhaps with less real warmth. She could speak to any number of people at once and hold their attention as though she were talking to one alone. 'Do you have satisfactory quarters?' she asked. 'I am so sorry that we can't offer you rooms here, but you see that houses in Kington are not very large,' she said sweeping her hand around the room. In truth, they had a perfectly adequate house, the largest that was available at the time that it was needed. While not precisely wealthy, Carlisle had made some money from prizes and would receive a great deal more when the courts had finished deliberating. Of course, the funds had to pass through the lawyers and the prize agent – not without a due proportion sticking to their hands along the way – before it reached his bank, and that took time. But his credit was excellent, and all of Jamaica knew the earning potential of a frigate captain in time of war. He could certainly afford the rent on any house in Kingston.

At that moment Black Rod entered the room to announce the arrival of tea, brought by the newly-acquired maid, a middle-aged indentured servant with a foreign accent. She had the look of one who had spent some time out of doors – her face was browned by the sun, and her skin lacked the delicacy that most women cultivated. She'd only been engaged the previous day. However, she seemed to know her way around a tea-tray, and Chiara served it as though she'd done so all her life, while in reality, it was a novelty to her, just one more oddity of these strange English people. Chalmers was the most talkative, Hosking being naturally reticent and Holbrooke as always having an attack of shyness in his captain's wife's company.

'Are you enjoying the delights of Kingston, Mrs Carlisle?' asked Chalmers, when they had each safely taken delivery of a delicate porcelain teacup and saucer. The finger-joints of sea officers weren't designed for this purpose, so Holbrooke and Hosking had to grip the whole handle between thumb and forefinger. Chalmers secretly wondered how long the joint between the cup and handle could withstand that kind of pressure. He withdrew his chair a foot or so, to remove himself from the splash zone. 'I expect you may find it a little lacking in sophistication when compared with Nice or Livorno.'

'It is a little rustic, I agree, but I've had no time to myself, no time at all.' Chiara looked sideways at her husband, looked away and then turned her whole face back to him. 'May I tell them, Edward? Oh, may I?'

The three guests exchanged mystified glances, while their captain pondered for no more than two seconds. In truth, there was little to consider. The balance of moral authority between him and his aristocratic, headstrong wife wasn't of the quality that would allow him to deny any request for very long.

'Yes, my dear,' he said with a smile. 'It'll be all over

Kingston, Spanish Town and Port Royal in a few days so those most concerned may certainly know first.'

'We are to take His Excellency the governor to St. Augustine!' exclaimed Chiara. She looked for a suitable reaction from the three men, but to them, it wasn't particularly noteworthy; a trip of about a month's duration through peaceful waters, and in any case, they couldn't start until *Medina* was seaworthy again. Chiara began to look disappointed at their reactions.

'I don't believe our guests have yet grasped the significance of the word *we* that you used, Chiara. They've made some assumptions that you may enjoy correcting,' said Carlisle, smiling.

'Of course!' cried Chiara, clapping her hands in delight. She attempted to explain, her command of English almost defeating her in her haste. 'This is – oh, what's the word? – something of a diplomatic mission, and with a Spanish countess travelling all that way in a British man-of-war, the admiral has determined that there should be a suitable companion. He's asked Edward if I may sail with you,' she said, 'to St. Augustine!'

The reaction was all that she could have hoped. They had been suitably amazed when Admiral Frankland had allowed Carlisle to convey his new wife from English Harbour to Port Royal, but that was little more than a shuttle across the Caribbean, six days of fair weather and little chance of meeting an enemy man-of-war. The admiral's decision was probably influenced by the guilt that he may have felt in the separation that the newly married couple would otherwise have to endure. However, this was something on a much grander scale. The voyage to St. Augustine would take them through the Yucatan Channel, around the northwestern tip of Cuba and northwards between the Bahamas and the mainland, following the Florida Stream. It was the same passage that the merchant convoy would take, avoiding the hard beat through the Windward Passage and, of the highest importance, bypassing the French naval base at Cape François on the northwest coast of Saint Domingue. In part, it followed the route that the Spanish treasure ships had taken for the last two hundred years, giving it an air of romance. *Medina* would presumably have to spend a few days at St. Augustine, the seat of the governor of Florida, then come back by the same way. The whole voyage would take a month, probably. It was almost unheard of for a commander-in-chief to allow a captain to take his wife on such a long voyage in wartime.

'Well, I congratulate you, ma'am. We'll have some fine sailing, but it'll be a long passage back to the Yucatan against the current.' Hosking was always the practical navigator, and he basked in the glory of having the features of this voyage at his fingertips without any prior knowledge of the plan and without the need to consult the pilots or charts.

'Ah, there I have you Mister Hosking,' exclaimed Carlisle in triumph. 'You're still guilty of making assumptions.' He observed his officers' faces. 'We'll return through the Windward Passage.'

Hosking looked less than pleased. This new route home exposed them to the French squadron based at Cape François. 'Very well, sir,' he replied, not wishing to relinquish the role of navigational oracle quite so quickly. 'Then it'll be a long leg north-northeast into the Atlantic until we can take a single tack outside the Bahamas, through Crooked Island Passage and then run through the Windward Passage and back to Jamaica. A few days faster than the Yucatan Channel, perhaps, but there are disadvantages …,' he didn't complete the sentence. It wasn't his place to reveal the dangers to his captain's wife.

Carlisle acknowledged the skill of his sailing master but didn't always appreciate his condescending manner in navigational matters, nor his tendency to offer his opinion on operational issues.

'But there is one further detail, gentlemen,' Carlisle

said, 'and I must insist on your discretion in this. I'm ordered to Cape François on the way home, to see what the French are doing.' He let that sink in for a moment. He could see that both Hosking and Holbrooke understood that what was previously thought of as a sort of yachting holiday had, at its end, a solid naval purpose. Of course, Admiral Townshend would take every opportunity to gain intelligence on the enemy, and after all, that was one of a frigate's main purposes. 'What will be our route in that case?' he asked Hosking, offering him the opportunity to shine.

'Well, sir, the Crooked Island Passage will see us too far west and to leeward of Cape François. We must beat further into the Atlantic and pass between the Inagua Islands and the Caicos Islands, the Caicos Passage, it's called. It's more difficult navigation, and I've never been that way, but it's perfectly normal for anyone sailing towards Saint Domingue. It'll place us north of Cape François, and we'll have the trade wind abaft the beam for the run in.' He looked thoughtful. 'It'll put a day or two on the passage, sir, so long as we don't get tangled up with the French.'

Chiara clapped her hands and smiled broadly. 'Bravo, Mister Hosking. I've been studying for the past half day, attempting to work out how we get to St. Augustine, and home again. And here I find you know the way without even a glimpse of a map.'

Hosking winced at hearing a sea-chart being referred to as a map, but he bowed graciously. Chalmers noticed that, with a few carefully-chosen words, Chiara had defused any hint of censure that the sailing master may have inferred from Carlisle's gentle teasing. Chalmers was a peacemaker himself, an inveterate healer of psychological wounds, and he recognised a kindred spirit. Perhaps the captain's wife would be an asset on this voyage. He noticed the door to the salon closing and caught a glimpse of Black Rod's coat sleeve as he held the door for the serving girl to leave the room with the tea tray.

'There is one thing that I don't understand,' said Holbrooke. 'Why do we not take His Excellency to Havana? Surely that would be the fastest way to return him to his countrymen, and we'll pass right by it.'

'He doesn't care to go to Havana,' replied Carlisle, who was unsure of his ground, 'he fears the delay that it'll cause. St. Augustine is his destination and unless we can find a Spanish ship willing to take him, then St. Augustine it is.'

Chiara held her hands wide in a very un-ladylike pose. 'I had no idea that you sailors had so much fun!' she said and laughed delightedly. Her pleasure was infectious, and soon all the men in the room joined her, even Hosking risked his dignity with a strange sort of barking sound which could politely be mistaken for laughter.

CHAPTER FIVE

His Excellency

Wednesday, twenty-second of June 1757
Kingston, Jamaica

With stately measure, Black Rod's deep voice intoned the name of the visitor. 'His Excellency Don Alonso Fernández de Heredia, governor of Florida.'

Don Alonso strode into the room that was fast becoming crowded with Captain Carlisle, Lady Chiara, Holbrooke, Hosking and Chalmers. He was a tall, handsome man in his late thirties with a neatly trimmed black beard in the best Spanish fashion. His face was browned by the tropical sun and his eyes swept across the room and its inhabitants from under level, sparse eyebrows. His pupils were jet-black, a blackness that was accentuated by the startling white of the surrounding sclera. Don Alonso was dressed in a suit of burgundy velvet shot through with silver threads, not unlike the outfit that he wore when he was rescued, but that suit had been rendered irreparable by the hurricane. This suit, however, was immaculate. He wore a silver-hilted small-sword and swept a large feathered hat from his head as he bowed on being introduced.

When they had last met, Don Alonso was a worried man, concerned for the safety of his family and of himself and suspicious of this English ship and her American captain. The officers of *Medina* had seen little of him during the two-day passage to Port Royal and what they did see hadn't impressed them. However, with his feet planted firmly on dry land, Don Alonso was a changed man. He'd immediately resumed the poise and authority that was characteristic of the Castilian grandee that he was.

Lesser men may have felt demeaned at being rescued from certain death – a death that he would have shared with his wife and daughter – by a commoner, and an English colonial commoner at that. Lesser men would have been further disadvantaged by knowing that it was the same English sea-officer who would deliver him and his family to their ultimate destination. That burden of obligation would have weighed heavily on the souls of most of mankind. However, Don Alonso lived in an altogether different world, and he'd never so far forgotten his God-given rank as to resent the everyday skills that other men had, and he had not. They had been given those skills for a purpose and, as far as he was concerned, that purpose was to carry out Don Alonso's wishes. His role was to command, and it was the duty of all inferior mortals to turn his orders into practical realities. He was a ruthless exploiter of other's talents and having sincerely offered his thanks – where it was necessary – he saw no further need to feel obligated. As a result, Don Alonso had no difficulty in expressing his gratitude for his deliverance to Captain Carlisle in the most gracious terms.

'It was merely my duty, Your Excellency,' replied Carlisle. Both men knew that these words were a conventional formula, but the difference was that Don Alonso believed that they also carried the force of natural law. Carlisle had indeed done no more than his duty and he, Don Alonso, had expressed his gratitude. There was no more to be said on the matter.

Carlisle made the introductions, and Don Alonso was enchanted to find that Chiara's Spanish was nearly fluent. 'May I enquire about the countess' recovery?' asked Chiara, fixing Don Alonso with the bold appraising gaze that she'd learned in the court of King Charles Emmanuel of Sardinia. She'd grown up dealing with men such as him, and for all that she loved her husband, she could see that in the subtleties of diplomacy he'd be no match for this Spaniard.

'The countess is still not at all well, I regret to say. She suffered badly in the hurricane, as your husband perhaps told you, and will take some weeks to recover.' Chiara inclined her head, more in recognition that he'd spoken than in agreement. She knew better than to agree to anything that was proposed by a man like Don Alonso until she knew the consequences of her acquiescence.

The sea-officers vividly remembered the countess being brought aboard *Medina* during the tail-end of the hurricane. The weather was still atrocious although not actually dangerous and it was undoubtedly no weather to be moving a very sick lady from one ship to another. However, she couldn't stay in the Spanish ship, rolling like a pig as it was, so *Medina* it had to be. She'd looked close to death – in fact, she probably was – when she was eventually hoisted aboard in a chair, with Jackson riding alongside her and keeping her firmly in place.

'Then may I offer my services if she needs some company?' asked Chiara.

'You are very good, Lady Chiara,' replied Don Alonso. 'The physician has suggested that in a few days she may welcome visitors, perhaps we may see you then? However, the countess won't be able to travel by sea for at least a month. Until she has recovered fully, the motion of a ship could prove fatal.' He turned to Carlisle. 'I understand, Captain, that I am to have the pleasure of being conveyed by you to St. Augustine and that your repairs will be complete in a month.'

That allayed any guilt that Carlisle felt about discussing his ship's destination with Chiara and his officers. If this Spaniard knew that *Medina* was bound for Florida, then the whole of the island would know within the day, if they didn't already. However, he knew that he must remind his officers of the secrecy of their return voyage, that was none of Don Alonso's business. He'd perhaps been too casual in releasing that information, but the temptation to goad his sailing master had been just too great.

'It will be my pleasure. Mister Hosking is already planning the voyage.' Don Alonso favoured Hosking with a half bow, a courtesy calculated to convey his thanks but also that he considered it no more than the sailing master's duty.

Carlisle was baffled by Don Alonso's impenetrable self-assurance. He'd have liked to be sure that the Spaniard understood the scale of the favour that the civilian government and the naval command in Jamaica were offering him, but it was hard to tell whether Don Alonso recognised anything other than his own importance. It made sense to Carlisle that Admiral Townshend should go to such trouble for the representative of a friendly power, even to the extent of dangerously depleting his frigate force, but it was galling that the recipient took it so much for granted. He knew that the French were busily trying to woo Spain away from her neutrality. His friend Augustus Hervey, whose brother the Duke of Bristol was ambassador to Madrid, had enthralled him with second-hand stories of the diplomacy and subterfuge that was being employed by the French. It was widely believed in the British government that the principal reason for the French choosing to invade Minorca and thus push Britain to war, was so that the island could be offered to Spain in exchange for an alliance. It was a measure of Spain's unreadiness for a war that Madrid should so far have resisted the proposal.

'I'm sure it needs no words from me, Your Excellency, to convey how happy I am to have the honour of conveying you to Florida. I was deeply concerned that you may make an attempt in *Nuestra Señora Del Rosario*, and then I had feared, when *Medina* was given the task, that it would only be as far as Havana.'

Don Alonso briefly wondered whether Carlisle was fishing for information, but he merely bowed. He knew from his recent visit to Madrid that there were compelling arguments for Spain joining France and Austria in an alliance against Britain and Prussia. There was the matter of Minorca – it was a national disgrace that Britain should have held it for nearly fifty years – and Gibraltar, both of which may be returned to Spain if the war went well. Yet Spanish ambitions didn't end there. Portugal was weak and ripe for invasion; it was an ally of Britain and could be quickly overrun. Yes, there would be war, but Madrid was not yet ready and wouldn't be for a few years. There was plenty of time for this half-Englishman to deliver him to St. Augustine without any danger of finding himself a guest in a hostile ship.

'I regret that it is impossible for the *Nuestra Señora Del Rosario* to convey me any further. If she is ever seaworthy again it will be long after I must return to my duties. I am told she requires significant internal structural repair as well as the repairs to her hull and a complete set of masts and sails. She is almost worthless.' This was the closest that Don Alonso would come to acknowledging the indisputable fact that Carlisle and his crew, according to the laws of salvage, owned a significant share of the wrecked ship. The Medinas could claim perhaps as much as half of the value of the vessel, although that would be for the Vice-Admiralty Court to decide, for its Spanish equivalent to contest and for the ship's insurers to appeal. Any money that eventually filtered through to the crew would be a very long time coming. In any case, it was probably only worth its scrap value.

'Well, it's an easy passage, Your Excellency, with following winds or currents the whole way. The greatest danger will come from hurricanes, although if there's any justice in this world, we've all had our share for this year.' Hosking looked grave; he saw nothing at all light-hearted about hurricanes. Don Alonso, however, was of a philosophical nature and smiled broadly.

'Certainly, we've had our share, and I wouldn't want to deprive any other seafarers of the exhilarating experience. I trust that any tropical storms will expend themselves in the

French colonies, far to the east!' Everyone could agree with that sentiment, and the talk became less constrained until Don Alonso departed after an hour.

'Mister Holbrooke, would you care to stay for a while, I've some business to discuss,' said Carlisle. This was a broad hint for Hosking and Chalmers to leave, and they said their farewells with a promise to come again.

'Please do,' said Chiara as she walked with them to the door. 'I'd welcome calls after ten o'clock any morning, particularly from such good friends.'

When the other men had left, Carlisle and Holbrooke settled into comfortable chairs, and the serving girl brought a rum punch. It was a good punch: Jamaican rum, cane sugar, lime juice and nutmeg, watered to taste. It just needed ice, but that was more than could be expected in seventeen degrees of latitude. In Carlisle's Virginia home they managed to keep a small amount of ice right through the year, maintaining something near sub-zero temperatures in purpose-built ice-houses dug deep into the soil. But that was many, many leagues north of Jamaica and here in the tropics, no ice could be found in any season of the year.

The two men enjoyed the first sips of the punch in preparation for their discussion. And yet, Chiara seemed inclined to linger. In fact, she showed no signs of departing the room.

'We will be talking business, my dear,' said Carlisle with a heavy hint that Chiara should leave them.

'Yes,' replied Chiara with a sweet smile, 'please don't feel that you're intruding,' and taking a seat beside the small table, she picked up a copy of the Jamaica Courant and pretended to read it. Carlisle sighed; he should have known that this willful woman of his wouldn't be so easily dismissed. He briefly considered moving into the dining room, but it would be too obviously a snub to his new wife, and there was the genuine danger – no, the near-certainty – that she'd follow them, with that same beguiling smile. Holbrooke maintained a rigid, immobile expression until Chiara looked up from her broadsheet and favoured him with a dazzling grin, which he could only return. Carlisle came very close to pomposity but steadied himself with a deep breath.

'Well, what do you think of him, Holbrooke?' he asked, deliberately not looking at his wife, who he felt sure would offer an opinion if given any encouragement.

'He's certainly a different man to the one that I met on board the wreck. He seems to have drawn strength from being ashore. I'd say that he's more of a soldier than a sailor and above all, he's a man who's used to being obeyed.'

'Just so,' replied Carlisle. 'He'll need watching on the voyage. The admiral warned me that my orders will include a clause about consulting His Excellency when appropriate. I'm concerned that if he knows or guesses that, he'll exploit it.'

'Are you sure that Spain isn't about to declare war?' asked Holbrooke. 'Don Alonso has just returned from Madrid; he'll have a better idea on that subject than anyone else on this side of the ocean.'

'My impression is that Spain will wait, and the admiral agrees with me. Their army isn't ready, and they need to build ships,' replied Carlisle, 'but Minorca is a powerful incentive. If the war lasts into the next decade, then I'm confident that Spain will join France against us. There's the Hapsburg family connection, apart from more practical considerations. I suppose there's a danger that we're being led into a trap and that Spain's war will start with the capture of a British frigate, but I don't believe so. There would be an international outcry if Spain so far abused British hospitality.'

Both men looked thoughtful. It would be a diplomatic juggling act, and they both knew that Don Alonso was not a man to readily acquiesce to other's views, even when a passenger in a foreign man-of-war. How far would Carlisle find his range of options constrained by this forceful guest?

Chiara broke the silence. 'May I offer an opinion, dear Edward,' she asked. It was clear to both the men that she would do so whatever Carlisle said, so making the best of it he replied in an almost welcoming tone. 'Certainly, my dear, what do you have to offer?'

Holbrooke was close to laughter. He may have the exalted situation of first lieutenant of a King's frigate, but he was only nineteen, and in principle, he was far too young for his position. His contemporaries were mostly men in their thirties and forties, but Carlisle trusted him and would have no other, and as there was only one lieutenant in the authorised establishment of a sixth-rate, he was the *de facto* first lieutenant. Yet Holbrooke hadn't entirely shaken off his youth and the sight of his captain being so adroitly managed came close to destroying his composure.

'I found Don Alonso perfectly charming, witty and handsome ...,' Carlisle groaned inwardly, is this what he had to look forward to? This level of conversation? He'd prefer that his wife remained silent, but if she must speak – and apparently, she must – couldn't she find something less embarrassing to say? Chiara, refusing to take notice of her husband's expression, continued with the same innocent smile, 'he's the model of a cultured Spanish courtier, and I very much look forward to travelling with him.' She paused, perhaps for effect. 'However, he is hiding something, and he is worried. I don't trust him, and nor should you!'

Carlisle and Holbrooke had been lulled by Chiara's soft words, but the last sentence was delivered with a hint of steel in her voice. Neither man spoke immediately, and it looked as though Chiara, having fired her broadside, would settle back to her newspaper, but Carlisle was intrigued.

'Why do you say that my dear. Do you have a specific concern?'

'I was watching his face. He looked straight at everyone who spoke, but when Mister Hosking referred to the passage around Cuba and past Havana, he looked away, he didn't want his expression to be read. There is something about our route that worries him, and that's not all. Have you noticed how he doesn't refer to the loss of the frigate that was escorting him? That must be a concern to him and yet he won't speak of it. At the very least it's an interesting topic for you sea-officers, and mere politeness would have suggested that he should mention it.'

'I don't see what could concern him about our route,' said Holbrooke. 'The admiral agreed that *Medina* should take him all the way to St. Augustine, but if we meet a Spanish man-of-war, it seems likely that he'll want to leave us. As I understand it, we're only taking him directly to St. Augustine for convenience and so that he's not delayed waiting for a suitable ship in Havana.'

'Ah, now you're touching on the greatest secret of them all,' replied Carlisle. 'I haven't mentioned this before now, but Admiral Townshend knows from other sources that His Excellency and the Captain-General of Cuba don't always agree. His Excellency ranks below the captain-general, who attempts to use his seniority to interfere in the governor's prerogatives in Florida. There's even talk that he's manoeuvring to subsume Florida into the Captaincy-General of Cuba. It's likely that Don Alonso has no desire to appear before the captain-general in the person of a helpless shipwrecked mariner. In fact, His Excellency has stated to the admiral that he'd be particularly grateful if he could be conveyed *directly* to St. Augustine without any communication with Havana or with the Spanish Navy.' Carlisle looked around at his audience. 'Have you ever heard anything so absurd?' he smiled, 'and yet it's true. You can see why, on the one hand, Don Alonso wants our help to reach St. Augustine un-noticed by Havana, while on the other hand he dares not admit to a foreign power his reason for doing so.' He turned to Chiara. 'My dear, I do believe you've exposed his weakness.'

'And now you have a trump card if he tries to interfere,' exclaimed Chiara, pleased to have her suspicions confirmed. 'It's likely that a mere hint of calling at Havana – our water is running low for example, or we need repairs – will bring him to obedience. Yet that doesn't address his second secret, the loss of his frigate. There's something there that still worries him and that he doesn't want to talk about.'

Holbrooke was pleased to be involved in these discussions, even with Lady Chiara involved – particularly with her involved if he was honest with himself. This talk of diplomatic issues and Chiara's evident familiarity with this level of discussion gave him a glimpse at the machinery that moved in realms above those of naval operations. He was starting to see the thought processes that sent squadrons across the oceans and determined the movements of his own *Medina*. It raised his sights above the level of a simple sailor.

'Then we must take the western side of the Yucatan Channel and catch the current that loops northwards and back to Cape Florida. We'll be well clear of Havana but within easy reach if we want to use that as a threat,' said Holbrooke. 'The current will favour us on that side of the channel in any case. The distance is greater, but the passage time will be less even though it'll take us closer to French Louisiana.'

'Very well,' declared Carlisle. 'Then it appears that we've successfully merged the skills of diplomacy,' he bowed to his wife, 'and seamanship to create a plan of action. Mister Holbrooke, would you let Mister Hosking know that I'd like to discuss the route in front of his charts tomorrow?'

'Perhaps, though, I shouldn't mention the reason for

avoiding Havana,' replied Holbrooke.

CHAPTER SIX

The Reception

Friday, twenty-second of July 1757
Kingston, Jamaica

The governor's residence was huge, even by Jamaican plantation standards. This evening it was brilliantly lit by torches set around its perimeter and at each torch was a servant, mostly indentured men and women from the English counties and African slaves, with here and there a soldier or sailor keeping watch. Captain Edward and Lady Chiara Carlisle arrived in a four-horse carriage that they had borrowed for the occasion. Holbrooke and Black Rod rode in the seat opposite them. Holbrooke was an invited guest while Black Rod would ensure that the driver didn't get drunk and that the carriage was at the door when they were ready to leave. For this was a significant diplomatic and social occasion. George Haldane, the governor of Jamaica, was saying his farewells to Don Alonso Fernández de Heredia and his wife and daughter. Don Alonso was Haldane's counterpart in Florida, and it was vital that he should be treated with all possible ceremony. Carlisle knew that except for Holbrooke, he was the most junior person present, whether it was counted by naval, military or civilian seniority. Neither he nor Holbrooke would have been invited if they weren't providing the transport to take Don Alonso home. For two weeks, Carlisle, Chiara and Holbrooke would be the only people of remotely comparable social status in contact with Don Alonso and his family.

'Captain Edward Carlisle and Lady Chiara Carlisle,' boomed the voice of the enormous Major-Domo, louder even than Black Rod. 'Lieutenant George Holbrooke.'

The governor's ballroom had been rigged for something not dissimilar to a royal levee. Haldane, Don Alonso and their ladies were stationed at the far end of the room in a sort of receiving line, with a queue of people waiting to be introduced. Rear Admiral of the Red Thomas Cotes, lately arrived as the new commander-in-chief, was also in the receiving line, looking unsure of his social and political position in relation to the two colonial governors. Vice Admiral Townshend and his lady were standing some way apart, putting a brave face on their banishment from the inner circle. They were nonentities, awaiting a ship to carry them home, and the society of Jamaica had already half-forgotten them. The cruel fact was that Townshend was hardly worth talking to now, his power and patronage had vanished the moment his flag was hauled down.

The shattering announcements of the Major-Domo were nothing more than an introduction to the room in general; the two governors paid no attention at all. The real business was being orchestrated by a much more discreet team of officials who were organising the visitors and passing those who were deemed suitable for an audience to a smartly-dressed soldier – presumably the governor's aide – who made a more personal introduction to the two governors.

One of the dubious benefits of marriage into minor nobility was that Carlisle had already met the governor and his wife. In fact, the Carlisles had been on the Jamaican social circuit since they had arrived on the island. Chiara adored social events. She'd been educated in courtly protocol form an early age and had spent a fair part of her youth around the influential men and women who followed King Charles Emanuel in his itinerate travels over his dispersed kingdom.

'Carlisle, how good to see you again, and Lady Chiara,' said Haldane as he bowed to kiss Chiara's proffered hand. 'I believe you know Don Alonso already, so I won't make introductions. Just take care of him and Countess Elena and see them safely to St. Augustine, won't you?'

George Haldane had little use for conversational niceties. He'd been a soldier in his youth and fought with distinction through the last war. He was wounded at Fontenoy and fought alongside King George at Dettingen. He campaigned with Cumberland in the Jacobite uprising of '45 and was at Lauffeld and Roucoux in '47. Haldane had been one of the army's youngest brigadier-generals before he resigned his commission for a career in politics.

'I won't rest until the doors of the Castillo San Marco are closed behind them, Your Excellency,' replied Carlisle. 'May I introduce Lieutenant Holbrooke? It was Mister Holbrooke who insisted on taking a boat to Don Alonso's ship before the hurricane had subsided. He certainly spared the countess another day of acute discomfort and quite probably saved her life.'

'Then I am grateful, Lieutenant Holbrooke, for without your heroism I would have been deprived of the countess' company.' He deftly moved the trio on to Don Alonso and addressed himself to the next in line, a heavy, red-faced planter who was distinguished not only by his enormous wealth but also by his tight grip on the levers of political power. He certainly deserved more of the governor's time than did a junior frigate captain and his first lieutenant.

'Good evening, Your Excellency,' said Carlisle. He hadn't met Don Alonso since his call at Carlisle's house a month ago.

'Good evening, Captain,' replied Don Alonso, returning the bow. The two men may not have met for a month, but Don Alonso had frequently seen Chiara when she visited his wife and had noted her aristocratic bearing. Intrigued, he'd made inquiries and what he learned had persuaded him that he must pay more attention to this otherwise unremarkable English captain. 'I don't believe you have met the Countess San Clemente Elena Marin de

Villanueva e Hijar,' he said as he introduced his wife. Countess Elena was an unremarkable woman and even allowing for her recent return from near-death, she looked much older than her husband. Her face was startlingly white in this room full of sunburned planters, sailors and soldiers and she looked shrivelled and worn. She leaned on the arm of a man in the uniform of the Spanish Royal Army whom Carlisle recognised from the day after the hurricane.

Carlisle bowed again, and Chiara made her courtesy. It appeared that the countess spoke no English, but Chiara was able to translate her vague gratitude for being saved from the sea and her hope that they would have a calm passage to Florida.

The next introduction was to a lady of such a contrast to the countess that Carlisle was momentarily disorientated. Maria Magdalena Fernandez de Heredia y Marin de Villanueva was as young and vibrant as her mother was middle-aged and dour. She'd inherited her father's commanding stance, his arresting manner and his looks, which in his daughter were translated into dark-haired, black flashing-eyed beauty.

Maria was a sort of younger, less finished version of Carlisle's wife. Maria confidently offered her hand to Carlisle and Holbrooke and her cheek to Chiara. She had a bold eye and held the gaze of each of the men as she spoke to them using correct but heavily-accented English. Maria can't have been past seventeen but displayed natural confidence that neither man was used to in young ladies. Chiara, on the contrary, was entirely accustomed to ladies like Maria. Indeed she'd been just such a person, and not so many years ago. She recognised that Maria, like herself, had been brought up to hold her own in a male-dominated society and by force of personality to demand the deference that her years wouldn't otherwise have warranted. Maria had not been so severely affected by the hurricane, but she'd stayed beside her mother's bed for the passage to Port Royal, and neither Carlisle nor Holbrooke had caught more than a glimpse of her before she disembarked with her father and mother.

Chiara knew the species and recognised the signs. Maria held her husband's hand just a second or two longer than was entirely correct, and her eyes didn't leave his face except to briefly acknowledge Chiara and Holbrooke. Edward Carlisle may not have really come to know Chiara during their brief months of marriage, but Chiara, with much more extensive experience of humanity in the round, knew her husband in detail. She watched Maria's frank advances and knew that Carlisle had few defences against this kind of assault. Chiara would have felt much more comfortable if it were Holbrooke's hand and Holbrooke's eye that she held. This young lady would need to be watched. And so would her husband.

Carlisle hadn't yet been introduced to Admiral Cotes. The captain of a frigate wasn't high on the priority list of people for a new commander-in-chief to meet, and if it weren't for this reception, they probably wouldn't have met before *Medina* sailed for St. Augustine.

'Pleased to meet you, Carlisle,' said the admiral, 'Lady Chiara, charmed,' he continued, kissing her hand. 'Mister Holbrooke, how do you do?' He let the social chit-chat take its course, and then beckoning to Carlisle, he led him some way apart. After all, he wasn't needed and felt that his dignity was imperilled by being the last in the receiving line, albeit the last behind two excellencies.

'I haven't had time to look into this cruise of yours, Carlisle,' he said, deliberately turning his back on Admiral Townshend who looked as though he'd join them, invited or not. 'It's highly unusual, and I'm not at all sure that it's the best use of one of my frigates.' He looked at Carlisle as though he blamed him for this irregularity. 'Still, I understand you have orders to return by way of Cape François, so it won't be a dead loss. Your orders can stand as written.'

'Thank you, sir. I didn't ask for this task…'

'Oh, it's not your fault, Carlisle. It's just a bit galling to hoist my flag and find that one of my best frigate captains – now don't try my patience with false modesty – has been sent away on what can best be described as a yachting trip. I imagine His Excellency feels the need to maintain friendly relations with the Spanish, but this is quite an imposition. Did you know that the wretched man positively declined to be put ashore in Havana?'

'I had heard that,' said Carlisle cautiously, 'some question of precedence between him and the Captain-General of Cuba I understand.'

'It's rather more than that, I'm told. The captain-general has been lobbying in Madrid for Florida to be subsumed into his little colonial empire. Don Alonso heard about it and immediately took passage for Spain to make his case for continued independence from Cuba. The issue, I understand, hasn't been resolved and Don Alonso now fears that he'll be detained on some pretext or other if ever he sets foot in Havana. He'll be very keen that you steer clear of Spanish national ships and he'll resist being moved into a Spanish merchantman if you should meet one going your way. You have him until you drop anchor under the guns of Castillo San Marco and there's no wriggling out of it. How that can ever help our relations with Spain is beyond my understanding. Surely it's better to have a captain-general as your friend rather than a colonial governor. But that's Haldane's business, not mine.'

Cotes paused and cast another furious glance at Townshend, who he blamed for agreeing to this voyage in the first place.

'It beggars belief. But I've told Haldane that the Don is to embark only his family and a maid. He's to have no aides, no orderlies, no damned soldiers. They can pay for their passage in whatever merchantman will take them, and

I trust the bottom falls out as soon as they've sunk the land,' he said with passion and not a little vindictiveness. 'You'll be better able to control His Excellency without his entourage interfering.' He gave the frigate captain a conspiratorial wink, a gesture that looked so incongruous that Carlisle almost laughed. 'But never mind, come back as quickly as you can, and you can take as many prizes as you like once you're rid of His Spanish Excellency. Those are *my* orders, so long as you make a good count of the French in Cape François. They're collecting together the biggest convoy for years, and I need to know what escort they have and how many merchantmen.' He looked thoughtful for a moment. 'I'll have to scratch together a squadron to blockade them once the hurricane season's over.' He stamped in frustration. 'And that's another thing, you're being sent away at the height of the season. I don't like it, not at all.'

'Oh, I've survived my hurricane for this year,' replied Carlisle casually, trying to lighten the mood. Everything he knew about commanders-in-chief on foreign stations told him that the present line of conversation would inevitably lead to the admiral venting his spleen on his frigate captain, fairly or unfairly. 'Hurricanes, like lightning, never strike the same person twice.'

Cotes looked as though he had something else to say, something less than pleasant, but he was interrupted by a fluttering fan as Maria Magdalena laid her gloved hand firmly on Carlisle's arm and led him away with the most perfunctory of apologies to the admiral. Carlisle looked over his shoulder, but the admiral had already forgotten him and had shifted his gimlet gaze onto a naval contractor that he spotted across the crowded room. A man to whom sharp practice was the only known way to conduct business and who had become a wealthy man providing calves at bullock prices and selling condemned butter back to the squadron's bosuns for greasing their yards. Carlisle saw something else as well; his wife was watching him. No, she was watching Maria Magdalena, with a very cool expression that he hadn't seen before. And out of the corner of his eye, he saw that Don Alonso had been watching the two men – the admiral and the frigate captain – as they were talking. Carlisle wondered whether he'd guessed what they were discussing. In all likelihood, yes, he decided. The admiral's evident anger, and his own defensiveness, would be easily interpreted even if Don Alonso hadn't caught any of their words.

Chiara discreetly watched her husband and Maria even as she chatted gaily and apparently without a care in the world to a succession of the great and the good of Jamaican society. Everyone was eager to be introduced to this new and exotic addition to their lonely outpost of empire. She watched, and she seethed, but not for anything would Chiara put her raging jealousy on display.

Chiara's huge advantage was that she'd observed this behaviour and its occasionally tragic consequences across the courts of half the Italian states. The situation was quite clear to her: Maria was infatuated with her husband. She probably didn't recognise her own feelings, but she did know how to monopolise the attention of a man, and she was displaying her whole arsenal of weapons right now: flattery, youthful good looks, a charming smile and the little apparently careless touches of her husband's hand as she was speaking to him. As far as Chiara could tell, Edward was at least mildly embarrassed by her attention. No, she was sure. He was looking for an escape, casting covert glances around the room while trying not to be overtly rude. She'd let him sweat for a little longer. Too long and he could start to enjoy the attention, too short and he wouldn't have learned the vital lesson that he needed to be able to deal with this sort of situation.

Maria's courtship – for that's what it was – continued. Chiara saw the occasional touching of his arm increase in frequency, Maria's laughter became livelier, and she stopped even pretending to look anywhere other than at her husband's face. 'She's actually holding his arm now,' Chiara observed, 'this has gone far enough.' She excused herself from the attention of a tall, lean colonel and his wife and took a circuit of the room ending at the spot where her husband, now visibly disturbed, was attempting to disentangle himself from Maria.

'My dear Maria, how pleasant to see you,' she exclaimed, as she took Maria's hand from her husband's arm and clasped it between her own two hands. 'We're so much looking forward to our cruise together, aren't we, Edward?' she asked.

Carlisle didn't recover quickly enough, he was in mild shock caused by traumatic stress. Chiara continued. 'It will be charming with your father and mother to keep us all company,' she said with heavy emphasis. 'Now, if you will excuse us, I'm afraid my husband has been neglecting his duties and monopolising your attention. We must speak to some of the sea-officers and you, I fear, must seek out your mother.'

At that Chiara took Carlisle firmly by the arm and steered him away, chattering happily as they left Maria alone, embarrassed and furious.

'How can I ever thank you, my dear?' asked Carlisle.

'I'll think of a way, you can be sure,' she replied. 'But you, my husband, must learn how to deal with predators such as Maria. She's relatively easy to dissuade; she's still young, but they become more proficient as they grow older. I should know,' she said with an enigmatic smile.

CHAPTER SEVEN

Grand Cayman

Monday, twenty-fifth of July 1757
Medina, at Sea. Pedro Bluff, Jamaica east-northeast 7 leagues

The last week in Port Royal had been frantic. The navy yard had returned *Medina* to her proper owner with tight seams and a bottom that had been so liberally smeared with white stuff that any discerning teredo worm and any frond of sea-grass wouldn't come within a cable of the noxious vessel. A new fore-topmast had been fitted, and all the standing rigging had been set up. It was a good, workmanlike job, but it left the task of storing, embarking the guns and setting up the sails and running rigging to *Medina's* crew. That was a week's work by anyone's standard and a hard week for a ship's company that had diligently spent every penny they owned and anything that they could borrow in the dubious delights of Port Royal. The city was a shadow of its former infamy in the time of Morgan and Myngs. Since then, an earthquake in 1692 had destroyed much of the waterfront and the adjoining houses, and a succession of hurricanes, floods and fires in the following years, had persuaded the great and good of Jamaica to move the capital to Kingston. However, what was left of Port Royal still held all that any seaman could desire. The result was a bleary-eyed crew that had to be driven to their work for the first few days before the worst effects of their debauchery had worn off.

'She's rigged as well as she's ever been, sir,' reported the bosun, visibly weakened after six days and nights of constant labour, 'and Chips has declared all the masts sound, so I do believe we're ready for sea.'

'Not a minute too soon, Mister Swinton,' replied Carlisle. He turned to Holbrooke, 'The men have done well. What do you think to shore-leave for each watch by turns?'

'There aren't many of them with any money left, sir. I believe most will choose to stay on board. What do you think, Bosun?'

'Aye, you're right, sir. But let it be their choice. We won't be back for a month, and at least they'll have been given the option.'

'Very well, Mister Holbrooke. Make it so.' He gazed up at the hundreds of lines that made up the rigging, reaching into the blue sky. It all looked taut and ready for sea, and he could think of no good reason to deprive those few men who, against all the odds, had a penny or two remaining in their pockets. Tuppence would get them dead drunk on kill-devil rum, or sixpence would get them a woman for a few hours. They had two days before Don Alonso was to arrive, so time for a night ashore for each watch.

Medina sailed late on a Monday afternoon through the southern passage, using the lull between the sea and land breezes when the northeast trade wind briefly reasserted itself even this close to the land. As they cleared the Three Fathom Bank, they started piling on the sail, t'gallants, staysails and stuns'ls. She was in all her glory of towering canvas when they passed Portland Point, and the sun was setting right on the bow as they altered course to the west. Night fell with all its tropical abruptness. Pedro Bluff passed as the morning watch came on deck, no more than a hint of greater darkness on their starboard side as they stretched out into the open Caribbean, northwest-by-west for Grand Cayman to deliver dispatches then on to the Yucatan Channel.

'This is delightful, Edward,' said Chiara as she leant against the starboard quarterdeck railing, the warm tropical breeze in her hair and the muted sounds of the sea against the hull. *Medina* had the wind two points abaft her starboard beam which was her best point of sailing, and it had the added benefit of reducing a stiff breeze to no more than light zephyrs over the deck. The frigate was eating up the miles towards their first destination of George Town in Grand Cayman, and at this exceptional rate of sailing, they should be there on Wednesday afternoon. They'd lie-to just long enough to deliver the dispatches then away for the hundred-mile gap between Cape Catoche on the tip of the Yucatan Peninsula and Cape St. Antonio at the western end of Cuba. Hosking had estimated that they'd be through the Yucatan Channel on Saturday.

'Just step up onto this hammock net would you my dear? The swabbers are making their way aft, and neither your shoes nor the hem of your dress will be improved by salt water.'

Chiara stepped lightly off the deck while the afterguard rushed through, knuckling their foreheads and murmuring 'if you please ma'am … with your permission.' First, the sweepers, then a general soaking with the deck hose, then the swabbers, and lastly squeegees to remove the surface water. The final drying could be left to the sun which was already a hand's-breadth above the horizon on their starboard quarter.

'Don Alonso, the countess and Maria are missing the best of the day, I fear,' said Chiara as she stepped back onto the deck. 'I hope they slept well in *our* cabin. But I suppose it was necessary that we moved out,' she looked at her husband for confirmation. It was inevitable that there should be at least a hint of rivalry between the two women, of similar background but having taken somewhat different paths in life.

'Yes, apart from the need to make our guests comfortable, the great cabin is the only space where all three could be decently accommodated. But the carpenter has done a good job of converting the dining cabin, don't you think?'

'Oh yes, I'm quite comfortable. My cot is a little snug,

but at least after all the time I've spent at sea I'm used to the motion.'

'Very true, my dear, you don't seem to suffer at all,' replied Carlisle, ruefully. It was hardly a secret in *Medina* that their captain was occasionally sick at the start of a voyage. He'd been lucky so far; the merest landlubber wouldn't have been inconvenienced by the frigate's motion before this steady trade wind. But it was infuriating that his wife appeared immune to sea-sickness.

'Forgive me Edward, but you don't appear to be very busy. When we sailed from Antigua to Jamaica, you were constantly running around, ordering changes of course, adjustments to sails, but now you appear completely at ease. I do believe you didn't leave the cabin at all last night.'

'Ha, you've discovered my guilty secret. I've turned the conduct of the ship over to George until we sight the Caymans. It'll be good for him, and it gives me more time with you,' he squeezed his wife's hand and was rewarded with a shy smile.

'You can also spend more time with our guests, of course,' she replied.

'Certainly, I can't neglect them. The governor was most particular about the need to treat the Spanish party with all courtesy,' he looked around the quarterdeck in case Don Alonso had come up from his cabin. 'You know that we must defer their entry into this war for as long as possible. My civility can't weigh heavily in Britain's favour, but any lack of courtesy could be used against us, even perhaps as a *casus belli*, the straw that breaks the camel's back.' He gazed out to windward where Jamaica lay over the horizon. 'And I remember what you said after we first met him, there is something that he isn't telling us. Just occasionally I catch him looking rather nervous, which I'm sure isn't his normal manner.'

Carlisle pondered for a moment, letting his mind wander freely. He wished that Don Alonso would keep that pest of a daughter away from him; he had enough to do without continually demonstrating his fidelity to Chiara.

The two days passed peacefully. Carlisle and Chiara dined with the governor on Tuesday and again on Wednesday, but the second meal was interrupted by a shout from the masthead that was heard in the great cabin. 'Sail Ho! Sail on the larboard quarter.'

'What do you make of her, Whittle,' shouted Holbrooke back to the masthead.

'A ship's t'gallant, it looks like, two points off the larboard quarter. There's the possibility of another beyond her, but if there is it's just her pole above the t'gallant and I can't be certain, sir.'

'Then keep an eye on them, Whittle, let me know if they alter course.'

'Aye, aye, sir,' came the reply drifting down from the masthead to the quarterdeck. Holbrooke turned to send the midshipman below to report to the captain when he was interrupted by another hail.

'Land Ho! Land two points on the starboard bow.'

Holbrooke ordered a change of course to head directly to the new sighting and walked down the ladder to report to the captain. The unknown ship or ships to the south-southeast were forgotten in the excitement of land being sighted. Anyway, they were probably Spanish merchantmen heading for the Gulf of Mexico and no business of *Medina's*. With the frigate's new course they'd soon drop back below the horizon.

Holbrooke knocked on the cabin door and swung it open without waiting for a reply. He knew that they'd all be seated at the table and he could save his captain the trouble of sending a servant or coming to the door himself.

'My apologies Your Excellency,' he said bowing towards Don Alonso, who acknowledged the lieutenant with an inclination of his head. Holbrooke turned to

Carlisle. 'The foretop lookout has sighted Grand Cayman, sir. It's about four leagues on the bow so we should be off George Town by eight bells.'

'Very well, Mister Holbrooke,' Carlisle replied. 'I'll leave it all to you. I believe the master has been here before, so you should have no difficulty.'

'He has indeed. We can lie-to a cable off George Town. We'll give them half an hour, and if they don't send a boat, I'll send the cutter in.'

'I heard Whittle make another report before the land was sighted, Mister Holbrooke,' he said questioningly. It was amazing how a hail from the masthead could be heard so clearly in the captain's apartments below the quarterdeck.

'Yes, sir, my apologies. It looks like a merchantman, possibly French but more likely Spanish, heading the same way as us. There may have been two of them, Whittle wasn't sure.'

Both men knew, and Don Alonso guessed, that even if they were French, *Medina* was under a prohibition against engaging in commerce warfare with the governor of Florida on board. The diplomatic storm that such an action would raise didn't bear thinking about.

'This is the normal route for my country's ships from New Granada to Mexico or to Florida,' interjected Don Alonso, 'and very often they travel in company.' He was evidently keen that Carlisle didn't investigate these new sightings. Perhaps he wanted to avoid any delay to their arrival at St. Augustine. Maybe if they were Spanish on their way to Florida it would raise the uncomfortable question of why he didn't take passage with them – they would likely call at Havana. However, Chiara was watching Don Alonso, and it seemed to her that there was something else, some reason to ignore those ships that he was unwilling to share with his hosts.

'Then we'll stand on for Grand Cayman, Mister Holbrooke.'

Chiara, alone of the company at dinner, saw the almost imperceptible look of relief that crossed Don Alonso's face.

Medina backed her main topsail a little over a cable off George Town. There was no visible fort, just a group of houses and a flagstaff from where a union flag had been hoisted when the frigate was a mile off the town. Looking closer, Holbrooke could see a pair of guns behind rudimentary earthworks, but that was all. No defence at all, really, in the face of a Spanish empire that still chafed after it had lost Jamaica and these islands to Cromwell's forces a hundred years ago.

True to his word, Carlisle had left the command of the ship to Holbrooke, and it was he who greeted the man in militia uniform who came on deck. There was no need to send mail out of the islands, they were served by a regular packet, and it was more likely to take a shorter route than a King's ship that had a dozen other calls on its time. In fact, there was no need for *Medina* to be delivering dispatches, the packet did that also, but as a matter of principle both the Governor of Jamaica and the Commander-in-Chief felt it a good policy to have a man-of-war visit from time to time, if nothing else to show the flag in this lonely outpost of empire.

'Captain Bodden, at your service, sir,' said the soldier holding out his hand to Holbrooke.

'Lieutenant Holbrooke, and it's good to have you on board Captain. May I introduce Captain Carlisle and Lady Carlisle,' he continued. Holbrooke wasn't at all sure whether he should introduce his captain first or Don Alonso, but he reasoned that in two weeks or less Don Alonso would have no influence over him at all, while Carlisle would be his mentor and source of preferment for the foreseeable future. He was saved from the problem of presenting Don Alonso when Carlisle stepped in to make the introductions.

'Your Excellency, may I present Captain Bodden, of the Cayman Militia?' asked Carlisle, making a guess at the soldier's regiment. 'Captain Bodden, this is Don Alonso Fernández de Heredia, Governor of Florida; his wife, Countess San Clemente Elena Marin de Villanueva e Hijar and their daughter Maria Magdalena Fernandez de Heredia y Marin de Villanueva.' Carlisle privately congratulated himself on delivering the introductions without stumbling over the titles. He was particularly pleased that he'd remembered not to refer to 'Spanish Florida' in case that implied that other nations had valid claims to all or part of that territory. None of those on the deck of *Medina* could imagine that in only six years, Florida would be traded to Britain for the return of Havana, that rich city having been taken by Britain during the period of Spain's disastrous entry into the present war.

Captain Bodden hesitated for a fraction of a second; he was utterly unprepared to meet a high official of a nation with which all the islanders still considered themselves at war. Old memories died hard in these isolated communities. However, he recovered himself and made the best bow he could, cursing himself that he'd only thrown on the semblance of a uniform over his normal daily short-clothes. Bodden looked like just what he was, a plantation owner surprised in his domestic tasks and hastily dressed as a soldier. Don Alonso noticed the hesitation and his return bow was low enough to satisfy protocol, but not so deep as to let anyone believe that he was impressed with this farmer-cum-soldier.

Bodden was evidently uneasy. He accepted the bag of dispatches and asked for them to be passed into the boat. He seemed inclined to linger, and it soon became evident that he had something to say that wasn't for Spanish ears. Carlisle looked pointedly at Holbrooke and with an inclination of his shoulder motioned to the quarterdeck ladder.

'Captain Bodden, would you join me for a moment?' asked Holbrooke. The soldier looked relieved and followed the lieutenant, casting a glance back over his shoulder at the Spaniard as though he still didn't believe his eyes. Don Alonso pointedly ignored him.

There were few suitable spaces left in the ship after Don Alonso's family had displaced Carlisle, leading to a cascade effect of discomfort for the remainder of the officers. However, Holbrooke had retained his cabin which was large enough for two, if they sat quietly and kept their arms still.

'You were clearly uncomfortable with the company on the quarterdeck,' said Holbrooke after they had squeezed into the cabin's only two chairs. 'I assume you've something to say?'

Bodden was a large man in his middle years. He was prominent in Cayman society, being a descendant of one of the original British settlers who, legend had it, was one of Cromwell's soldiers at the capture of the islands from the Spanish in the middle of the last century. Bodden was also a successful planter with land all over the island. But for all that he'd been taken aback by the presence of a Spanish governor and his family and had been unable to find the right words to request a private conversation. He was grateful to Holbrooke and prepared to like him.

'Aye, thanks for saving me, Holbrooke. I was surprised to see a Don in a King's ship.' He produced an enormous red handkerchief and mopped his brow. It was airless in Holbrooke's tiny quarters, and Bodden rarely wore the heavy wool uniform coat that was scratching horribly where it touched his skin.

'But we're not at war, not yet at least,' replied Holbrooke, signalling for drinks from Smart, who had anticipated being called.

'You wouldn't take that view if you lived in these islands,' said Bodden. 'You'll have seen our defences, and incidentally so will El Supremo up there. We wouldn't survive an attack by a longboat full of nuns. The Spaniards haven't forgotten that they once owned everything in this sea and it's only a matter of time before they join with France to get some of it back. If you lived on the Caymans, you wouldn't trust a Spaniard an inch.' Holbrooke nodded in understanding.

'However, you were correct, there is something I wanted to tell you, and it's not for Spanish ears.' He looked at the cabin bulkheads, they were made of thin deal planks that would hardly impede the slightest sound. He drew closer to Holbrooke. 'We had some unexpected visitors last month.'

Holbrooke adopted an expression of polite interest. Clearly, unexpected visitors were a matter for astonishment, without needing to know their errand. Life on a small, remote island such as this must be genuinely insular, in the worst sense of the word. Would this soldier ever get to the point? He didn't have to wait much longer. With a deep intake of breath, Bodden said 'Dutch privateers! Two of them, ship-rigged with low freeboards and not a bit of deck-hamper, no casks, no bales, no timber. They looked as though they were stripped down for fighting. Oh, they called themselves merchantmen, but they had nothing to trade and offered no explanation how they were so far out of any possible trade routes for Hollanders.'

There was another long pause while the soldier waited for a reaction. Holbrooke felt the moral pressure building up, and in desperation, for want of anything better, said 'Dutch? How terrible. What did you do?' But Bodden didn't catch the facetiousness of his comment and rolled straight over it. Holbrooke inwardly resolved never, ever to retire to an island.

'Dutch indeed, and do you know what they were looking for?' But Holbrooke was wise to this line of conversation by now, and he merely returned the soldiers manic stare, waiting for him to elaborate.

'Spaniards! They were asking if a Spanish ship had come this way. I made a note of its name,' he said rifling through the pockets of his civilian waistcoat that he'd not seen fit to change for a uniform equivalent. 'Ah, here it is, they were very insistent that I should write it accurately, they said they'd be back again, and I didn't want any trouble.' He passed a grimy piece of paper to Holbrooke, who took it and, stifling a yawn of boredom, read the name.

Nuestra Señora Del Rosario. In English, *Our Lady of the Rosary.*

That woke Holbrooke with a start. Unless there were two of that name, that was the ship that had carried Don Alonso across the Atlantic, the same that Holbrooke had boarded in the tail-end of a hurricane and was now awaiting condemnation in Port Royal. The vessel in which Holbrooke, along with all the other Medinas, had a financial interest after her salvage. He recovered himself before he let the soldier see his renewed interest. Whatever came of this, it could hardly be the concern of this planter. However, Holbrooke quickly realised that any show of interest would likely be considered quite normal by Bodden, to whom any disturbance in the life of the island must be momentous.

'That's interesting,' he said to Bodden, affecting a polite disinterest. 'In case we meet them, please tell me just what they said and what happened.'

'Well, they were looking for this Spanish ship, they wouldn't say why, but given their obvious profession it was certain that they didn't want to invite them to tea.' He looked knowingly at Holbrooke. 'They thought she may have been driven here by the hurricane last month, but of course, we've seen nothing of a Spanish ship. They said they'd been badly handled by the hurricane, but the damage looked more like they'd been in action. In any case, they asked civil enough, so we sold them some provisions and water, and some canvas and cordage, and they went on their way.'

'Which direction did they sail?' asked Holbrooke.

'Southeast, as close to the wind as they could lie. They said they were bound for Willemstad, but if that was true, it was mighty strange as they came from the east. We're a long way to leeward for a social visit.' The soldier stared at Holbrooke, evidently expecting some reaction.

'Well, they'd have no business west of here in the Gulf. Everything beyond the Yucatan Channel is either Spanish or the French and neither will trade with the Dutch for fear of them taking an interest in the area,' Holbrooke replied. Southeast would also be a course for Jamaica, with only one tack needed to make any of the small harbours in the west of the island, but he didn't want to discuss that with the soldier.

'Is that all, nothing else?' asked Holbrooke. 'I only ask in case we meet them; there's no cause for a King's ship to get involved.'

'Nothing,' said the soldier rising with difficulty from the chair and careful not to break his skull on the deckhead. 'Nothing else at all … except that I heard them talking among themselves and they mentioned a name, a Spanish name, and now I think of it, the name sounded like your governor up there,' and he pointed at the deck above. 'But all those Spanish names sound alike, Don something-or-other, but it *did* sound like the same name.'

Holbrooke led the soldier to the waist and back into his boat. Don Alonso didn't offer any farewells, and Carlisle chose to leave it to his first lieutenant.

Medina's main topsail yard was hauled around to catch the wind, and she gathered way on the starboard tack, northwest-by-west to leave Cape Catoche two leagues to leeward.

CHAPTER EIGHT

Ocean Currents

Saturday, thirtieth of July 1757
Medina, at Sea. Cape Catoche, Yucatan south 20 leagues

Medina enjoyed a fast passage after leaving George Town. With a steady wind, she made seven knots day and night and passed into the Gulf of Mexico on Saturday before the forenoon watch had ended. They ate their dinner in a new sea, a sea where the steady trade wind gave way to variables that baffled mariners in their lack of consistency. Here the ocean currents held sway, creating the all-important yet unseen highways of the sea. The Spaniards had sailed these waters for a quarter of a millennium and knew them well, but if Don Alonso had any knowledge of ocean currents, he was wisely keeping it to himself. Even now, in the declining years of their American Empire, the Spanish kept their secrets of navigation close.

Carlisle, Holbrooke and Hosking were crammed into the tiny space which served as the master's sea-cabin, the storage space for navigational instruments and the charthouse.

'I've never sailed the Gulf before,' admitted Hosking, 'but I've spoken to many who have.' There was the merest hint of a challenge in his voice, in case anyone doubted his competence.

'We all know about the Florida Stream that starts in the waters to the north of Havana,' he pointed at the chart, 'and flows north between Florida and the Bahamas, right past St. Augustine and eventually becomes the stream that runs up the coast of Georgia, Carolina and Virginia and across the Atlantic.' He swept his hand north up the American coast and east across the Atlantic towards

Britain in an expansive gesture. 'Well, the Florida Stream is fed from the waters of the Gulf of Mexico, starting with the flow from the Caribbean through the Yucatan Channel. The thing is, the current doesn't take a direct path, it loops northwest and then right around,' he traced a great bight filling the eastern side of the Gulf, 'until it runs southeast and forms the start of the Florida Stream. So, you see, this loop, the Florida Stream and the Atlantic Stream are really all one flow of water that runs right from here to the western coast of the British Isles.'

Hosking straightened himself in triumph. His greatest joy was to be able to enlighten the navigationally uneducated. Previous captains and first lieutenants had been poor subjects, content to leave navigation to the master, but these two would stay to listen without being physically constrained. 'Without this loop,' he continued, 'the Florida Straits would be a southbound passage, but in fact, the strong current makes it a northbound passage. That's why, sir, we must now head northwest, as though sailing for the mouth of the Mississippi and French Louisiana, and then follow the current around and so past Havana and into the Florida Straits.'

Carlisle looked dubious, but Holbrooke had heard this before. His father had been a sailing master and had navigated these waters in the last war. He could remember being told something about a loop current that Ponce de Leon, that revered Spanish explorer, had discovered over two-hundred years ago. Succeeding generations of Spaniards had attempted to keep the secret, but through captured ships' logs and disaffected informers it had gradually seeped out and was now quite well known by Britain, France, Holland and Portugal.

'How will we know when we're in this stream, Mister Hosking,' asked Carlisle.

'Oh, we'll know, sir. The current runs strongly across the wind once we're past the Yucatan and it raises quite a chop.' Carlisle thought ruefully of his sea-legs that hadn't yet been tested on this voyage. 'And then our noon sights will help us. The current runs at around three knots, getting up to four as we pass Havana, so we can compare our noon latitude with our dead reckoning. Once we're in it, it's easy to follow.'

'Very well Mister Hosking, make it so. Let me know when you've found your loop. Meanwhile, I'll return to my damned diplomatic duties. Wish me good fortune.'

The master's sea-cabin was a blessed refuge to Carlisle who spent his days avoiding His Excellency's wife, but more so his eager daughter. Maria had taken a while to recover from her brush with Chiara at the governor's reception. For a few days, she'd avoided Carlisle and most notably his wife. But her confidence had returned with the resilience of youth and she'd gradually sought his company more and more overtly. Chiara wasn't too much concerned. In the confines of a frigate and with the weight of naval discipline behind her, she felt that she could quite easily control the situation. She hadn't yet been moved to intervene between her husband and Maria a second time, to *frap her down*, as the sailors would say.

Nevertheless, the continued vigilance was playing on Carlisle's nerves, and he spent more and more time in the parts of the ship where his guests' presence would raise eyebrows. The rodents that inhabited the cable tier were amazed to see him, ostensibly examining the cable, and they scampered away indignantly. The dogwatch dice-players were dismayed when he climbed into the foretop, and the midshipmen were horrified when he paid them a visit in the cockpit. But eventually, he had to return to the great cabin where he took his meals with Chiara and his guests, and it was there that the governor's womenfolk could be sure of finding him.

'Captain, can nothing be done about the draught in my cabin,' asked a petulant Countess Elena for at least the third time, 'and is it essential that the sailors should walk so heavily above my head? I cannot sleep at all.'

Don Alonso was no help: he merely nodded at Carlisle as though endorsing his wife's complaint.

'Pass the word for the carpenter,' Carlisle shouted to the sentry, in exasperation, 'and my compliments to Mister Hosking. I would be pleased if he ordered that the quarterdeck is out of bounds after pipe down to all except the quartermaster and steersmen, and they're to discard their shoes.'

'Captain, I would so much like to be shown how the ship is steered,' asked Maria, fluttering her eyelashes, 'I'm sure that you know better than any man on board how it is done.' Don Alonso chose to ignore the increasingly desperate attempts of his daughter to seduce their host. However, Carlisle had developed a robust defensive manoeuvre for requests of this nature.

'Pass the word for Mister Angelini,' he called. 'Midshipman Angelini is the finest steersman in the ship,' he explained to the whole table, crossing his fingers behind his back. To his knowledge, young Enrico had not yet been introduced to that particular seaman's art, but he was adept at handling young ladies, disturbingly so sometimes.

Chiara watched all this with detached amusement. She no longer feared for her husband's fidelity, but she did wish that he'd develop better strategies for dealing with these increasingly common situations. At present, he looked exactly what he was, a man with few defences against a determined woman other than to thrust someone else into the line of fire. She exchanged knowing glances with Chalmers, a regular guest at lunch since Don Alonso embarked. Somehow, she felt that David Chalmers understood her better than anyone else in *Medina*. He seemed to pierce her thoughts and empathise, with a wry smile not far from the surface. Chiara had always known that people were Chalmers' chief interest. He watched them with care, and she could almost see his mind working, analysing their motives, anticipating their reactions and categorising them according to some system of his own. She was certain that the chaplain knew all about the triangular relationship at work here: Maria's youthful infatuation and clumsy attempts at seduction, Carlisle's naivety and guilt, and her own jealousy and determination. Yes, Chalmers knew, she could see it in his lack of facial expression and his apparent – but not actual – inattention to the thrust, parry and riposte of the conversation.

'What do you mean, Mister Angelini,' asked Lynton, the president of the cockpit mess, in his most imperious voice, 'by placing your arm around the waist of a young lady while imposing on her credulity to the extent of pretending to know how to steer the ship? Perhaps you could explain your actions to your messmates.'

Enrico had rapidly come to understand the ways of his new British friends, but he hadn't yet learned to recognise unfailingly when he was being made game of. He knew, in principle, that Lynton had some sort of authority over him, but whether he was exercising that now, or whether this was just another attempt to embarrass him before his shipmates, he wasn't too sure. On the one hand, there was the very real possibility that he could be sent to the masthead with no supper if he treated the question as a jest when in fact it was a genuine inquiry carrying an implied rebuke. But on the other hand, if it was a jest and he treated it seriously, his friends' laughter would be heard throughout the ship. However, what he *had* learned was that nobody questioned the captain and that to invoke his authority trumped almost all hands. Until, of course, the day when somebody chose to ask the captain whether he had indeed ordered the act; Enrico decided that this wasn't such a case.

'Sir,' he replied gravely, 'the captain judged that my poor level of knowledge was sufficient for the task and he further gave me strict orders to ensure that the lady didn't fall. I regret if I misinterpreted those orders and was over-zealous in my obedience, I beg your pardon.'

The mess was silent. Then Simmonds started sniggering and soon the whole table was lost in laughter. It took Enrico a moment to realise that they weren't laughing *at* him but were showing their appreciation for the way that he turned the question back on Lynton.

Lynton banged on the table. 'Silence,' he roared. 'Mister Angelini, on consideration, I believe that you carried out your orders diligently.' The mess gave an involuntary groan, they were hoping that Enrico would be fined so that they could drink on his number. 'However, in touching a young lady's waist on the quarterdeck, you've enjoyed yourself unreasonably, beyond anything that a midshipman in His Britannic Majesty's navy has a right to expect. Therefore, I impose a penalty of two bottles of wine to be paid immediately.'

'Captain, there's that demonic howling again,' complained the countess. 'Is there nothing that can be done about it? I'm sure my nerves won't stand much more of this.'

Jackson and Swinton were sitting in the tiny bosun's cabin under the fo'c'sle. Swinton had lowered his folding table and had laid out all his books: his records of stores received, rope and tallow expended, slush taken from the galley coppers, sails condemned, routine cable inspections and all the other returns that he had to make to the Navy Board, through Captain Carlisle and his clerk, every two months.

'Now then mate, where would you like to start?' The bosun had been teaching Jackson the finer points of his duties on-and-off for the past three months, ever since they'd shared a bottle ashore in Port Royal and Jackson had let slip his ambition to achieve a bosun's warrant. Swinton had never heard the word *mentor*, but he liked Jackson and was eager to help, in his own way. He was a slow and methodical man, and Jackson had already endured long hours of monologue on subjects that he knew perfectly well. They had crawled over every part of the ship from the main truck to the heel of the mizzen mast and from the jib-boom cap to the rudder pintles. It wasn't exactly wasted on Jackson – although he'd grown up learning the complexities of a ship's rigging – because the bosun looked at things differently. He was concerned with the maintenance of the masts, sails, spars and cordage, and not just their functions.

However, today they were making a start on the paperwork. It wasn't usual for a prospective bosun to be examined on his bookkeeping, but Jackson didn't want to take any chances. He knew he'd have to wait a long time if he dropped his first opportunity, and he could sense that it was approaching. He could see *his* officer, Holbrooke, maturing fast and with the rate at which *Medina* saw action, and the speed with which the Jamaica Squadron was growing he judged that with a little luck it would only be a matter of months.

It wasn't long before Jackson realised that however good Swinton was at his more practical duties, the man was barely literate, and his books were an illegible mess. It was evident that Carlisle's clerk, the long-suffering Frederick Simmonds, must have spent many frustrating hours putting Swinton's books in order before they were dispatched. And it was of the first importance that the accounts should be presented correctly. None of the commission or warrant officers could be paid until they'd cleared their books, and the sharp-eyed clerks in Seething Lane had a lifetime of experience in spotting errors and evasions.

Swinton was aware of his weakness where writing and book-keeping were concerned, and he'd tried to improve, but his heart wasn't really in it. He wanted to be perched on a yardarm repairing a frayed horse in a gale, not sat in his cabin attempting to make sense of his columns of figures.

'It's all very well, this mad lust after recording everything,' said Swinton, dragging his fingers through his thinning hair, 'but I'm not getting any younger and these figures just don't add up like they should.'

'The captain's clerk, Simmonds, he must help, surely?' asked Jackson, running his finger down a column of numbers that appeared to have been picked randomly from thin air.

'He does, he does, but he's started to be a bit saucy about it, and I don't like his tone sometimes. You wouldn't think I'd been at sea before he was breeched,' he replied looking glum. 'I don't rightly like to show him the books any more. The trouble is that I know the damned Navy Board will be down on me one of these days.'

Jackson continued tracing the evolution of the numbers in the column. 'Ah, I've found the problem. You've added instead of taken away here,' he said and pointed at the errant figure. 'If you change that it'll all be right.'

Swinton looked suspiciously at the entry that Jackson was pointing out.

'You're good at this, better than me at any rate,' said Swinton, looking like he'd say more but thought better of it.

'Well, you've been very kind to me Mister Swinton, and I've a head for numbers, and I write a fair hand. How about I help you with your books as repayment for your teaching me the bosun's art? I can get these into shape in a few hours, and they'll be ready for the King's own bookkeeper to inspect before we sight Jamaica again.'

CHAPTER NINE

The Dutchmen

Saturday, thirtieth of July 1757
Medina, at Sea. Cape Catoche, Yucatan south-southeast 30 leagues

It was late in the last dog watch, and the sun was slipping towards the horizon on the larboard bow. Almost the entire ship's company was on deck, for there was a hornpipe competition on the fo'c'sle, with the more agile sailors showing off their steps to the accompaniment of a squeaky fiddle. Even Don Alonso and his family had made an appearance; they were desperate for some form of entertainment after five days at sea with nothing to distinguish one from the other. The short visit to Grand Cayman had done little to relieve their boredom, and now this outlandish performance drew them out of their stifling quarters and onto the deck. Eli was the master of ceremonies and the judge, and he'd just demolished the technique of a hopeful young topman. Eli's use of language was hard to follow for anyone but an English-speaking seaman, which was just as well because few of his adjectives were suitable for the ladies' ears. He held the thirty-second glass in his horny hand and turned it with a sharp rap onto the ship's belfry as a signal to the fiddler and the next hopeful. The fiddle struck its notes and the sailor, a nervous foretopman in Jackson's mess, stepped out.

'Sail Ho!' shouted the foretop lookout, 'sail three points on the starboard bow.' It was Whittle again, the ship's lucky mascot and almost inevitably the first man to sight prizes.

The fiddle stopped abruptly, the foretopman paused dramatically in mid-step, and every eye turned to the masthead. The all knew that they had passed from the

Caribbean, a sea in which the British Navy had a significant presence, into the Gulf of Mexico where France and Spain ruled. It was an even chance that the sail was Spanish, but it could equally be French, on passage from Louisiana to the Caribbean. Carlisle was under strict orders: no belligerent acts against the French until Don Alonso and his family were safely ashore. That meant that even if this was a valuable French merchantman loaded with furs, tobacco and indigo, he must leave her alone. However, the crew didn't know that, and each face showed an eager expectation. After all, Carlisle had led them to profitable prizes before.

'Up you go, Mister Angelini. Take the spyglass and let me know what you see,' said Holbrooke to the midshipman of the watch. It was unlikely that Enrico would see anything that Whittle couldn't, but it was good for his education. When he was entered on the ship's books five months ago, he'd been terrified of going aloft, and it had taken some patience and a little brutality to persuade him that it was a necessary skill for young gentlemen in His Majesty's navy. He still didn't have the agility and fearlessness of a seasoned topman, but at least he no longer brought disgrace upon the ship. Chiara hid her feelings well; she'd never become used to seeing her younger cousin risking himself among that confusion of masts, ropes and sails.

Whittle saw what was happening and took another long look at the sail. Perhaps there was something else that he could add before this unwanted help arrived. He stared hard at the white square; there was still plenty of light from the setting sun, and he could see a distinct horizon. Was that something just a little to the right of the sail? Yes, there it was again, just showing as *Medina* rose on the swell.

'Deck there! I see two sails. T'gallants I believe. They're about three miles apart, but they don't look like merchantmen.'

That changed things. They had started to sound very

much like Frenchmen, perhaps a pair of frigates taking the faster route to Cape François on the northern side of Saint Domingue or they could be on passage to Fort Royal on Martinique. Holbrooke waited impatiently for Enrico to deliver his verdict with the higher magnification of a spyglass. Carlisle stood imperturbably on the quarterdeck. He'd turned over the conduct of the frigate to his first lieutenant, and he wasn't going to take it back until there was some imminent danger. Actually, he thought that Holbrooke was taking exactly the right action. Let the midshipman report, and if they still looked like men-of-war, that was the time to take action.

'Two t'gallants sir,' shouted Enrico. His voice was surprisingly loud for a young man, and he wasn't overawed by authority. Holbrooke could see that after an initial inspection, he'd passed the telescope to Whittle. That was very wise; the able seaman from Virginia had excellent eyesight and more experience as a lookout, but he was diplomatically letting the midshipman make the reports. Holbrooke was pleased to see that simple act of trust between the able seaman and the midshipman. Enrico was earning his authority, and he could go far in the service if it weren't for the unfortunate fact of his religion.

'They're not merchantmen, but they don't look like men-of-war either. Privateers perhaps,' called Enrico.

Holbrooke wasted no more time. With a brief glance at Carlisle, who nodded almost imperceptibly, he raised his voice to his best quarterdeck bellow. 'Hands to quarters, clear for action!'

The hornpipe dancers and their audience scattered. Within a minute the sound of bulkheads being cleared away rang through the ship, beechwood mallets against hard oak wedges. If Don Alonso and his party thought that they could return to the cabin, they were sadly mistaken. The cabin had disappeared before they could have decently made their way down the ladder. The only evidence of its former existence was Carlisle's servant assisted by some of the idlers carrying bundles of belongings down to the hold while the carpenter and his crew ran below carrying the flimsy partitions. Within ten minutes the upper deck was clear of obstacles and all that could be seen was two uninterrupted rows of nine-pounder guns, their crews busily loosening their lashings and checking their equipment.

'I'll take our guests to the wardroom until we know the situation, Mister Holbrooke. Call me when you've identified those ships.' For ships, they were; fore and main t'gallants were now plainly visible, and the peak of a mizzen was just discernible as they rose on the swell.

'What do you think, Mister Hosking?' asked Holbrooke. He knew that Hosking had spent most of the last war in the islands and had seen all the great variety of craft that this region had to offer.

'Not men-of-war, at least not of a like that I've seen before, and not merchantmen either. They look very businesslike, strung out as though they're searching for something.'

Holbrooke could see what he meant. There was an undefinable quality to the way those ships were sailing; they looked professional, competent and determined.

'Privateers for a guinea,' said Hosking, 'but neither French nor Spanish, I fancy,' he declared thoughtfully. 'I recognise those old fashioned t'gallant masts, you see how short they are compared to the topmasts?' he said to Holbrooke with the spyglass still firmly held to his eye. 'Dutch privateers from St. Eustatius, but what they're doing here I can't tell, and what right do they have to be cruising in the Gulf when Holland isn't at war?'

'How many guns?' asked Holbrooke.

'Eight a side, if they're the same that sailed out of St. Eustatius in the last war, eight-pounders, and some swivel guns. They look very much as I remember them, wide and low, not very fast but heavily armed for their size. They played hell with the French and Spanish trade right through to the peace. They've probably been slaving since '48, but they can't be doing that now. Neither the French nor Spanish will tolerate a Dutchman running slaves into their colonies.'

'Mister Wishart. My compliments to Captain Carlisle, and would he step on deck, at his convenience?'

'Well, I can't see that they're much threat to us. Holland has no part in this war, and even if they did, it's hardly likely that two privateers would take on a King's frigate,' said Hosking, snapping shut his spyglass. 'But it's good exercise for the men, and it shows the Don that this is a fighting ship, not a passenger ferry.'

Holbrooke wasn't certain. He'd never seen privateers approach a man-of-war with such an outward show of hostility, and he was almost sure that they'd come a point or two off the wind to intercept.

'Dutchmen, then,' said Carlisle, striding onto the quarterdeck with Don Alonso a few paces behind. 'And what would Dutchmen want with us?'

Don Alonso was behind Carlisle, so the captain missed the play of emotions on the Spaniard's face, but Holbrooke didn't. He couldn't immediately interpret it, but at the news that these ships were Dutch, Don Alonso reacted with a mixture of surprise and alarm, quickly concealed under his habitual mask of aristocratic unconcern.

'That I don't know, sir, but I don't like the look of them. They're clearly on a search line, and they altered course when they saw us. They'll be with us in fifteen minutes. It'll do no harm to be closed up with our guns run out when we hail them. I've run up our colours,' said Holbrooke.

Carlisle looked astern at the red ensign whipping in the breeze, and then up at the vast spread of canvas. Holbrooke interpreted the look correctly 'I'll get the stuns'ls and t'gallants in, sir,' he said.

With a worked-up crew and under the gaze of a foreign

gentleman, the Medinas reduced the ship to fighting sail in less than five minutes. The frigate's actions would undoubtedly be visible to these predators, and their meaning obvious. Whatever the two privateers intended, *Medina* was ready to fight.

'I'll take the ship now, Mister Holbrooke,' said Carlisle.

'Mister Hosking, I wish to be within hailing range and to windward of the easterly of those two. We mustn't allow them to get either side of us.'

'Aye-aye, sir,' replied the sailing master. 'Come up a point, quartermaster,' he said over his shoulder, 'and we'll take a fathom in on the sheets,' he said to the mate-of-the-watch.

With a closing speed of over twelve knots, the three ships converged rapidly. The lead ship of the two, the one furthest to windward, hoisted its ensign – red, white and blue horizontal stripes – so unless there was an elaborate bluff in play, their identity was confirmed. At five cables, the ensign was briefly dipped which surprised those on the deck of *Medina*. Dipping the ensign to a King's ship was an old custom which had fueled conflict between Britain and Holland for centuries. It had fallen out of fashion and King's ships no longer insisted on that courtesy, particularly outside the narrow seas that surrounded the British Isles. The signal midshipman was taken unawares, and it took a sharp word to propel him to the taffrail to return the salute. The privateer put down her helm and came neatly about to parallel *Medina's* course. Her guns hadn't been run out, but a great many men were crowding her decks, more than would be needed for anything other than privateering.

'Lie-to, Mister Hosking, we'll hear what he has to say.'

The two ships backed their mainsails and main topsails and lay easily beam-on to the weak remnants of the trade wind, rising and falling as the long swell ran under their keels.

'What ship, where bound?' shouted Holbrooke across the gap, his voice easily carrying the conventional hail downwind. The nearest ship looked trim and efficient, but he could see the scars of a recent fight. It looked like two gun ports had been beaten into one, and the missing planking had been replaced by new timber. They'd attempted to match the paintwork of the rest of the hull, but without complete success.

The Dutchman's reply wasn't intelligible, his voice was distorted in its fight upwind, and the problem was exacerbated by his accent. However, his intention was apparent as he hauled his boat alongside. With the crew in the boat, only one figure stepped the short distance down from the ship's gunwale, the same man that had attempted to reply to Holbrooke's hail. He was tall with a thick waist and sparse, grey hair, and dressed in a plain blue suit. It was a hard pull against the wind, the crew and passenger suffering from the blown spray and the occasional slap of a wave making its way inboard. *Medina* prepared to meet the visitor with manropes to help with the climb up the deck.

'Come alongside,' shouted Holbrooke as the boat was under the quarterdeck.

The man in blue shook his head emphatically. 'I can talk from here, captain,' he said, in reasonable but accented English.

Holbrooke looked over his shoulder at Carlisle, who nodded briefly to indicate that he'd let his first lieutenant handle the conversation.

'Very well. I am Lieutenant Holbrooke of His Britannic Majesty's frigate *Medina*. Who are you, what are the names of your ships and what is your business?'

The Dutchman puffed out his chest and drew in a great gulp of air. 'You are holding my prisoner, Don Alonso. I will give you my name and the names of my ships when we have agreed on the arrangements for transferring the Spaniard.' Having delivered his message, he stood defiantly in the stern-sheets, his feet placed wide apart, swaying easily as he kept his balance in the pitching and rolling boat.

Carlisle swung around to look at Don Alonso. If the Spaniard was surprised, it didn't show. He looked like a man who was hearing just what he expected to hear, although it was always difficult to read Don Alonso's thoughts. Carlisle stepped to the rail. 'This is Captain Carlisle,' he called down to the boat, 'come on board, and you can explain your mission in comfort.'

At that moment Don Alonso also stepped up to the gunwale and looked down into the boat. The man in blue saw him immediately and stiffened. He evidently recognised his quarry. Whether Don Alonso recognised the Dutchman was impossible to say.

'I see the criminal walks your deck freely,' said the Dutchman. 'You clearly have no idea what a viper you are harbouring, but I'll take him now, and then we'll be on our way.'

'Will you come on board,' replied Carlisle, 'I won't carry out this conversation any longer unless you do.'

'No, sir,' replied the man in blue. 'There is nothing to discuss. Give me the Spanish dog. I have a letter of marque that specifically allows me to hunt him down.'

Carlisle stepped away from the rail. 'Keep him talking, Mister Holbrooke, but don't agree to anything and don't give him any information.' He turned to Don Alonso. 'Your Excellency, please step to the taffrail.'

They stood beneath the ensign that was bravely streaming away to leeward. Out of the corner of his eye, Carlisle spotted Chiara and Chalmers quietly climbing the ladder to the quarterdeck. There was no immediate threat, and they wouldn't be in any danger.

Don Alonso broke first, the moral pressure on him to speak was irresistible 'You will be curious, no doubt Captain,' he said after a short pause, 'you will be wondering what I know of these Dutch pirates.'

'Indeed, I am,' replied Carlisle who waited for Don Alonso to continue. He could hear Holbrooke in the background delivering short non-committal answers to the boat that held its position alongside.

'In the last war I was engaged against the Dutch, and I am aware that letters of Marque and Reprisal were issued specifically against me. Of course, they expired with the peace treaty in 1748, so this attempt on my person is no more than piracy. I understand that the governor at St. Eustatius has illegally re-issued the letters, even though we are not at war. That pirate,' he looked down at the boat, 'knows that a ransom will be paid for me. He knows that there is no peace between Spain and Holland beyond the line.'

Carlisle watched the Spaniard intently, and he waited for a moment for the appeal from his guest – the plea that he should not be turned over to the Dutchman. But Don Alonso was too proud, and perhaps too sure of Carlisle's orders, to demean himself. He merely returned Carlisle's gaze.

'Thank you, Your Excellency. I have two more questions if you please,' this was becoming a test of wills. 'First, do you know who this person is?' he moved his head to indicate the man in blue, 'and second,' he said, carefully observing Don Alonso's reactions, 'are you surprised by this encounter, or were you expecting it?'

Don Alonso stared across at the Dutch ship for a moment, conflicting emotions playing across his face. He was evidently taking care over his answer, but was he pausing to frame his response correctly, or, more likely, was he deciding how much of the truth to reveal?

'To answer your first question, Captain, no, I do not know that man nor can I guess his identity.' He was still staring at the Dutch ship, not looking directly at Carlisle. 'As for your second question. I saw them a week before the hurricane, to the south-east of Tobago. You may remember me mentioning that we had lost contact with the frigate that had escorted us from Cadiz. When these two ships showed obvious hostile intent, I ordered the *Argonauta* to prevent them from following us into the Caribbean Sea. The *Argonauta* is a fast, new, thirty-gun frigate and I had expected that she would easily deal these pirates. However, I have heard nothing of her since the time we parted company. It appears that those two have taken some damage, and yet here they are. I fear the worst for *Argonauta*, but how could they have defeated a thirty-gun ship of the Spanish navy?'

'Their trade is privateering, Your Excellency, although today they appear perhaps as pirates. You see how many men are on the deck? They would have taken *Argonauta* from both sides, braving the cannon fire – you can see their scars – until they were alongside, and then it would all have been over in ten minutes. They must have more than double our number of men. *Argonauta* is probably being sold in St. Eustatius, and her crew ...' Carlisle shrugged his shoulders.

'Then what do you intend now, Captain ...'

Don Alonso was cut off in mid-sentence by Holbrooke who had walked quietly towards them.

'The second ship has come hard on the wind, sir. It appears that she's attempting to get to windward of us.'

The first privateer's boat, seeing that Holbrooke had observed its consort's manoeuvre, was rapidly retreating, it's oars bending under the pressure of the strong arms of the rowers.

Carlisle looked down to the waist. The gunner was standing eagerly beside the number five gun, adjusting the elevation and carefully heaving the great gun around with a hand-spike. He felt his captain's eyes upon him, raised his head and nodded emphatically. So, Carlisle had a choice. He could sink the boat, either kill or capture the man in the blue suit and possibly end this ridiculous situation here and now. He looked from the gun to the boat and on to the two ships with a sweeping glance. No, he couldn't do it. He had only the word of Don Alonso that these were pirates, and that wasn't enough evidence to warrant the killing of a dozen men.

'Mister Hosking, we'll continue on our passage. Haul aft the sheets and let's be on our way.' He turned to the first lieutenant. 'Mister Holbrooke, the hands will remain at quarters, and the ship will remain cleared for action. Pass the word for the carpenter, the partitions to my dining cabin are to be replaced immediately.' Carlisle delivered this in his normal quarterdeck tone so that there should be no doubt, but separately and more confidentially he said to Holbrooke, 'I need the privacy of the great cabin to get to the bottom of this mystery.'

Carlisle waited patiently on the quarterdeck. He could hear the cabin partitions being replaced and he saw the gun crews who were stationed there being hurried forward.

'Mister Holbrooke, please rig the boarding nets as soon as the Dutchmen can't see what you're doing. We should be able to put a few miles between us by the time they've arranged themselves.'

Chris Durbin

CHAPTER TEN

Privateers or Pirates?

Saturday, thirtieth of July 1757
Medina, at Sea. Cape Catoche, Yucatan south-southeast 35 leagues

The two Dutch privateers were soon left behind, the one having taken some time to retrieve his boat's crew while the other lost position by trying to tack around *Medina's* stern. As the sun set to larboard, they were three miles astern and crowding on sails to catch up.

Carlisle needed to talk this through with his first lieutenant. 'Mister Hosking. You'll entertain His Excellency on deck, if you please, and see that the sentry is set at the cabin,' he said loud enough for Don Alonso to hear. Even this thick-skinned Spaniard, used to command rather than obey, would hesitate before interrupting their meeting. And if he chose to ignore the heavy hint, Carlisle knew that he could rely upon the marine sentry to keep unwanted visitors at bay.

He'd only been in the cabin a minute when Holbrooke opened the door. 'If you please, sir, Mister Chalmers is having difficulty in preventing Lady Chiara joining us, …' he tailed off indecisively. Holbrooke knew enough of married life to know that there was no glory to be gained in involving himself in a disagreement between husband and wife, particularly when the husband in question was also his captain.

Carlisle looked at him sharply, 'was he being manoeuvred?' he asked himself. Holbrooke's expression revealed nothing, and on balance, he decided that his first lieutenant was doing no more than his duty – albeit under trying circumstances. Carlisle reflected on the dubious balance of benefits in a captain bringing his wife to sea. Perhaps it would be easier if he had a normal wife, who wasn't a headstrong Italian aristocrat, brought up without the due respect for the boundaries between a man's work and his family life.

'Very well,' he replied, looking carefully for any revealing change of expression, 'the chaplain and Lady Chiara may join us, show them in.' Holbrooke's face revealed nothing except relief that he hadn't been savaged.

When Chiara entered the cabin, Carlisle's had succeeded in arranging his face into an expression that could – with a generous mind – be interpreted as welcoming. Chiara knew her husband well, she knew that he'd prefer that she didn't involve herself in naval matters, but she was constitutionally incapable of remaining on the sidelines. She'd been brought up in a family where all issues were discussed communally and where, by sheer force of will, the women were as involved in decisions as the men. Chiara loved her husband very much, but she wasn't planning to give up the right to a say in their affairs. She correctly interpreted her husband's expression, but the effect on Chiara was unlike that on any other person that Holbrooke had met. In the face of her husband's obvious disapproval, she merely became more charming, her smile broadened, and she gave every impression of being nothing more than a hostess, while all the time staking her claim to be taken seriously.

'My dear, please take a seat,' said Carlisle, motioning to the easy-chair that had been set beside the window, away from the table where he'd discuss his plans with his first lieutenant. He was fighting to keep his voice welcoming.

'I believe Mister Chalmers would appreciate the comfortable seat, dear,' she said as she ignored the chair that was offered, the place that would have kept her at the periphery of the conversation, and instead chose one of the dining chairs that had been set around the hastily-erected table. Holbrooke and Chalmers studiously avoided eye-contact; they were becoming skilled at keeping a neutral expression.

Carlisle had no defence against this tactic, this outward meekness concealing a determined interior. 'Very well,' he said and did the only thing that he could do without causing an embarrassing scene. He took the second seat around the table, and Holbrooke gingerly took the third.

'Well, it appears that these Dutch gentlemen aren't entirely unknown to Don Alonso,' said Carlisle. 'They have a letter of marque – almost certainly not a legally valid document – and I can only assume that they hope to make a great deal of money from his ransom. However, my orders,' he almost said *my duty*, but realised that it would sound pompous, not least to his wife who he suspected may also find it irrelevant and otiose, 'are quite clear. I must deliver Don Alonso, his wife and his daughter to St. Augustine. By the look on that Dutchman's face, if we're to fulfil those orders, I believe we'll be forced to fight.'

'Do you believe it'll come to that, sir?' asked Holbrooke. 'It seems very risky for the Dutch.'

'Yes, you're right Mister Holbrooke, their actions would undoubtedly be deemed piracy at the Vice-Admiralty court in Jamaica, and I doubt whether the captain-general in Havana would even give him the courtesy of a trial. And yet they appeared determined and now as you see,' he gestured out of the wide windows of the cabin, where the two ships were visible, 'they're in hot pursuit. I doubt whether they'll be asking so politely the next time.'

'I wasn't thinking of the legality, sir,' he said, 'but of their force. Here in the open ocean, they have a poor chance of prevailing, don't you think?'

'Indeed, gun-for-gun they stand little chance, but if once they get on our decks... well, we all know the reputation of pirates in hand-to-hand fighting. But they must know that we'll do everything we can to reduce them before they can board us.'

'Surely, then, there is more at stake than a ransom, to justify that risk? The Spanish won't take that lightly, and these Dutchmen will be hunted wherever they hide,' said Chalmers. 'It's hard to see how they can get away with this. St. Eustatius will be no secure hiding place if they take a British frigate and ransom a Spanish governor when their country is at peace.'

Chiara, who had remained uncharacteristically silent until now, interrupted. 'My dear, would you like to hear what I learned from the countess?' she asked, in a small voice that anyone who didn't know her would take for wifely submission.

Carlisle nodded cautiously, not wishing to commit himself to ask for his wife's help in naval matters. However, he was aware that her Spanish was nearly fluent while the countess spoke no English. That would have helped to forge some sort of bond over the four weeks in Port Royal, and any relationship ashore would inevitably have been intensified in the week since they had sailed from Jamaica. It could do no harm to hear what his wife had to say.

'It appears that there's more to this than Don Alonso has revealed,' said Chiara. 'The countess told me in some confidence,' she looked at her husband and the other two men with an unspoken question, *will you keep this confidence*, and was evidently satisfied with what she saw, 'that this is a blood-feud between a wealthy merchant from Holland – the man in the boat I imagine, he of the blue suit – and Don Alonso. It dates to the final years of the last war when it appears that Don Alonso was instrumental in the death of that man's son.'

She had their attention now. They all knew that the killing of a son in anything other than fair combat could drive a man to desperate measures. The warrior code of those who fought at sea demanded revenge.

'A Dutch privateer had been taken,' Chiara continued, 'and all the prisoners were handed to the nearest military unit in an out-of-the-way corner of northwest Spain, including the captain who was the son of our man in the blue coat. Don Alonso commanded that Spanish army unit. The Dutchman's son was unable to produce either a commission or a letter of marque, which he claimed to have lost in the fighting. At a court martial, the captain and his principal officers were found guilty of piracy; naturally, they were hanged. Although Don Alonso convened the court martial, he did not himself sit on the board. However, by chance all the members of the board have died, either during the war or since its end. Don Alonso is the last surviving Spaniard whom the Dutchman can blame for his son's death. That's why this Dutchman wants Don Alonso, not for ransom, but to hang him in retaliation. And that's why, even in peacetime, Don Alonso won't travel without a powerful escort. He and his family have lived with this threat for the past nine years.'

Chiara finished her speech and, laying one hand demurely over the other in her lap, her back straight on the chair as her governess had taught her, waited for her husband's response. She waited in vain. There was a stunned silence in the cabin, as each man took in what he'd heard. Each was considering the wrong decisions that they'd have made if this information wasn't available to them.

Chalmers spoke first. 'In which case, we can't look for any sort of reasonable behaviour from the privateers. I watched our friend in the boat; he was barely able to hold in his seething anger. If the imposing sight of a King's frigate towering above him doesn't bring him to his senses, then nothing will. A blood-feud indeed.'

'If this is a blood-feud,' said Holbrooke, 'and if it's gone on for nine years, it's unlikely that he'll baulk at attacking us when he has twice our number of men and the advantage of two ships.' His mind was already thinking through the tactics for the coming fight. 'We must keep them at arm's length and pound them with our greater firepower.'

Chalmers was looking thoughtful, and he could be seen

making rapid calculations, his lips moving as he added and multiplied. 'Forgive me if I don't fully understand,' he said, tentatively. '*Medina* has twenty-four nine-pound guns and four three-pounders. That makes a total weight of two hundred and twenty-eight pounds.'

'That's correct,' said Holbrooke. 'We're called a nine-pounder twenty-eight-gun frigate, but the four that are on the quarterdeck are only three-pounders. They're hardly broadside guns at all, we use them with canister to clear our opponent's deck.'

'Well, if Mister Hosking's recollection is true and each of those privateers – or pirates – has sixteen eight-pounders, that makes a hundred and twenty-eight pounds of broadside weight. There are two of them which makes two hundred and fifty-six pounds. Yet you say we have greater firepower?'

'You're right, of course, Chalmers,' said Carlisle smiling, 'by sheer arithmetic those two have the advantage of us. We use the term *weight of broadside*, but we mean all the factors that contribute to the disparity in power. Consider, to bring all that weight to bear, they must be in a position where they can attack us simultaneously, and I don't intend to let that happen. To make matters worse for them, *Medina* is much heavier-built, her scantlings are much stronger precisely so that she can mount the larger guns and more of them. Our shot has perhaps four times the chance of penetrating their sides as they have of piercing ours. I'm not saying that eight-pounders will bounce off our sides – they won't – but our nine-pounders will smash their fragile planking and cause huge damage to their gun crews. No, they can't stand against us broadside-to-broadside, and they know it.'

'Then forgive my ignorance, sir, but how will they attack us?'

'It's not very sophisticated I'm afraid, Chalmers,' replied Carlisle, 'the tactics haven't changed since the heyday of the pirates fifty years ago. Morgan and Rackham would have done just the same. They'll try to get either side of us, and when they're in position, they'll bear down to board us on both sides as near simultaneously as the can contrive. Just before they're alongside, they'll fire their broadsides and then abandon the guns, they won't attempt to reload. It'll be all hands to the boarding party, and they'll hack their way through and around our boarding nets.'

'That sounds a difficult manoeuvre. What will they do if they can't attack from both sides?' asked Chalmers.

'They'll make the best of a bad job and attack from whichever direction they can. Speed is everything, and the longer they spend approaching us, the more time we have to reduce them with our cannon.'

'A bloody business then, perhaps I should arm myself.'

'You should, Chalmers. They won't stop to see your credentials once they have a toe-hold on our deck. I'll be arming every man on board.'

Chiara listened carefully. She wasn't going to be defenceless, not when she knew where her husband kept his spare pistols, but she kept her plans to herself.

Carlisle walked to the windows and looked out. There were the two Dutchmen, three miles astern. They still had that purposeful air, but now they weren't in a search line, they were just a few cables apart and had set all their sails in pursuit. They had a predatory air and didn't look like they were going to give up easily.

'Well, my dear, we must all thank you for this intelligence,' he said, as graciously as he could. He turned to Holbrooke, 'They look to be faster than us by about a knot I'd guess. They'll be up with us before midnight.'

CHAPTER ELEVEN

A Desperate Fight

Saturday, thirtieth of July 1757
Medina, at Sea. Cape Catoche, Yucatan south-by-east 42 leagues

The quartermaster's muted voice barely disturbed the silence. 'Turn the glass and strike the bell.' Six bells in the first watch, eleven o'clock at night. It would be just an hour left to the change of the watch, if the ship were not already at quarters with all hands at their stations, alert or dozing according to the requirements of their duty. *Medina* was reaching towards the north on the starboard tack, tracking the loop current as it swung in its great arc through the eastern Gulf of Mexico. There was little noise on deck. All the preparations for action had been taken, and the frigate was as ready as she'd ever be. Yet, there was a strange feeling about the ship. *Medina* and her company had been in action before, when they'd battled a powerful fortress in Grenada and only a few months ago they'd captured a French frigate off Montserrat; they were well used to the inevitable death and destruction when opposing forces met. This time, however, the logic of war was missing. They could all understand the motivations of a King's ship fighting its country's wars, or a privateer cruising for profit, but this concept of a blood-feud was unfamiliar and troubling. There was no telling how far the fight would go, how many casualties were acceptable before honour was satisfied. There were few secrets on a small frigate when it was cleared for action, and every man on board knew why they were being pursued. They knew, and they didn't much like it.

Don Alonso stood alone on the quarterdeck. His wife and daughter had been sent to the orlop where they would be safest, but his pride wouldn't let him seek safety below.

He was standing where he'd been for the past two hours, at the taffrail watching the approaching Dutchmen.

Carlisle said a few words to Holbrooke and walked back to join the Spaniard. 'Your Excellency,' he said, 'may I have a few words?'

'By all means, Captain. There is no hope of privacy until this business is finished, but at least here we will be left in peace.'

Carlisle moved to Don Alonso's side, and for a moment they both watched the two pursuing ships. Although the sun had set long ago, it was a clear night, and the moon and stars gave enough light to see their adversaries, now only a mile astern. They were positioned on either quarter of *Medina*, and it was quite clear that they planned to board the frigate from both sides. It was an unimaginative tactic, but they had few options. They couldn't match the frigate's weight of broadside, but if they could get their grappling irons across, then they'd have the advantage of numbers.

Carlisle knew that he must have this conversation with Don Alonso, but it was difficult to know how to broach the question. Perhaps he let the silence run on a few seconds more than he should because he was pre-empted.

'I can guess at only two reasons why you feel the need to speak now, with a bloody battle perhaps only an hour away,' he said. 'Either you are here to request that I surrender myself and save your ship the trouble of fighting against people with whom you have no quarrel,' he saw a flash of anger in Carlisle's face, 'but your honour and your orders prevent you from taking that easy course, isn't that so?'

Carlisle nodded slowly in agreement; Don Alonso had captured the essence of Carlisle's problem.

'Then I must assume that you have come to ask me whether I would rather surrender myself to these pirates than take the risk that, should they prevail in this fight, they take revenge upon my wife and daughter.'

Carlisle nodded again, that was precisely his errand. The Dutchman had asked only for Don Alonso, not his family. It was only right that he should be given the opportunity to make his family safe.

'Then let me save you the trouble, Captain,' he said, turning to face Carlisle with a forced smile. 'You don't look like a man who flees from his duty, and nor am I. Neither of us is afraid to fight, but we would both prefer to fight on our King's business. This skirmishing with pirates has little honour in it. And yet, in these of all seas, it is more essential than ever that civilised people stand against the anarchy that the likes of those people,' and he flung his arm towards the ships astern, 'would impose.'

Don Alonso's face took on a hard, determined edge.

'This is not about Spain or England or Holland, it is not about our honour or our families, it is about law and the ability for ships to sail the seas unmolested. There will come a day when we have an enduring peace between our empires; yes, even here, beyond the line. I have no wish to exchange that dream of international amity for a dog-eat-dog fight for blood and profit. So, you see, Captain, we must fight. I heard stories about you in Port Royal. They called you a fighting captain and told me that you have won against the odds before. Captain Carlisle, I expect you to do so again.'

Carlisle recognised the natural orator – no the natural leader – and he was making a very compelling case. In truth, Carlisle was relieved. Although he didn't relish this fight, he was even less looking forward to reporting to Admiral Cotes and the governor of Jamaica that he'd surrendered to his enemies the man that they had placed under his protection. Nothing could take away the smear that such an action would leave against his name, even if Don Alonso had consented to the exchange to save his family.

'Then your hand on it, Your Excellency,' said Carlisle, 'and let's rid the seas of a few more pirates.'

The two men shook hands under the red ensign that flew defiantly from its staff, recognising in each other, for the first time, kindred spirits that were separated only by nationality.

'I'll tell my officers my plan now. Would you care to join us?' asked Carlisle.

'With the greatest pleasure, sir.'

The officers came aft, all those whose business was fighting or handling the ship: the first lieutenant, the marine lieutenant, the master, the gunner, the bosun and the two master's mates. The chaplain came unbidden, leading the four midshipmen and muttering something barely audible about the need to educate them in their profession. Carlisle stood beside Don Alonso, a gesture of solidarity in case any of *Medina's* officers should doubt whether this fight was their concern.

'Gentlemen, you all see where we stand,' said Carlisle, looking from face to face and then gesturing to the two ships astern. 'Each of those ships carries as many men as we do. If we let them alongside us, it'll be a hard and bloody fight. I don't intend to allow that. There are two of them, but I shall use their numbers against them.' All these men had followed Carlisle into battle on previous occasions, and he'd always won by guile, rather than brute strength. They gathered in closer.

Seven bells and the Dutchmen were only a few hundred yards astern. To the casual onlooker, it appeared that they were shepherding the frigate, one on each side of her wake, preventing an escape. Their intention was apparent. They'd grit their teeth and endure *Medina's* broadsides – which would surely start soon – until their bows were abreast the frigate's waist. Then, at a signal, perhaps a flag or the loosing of a topsail, they'd put their helms over and crash alongside. The frigate's boarding nets would slow them, but not for long, and two or three hundred seasoned privateers on *Medina's* deck would soon decide the contest.

Carlisle needed to break up the symmetry of their attack.

'Mister Hosking, come three points to starboard, bring her close to the wind,' he ordered.

'Mister Holbrooke. Stand by the starboard battery.' He hoped that the Dutchman would take this as his final manoeuvre and assume that he'd set his teeth into the junior of the two ships, the one that wasn't commanded by the man in the blue suit.

As *Medina* hardened up her sheets and tacks and showed her long battery, the privateer on her starboard side edged away. They'd probably rehearsed this move, to prevent the frigate fatally engaging one before the other could come into action.

Holbrooke observed the angles. At the point where the whole battery could see the target, he blew his whistle. The twelve nine-pounders fired almost as one with the sharper sound of the quarterdeck three-pounders joining a second or so later. The Dutchman had made the right move; instead of her vulnerable bows, *Medina's* shot ploughed into her sides. She was smaller and lighter than the frigate, but nevertheless, few of the shot did much damage even at that close range.

Carlisle looked over his shoulder at the other ship, the leader of this piratical squadron. She hadn't yet turned, she was waiting to determine what *Medina* would do next. It was in the interests of the Dutchmen to turn this into a melee, where the frigate's superior firepower would be nullified in the chaos of a close action, and where a boarding could come out of the smoke without notice. However, the man in the blue suit wanted to hold off for a moment. Apparently, he thought there was time enough to get his ships in the best position for the attack; after all, the frigate couldn't escape.

However, Carlisle had other ideas, and he had the advantage that all his force was under his eye and immediately obedient to his orders. He knew that his task was to make order out of the chaos that the enemy would try to impose upon him. He watched with satisfaction as the junior Dutchman was forced away to starboard, paralleling the frigate with the wind hard on his starboard bows. Now was the time to take the initiative away from the attackers.

'One more broadside, Mister Holbrooke,' he shouted. 'Are you ready Mister Hosking?'

'Ready, aye, ready,' replied the sailing master.

Medina was taking hits from the Dutchman. They were only eight-pound shot, and they couldn't penetrate the frigate's sides at that range, but Carlisle could see a few casualties where a ball had come in through one of the gun ports in the waist. One man was being dragged below to the cockpit, blood streaming from a wound to his leg, another was being bandaged by his mate.

Carlisle was taken by surprise by the second broadside. There had been no warning whistle, Holbrooke having ordered that each gun should fire as it was ready. He caught Don Alonso out of the corner of his eye, standing beside the hammock netting, apparently unconcerned by the Dutchman's fire. Carlisle waited for the right moment and saw just the first hint of the senior Dutchman starting to put his helm down to join the fight. So far, so good, and it looked like he'd persuaded his enemies that he was trying to escape to the north and east. Time to introduce his own chaos to the fight.

'Now, Mister Hosking. Lay me across that gentleman's bows.' The junior privateer, by following *Medina* onto the wind had put himself in a position where he couldn't get to the north of *Medina*. The senior privateer, meanwhile, was about to be given a lesson in concentrated firepower. 'As close as you can get, master.'

'Aye, aye, sir,' replied Hosking. 'I'll shave his bowsprit cap for you.'

Medina came off the wind with a rush. Round she came

onto a dead run. The senior privateer was staring death in the face; he'd told his crew to harden onto the wind, not to go about. There was no time to amend the order, he'd have to face a raking fire on his bow. The Dutch ships were of an older design, with a beakhead bulkhead, little more than a light partition across the bows that was pierced for access to the heads and bowsprit, rather than the modern built-up rounded bow that was made for protection. With *Medina's* superior height, her shot would be almost unimpeded on its journey along the gundeck. Holbrooke's twelve nine-pounders of the larboard battery were all aiming at the same compact area.

The weeks of training were paying off. The gun crews moved swiftly from starboard to larboard to join the second gun captain who had nothing to do but to ensure that the guns were ready for this moment. They knew what they were aiming at, not the tiny target of a foremast, but the beakhead bulkhead, and at this range, half pistol-shot, even with *Medina* moving at six knots across the privateer's bow, they could hardly miss.

Bang! Number one gun fired, then all down the side the remaining eleven fired as they saw the target. These were the fruits of intensive training when each gun captain ignored the noise and smoke and waited until the mark was clearly visible through his gun port. One or two of the shots missed, but at least eight nine-pound balls shattered the bulkhead and carried a trail of death and dismemberment the length of the privateer, upsetting guns and killing and maiming the crew.

This was the battle that Carlisle wanted, a battle where he grabbed the initiative, where he determined what would happen next. As they hurtled past the privateer, he saw its captain on the quarterdeck, the man in the blue suit, pushing men into their positions and shouting orders. There were twenty or thirty musketeers on the fo'c'sle and in the waist; some of them had been knocked over by *Medina's* broadside, and some stood stupidly, confused by the pace of the battle. But a few were effective, and they raised their weapons and took aim at *Medina's* quarterdeck as the frigate sped past them. He heard the popping of the small arms and the answering, louder reports from close at hand as his own marines joined the contest. Carlisle heard a gasp behind him. It sounded like someone on the quarterdeck had been hit, but he didn't have time to turn around.

'Mister Hosking. Bring her about and lay me alongside the Dutchman at a cable's range, we'll show him how a nine-pound battery should be handled.'

'Starboard battery, Holbrooke.' But his words weren't needed, and the crews were already changing sides, back to the starboard battery that had been reloaded in their absence. They only had to run the guns out – a task beyond the second gun captains that had been left behind – and they'd be ready to engage.

The junior privateer was temporarily out of the fight, not severely damaged, but unable to see where to re-enter the fray. She'd need watching, but it would take precious minutes for her to sail around her consort to take *Medina* on her larboard side. The privateer's only tactic, their only hope really, had been to board *Medina* from both sides simultaneously, or if that wasn't possible to run her aboard from the head and stern. Carlisle had frustrated their first attempt, but it was clear that they wouldn't give up easily.

'Aim for her hull, Mister Holbrooke, and then reload with chain. At this range, we should be able to take down some spars.'

Carlisle had a moment to look around him. He saw the damage to his ship's gunwales, he saw half a dozen wounded being taken below, and one man, the loader for one of the three-pounders, lying still under the hammock railings, a trail of blood showing where he'd been dragged from his gun.

'Where's Don Alonso?' he asked Eli, the quartermaster.

'Taken below, sir. A musket ball caught him in the

chest, he looked right poorly.' Eli had fought the Spanish in the last war and had little sympathy for the governor's wounds.

'Midshipman Smith!' shouted Carlisle, 'go below and bring me back a report on Don Alonso. Run!' He wasn't sure how the Spaniard's condition would change the terms of this fight, but still, he needed to know.

The senior privateer was game enough. Carlisle could see the captain shouting for boarders. The danger here was that *Medina* was now in the leeward position, and the Dutchman could dictate when to close the range, to crash alongside and board with her large crew. If they once got a foothold in *Medina*, and if they could hold on for the first five or ten minutes, the junior privateer would be alongside, and the battle would deteriorate into a brawl, a bloody street-fight that would favour the privateers.

'Open the range a little, Mister Hosking. We need to have room to react if our friend there bears down upon us.'

With a start, he realised that he didn't know where the junior privateer was. If she'd managed to work her way ahead of *Medina*, then it could be awkward. It was difficult to see through the growing bank of smoke, but was that her topsail that he could see through the murk, advancing past the senior privateer's bowsprit? Carlisle stared into the thick atmosphere. Yes, the second privateer had chosen to pass ahead of her leader and was hoping to do so unnoticed. All three ships were heading north with the wind on their starboard beams, the second privateer to windward and *Medina* to leeward with the lead privateer between them.

'Mister Hosking, I wish to pass astern of that privateer,' he pointed to the leader of the Dutchmen, now three cables to windward, 'bring the ship about.'

'May I suggest we veer, sir? That'll give us more separation,' and he pointed at the ship to windward.

Hosking was an excellent sailing master, and more aggressive than most, but his chief concern was the safety of the ship, whereas Carlisle's duty was to engage the enemy.

'Thank you for your advice, Mister Hosking,' he said with formality, 'nevertheless, we'll tack. We can finish this one off as we pass her stern.'

Hosking shrugged and gave the orders. The bosun's call summoned from the guns those men whose duties at quarters included sail handling and there was a rush of feet to the tacks and sheets. *Medina's* bow moved fast to starboard. The privateer saw what was happening and spotted her opportunity. If she could crash into *Medina* as she passed through the wind, she could hold the frigate until the second Dutchman came up. But Carlisle had anticipated that move. He'd seen that the privateer had nobody at the sheets and that she'd need to pass her stern right through the wind to execute that manoeuvre. *Medina*, with her superior discipline and training, would be too fast – he hoped.

As *Medina's* sails filled on the larboard tack, with her head to the east-southeast, he saw the privateer put over his own helm. Too late. *Medina's* fresh larboard battery was ready, double-shotted with chain and bar shot.

Even with a man from each gun away trimming the sails, the remaining crews were enough for the task. For a brief moment, both ships were passing each other on opposite tacks at half a cable range. *Medina's* broadside was shattering. Holbrooke had anticipated Carlisle's plan, and all the guns were at maximum elevation. The chain and bar shot ripped through the Dutchman's masts, sails and rigging. There was a wild cheer as her mizzen was shot through just above deck-level and in falling dragged her main topmast in a tangled mess over her larboard side. The Dutch boarders were hopelessly entangled and the ship, without any balancing sails aft, swung swiftly back to starboard. For a brief few seconds, *Medina* had the perfect opportunity to rake her from aft as she showed her exposed stern, but the larboard battery hadn't reloaded, and only the marines could add their musket fire to the confusion on the privateer's deck. The second privateer was hopelessly out of position with her leader between her and their intended victim.

'I'll load with ball, sir,' shouted Holbrooke. 'We can finish off this one before the second can get around her.'

Carlisle was tempted for a moment, but only briefly.

'Reload by all means Mister Holbrooke, but we won't be bothering these gentlemen again today unless they insist.'

Carlisle had already thought this through. Britain wasn't at war with Holland, and although these two ships were arguably pirates – and all King's officers had a general duty to suppress piracy – his orders were quite clear, and his chief responsibility was to deliver Don Alonso and his family safely to St. Augustine.

'Take us a mile to windward and then lie-to Mister Hosking.'

Carlisle realised that he'd been ignoring Midshipman Smith who'd been trying to speak to him for the past five minutes. He remembered that he'd sent the young man to determine Don Alonso's condition.

'If you please, sir, the doctor says that His Excellency isn't in immediate danger. A musket ball struck his chest but didn't penetrate his ribs. He's conscious and being bandaged.' The midshipman looked a little pale. Perhaps this was the first time that he'd been into the cockpit during a battle, the first time that he'd seen the shattered bodies, the blood and the severed limbs that were the consequence of a sea-fight.

'Very well, Mister Smith, now run down to the waist and ask Mister Holbrooke to join me on the quarterdeck.'

The silence was profound after the last fifteen minutes of intense fire from the great guns and the muskets.

Carlisle was aware of the sound of the breeze in the rigging as *Medina* lay-to with the fitful trade wind on her beam. To leeward he could see the lead privateer struggling to make some order out of the chaos of broken spars and torn sails. He watched the wreckage of the main topmast slip over the side, the additional weight bringing down the fore topmast. At a mile to windward, not a sound could be heard, and the agony of the shattered ship was played out in a dreamlike silence.

'Well, gentlemen, you're probably wondering what our next move will be.' Holbrooke watched him attentively, his pulse still running high from the action, and half-hoping that *Medina* would charge back into battle to finish off at least one of the Dutch ships. Hosking had his usual slightly detached air, accentuated, as always, when his advice had been disregarded.

'Much as I'd like to take these gentlemen back to Port Royal in irons, and see them tried as pirates, that's not our business today. We must see Don Alonso safely into St. Augustine. Nevertheless, I won't have them believe me to be shy so we'll lie here for half an hour to give them the opportunity to try their luck again. I'd like a report on damage and casualties within fifteen minutes, Mister Holbrooke, if you please.'

'Aye, aye, sir,' replied Holbrooke. He looked around, it was evident that the quarterdeck had taken the worst of the enemy's fire and there was damage to the hammock nets and the taffrail and some ugly dark smears on the deck where wounded men had been dragged away.

'Mister Hosking. Hold us in this position and let me know if the Dutchmen make any moves in our direction. I'll be in the cockpit and will then visit the orlop. I see the bosun has those halyards in hand.'

CHAPTER TWELVE

St. Augustine

Wednesday, third of August 1757
Medina. Off the Castillo San Marco, St. Augustine

Morgan paced the forward end of the quarterdeck, intoning the age-old chant to regulate the interval between guns in a salute. 'If I wasn't a gunner, I wouldn't be here, fire *one*! If I wasn't a gunner, I wouldn't be here, fire *two*!'

Medina was approaching her berth in the anchorage off the Castillo San Marco. The frigate had arrived off the maze of shallow banks that protected the entrance to the harbour of St. Augustine as the sun was just appearing over the broad Atlantic. Holbrooke and Chalmers had taken the cutter in to state their business and to arrange salutes. The commander of the castle was frankly amazed and initially suspicious, and it had tested the chaplain's mastery of Spanish to explain that the governor of Florida, Don Alonso himself, was on board with his family. The Spanish colonel had almost given Don Alonso up for lost. He was a month late and, in that time, they had heard no news of either the *Argonauta* or the *Nuestra Señora Del Rosario*. St. Augustine had suffered the tail end of the hurricane in June and that, combined with the lack of news, had caused them to fear the worst. It took half an hour to persuade them, but when he was satisfied that these two Englishmen – and one of them looked suspiciously like a heretical priest – were telling the truth, he swung into immediate action. The port's best pilot was dispatched to *Medina* to bring her safely into harbour, and the batteries were manned for a salute. Nineteen guns for a governor, and unusually for a foreign man-of-war, the castle would initiate the exchange of salutes.

Carlisle stood beside Don Alonso's chair on the quarterdeck. The governor had recovered remarkably quickly, proving his courage and fortitude and winning the admiration of the Medinas. However, his recovery wasn't a foregone conclusion, and he owed his very survival to *Medina's* surgeon.

Carlton could see that the ball had not passed through his body but was lodged somewhere in his right side. He'd followed the black, red and blue track of the bruising right across his chest from the entry wound and probing deep he'd found the musket ball lodged in Don Alonso's right armpit. Carlton had extracted the ball in the cockpit, by the light of a lantern, surrounded by the few other wounded and assisted by Chalmers. Don Alonso had hardly flinched as the cold steel bit into the living flesh. He'd been fortunate; two cracked ribs and a moderate loss of blood had been a small price to pay for being hit in the chest by an ounce of lead travelling at six hundred feet per second. He was lucky that it was a glancing blow and that his sternum had survived the impact. By medical logic, Don Alonso should have been below in a cot, moaning feebly, but nothing short of death would have kept him off the deck when he was being saluted by his own castle. He was pale and visibly weak, but he managed a smile and a gracious inclination of his head to Carlisle and Lady Chiara. He owed much to Chiara. His own wife, on setting foot in a ship, lost any semblance of practical usefulness that she may have commanded ashore, and his daughter was principally concerned with caring for her mother in the intervals when she wasn't following Carlisle around the deck, looking wistfully at the tall captain. It was Chiara who had nursed the governor, changed his bandages and cajoled him into eating. It was thanks to Chiara that he was in a fit state to be taken ashore without the need for a stretcher.

'Good morning Your Excellency,' said Carlisle. He

hadn't seen Don Alonso since the previous evening and was surprised to see him so well. 'As you see, we have anchored and here is a boat to take you ashore.'

It was a remarkable scene. Castillo San Marco glistened in the bright sunshine. Its walls were made of *Coquina*, a stone that was formed of ancient shells bonded together, and its myriad silvery grains reflected the light so that it was painful to look at it directly.

Medina was anchored right under the fort's guns. It was easy to see why all attempts at siege had so far failed. The river was so narrow that any attacking ship would be destroyed by the Spanish gunners before they could manoeuvre into position to bombard the fort. And even if a hostile ship should come unscathed to that position, one of the properties of *Coquina* was that it absorbed the shock of impacts. It wasn't a question of cannon balls bouncing off, they just failed to cause the sort of damage that was expected. The only possibility was to establish a battery on the higher land across the river, but that would hardly answer against such strong battlements. It gave Carlisle an uneasy feeling lying there under the Spanish guns. If Don Alonso had played them false, if Spain had already declared war, then *Medina* would be hard-pressed to make her escape from this elegant trap.

The barge that approached was worthy of a Spanish colonial governor. It rowed six oars on each side, but the liveried rowers were all in the forward part. The space from amidships right aft to the transom was covered by a gaudy canopy held up by four posts. There were tassels at each corner of the canopy, and below it, the inward-facing seats were cushioned in red fabric. The flag of the ruling house of Spain, the Bourbon arms on a white background, flew from a staff on the transom.

As the last of *Medina's* gun salutes echoed back from the tall walls of the castle, the barge hooked onto the larboard side of the frigate. Carlisle had alerted the bosun to the need for chairs slung from the yards to move Don

Alonso and his family from the frigate into the boat, but he'd reckoned without the awe in which the office of the governor of Florida was held. The barge was broad, and the space between the oarsmen was taken up with a folding accommodation ladder. At first, it appeared that rigging the ladder would take some time, but within two minutes it was complete, a rigid contraption that locked onto the gunwale of the barge and provided a convenient, dignified and safe means for people of consequence – and the governor indeed met the description – to embark or disembark. All they had to do was to time the short step from the deck of *Medina* onto the accommodation ladder; the rest was just a stately descent. *Medina's* bosun looked at it scornfully. 'It's all very well for this here harbour – more like a lake really – but I'd like to see how that device would survive even a flat day at Spithead,' he said to anyone who would listen.

First up the ladder was the colonel whom Chalmers had already indicated to Carlisle as the commander of the Castillo San Marco, closely followed by an army doctor. From that moment, Carlisle lost all authority over Don Alonso and his family. The efficient Spanish army took over, and Don Alonso was carefully handed down into the boat, followed by his wife and daughter. His baggage, such of it that had survived the hurricane, would follow later.

'You will stay in St. Augustine a few days, Captain?' asked Don Alonso. 'I owe you a debt of gratitude that it will be hard to repay, but I will do my poor best.'

Medina spent five days in St. Augustine. Never had a British ship been so welcome; in fact, never had a British ship been welcome at all in the capital of *Spanish* Florida. Twice in that century, the southern British colonies had laid siege to Castillo San Marco, the last time only seventeen years before *Medina's* visit, and the memories were still fresh. That both attacks had failed hardly mattered. The people of the town had been forced to take refuge in the castle, and their homes had been first levelled by the Spanish army to clear the fields of fire, and then the work was completed by the attackers who pillaged ruthlessly. Both sieges resulted in a castle that remained more-or-less intact, a town that was wholly destroyed and a populace that had to rebuild their homes and farms from the ground up.

However, Don Alonso ruled the colony with powers that were not unlike those that King Ferdinand, his master, enjoyed in Spain. He was the absolute ruler of this distant and half-forgotten colony, and if he said that *Medina* and its crew were welcome, there were none in St. Augustine who would dare to contradict him. The taverns were thrown open to those of the crew who were given leave. They complained that all they could get was wine, there was no beer and very little rum available, but nevertheless, they made the most of this unexpected welcome. In a way, it wasn't unlike a run ashore in Cadiz or Cartagena in Old Spain: the same wine shops, the same heat, the same grinding poverty existing cheek-by-jowl with conspicuous wealth. By Sunday, *Medina* was an inch or two deeper in the water, weighed down with fresh fruit and vegetables, her water butts refilled and enough wood to keep the galley fire burning until they should reach Port Royal.

Carlisle had caught sight of Maria at each of the formal events during their stay in St. Augustine, the dinners, the celebratory mass and the receptions, but here on home territory, she'd been returned to the discipline of a chaperone. This lady of indeterminate age had evidently been well-briefed, and she hadn't allowed Maria to pass close enough to Carlisle to exchange even a word. Much to his relief, Carlisle was favoured by nothing more than a wistful glance.

At dinner on Sunday the unfortunate young lady had been ushered out of the room when her composure left her, and she threatened to collapse, her passing marked by a strangled sob and the clucking of her chaperone. Chiara noted all this with satisfaction. She didn't blame her husband and neither did she blame Maria. In fact, Chiara could have forecast how it would end, the whole affair had the stately inevitability of a Greek tragedy. It was even amusing in a way, but she was glad that it had passed without any lasting damage. Looking around at all the young Spanish officers, she could confidently forecast that Maria's despair wouldn't last out the month, probably not even the week.

'Well, Captain,' said Don Alonso as they sat together after an early breakfast on Monday morning, 'I shall miss your company, and that of Lady Chiara, but you have a war to return to, and it's not possible that King George has so many ships of this quality that he can spare *Medina* indefinitely. The weather looks fair but beware of hurricanes, the season is still young.'

'I regret that's so,' said Carlisle, wondering what Don Alonso knew or guessed about his orders to return home by way of the Caicos Passage and Cape François. 'Admiral Cotes will be fretting for lack of frigates and my men are growing fat on Florida's hospitality.'

Both men looked out beyond the castle's walls to *Medina* in the harbour. The governor's personal barge was at the jetty waiting for Carlisle, *Medina's* anchor had been heaved in short, the Spanish pilot was on board, and the frigate would be feeling the Atlantic swell within half an hour of them finishing their coffee. This was a private breakfast. The formal farewells had been said at dinner on Sunday, after Mass at the castle's chapel, which Chiara, Carlisle and Chalmers had attended. Chiara, of course, was a Catholic, and Carlisle attended out of respect and support to his wife. Chalmers, meanwhile, seized the opportunity to participate in a Catholic mass without the risk of being censured, which would surely have been the least he could expect if he'd attended a mass in England. So, this was the final farewell, but Carlisle had the distinct feeling that there were some things that Don Alonso wanted to say to him, issues that couldn't be discussed in public.

'You'll be aware, captain, that I have engineered this last meeting so that I can speak freely to you in private,' said Don Alonso in his habitually straightforward manner. It almost seemed that he'd been reading Carlisle's thoughts. 'There are three matters I want to raise. First, and most sincerely to thank you. You have saved my life on two occasions, but of greater importance, you saved the lives of my wife and daughter, whom I treasure above all else.'

Carlisle watched Don Alonso carefully. He was sure that the governor valued his daughter's life, perhaps even over his own, but he wasn't at all sure that his devotion extended to his wife, and he was confident that many of the ladies of the governor's court could attest to that.

'Second, to express my sincere hope that Britain and Spain won't go to war again this century,' said Don Alonso, with a conspiratorial air. 'It will come as no surprise to you that our mutual friends, the French, are working hard to bring Spain into the war and create a Hapsburg family alliance against your country. The invasion of Minorca, of course, was principally so that France could offer the island to Spain in exchange for our support in the war. However, it is not in my country's interests to fight Britain again, and I want to express my fervent hope that we will remain at peace, if only so that I can welcome *Medina* to St. Augustine again.'

Carlisle bowed. It wasn't his place as a junior post-captain to comment on matters of high diplomacy, and from the expression on Don Alonso's face, his host knew that very well. In any case, he strongly suspected that the governor knew more than he was saying about Spain's real attitude to this latest war.

'And third, Captain, a warning.'

Carlisle moved uncomfortably in his chair as he waited

for Don Alonso to continue.

'A caution is perhaps a better word to use, but anyway, you would do well to heed it,' he said, stroking his beard. Carlisle had never seen Don Alonso stroke his beard, it was generally considered impolite, and in this case, it lent a hint of drama to the Spaniard's delivery of his warning.

'The Dutch pirate, as you know, is a resolute man. He is not only determined, but he is also vindictive. I would not be surprised if he extends his vendetta to include you and your crew. You must be on your guard! *Medina* is powerful enough to resist the two Dutch ships in the open sea, but he will attempt to use surprise to overpower you, and I believe he will stop at nothing. My family and I are safe enough in Florida, and I will not put to sea again without an adequate escort, but I am afraid that while he cannot strike at me, he may make an attempt on you. Be on your guard, Captain!'

Carlisle considered for a moment. Did Don Alonso know that his wife had revealed to Chiara the reason that these Dutchmen were hunting him across the Caribbean and the Gulf of Mexico? Why they'd been pursuing him for the past nine years? From the slight conspiratorial smile on his face, it appeared that he did, but for some reason didn't wish to acknowledge it. Probably he'd contrived the conversation between the two women so that his role was deniable. Carlisle held his gaze for a few seconds. Evidently, the knowledge was shared, and it was better not to press the point.

They parted with a most cordial handshake, and as *Medina's* anchor broke away from the mud of the Matanzas River, the Castillo's batteries fired a parting salute that shook the slates on the roofs of the houses of the town. *Medina* dropped her pilot into the accompanying cutter when they were clear of the river mouth and then she stood out into the open ocean. When she was out of sight of land, she put the wind on her beam and reached away towards Savannah in the British colony of Georgia, some hundred and fifty miles to the north. If Don Alonso had guessed that they were bound for Savannah, he politely didn't show it. Although Britain and Spain were at peace, that fact hardly mattered to the colonies of Florida and Georgia who carried out a constant and bitter feud across the border. As far as Florida was concerned, Georgia was a hostile colony with which they shared an ill-defined and often contested border. No peace beyond the line indeed.

CHAPTER THIRTEEN

The Angelini Cousins

Wednesday, tenth of August 1757
Medina, at Sea. Tybee Island, Georgia west 12 leagues

M edina was under full sail, moving steadily
eastwards out into the Atlantic. She'd weighed
her anchor and left Savannah Sound soon after
first light, glad to shake off the intense, sticky heat, the
mosquitos and the barely-concealed hostility of the
colonists. The Province of Georgia was a new colony, only
thirty-five years old, and it sat precariously between the
established territory of Carolina and Spanish Florida.
Indeed, part of the reason for Georgia's existence was as a
buffer between the British and Spanish colonies on the
eastern seaboard of America. The Georgia militia had laid
siege to Castillo San Marco only seventeen years before,
and the defeat and the loss of so many colonists was still
fresh in the memory of the inhabitants of Savannah. When
this *Virginian* captain came sailing in out of the blue with
the news that he'd saved the lives of the governor of
Florida and his family and restored them to their home, it
was understandable that he should find little friendliness in
Savannah. *Medina* had stayed barely twenty-four hours and
had not sailed up the Savannah River at all, remaining at
anchor in the sound where at least there was some breeze
and fewer biting insects.

'Good evening Mister Hosking. I hope this cool sea air
agrees with you after the coast of America.'

'It certainly does ma'am.' The sailing master had
reverted to his usual offshore rig of duck trousers and a
linen shirt, and he was apparently the better for it. Even
twelve miles downriver from the colonial capital, he'd felt
the need to wear his blue coat and hat to maintain the

dignity of the ship while it was at anchor.

'Captain Carlisle tells me that it will take two weeks to return to Port Royal,' said Chiara.

'That it will ma'am, a fortnight if we can get through these variables and back into the northeast trade winds without too much delay. We have an errand to perform at Cape François that will add a day or two, so I can't promise that we will be stretching out our cable before the last week of the month.'

'Are we then in the variables that you spoke of?' Chiara asked, 'and yet we appear to be sailing at a reasonable speed.'

'Well, here's the problem, ma'am,' said the sailing master. He was always happy to display his knowledge and here he saw a great opportunity and a willing listener.

'Mister Smith,' he said to the midshipman of the watch, who was loitering only a few paces away. 'Jump below to my cabin and bring me the chart that you'll see on my desk.'

'Aye, aye, sir,' replied the midshipman who sprinted for the quarterdeck ladder and thence below. He returned so fast that Hosking hadn't even managed to start another sentence. It was wonderful how all these young men were so eager to show their zeal and energy when the captain's wife was on deck.

'Now, hold this down on the binnacle, both hands for the chart, don't worry about yourself.'

In an hour it would be dark, but so abrupt was the transition from day to night this close to the tropics, that the chart could be seen clearly in the slanting light.

'Now, we're here, more-or-less,' said Hosking, his finger to the chart some thirty-five miles off the coast, on the same latitude as Savannah which they had left twelve hours ago. 'Our orders are to return to Port Royal here,' and his finger traced a straight line cutting south and a little east, back through the Florida Straits, clipping the western edge of the Bahamas, crossing Cuba and Jamaica to the island's southwestern corner where Port Royal could just be identified as a notch in the coastline. 'Now, if we could fly there at our average speed of, say, six knots, we'd make it in just seven days, it's less than a thousand miles south of here.'

Chiara nodded. This much she knew already having studied her husband's chart, but she didn't want to interrupt Hosking while he was so talkative. She wanted to hear the details that only navigators knew and if it took a little charm to extract it from this seasoned sailor, then so be it.

'I'm sure you have a plan that prevents us being wrecked on any of those islands, Mister Hosking,' she said with a smile.

'Aye, I do,' he replied, not sensing the irony in Chiara's voice. 'We've to look at the French navy in Cape François,' he pointed to a tiny indent in the northwest coast of Hispaniola, 'and then we can take the Windward Passage between Cuba and French Hispaniola – they call it Saint Domingue nowadays – and then around the eastern end of Jamaica and so to Port Royal.'

Chiara recognised the geographical logic, but it was the subtlety of winds and tides that interested her.

'We're well out of the northeast trades here and won't pick them up until we're about twenty-eight degrees above the equator,' Hosking traced a horizontal line across the chart from at St. Augustine. 'Further north from here the westerlies rule but between the westerlies and the trade winds we have this band of variables. We can't head straight south to pick up the trade winds because that would put us too far west and we'd have to beat against the wind to make our way to the east. So, we must head out into the Atlantic for perhaps three or four days before we set our head to the south and aim for this gap between the Caicos Islands and the easterly Bahamas.'

Chiara frowned. She could see the problem immediately. For centuries mariners had been able to fix their latitude with some certainty, particularly in areas where the sun was less likely to be obscured. But if *Medina* was to head east into the trackless wastes of the Atlantic, she needed to know her longitude to determine when to head south for the coast of Hispaniola. Chiara knew very well that there was no reliable way of directly measuring longitude.

'How will you determine when we should turn to the south, Mister Hosking,' she asked, studying the chart and running her finger along their intended track. 'You speak of three or four days, but a day of error, either way, will cause us to entirely miss this passage.'

'Ah, well it all comes back to the old ways of navigating,' said Hosking. 'We have our log to tell our speed,' and he pointed to the line coiled and made fast to the taffrail, 'and we have our compass,' he said thumping on the binnacle. 'Midshipman Smith here will note our course and speed each half-hour on this traverse board,' and he held up a flat piece of wood marked with a compass rose and pierced by regularly-spaced holes, some of which had tethered pegs inserted. 'And we know how much leeway *Medina* makes, so with those pieces of knowledge we can tell how far we've moved through the water and in which direction.'

'Then the unknown factor is the ocean current. Is that correct?' asked Chiara.

Hosking gave Chiara a quizzical look. She appeared to know more about navigation than he'd assumed. At least her questions were intelligent. The sailing master stiffened slightly. He was quite relaxed when he could be somewhat condescending about his skills, but he wasn't so happy with this air of critical enquiry. Chiara, ever sensitive to mood, spotted the change immediately and suppressed a smile. If she wanted any more information, she'd have to play this carefully.

'I remember you explaining the currents back in Port Royal, but perhaps I wasn't quite attending,' she said, casting her eyes down modestly in imitation of a pupil who has been caught daydreaming.

'Well,' said Hosking, somewhat mollified to find that his captain's wife could attribute what little knowledge she had to his own instruction, 'of course we have the current behind us today, but we're cutting across the stream slantwise, so although it's helping us along, we'll soon be out of it. Then we'll just have to trim the sails and shape our course as the wind dictates. We'll maintain our latitude by the noon sun-sights, and we'll reckon our longitude from the log and compass, with a correction for the stream. When by that reckoning we reach the meridian of the passage, about seventy-one degrees west of Greenwich, then we'll turn south.'

'Will you be able to see these islands as we approach?' she pointed to the Caicos Islands to the east and the Inagua Islands to the west, 'are they very high?'

'Why, no, bless you, ma'am. Those are the lowest-lying islands you can imagine. We'll be careful to approach by day and keep a good lookout. I'll recommend to the captain that he points the ship a little to the east of the passage, straight at the Caicos Islands,' he said, pointing at the small archipelago to the north of Hispaniola. Hosking was gratified by a puzzled look from Chiara, 'so that when we *do* sight land right ahead' – he tapped the wood of the binnacle as a private superstition – 'we'll know which way to turn for the passage. And we'll be to windward of Cape François.'

Chiara nodded in understanding. 'I see. If you were to point directly at the passage but were a few miles off in your reckoning, when you see land ahead you won't know which way to turn unless you can identify it.'

'Exactly. Now, we must get through that passage in the daylight, minding the Caicos to the east and this mess of islands and reefs to the west, it's far too dangerous at night, then we'll be able to approach Cape François overnight and be in position in the morning watch. A quick look into the harbour, then we'll put our stern to the wind and run past Tortuga and into the Windward Passage. The current, what there is of it, should be with us, and we can hope for some wind from the east. In which case, two days should see us home.'

'You make it sound so easy, Mister Hosking, but I'm sure it isn't. Yet I feel at ease with you in charge of the navigation. Captain Carlisle is very fortunate to be sailing with you.'

Hosking wasn't used to compliments and particularly not an informed professional compliment from a woman. He hardly knew how to react. He started to scowl, then caught himself and bowed as graciously as he knew how.

'Thank you, ma'am, it's been a pleasure. Now perhaps you'll excuse me as the watch is about to change,' and Hosking retreated from this unknown situation into the familiar details of the profession that he knew so well.

Chiara had to turn away so that the smile on her face, which was rapidly turning into an uncontrollable giggle, wouldn't be seen. She wouldn't, for all the world, mock this man, whom life at sea had left poorly equipped to deal with inquisitive young women.

It wasn't appropriate for Chiara to meet her cousin in the cockpit, where he messed with the other midshipmen and the petty officers who aspired to gentlemanly status. Nor could she invite Enrico to the cabin unless Carlisle was hosting him for breakfast or dinner. However, they had found a way around the problem by meeting in the last dogwatch at the leeward side of the quarterdeck, there to exchange news and keep in touch. For whereas Chiara was a passenger, Enrico was a member of the ship's company, duly entered in the books and subject to the articles of war. Not only was he part of the crew, but in *Medina*, his social status was immeasurably lower than the captain's wife, and it had taken them both a little while to understand that and to come to terms with the restrictions that it placed upon them.

This evening, Chiara was looking forward to their meeting with more than usual anticipation; she was eager to display her new-found knowledge to her younger cousin. Before they left Nice together, Chiara's understanding of warfare had eclipsed Enrico's despite his commission as an ensign in the army of Sardinia. For Chiara had survived an attack on her ship in the Mediterranean, even though the supposed attacker had later been found to be a friend, and she'd witnessed Carlisle's attempt to catch the aggressor, where cannon had actually fired, and the attacker's xebec was damaged. Enrico's short service in King Charles Emmanuel's army had provided no such excitement. But since he'd been taken into *Medina* as a midshipman, he'd taken part in a battle at sea, had managed a section of four guns and had seen men die around him. The balance of warlike experience had shifted in Enrico's favour, and his cousin was keen to redress the balance by displaying her navigational knowledge. She looked around to ensure that the master couldn't hear them.

'Good evening, Enrico,' she said with an innocent smile, 'when are you next on watch?' They'd agreed to speak English whenever they met to help imprint the language in their minds.

'Good evening Chiara,' he replied. He had to be careful, it would never do to refer to the captain's wife by her Christian name if the captain was listening. Enrico had started his new life in *Medina* with an aristocratic disdain for commoners. He was prepared to tolerate Carlisle's command, but in those early days, he knew deep inside himself that his breeding made him superior. Six months in the rough and tumble of the cockpit had gone a long way to change his opinion. It wasn't that he thought less of himself, but he'd come to appreciate the skills of the ship's officers: the first lieutenant, the master, the bosun, the gunner and all the others. But Carlisle was different. For the first few months he'd learned to fear the captain, then by degrees to admire him, and now his regard for his captain came close to veneration. Chiara was still his cousin, an older cousin, but they had played together as children, and it was difficult to move on from that relationship. Nevertheless, Enrico found that he couldn't speak to her as he used to, and he'd always have a quick all-around scan for the captain when they met. Chiara, of course, had noticed this and exploited it.

'Good evening, I have the first watch, so I'll be back on deck in an hour, but I must have a bite of supper before then.' He was fast learning the patois of the sailor and no longer saw any incongruity in speaking of the *deck* in two separate personas; as a solid wooden object upon which he was at that moment standing and as a term to describe his duty station.

'Then you have time to help me a little,' she said with her sweetest, most innocent smile. Enrico nodded inscrutably. That was something else he'd learned along with the hard knocks in the midshipman's berth, and in any case, he knew his cousin's treacherous smiles of old.

'I'm puzzled as to why we appear to be heading east when Port Royal is almost south of here. Can you explain it please, you must know so much about navigation?' She studied his face carefully for the first signs of evasion.

Enrico thought fast. Another of life's lessons in the cockpit was never to admit that you don't know anything and always to play a losing hand to the end; you never knew what the fates would throw down to save you. 'Ah, that is because of the prevailing wind and the Atlantic stream, not to mention the magnetic variation and the phase of the moon,' he said loftily. 'It would take some hours to explain it all to you, and I regret that I wouldn't be able to do the subject justice in the few moments that I have left.'

'Oh, but we have a minute or two. Pray, what is the prevailing wind in this latitude? From which direction does it blow?

'Well, it all depends on the season and on the strength of the current. It's changeable today, but I expect it to blow more steadily tomorrow.'

'Then you expect that we will meet the trade winds again, tomorrow?' she asked with that vague air of unconcern that Enrico knew so well, 'how strange that we will meet the trade winds this far north. How unusual.'

Enrico felt – no, he knew – that he was being led into a trap, but the midshipman didn't know how to evade it without admitting that he had no idea what winds he could expect on this passage. It was all the same to him; an arctic blast or a tropical breeze. He'd still have to turn out at midnight and pace the deck for his four hours, he'd lay out on the yards with the common seamen, and he'd eat the monotonous but hearty food of the cockpit and drink the small beer. It wasn't that he disdained the higher learning of his new profession, it was just that it would do him no good until he'd mastered the basics of seamanship. Enrico knew that this evening he'd been dealt a losing hand and his opponent was playing hers ruthlessly, but he pressed on, playing his hand through and relying on a kindly fate to save him.

'At this time of year,' he started, affecting to test the breeze with his forefinger, 'the northeast trade wind …'

'All Hands,' roared the bosun, 'all hands to put the ship about. Rouse out, tacks and sheets, bowlines there!'

Enrico bowed briefly to his cousin and without a further word, and in relief, sprinted for the shrouds and raced up to his post in the maintop. It was a lesson well-learned. Play a losing hand to the end, particularly at sea; you never knew what was over the horizon.

Chiara retreated to the taffrail where she knew she was least likely to be in the way. She'd scored her point; Enrico had felt the button of her épée pressing on his tunic. It would have been better if she'd been able to twist it a little, but she was satisfied.

CHAPTER FOURTEEN

The Caicos Islands

Thursday, eighteenth of August 1757
Medina, at Sea. Caicos Islands south 3 leagues

The masthead lookout had sighted the low-lying Caicos Islands an hour after sunrise, nine miles distant and only a point on the larboard bow. Hosking had maintained an outward imperturbable demeanour, but he hadn't left the deck since sunset and the last hour, when nothing was to be seen, no hint of land just over the horizon, had taken its toll. He grunted in response and made his laboured way to the maintop.

'Brail the foretopsail,' he shouted grumpily to the deck, 'I can't see a bleeding thing. How do you expect me to see through four-weight canvas? Mister Smith, sharpen up those waisters.' Clearly, the whole ship would have to suffer for the master's sleepless night.

Hosking scanned the horizon on the larboard bow. Although he was forty feet lower than the lookout – the masthead was no place for a man of his years and dignity – *Medina* had advanced a mile in the ten minutes since the hail had reached the quarterdeck. The sailing master could just see the faintest interruption in the ruler-straight line of the southern horizon, and now that it was brought to his attention, there was the hint of thickening cloud over the islands. He raised the telescope to his eye and studied the contours of the land.

Hosking hated these meridian landfalls. When he was looking for a landfall in an easterly or westerly direction, he could just run along the appropriate line of latitude and as long as he'd aimed-off a little, he could be reasonably confident of the identity of whatever he first saw. But when he had to approach from the north or south, not

143

only would he be unsure of his own longitude, but the longitude of the landfall would probably have been set down inaccurately in the charts. It was all very well giving the impression that navigation was a well-ordered science, but in reality, it was an art and an inexact one at that. Hosking was staking his professional reputation on correctly identifying these undistinguished sand-dunes. He knew he hadn't come far enough south to be in sight of mainland Hispaniola, the only real question was whether he was too far west. It was unlikely, he decided. They had come too far south by his reckoning for these islands to be the eastern Bahamas. As he pondered, more land came into sight to the east and west of the original sighting. It was evidently a significant archipelago and could only be the Caicos Islands. He thought, perhaps, that he was further east than he'd intended, but nobody needed to know that. The captain and first lieutenant may guess, but they'd say nothing to undermine the ship's company's faith in the master's navigation.

'Captain, sir!' Hosking shouted to the quarterdeck. The eyes of every man on deck turned upwards, a landfall was always an important event in the life of this small community. 'That's the Caicos Islands stretching right ahead of us, two points on either bow. If we put the ship before the wind, we can follow them around to the western end. I'll stay here for a while to get my bearings. Could you send Mister Angelini up with my chart of the Caicos?'

'Very well, Mister Hosking,' replied Carlisle. Enrico was already halfway to the maintop with the precious chart tightly rolled and securely stowed inside his shirt.

Carlisle and Holbrooke watched from the quarterdeck rail as the tacks and sheets were eased, and the steersman turned the ship a few points to starboard, putting the wind a point on the starboard quarter. Although the moderate breeze from astern was pushing *Medina* southwest at nine or ten knots, the ship's speed and the wind speed were so similar that the familiar and usually unnoticed sound of the wind in the rigging was stilled. Only the ripple of water passing down the hull broke the silence.

'Stuns'ls, sir?' asked Holbrooke, his voice making Carlisle start.

'Yes, by all means, Mister Holbrooke. I'd like to be squarely in the passage well before sunset. With a good departure from West Caicos and a certainty that we're clear of the Inagua Islands we can be safely inside the Caicos Bank and raising Cape François at first light.'

'Aye, aye, sir,' and Holbrooke turned to give the orders. It wasn't necessary, of course. The watch on deck could see the situation; there was still an hour to go before the change of watch, and they were happy to have the exercise. They poured aloft in a steady stream, the main topmen swarming over the master and the midshipman as they tried to resolve the points of land against the chart. Within five minutes the desired sails were set, main and main topsail stuns'ls, and foretopsail stuns'ls, increasing *Medina's* speed by a knot.

'Jackson, pass the word to the masthead to watch the water ahead for any sign of a shallow patch. We shouldn't even be in soundings here, but we're sailing too fast for the deep-sea lead, and I don't want to take chances.'

'Aye, aye, sir.' Jackson ran lightly up the shrouds to the lookout perched on the fore topmast trestle-trees.

'Mister Hosking,' shouted Holbrooke to the maintop, 'how close may we approach these islands?'

'Two miles will keep us clear,' the master replied. 'There's a reef less than half a mile offshore, and it's deep water right up to the coral.'

Holbrooke could see the islands from the deck now, an uninterrupted line of low-lying land from three points on the larboard bow right around to the larboard beam. On this course, *Medina* would clear the furthest point that they could see by about a league. If West Caicos was beyond that point, as the master seemed to believe, then they'd leave it a few miles on the beam and turn into the Caicos Passage between the Bahamas and the Caicos Islands. The timing looked good. All the tricky navigation should be over before sunset, and then they'd be in clear water with only Cape François ahead.

This was the finest of sailing. All that day *Medina* coasted along the northern shore of the Caicos archipelago, enjoying the sight of a low sandy shore fringed with palm trees. Hosking's suspicion had proven correct. The frigate had made landfall further east than he'd anticipated, but by aiming off to the east during the approach, he knew that the land that he saw could only reasonably be the Caicos Islands, and therefore a turn to the west would bring them to the passage. The master's chart of the Caicos, only a dozen years old, had been pinned to a grating and set up on the quarterdeck. There was no flying spray to endanger it, and the midshipman of the watch was under the strictest orders to hurry it below at the slightest sign of any untoward activity.

Meanwhile, the chart was being used to instruct the young gentlemen in the art of recognising a three-dimensional shoreline from a two-dimensional representation on paper. When Hosking had exhausted that means of tormenting them, he'd set them to sketching the views and referencing the few prominent points to the charted locations. This wasn't being done merely for the benefit of the midshipmen and master's mates. Hosking, like most masters of men-of-war, produced charts and sketches of all unfrequented shorelines and returned them to the Navy Board. There was no Admiralty direction for this, but it was generally considered the duty of every sailing master to contribute to the growing body of knowledge of foreign landfalls. There was talk of a hydrographic office being set up and captains and masters being *required* to send in their soundings and sketches, but nothing had yet been done. This was all part of the new enthusiasm for charting the expanded range of the British navy, as it reached out from the narrow seas into the global oceans.

'This is delightful,' said Chiara, as they sat side-by-side on the windward side of the quarterdeck. 'If it were always like this I would take the King's shilling and forego the land for this sparkling sea and sky.' She stretched her arms to the sun and laughed out loud. The master frowned, his gaze fixed steadfastly away towards the low shore, disavowing this unseemly behaviour on the holy planks of the quarterdeck. But the quartermaster smiled covertly, and the two steersmen grinned broadly. The captain's wife had become a favourite of the lower deck, and if she wished to laugh on the quarterdeck, then that was perfectly fine with them.

'Are you anticipating any difficulty with the French, my dear?' she asked.

'No, I don't believe so. This is the least likely direction for a British man-of-war to approach Cape François. If we'd come from Port Royal, we'd approach from the west, through the Windward Passage. If from English Harbour, then we'd have coasted westwards along the northern coast of Hispaniola. We're only taking this route because of our visit to St. Augustine and Savannah, and the French could hardly know about that. No, it'll be sheer bad luck if we meet a Frenchman today and I intend to be so early off the Cape tomorrow that they won't have had their breakfast,' he smiled, 'and you know that no self-respecting Frenchman will be active before breakfast. We'll approach to within a few miles, make our count and be away before they know they're being watched. We'll be in Port Royal on Monday.'

'Well, with weather like this, I could wish that Port Royal was a year away.'

Holbrooke idly watched the small knot of midshipmen and master's mates sitting cross-legged on the quarterdeck sketching the landfall. He'd never been good at drawing; even at the naval academy, his efforts had called forth the scorn and wrath of the master and the instructors. Luckily, he'd never sailed under a master like Hosking who insisted that every young officer should contribute to his stock of drawings. There were six young men in total making sketches. Holbrooke walked between them looking over their shoulders. Some tried to hide their work by affecting to move their paper to a different angle as he passed by, but a sharp word brought them to order. Some of them were actually quite good, far better than he could have done himself, Holbrooke admitted, but at least two of them were utterly worthless, a criminal waste of paper and lead. The last that he looked at was Enrico's. The younger Angelini was unaware of his first lieutenant's approach and was wholly absorbed in his work. The half-finished result was breathtaking. Holbrooke looked from the paper up to the shore and then back again. It was quite remarkable how Enrico had rendered the three-dimensional scene onto a two-dimensional surface. The outline of the land was exact, true to life, but the real beauty was in the way that he'd used subtle shading to show how the ground rose and fell and give an impression of depth to the sketch. It was even more remarkable because the Caicos Islands as seen from the north had little to distinguish them, just gently undulating sand-dunes, a few palm trees and the distinctive Caicos pines, looking wholly out of place under the tropical sun. Yet Enrico had managed to create a picture that could be used by any navigator to determine which part of the island he was looking at. Evidently, the young Sardinian had a real artistic talent.

'Aye, he has a good eye and hand,' said Hosking when they were out of hearing of the group. 'I'll be sending his work to the Navy Board without any corrections, and I'll give him credit for them. Our children and grandchildren, if they pass this way, will be using his sketches. I doubt there have been any like them before and I doubt there'll be any better in the future.'

'I'm pleased about that,' said Holbrooke. 'He isn't finding life at sea very easy at all. I think he had the idea that it would be like being an ensign in the Sardinian army, where it appears that nothing was expected of him in the way of actual knowledge of his profession.'

'He's four years late, at least, for coming to sea, so we should make some allowances,' said Hosking. 'He's trying, but it's hard. Nevertheless, he's quick and clever, and I've hopes for him. Certainly, his mathematics is way beyond the ordinary.'

'Is it? I'd no idea. I've seen his journal, but that's a little unfair as he's only just coming to grips with spoken English, and we should expect his written work to take a little longer.'

'I'll send you his day's workings tomorrow, sir, and you can see for yourself. He's a natural.'

'Are you discussing my cousin?' asked Chiara as she strolled up to join them.

'We are, ma'am,' replied Hosking, bowing. 'The lad has a rare talent for drawing.'

'Oh, I hadn't realised that drawing was a necessary skill for sea-officers, Mister Hosking, but I see that all the young gentlemen are engaged in it.'

Hosking explained to Chiara the need for sketches of landfalls, taking the time to show her the different standards of work and comparing them to Enrico's, much to his dismay as he still saw himself as an equal to his cousin, not a young man under instruction being displayed to the visiting gentlefolk.

'Mister Hosking, the purser's asking that you come and look at a cask of beef, he wants to condemn it,' said a breathless boy who had just run from the hold to the quarterdeck without pausing. Too late he saw that the master was talking to the captain's wife and in his haste to make a bow he tripped over a ring-bolt that ordinarily secured the tackle for one of the three-pounders and fell flat on his face. In picking him up and dusting him off, Chiara missed Hosking's apologies and found herself briefly alone at the quarterdeck rail. She didn't feel like solitude on this beautiful day, so she turned to Holbrooke who was still examining the sketches.

'George,' she said drawing Holbrooke away from the young gentlemen, 'would it be in order if I asked how my cousin is coming along? It's so difficult for me to judge whether he's progressing as a mariner.'

Holbrooke laughed, 'I'd be happy to give you my opinion, although of course he's on the ship's books as the captain's servant and strictly not my concern.'

'But I thought he was a midshipman,' she said with a frown.

'And so he is, ma'am. The captain's rated him midshipman, and as you see, he messes with the others and walks the quarterdeck. However, when he joined *Medina*, we already had our full establishment of midshipmen, so he's on the books as a captain's servant.'

'Is that allowed? Doesn't the Admiralty see through this trick?'

'Oh, their Lordships don't care, so long as they don't have to pay him as a midshipman. I expect the captain will make it all right as soon as there's a vacancy. It'll only take someone to drop out above him, any of the master's mates or midshipmen, and his rank will become official,' said Holbrooke, gazing absently at the passing shoreline. 'Sooner or later one will be taken ill, or pass for lieutenant, or he'll just be moved to another ship. The midshipman's berths are entirely at the captain's discretion, you know.'

'Then he's doing well, I gather, he's not disgracing his family? It's just that he seems so far behind the others.'

'He's certainly not disgracing you, ma'am. Yes, he is behind, but then he's late in coming to sea. There's a huge amount to learn, and of course, no amount of learning can be a substitute for experience at sea,' said Holbrooke with his tongue firmly in his cheek. He'd spent three years in the naval academy while his contemporaries were at sea. 'He's intelligent and strong, and most of all the men are starting to respect him. He'll do well.'

'Forgive all these questions, George, but is there a future for him in the navy? I really don't know whether he regards this as his new career or just a few months or years of a different experience before he returns to Sardinia, but he must soon start thinking about it.'

Holbrooke paused to formulate his answer. 'Well, he has the ability to pass a lieutenant's board, and with the captain becoming so well respected in the service, he has the patronage to be commissioned and sent back to a ship as a lieutenant. However, to be commissioned one must renounce the Pope and swear an oath to that effect. I imagine that's a barrier that Enrico will be unable to pass.'

'Yes, yes I believe it is,' said Chiara sadly. 'Then he must enjoy this experience while he can and return to King Charles Emmanuel's army with skills that no others will be able to match. Imagine the figure that he'll cut in command of a galley!'

Chris Durbin

CHAPTER FIFTEEN

Ambush

Thursday, eighteenth of August 1757
Medina, at Sea. West Caicos Island east 5 miles

Medina rounded West Caicos at six bells in the forenoon watch and put the wind on her larboard quarter. The Caicos Passage was clear of ships; there wasn't a sail in sight.

'There's a westerly current here sir,' said Hosking. 'It runs between Hispaniola and the Caicos and on into the Old Straits of Bahama. We felt its last gasps as it joined the Florida Stream and swept us north to St. Augustine. We'll need to make a little easting to compensate, southeast-by-south for the Cape. If this wind holds, we'll be there at the start of the morning watch, but we'll need to keep the stuns'ls on her.'

'Very well Mister Hosking, make it so,' said Carlisle. He looked around the horizon, and his eyes lingered on the island to larboard, West Caicos. Carlisle knew there was an anchorage close to the southwest corner of the island, used by fishermen and the occasional merchantman, but there was a small bluff, a large sand-dune really, that was obscuring the view. Perhaps there was the hint of some masts showing over the land, but he couldn't be sure. The islands were essentially uninhabited, and he wasn't even sure which of the colonial powers currently had a claim to them. He couldn't see anything at all now – it was probably nothing.

'Mister Holbrooke, I'll be in my cabin. Keep an eye on the anchorage behind West Caicos.'

Holbrooke and Hosking paced the weather side of the quarterdeck, discussing the probable winds and currents in this odd corner of the West Indies. It wasn't at all frequented by British men-of-war and Hosking was already mentally composing the note that he'd send back to the Admiralty, accompanied by Enrico's sketches. They turned at the quarterdeck rail, each man rotating towards the other so that their conversation wasn't interrupted. Holbrooke, who happened to have taken the inboard track, naturally turned to his left and briefly faced the island. What he saw stopped him in his tracks. He whipped his telescope to his eye; it took him only a second to confirm what he already feared.

'Beat to quarters,' he bellowed, 'clear for action.' In a quieter voice over his shoulder, 'Mister Angelini, my compliments to Captain ....'

But Carlisle was already bounding up the quarterdeck ladder. He'd felt uneasy as he went below and had been infuriating Chiara by pacing the cabin and peering nervously out of the window.

'It's the Dutchmen, sir,' said Holbrooke, pointing to windward at the two sleek, black hulls moving out to sea past the southern end of the island. They'd evidently been waiting for *Medina*, and they'd slipped their anchors and set sail as soon as they saw that the frigate was committed to the passage.

'What on earth do they want with us?' asked Carlisle to nobody in particular. He thumped his fist in exasperation on the cap of the quarterdeck rail, 'they must know that Don Alonso is safely ashore.'

'He's a bloody-minded character, sir,' said Chalmers who had come to the quarterdeck on first hearing Holbrooke's shout. 'He's been deprived of his revenge against the Spaniard and has transferred his anger to us.'

'You may be right, Mister Chalmers,' said Carlisle, savagely, 'but I have no constraints now, and I have a general instruction to suppress piracy. He won't limp away from this fight, by God he won't!'

Chalmers was shocked. He'd never seen Carlisle look so fierce. He looked around at the other sea officers.

Holbrooke also looked aggressive, even the ordinarily stoic Hosking looked angry. It dawned upon Chalmers that this Dutchman had stepped over some subtle line that all but he had understood. They were fighting and inflicting casualties without the backing of a legitimate government. The word *piracy* was overused in broadsheets and popular fiction, but for the first time, the full impact of the crime came home to Chalmers. It was beyond the pale to seafarers; they didn't like the unpredictable brutality of the breed. The chaplain knew that Carlisle disliked corporal punishment – the cat wasn't out of the bag in *Medina* more than once a month – and he abhorred capital punishment. He had witnessed Carlisle trying every ploy to be unavailable for courts martial where the death penalty may have to be awarded, but it was clear that he'd have no such qualms where actual piracy was involved.

'Don't furl the stuns'ls Mister Hosking, we'll keep all sail on her for the time being.'

All around them was frenetic activity: guns being freed of their lashings, boarding nets and splinter nets being rigged and everywhere the sound of hammering as all the light wooden and canvas partitions were struck below.

The two Dutch pirates were only three miles to windward, and if *Medina* accepted battle immediately, they could be alongside in no more than twenty minutes. Carlisle studied them through his telescope; they certainly looked determined. Their decks were crowded with men, but they had little protection, no hammocks along their gunwales and no boarding nets or splinter nets. Evidently, their plan was entirely offensive, a rapid descent on their prey, a crashing meeting between the two hulls and a wild charge of boarders that few vessels afloat could resist.

'Well Mister Holbrooke, they haven't changed their tactics, and we beat them last time, so we won't change ours. We mustn't let them get either side of us, and we must smash them from long range. Load both batteries with ball if you please.'

With an eye to his telescope and wholly taken up with the coming fight, he didn't notice the silent approach of his wife until she touched him on the arm, making him start with surprise. He realised guiltily that he'd forgotten all about her, hadn't taken her presence into account at all. How long had she been on the quarterdeck, he wondered? Had she heard him say – so rashly – that he had no constraints in his handling of this battle? No constraints, when his wife was on board?

His immediate reaction was to hustle her unceremoniously below to the orlop deck or even further below into the hold where she'd be out of danger. But in a flash of empathy, he realised that it just wouldn't do. His wife had been so supportive of him, so helpful, so much a part of the team, that she deserved better, even with the enemy so close and so evidently determined to fight.

'Chiara, my dear,' he said holding her hand, 'you see that we must fight these pirates again.' He pointed at the two ships, now little more than two miles away. It was curious just how belligerent they looked. There weren't actually very different to a whole range of ships – merchantmen, privateers, slavers – that could be seen any day around Port Royal, but there was something lethal and purposeful about them. They couldn't be mistaken for any vessels upon their lawful occasions.

'Are they really the same that we met in the Gulf of Mexico, dear?' she asked.

'They are, but this time I must rid the seas of this menace. Will you go below when the fighting starts? Perhaps Mister Chalmers would be good enough to escort you and see to your comfort.'

'Then may I stay for a while?' she asked. 'When do you expect to fight?'

'Oh, an hour from now. It's entirely at our discretion, even though the Dutchmen have the weather gage. I'll lead them on for a while to get clear of the island. Stay on the quarterdeck at least until we turn towards them.'

155

'Mister Hosking, we'll conduct this business with plenty of sea-room. Put us before the wind.'

'Aye, sir, but it'll appear that we're declining to fight.'

'That's exactly my plan. They know that today we can run two-and-a-half miles to their two. Just look at the jury mizzen on the leader, and his topmasts aren't much better, it's hardly a dockyard job, and they daren't split too far apart. That was a good day's work we did in the Gulf. We have as much time as we want now.'

He took another long look through his telescope. 'Join us if you please Mister Holbrooke.'

Clustered around the taffrail, with the two Dutch pirates in sight right astern, Carlisle outlined his plan. He looked every inch the fighting captain and the prospect of action had brought out a hint of determination that Holbrooke hadn't noticed before. He'd never thought of his captain as particularly aggressive, but he knew now that he'd been wrong. There was something of the buccaneer in Carlisle that only needed a little prodding to be brought to the surface. It was there now, for all to see.

'I have to assume that he knows why we're here. It's quite clear that he's known our movements from the beginning. I wondered how they had found us in the Yucatan Channel, it was almost like a pre-planned rendezvous. We can investigate the source of that intelligence later, but for now, I must assume that they know that I have to look into Cape François before making for the Windward Passage.'

'We're heading four points off our true course for the Cape, more like six points when we take the stream into account,' said Hosking.

'Yes master,' said Carlisle 'and just look at their heading now,' he turned to face the enemy. 'They're heading directly to Cape François to cut us off.'

They all looked and could see the truth of Carlisle's words. The two pursuing ships had brought the wind onto their larboard quarters and were heading south under all the sail that they could carry. If they wanted to force an engagement – and it looked like they did – then this was the best way to arrange it. They were cutting across *Medina's* wake in an attempt to get to the west of their prey. The Dutch captain would know that Carlisle wouldn't defy his orders and run straight for the passage and Port Royal. But how on earth did he know those orders?

'When they're ten miles clear of the islands, we'll turn and head straight for them. Mister Holbrooke, issue the boarders with their weapons as we close. However, I don't intend to be boarded, and I don't plan to board them until they've struck or until they're so depleted that they can't resist us. I'll sink them if I can.'

Holbrooke nodded in understanding. 'We'll aim for their hulls with the cannon and sweep their decks with the swivel guns.'

'Just so,' replied Carlisle. 'Send the bosun around to check the boarding nets, just in case.'

'Mister Hosking, you know the drill. They mustn't be allowed to trap us between them, and they mustn't be allowed to board. We have the perfect opportunity to get to windward now, so when we turn, your first concern is to take the weather gage, then we can dictate the next move. I want to have them in a position where they are compelled to beat up to us, and if they don't do that, we'll run down to them.'

The scene was unnaturally peaceful. The frigate was cleared for action, all the men were at their stations, and the warrant and petty officers had finished their last-minute inspections of the weapons and defensive measures. *Medina* was running southwest under a brilliant blue sky and a moderate northeasterly breeze. Carlisle took one last look at the enemy, now four miles away to windward.

'My dear, you should go below now,' he said to his

wife. 'We'll be firing on them in twenty minutes, and we'll be at close quarters in thirty.'

Defying all convention, Chiara reached up and kissed him on the cheek. She turned wordlessly away, a nagging fear in her mind, to be taken below by Chalmers. Strangely moved, and with a heavy heart, Carlisle watched her almost stumble at the quarterdeck ladder, recover herself and walk stiffly below. Then he turned back to the business of war.

'Let's get the stuns'ls out of the way and bring her onto the wind, Mister Hosking.'

The bosun had been waiting for this order, and before the words were out of Carlisle's mouth, he was issuing the few instructions that were necessary for such a well-trained crew to accomplish this routine task. The topmen were already at their stations. They saw the exchange of words on the quarterdeck and the meaningful looks aloft. In a few seconds they had run out along the yards, dropped their feet down onto the horses and within less than a minute the stuns'l booms had been retracted, and the tall, thin sails stowed securely in the tops.

Medina came gracefully onto the wind and heeled to the breeze. The whole scene changed in an instant. No longer was the deck a place of peace; it had taken a much harder aspect, with capfuls of spray arching over the bow to wet the crews at their guns. Carlisle observed his adversaries through narrowed eyes. They'd seen the danger of letting *Medina* get to windward. The frigate was evidently faster than even the undamaged Dutch ship and with the advantage of the wind would be able to dictate the pace of the battle. However, they didn't appear deterred. A bloody-minded crowd indeed.

'They're splitting,' said Holbrooke. 'The faster one is coming onto the wind, it looks like he's trying a luffing match with us.'

'Then let's humour him, gentlemen. If he concentrates

on us and not his leader's movements, we can draw him to windward and deal with them separately. Give them a little encouragement Mister Hosking.'

'Fall off a point,' Hosking growled to Eli, the quartermaster, 'but don't start the sheets, let them believe that's the highest that we can point.'

Eli gave the helm order with a motion of his hand. His steersmen were the best in the ship, selected for their experience and steadiness. It was advertised as an honour, but everyone knew that the quarterdeck was the most dangerous place in a battle. The captain, the master, the quartermaster and the steersmen had little protection from the enemy shot and were always the prime targets for marksmen. Furthermore, they couldn't even duck when the shot started coming inboard. For the captain and the master, it would be an unthinkable dereliction of their duty while for the quartermaster and steersmen, it was so obviously vital that they concentrated on steering that the thought of taking cover wouldn't even cross their minds.

Hosking took a bearing of their immediate adversary. With *Medina* on the larboard tack and the Dutchman on the starboard tack, it was easy to see who was winning the race. If the dutchman's bearing drew left, he was winning, if it drew right, the frigate was winning. If the bearing remained steady, then they were on a collision course. And that was precisely what Carlisle wanted.

Carlisle turned with a smile on his face. 'Sometimes, just occasionally, I'm glad that I'm in a service that has some understanding of discipline and gives some structure to its fighting.'

They all looked at their captain, expecting a profound discourse on the art of war.

'They've lost,' he said, thumping old Eli on the back in a companionable fashion. 'The leader must have shouted something like *get to windward of the Englishman*! And his companion, there in the faster ship has taken him at his word. But now, the leader sees that even if his consort can get to windward – and we know that he can't – they'll be so far separated that with our far greater firepower, it'll be two separate battles that they'll be fighting. But now, the leader has no way of recalling his friend, who isn't even looking back but concentrating on winning the luffing race. Unless he gives up now and concedes the weather gage, we've won!'

Carlisle beamed at his team, even Hosking managed a thin smile.

'So, let's let his bearing draw very slowly left Mister Hosking,' he looked significantly at the steersmen and Eli, 'make him think he's winning the race. A cable before we collide, we'll luff him and rake his bow.'

'But he can put his helm up at any time, or he can tack,' objected Hosking.

Carlisle nodded to Holbrooke.

'But if he does either of those things – and he won't,' said the first lieutenant with emphasis, 'he'll have failed in both of his objectives: to get to windward and to trap us between the two Dutchmen. He'll put himself and his leader in the worst possible position before a shot is fired. The real beauty is that there is nothing that he can do to stop it.' Eli winked and looked significantly at his unnaturally stiff luffs, the subterfuge that kept the Dutchman striving for the windward position. 'And by trying for the windward position,' Holbrooke continued, 'he's making matters worse, drawing the two ships further and further apart.'

Hosking sniffed disapprovingly. It was his responsibility to handle the ship, not to fight it, and deep down he cherished the certainty that his was the higher calling. These gentlemen could do as they wished with their cannon and cutlasses, but he knew that their success or failure was largely in his hands.

'I believe we can reserve the first broadside until we cross her bows, Mister Holbrooke. You've time to double-shot the larboard battery, so make it so, if you please.'

Having given his orders, Carlisle took up his telescope and studied the approaching ship. She was no match for *Medina*; even the two combined had a puny weight of broadside compared with the frigate. The Dutchman must by now have the idea that she could cross *Medina's* bows and force a collision. She probably had as many people as *Medina*, and unlike a King's frigate, they'd all be fighting men, every one of them motivated by the value of the frigate's hull and the ransom of the crew, even after their leader had extracted whatever revenge he had in mind. They could surely hold their own on *Medina's* deck until their consort could beat up to board from the other side. If that happened, *Medina* could fight for honour, but the result would be foretold. He trained his telescope to the right. The leader of the two was struggling hard to windward, but her jury mizzen wasn't doing its job in keeping her head up, and she'd had to reduce her headsails to compensate. *Medina* had at least fifteen minutes grace to batter the first ship before the second joined the fight.

'Mister Holbrooke,' Carlisle shouted, 'the swivels are to fire on the Dutchman's quarterdeck. If they can see it as we approach, so much the better, but if they can't, they're to hold their fire until we've crossed her bow.'

Holbrooke raised his hat in acknowledgement. He was standing at the quarterdeck rail where he could best command his batteries. He looked down at the guns and was amused to see Enrico practising lunges with his sword at the base of the mainmast. Most officers swapped their small-sword for something more substantial when boarding was possible, but that appeared to be outside the young Angelini's code of conduct. Holbrooke had to admit that he looked deadly with that slim weapon, and most of the guns crews were watching him with something approaching admiration. It was all very well, but far better if the young man didn't get a chance to use his skills. Holbrooke hoped that he'd be able to defeat them at long range, not stand toe-to-toe with a pirate crew on his deck.

Chris Durbin

'Mister Hook, if you see any targets on her fo'c'sle you may engage; otherwise, reserve your fire for the quarterdeck,' said Carlisle.

'Aye, aye, sir,' replied the Marine Lieutenant, who, having deployed his men, was studiously avoiding unnerving them with unnecessary orders, 'they'll be obedient to my command.' Hook looked calm and competent, as though he was indifferent to the blood-letting that was about to happen.

'What do you think, Mister Hosking?'

'Another half cable, sir,' he replied.

Eli and the steersmen were awaiting the order. All they had to do was turn onto the wind. There was no sail-trimming required, and they had a point-and-a-half in hand before they were in danger of pointing too high.

'Now, I believe, sir,' said Hosking, looking from the Dutchman to the frigate's sails.

'Make it so, master,' said Carlisle, watching the enemy with deadly intensity.

Eli made his cryptic hand motion to the helmsmen, and *Medina's* bow turned swiftly to larboard. The Dutchman's peril was now evident. If she tacked, she'd offer her vulnerable stern to raking fire from the formidable batteries of the frigate. Her obvious alternative was to pay off and force a collision, then the wild rush of the piratical crew would sweep *Medina's* boarding nets away, and they'd be on her deck in a minute. But the Dutchman just didn't have enough speed to intercept *Medina*. Before the frigate hardened onto the wind, she could just about have made it, and perhaps that was her plan, but now she'd fall short and expose her starboard side to *Medina's* fire.

Carlisle could see the Dutch captain looking over his quarterdeck rail and could detect his indecision. At the last moment possible and with a despairing wave at his helm, he chose the second option. The ship had no wheel, but an old-fashioned tiller. The two steersmen leaned into the wooden bar and pushed it hard to starboard, and the ship turned fast towards *Medina*. It was probably their best decision, but Carlisle still intended to make them pay for it.

'Fire!' shouted Holbrooke as the pirate's bows swung across *Medina's* starboard beam. The battery responded almost as one, and the whole broadside came crashing into the Dutchman's head and bowsprit. One lucky shot was a little late and aimed lower than the rest. In normal circumstances that would have earned a rebuke for the gun captain, but in this case, that single ball opened the butt of a plank on the starboard bow. It wouldn't have been serious if the ship had been on the downward roll at the time of impact, but by ill-fortune, the bow had been lifted by the action the rapid turn, and as it rolled back underwater, the sea found the hole and started to rush in. None of that was yet known to the Dutch captain who, despite the obvious damage that he could see, was determined to hold *Medina* until his leader could work his way up to join him. The Dutchman's eight-pounders were firing furiously, but with more speed than precision, and every man who had a musket was aiming at the frigate that was rushing past them.

Carlisle could see that his immediate adversary was unable to manoeuvre. Even from the deck of *Medina*, he could see the water pouring into the bow under the wreckage of the bowsprit and head. Perhaps the Dutch captain was still not aware of the state of his ship, but he soon would be.

'Mister Hosking! Bring the ship about. Mister Holbrooke! Stand by the larboard battery. We'll finish her on the next pass.'

The Dutchman was indeed in dire straits, her head to the wind and a tangle of rigging strewn about the forward part of the ship. Carlisle could see that he was making no attempt at repairs, but all his available men were at the gunwales with muskets or manning the guns in her waist. That was sensible; this part of the battle would be over before any meaningful repairs were completed and they could at least cause some degree of damage to *Medina* before her consort came to grips. Nevertheless, this must be a particularly obstinate crew to persevere when all was lost. But then, Carlisle reflected, they really had no choice. All the colonial nations were united in their determination to stamp out the last remnants of piracy in the Caribbean, and only the gallows awaited them if they were captured.

Medina came about smoothly. She'd taken only superficial damage from the Dutchman's cannon, which were poorly pointed and seemed to lack any firm leadership. Probably the pirates considered their broadside as a single-shot weapon to be used once before boarding and then abandoned. As the frigate bore down upon its motionless prey, the men on the quarterdeck could all see that the Dutchman was settling by the bows. It was unlikely that she'd sink in this kind weather, but without immediate attention to damage control she'd settle to her gunwales and be carried by the wind and current to founder on the Inagua Islands or the western tip of Cuba. In any case, without help, she was finished as a sea rover, but Carlisle wasn't feeling benevolent.

'Are you ready Mister Holbrooke?'

'Ready, aye, ready,' he replied, looking down at his larboard battery. What he saw cheered him; there was an uninterrupted row of guns, each with its crew poised to unleash a death blow on the enemy.

Carlisle was staying to windward on the principle of not getting between the two enemy ships – and looking to leeward he could see that the leader had made a surprising amount of way upwind. In another five minutes, he'd be fighting two ships simultaneously.

The larboard battery fired a rippling broadside from forward to aft. Holbrooke had found that he had the time to double-shot the guns, sacrificing range for hitting power. He was rewarded as gaping holes opened in the Dutchman's side, smashing through the planking to shatter timbers and knees. He could see guns overturned and gaps in the ranks of musketeers, who were still firing hopefully at their tormentor even though it was almost out of range.

'Reload the larboard battery,' he shouted and looked back to ask his captain what he intended next. But what he saw shocked him. Carlisle was lying bedside the binnacle in a growing pool of blood. Hosking and Chalmers were beside him, and Eli was looking around for orders.

'Mister Wishart take over command of the batteries,' he shouted at the midshipman and ran the few paces back to where Carlisle lay. He could see immediately that it was a severe wound, apparently to his chest. It was remarkably like the injury that Don Alonso had received, or so it appeared at first sight. Holbrooke knelt briefly beside his captain. He was breathing and conscious. Carlisle grasped his sleeve and pulled the younger man's face close to his own.

'Don't let them on our deck, Holbrooke, fight them at the boarding nets. You must keep them away and sink them. Go, go, take command,' and he gasped and lay back, his strength fading fast.

CHAPTER SIXTEEN

Counter-Attack

Thursday, eighteenth of August 1757
Medina, at Sea. West Caicos Island northeast 3 leagues

Holbrooke stood uncertainly beside the binnacle and for a moment looked bewildered. He doubted his readiness for this responsibility. Was he just acting a part? What would happen if he failed? He looked around at the deck of the frigate, at the Dutch pirate moving aggressively towards them and he caught Chalmers' eye. The chaplain was already covered in his captain's blood, and yet he had the time to look up from his task, and he stared meaningfully at Holbrooke. 'Take command!' his look said, 'we're all relying on you now.' It was only a momentary exchange, less than a second, but it stiffened the lieutenant at the time when he most needed it. Holbrooke nodded at Chalmers and turned to face his responsibilities.

It had been less than half a minute that the frigate had no clear command, but so much had changed. *Medina*, bereft of orders, had continued south-westwards, away from the stricken pirate ship but now dangerously close to the leader. He could see the Dutchman's boarding parties mustering at her waist; he could see the rapidly closing gap between the frigate and the pirate ship. There was little time left, in a minute the two ships would collide. If he tacked, *Medina* would slow down enough for the Dutchman to get his grappling irons across onto the quarterdeck; there was no room to veer, and if he merely hauled his wind, the Dutchman would luff and come crashing into the frigate's larboard side. There were no good options. He looked at the wild men gathering on the bow of the pirate ship and made his decision.

'Bring her about, Mister Hosking,' he shouted. 'Boarders to the quarterdeck,' he roared down at the waist. 'Swivels, clear that ship's fo'c'sle. Mister Hook. Concentrate your fire on those men in her waist.'

Holbrooke had laboured long and hard at the watch and station bill, allocating men to their stations in any of half a dozen situations, so that each man knew that as well as his station at quarters, he had to be ready to respond when specific orders were given. Now those hours of preparation paid off. Some ran from their guns to the sails, some took up boarding pikes, some cutlasses, tomahawks or pistols. In a few moments, Holbrooke had a hard core of armed men at the quarterdeck ready to repel the inevitable invasion.

Medina swung swiftly through the eye of the wind, but her speed through the water diminished, and the Dutchman seemed to accelerate towards the frigate's stern. The noise was tremendous as *Medina's* swivel guns poured their lethal charges of canister into the packed masses. The Dutchman's jib-boom came past *Medina's* taffrail and jutted menacingly towards the starboard side of the quarterdeck. Holbrooke could see a few daring men perched on the bowsprit swinging grappling irons. At least six were thrown at *Medina*. Two fell short, two or three bounced off the hammock nets, but two more caught in the metal cranes that suspended the hammock nets and were instantly hauled taut. It was no use trying to cut them free because the last fathom before the grapnel was a heavy iron chain. The pirate ship hauled itself closer and closer to *Medina*.

'Stand clear, sir!' shouted a voice beside him and Holbrooke was almost knocked over as the swivel gun on the quarterdeck trained on its target. The seaman in charge took aim. There was nothing sophisticated about a swivel-gun's sight; he just squinted along the barrel and heaved it around until he found his target. It discharged with a dull thud and a spurt of black powder smoke that escaped through the gap between the mug and the breech. An instant later, the Dutchmen who were hauling at one of the lines for the grappling irons were torn apart by the canister shot and fell from the bowsprit, one into the netting while the other fell clear into the rushing water below. With only one grapnel left, the rate that the two ships were drawing together momentarily slackened, but fresh men rushed over the body of their stricken shipmate. Ignoring his death agonies, they took his place to heave on the line. The two ships drew even closer together.

'Boarders to the gunwales, starboard side,' shouted Holbrooke. 'Mister Hook, form up your marines behind them and be ready for volley fire.'

Holbrooke was determined to take the initiative. He remembered the way that his charge across the disengaged side of *Vulcain*, in the Mediterranean only a year ago, had turned the battle. He had no smaller vessel to make that outflanking move, but perhaps there was another way.

'Mister Wishart, Jackson, Angelini,' they hurried at his call. 'Take a dozen men from what's left of the aft guns crews. Take all the pistols and cutlasses you can find and board the Dutchman through his gun ports. Fight your way to his deck and take them from behind. Don't stop for anything.'

Wishart and Jackson looked at each other; Enrico appeared eager, a wild light of battle in his eyes.

Holbrooke grabbed Jackson's shoulder. 'Remember *Vulcain*! You can win this for us, the same as we did that time.'

Jackson nodded to Holbrooke and turned to the younger men, his officers. 'Let's go,' he said, and they ran down into the waist, calling men's names as they went.

There was a rush of men to the starboard quarter, and behind him, Holbrooke could hear the booted tread as Sergeant Wilson called the cadence to form three ranks, a solid impediment to the Dutch boarders.

'Fix bayonets Sergeant Wilson,' ordered Lieutenant Hook in a calm, steady voice. The rasp and click of the bayonets being secured to the muskets sounded loud in the unnatural hush. A boarding was imminent, and everyone was saving their powder for the final rush.

'I'll give them one more volley if you please, sir,' said Hook from behind Holbrooke's back.

'Boarders lie down,' shouted Holbrooke. There was a moment of confusion, but his steady petty officers, led by Morgan, the master gunner, pushed and thumped the excited men until they had all dropped below the level of the gunwale.

'Present your muskets – take aim – fire!' intoned Sergeant Wilson. That disciplined volley wreaked havoc in the ranks of the Dutch boarders, killing or wounding almost all in the front rank. One of the Medinas, an otherwise reliable able seaman, hadn't ducked low enough and a musket ball took off the top of his head, spraying blood and fragments of bone over his neighbours. He dropped without a sound and lay in his own blood under the hammocks, a victim of his shipmate's musket.

But still, the Dutchmen hauled at the lines and the narrowing gap would soon be small enough for men to leap across. The marines reloaded, and the Medinas crouched under the gunwale, ready to spring up and grapple with the first, most daring boarders.

So far, the frigate's people had taken few casualties, but Holbrooke knew that it couldn't last. He felt horribly exposed himself, but at least the Dutch sharpshooters had paused, pushing forward now to join the boarders.

When it came, the impact was surprisingly soft as the two ships nudged gently together. There was a breathless pause and then a wild shout from the Dutch ship, and the boarders threw themselves at *Medina's* netting, swinging cutlasses, knives and axes.

'Boarders down!' This time it was Hook giving the

order in a shattering bellow. Sergeant Wilson repeated his sequence of orders, and another devastating volley hit the Dutch boarders as they were at their most vulnerable, hacking away at the boarding nets, caught like flies in a web. More Dutchmen fell but spurred by the desperation that knows that the hand of all civilisation is against them, a fresh wave of boarders threw themselves at the netting. The Medinas stood up to the challenge, thrusting with boarding pikes, slashing with cutlasses and firing their pistols at such close range that their opponents' clothing was scorched by the muzzle flash. It was murder, but still they came.

Holbrooke could see that the boarding nets wouldn't last much longer against this frenzied attack and his seamen were tiring. 'Mister Hook. Bayonets,' he shouted above the din. 'Medinas down or away.'

Those that could disengage from their enemies fled forward or aft. Those that couldn't crouched low as the tide of red uniforms charged over them, pushing through the netting with their bayonets. The battle had become a free-for-all, any hope of order had been lost as the sailors and marines fought side by side in a desperate attempt to prevent the Dutch pirates making a breach in the netting. But Holbrooke could see that a breach would be made, as rope by rope, the strands of the boarding nets were cut away. Soon he could see bodies trying to squeeze through the gaps, each one impaled by a bayonet or hacked by a cutlass, but for every Dutchman that was felled, another took his place. It couldn't last, and soon a practicable breach would be made.

Holbrooke jumped atop the binnacle. 'Wishart, Jackson!' he shouted as loud as he could. 'Now's the time!'

At first, there was no answering call, and he started to despair, perhaps his flanking party were all lying dead on the Dutchman's gundeck. Then he saw them. A line of men was forming up stealthily, crouching low on the far side of the Dutchman's fo'c'sle. He saw Wishart and

Jackson step to the fore while Enrico stood slightly apart on the right flank swinging his small-sword most professionally. He saw, rather than heard, their loud simultaneous shout of '*Medina*!' and then they surged forward. Wishart and Jackson were instantly at close quarters with the Dutchmen, using their weapons like choppers, raining blows on heads and shoulders. Enrico, however, was displaying the fruits of his expensive fencing lessons and was giving himself space to use the point of his sword. In quick succession two of the enemy fell to lightning-fast thrusts as he guarded the flank of the counter-attack.

At first, only the rear ranks of the boarders recognised the problem as they fell to the unexpected blows from behind, then gradually, man-by-man, the whole body of Dutchmen became aware of this new menace in their rear. Pressed against the boarding nets, pinned in position by those behind them who were trying to evade the wicked blows of Wishart and Jackson's party and the flashing blade of Enrico, the leaders attempted to turn. All thought of *Medina's* deck was forgotten. Those who hadn't panicked were intent now on securing their own deck.

Holbrooke cast around for the bosun. 'Furl the boarding nets, as fast as you can.' He knew that the nets had been rigged with slip-knots below the gunwales where the enemy couldn't reach them, and once they were released it was a simple matter to haul down on the brails that led from the skirts of the nets to the mizzen top. The bosun shouted his orders, the slip-knots at the forward end of the quarterdeck were released, but the knots beside the taffrail were jammed. It didn't matter, the forward brails were hauled up, and there was enough space for the Medinas to pour through. Holbrooke leapt onto the gunwale waving his sword.

'Medinas to me,' he shouted, 'away boarders!'

The Dutchmen were trapped. Wishart, Enrico and Jackson with their steadfast band kept them from retreating, pinning them against the fo'c'sle railing, while an unstoppable horde of sailors and marines vaulted across the gap. Holbrooke slashed from left to right. There was no science to this fighting, no space for approved fencing moves. The hilt of his sword smashed into a man's face was as useful as its point or edge. Slowly the Medinas squeezed the Dutchmen. Some escaped aft, some took refuge on the bowsprit, but of the remainder, few pleaded for quarter, and to even fewer was it granted. It seemed like hours, but the fighting was over in five minutes. At some point Holbrooke found Jackson beside him; he'd fought his way to his lieutenant's side, as he'd done on the deck of *Vulcain*.

'Just like old times, sir,' he said with a smile.

The Dutchman's ranks were thinning fast; the last few were herded against the fo'c'sle rail, their weapons dropped, and hands raised. Even then, Holbrooke saw a sailor thrust his boarding pike into a belly and watched helplessly as the man fell to the deck, a great red patch spreading across his shirt.

Perhaps he was luckier than his fellows; there'd be no Port Royal gallows waiting for him. Seeing that it was all over, he fumbled in his pocket for his whistle. His fingers couldn't quite grasp it, and in those few clumsy seconds, two more Dutchmen were felled. At last, he hauled the whistle clear of his pocket and blew a single blast. All sailors knew the meaning of that, even the Dutchmen – *Still*. The fighting madness retreated, and only dull anger was left for their fallen shipmates.

That scene was etched on Holbrooke's memory, and he'd be able to recall it to his last days. The dead and dying were lying in heaps, mostly along the Dutchman's fo'c'sle gunwale where they had fallen in their dozens while trying to board *Medina*, and there was a random scattering of bodies all along the deck. There was curiously little blood to be seen, just a few crimson patches where a dying man had fallen on his back. The small knot of the surviving enemy, now frightened and bewildered, was hemmed in by the red uniforms of the marines and the blue and white of the seamen. But there were shockingly few Dutchmen left standing, less than twenty, he thought. Over the whole, a pall of smoke persisted even with the wind whipping across the deck.

'Wish you joy of your victory,' shouted Hosking from *Medina's* quarterdeck. A more inappropriate word than *Joy* he couldn't have chosen, in Holbrooke's opinion, as he looked around at the dead, dying and maimed. 'The other fellow's fled. He's hoisted what sail he can and is running fast for the Old Straits of Bahama.'

Holbrooke looked over *Medina's* quarter to see the damaged Dutchman, her mizzen furled to keep her head away from the wind, disappearing fast to leeward in the direction of Cuba.

CHAPTER SEVENTEEN

The Lone Pine Tree

Thursday, eighteenth of August 1757
Medina, at Anchor. West Caicos

The cabin was bathed in the last of the daylight as *Medina* swung to her anchor off the southern point of West Caicos. The figure lying in the cot looked pale, but alert, his head resting on a pillow and a sheet spread over his lower body. His upper body was mostly covered with an extensive crisscross of bandages that covered his chest and his right shoulder.

'… and so, as you directed, not a single Dutchman stepped on *Medina's* deck. The few that live are battened below decks on their own ship with Sergeant Wilson and a brace of swivel guns keeping watch over them.'

Carlisle attempted a smile, but it was more of a grimace as he winced in pain. 'What of their captain, the man in the blue suit?' he asked.

'We found his body in the first rank of their boarders. He'd been pistoled and slashed with a cutlass,' Holbrooke made a sweeping motion across his head and chest, 'but it was a bayonet that killed him. Wilson is claiming the credit.'

'Very well, then how many remain?'

'Fourteen, and they're all more-or-less wounded. The doctor is seeing them one at a time under heavy guard, but they're as meek as lambs now. Schoonderwoerd of the foretop is with the doctor – he speaks the language – and he says they're busy polishing their defence, telling each other how it was the skipper and his mate that lured them from privateering into pirating. It may even be true; Schoonderwoerd believes so.'

'Much good it'll do them in Port Royal, but the best of

luck to them. I tend to the view that there are no bad followers, only bad leaders,' said Carlisle weakly.

'Our prize is little damaged,' said Holbrooke. 'She's the *Torenvalk* – *Kestrel* in English – from St. Eustatius as Hosking said, sixteen eight-pounders and a few swivels. There's a letter of marque with what is claimed to be the governor's signature, but it's not in a sensible legal form and in any case, it's years out of date. She's a fair prize. The other was last seen heading for the Old Straits of Bahama, but where she'll find a friendly port to the west, I don't know. They'll be lucky if Don Alonso doesn't find them; I can't see him offering much mercy.'

'The captain must rest now, Mister Holbrooke,' interrupted Chiara, who was seated beside his cot. 'He needs to regain his strength.'

Carlisle waved his hand, 'just one more question, my dear, then I'll let Mister Holbrooke go.' He turned his face to his first lieutenant. 'What of our casualties?'

Holbrooke looked grave, 'we lost some good men, aye and good friends, but our losses are few compared with the enemy. Six dead,' he named them, able seamen, ordinary seamen and a marine, good men and not so good, but each missed, 'and another fifteen wounded, but the doctor believes they all have a fair chance of survival.'

Carlisle looked briefly troubled, then his face cleared. 'It's a famous victory for you Holbrooke. If that had been a national ship, you could have expected promotion …' but Carlisle was talking to the deckhead because Chiara had silently ushered Holbrooke out of the cabin. Carlisle swung gently in his cot, dreaming feverishly of slashing cutlasses and barking muskets, and all his dead shipmates rolling in the red, red sea in *Medina's* wake as the frigate swayed to the mild land breeze, and the sun sank over the tip of West Caicos Island.

'Well, bosun, how much longer do you need to make the *Torenvalk* fit for sea? I want to send Mister Wishart away in her before the forenoon watch on Saturday. That gives you a clear day. We'll escort him through the day and see him off towards the Windward Passage before we run down to Cape François,' said Holbrooke as he watched the hive of activity that their prize had become.

'Aye, we'll have her spick and span before then. The moon is only just past new, but with this clear sky, we'll have enough starlight to work. She'll be good for the couple of days it will take to run down to Port Royal. The shipwrights will have some work to do, but she'll make a fine sloop if she's bought into the service. Will we get prize money for her, sir?'

'That'll be up to the Vice-Admiralty Court in Port Royal. If she's declared a pirate, then we'll get head money for this ship, but probably not for the one that got away. But prize money? That's an interesting point. We're at war, and the prize order has been granted, but as we're not at war with Holland. There are some legal niceties there that I'm not familiar with. We'll just have to see, Mister Swinton. But one thing I know, the better condition that the *Torenvalk* is in when she reaches port, the more the Admiral will pay for her.'

'In that case, I'll just stir up Chips as well as my own crew,' chuckled the bosun. 'He can at least make her look pretty again. How many heads will we be claiming for?'

'It's astonishing, Mister Swinton. My tally comes to two hundred and twenty-three, counting in all the dead we could find. We discovered a muster list that shows a total of four hundred and nineteen for the two ships, so allowing that a few went over the side in the fight, we should be able to claim two hundred and thirty.'

'It must have been tight berthing in those little ships,' said Swinton, 'but I expect they reckon on no more than a week at sea under normal circumstances. I'll be away then, sir, to make all taut before tomorrow.'

Holbrooke watched the bosun being rowed the half cable to the prize and could clearly see him figuring on a scrap of paper and occasionally scratching his head. Holbrooke knew just what he was doing; if there were two hundred and thirty men in *Torenvalk* at five pounds a head, one-eighth of which went to the warrant officers – bosun, gunner, carpenter, surgeon, purser – and the chaplain and marine lieutenant, then Mister Swinton would be personally richer by about twenty pounds. Not a bad day's work, and then there may be prize money as well, and that handsome ship was probably worth two thousand pounds. Some favourite of the Admiral's would be delighted to be given her as a command once she'd been armed to the navy's establishment of guns. And with that command would come a temporary promotion to commander, which would undoubtedly be confirmed by their Lordships with so many ships to be officered and manned as the war escalated. Holbrooke sighed. He wasn't even remotely a favourite of the Admiral's, nor would he ever be as long as he was the first lieutenant of a frigate – out of sight and out of mind.

Down below, in the great cabin, Carlisle was snoring. The surgeon had given him a dose of tincture of opium – laudanum – the equivalent of three grains, and after an hour of nervous vitality, he'd fallen into a deep sleep.

'How's your patient, Mister Carlton?' asked Holbrooke, after bowing to Chiara, who sat beside the cot, holding Carlisle's hand.

'He'll do very well, I believe. The ball scored his chest, breaking three ribs and cracking the right clavicle.' Holbrooke looked questioningly at him. 'The collar-bone,' he elaborated. 'The ball exited through the shoulder missing the important vessels. Aye, he'll do very well. I understand that we should be in Port Royal on Tuesday. Is that correct, Mister Holbrooke?'

'It is. I must escort the *Torenvalk* on her way, then look into Cape François, but I won't linger. We'll weigh anchor in the morning watch on Saturday.'

Chris Durbin

'Then I'll tell you what I've already told Lady Chiara,' he said, casting a glance at the captain's wife. 'I'll keep the captain sedated as long as I dare, but if it comes to a fever I'll have to stop the laudanum …'

'Do you expect a fever?' interrupted Holbrooke.

The surgeon made a half-rotating motion of his wrist. 'Perhaps; it occurs as often as not in these cases. If a fever comes on, I expect it to start tomorrow and continue for two or three days. It'll be over before we reach port. I've warned Lady Chiara that he may not be quite himself while the fever lasts, but he's strong and not in any great danger.'

Holbrooke looked carefully at his captain's face, pale and sweating slightly, but in this heat, they all sweltered all the time. 'And his recovery, Mister Carlton, how long before he's fit to go back to sea?'

The surgeon looked sideways at Chiara. She'd asked the same question, and he'd avoided answering. However, he understood that the management of the ship to some extent depended on the ability of the captain to command. 'The wound is clean and open, it'll heal in a few weeks. The ribs will knit back together in a month or so, but the clavicle will take longer. I wouldn't like to see him back on the deck of a ship for three months,' he said positively.

Chiara looked worried, but she brightened at the thought of having her husband ashore for three months. She knew that Admiral Cotes would want his frigate back to sea as soon as possible, and she now knew enough about the fabric of ships to know that with a day or two for essential repairs and breaming, *Medina* would be back at sea two weeks after they arrived at Port Royal.

'Well, I'll leave you now ma'am.' Holbrooke bowed to Chiara who distractedly inclined her head in reply.

'Is it convenient to visit the sickbay now Mister Carlton?'

The sickbay was a far cry from the great cabin, but Carlton, his mate and the loblolly-boy had made *Medina's* wounded comfortable. Of the fifteen with injuries that were sufficiently serious to be noticed, eight of them had been discharged to their messes with orders to report to the sick bay for dressing changes each day. There was a significant incentive to stay out of the sickbay: the rum ration was denied to those in the care of the surgeon, whereas in their messes no such restriction applied. Of the remainder, two were amputations, a foot and an arm, one had a suspected fractured skull, two had simple fractures, and the other two had deep wounds. Only the amputees had been given laudanum, and they were sleeping soundly; the remainder were talkative. If it had been the captain visiting, they'd have lain stiff in their cots, affecting a swooning weakness whether they felt that way or not. It would have seemed bad form in front of the captain to be anything other than near death. However, the first lieutenant was a whole degree lower in awful majesty. The people of *Medina* generally liked Holbrooke. They thought him very young to be a first lieutenant, but he put on no airs in front of them, and they recognised his competence.

'We showed those butter-balls, sir. God, it was like a slaughter-house on that deck!' said one young seaman sporting a splint to his ankle. Holbrooke looked at Carlton who made the same rotating gesture with his hand below the seaman's eye-line. Carlton wasn't convinced that he could save the foot, but at least an amputation would be below the knee; he'd know before they reached Port Royal.

'I heard the bosun say that there'd be head money, and maybe prize money too,' said an older seaman, winking at Holbrooke. 'There's a lady in Port Royal as will be mighty glad to see me with a pocketful of coins.' That raised a laugh. Dobbs' preferred entertainment while ashore was well-known in the ship, and after a month ashore with a few pounds to his name, he'd be pretty well known throughout the bordellos of Port Royal.

'Just you concentrate on healing that wound,' said Holbrooke, pointing to the bandage wrapped around his stomach. 'The ladies of Port Royal will manage quite well without you.'

'Now sir, you know that's not true,' he replied, 'no lady can manage without me!' and he favoured his first lieutenant with a lewd smirk.

'I think I've seen enough, Mister Carlton; let me know how they do. In any case, I'll have a report before the forenoon watch while we're at sea,' said Holbrooke loudly enough for all in the sick bay to hear. It did no harm for these men with honourable wounds to know that their first lieutenant was concerned with their welfare.

Holbrooke walked back towards his cabin as the light was fading. He was dog-tired, but there was one further duty before he could surrender to a few hours of sleep. 'Pass the word for the chaplain!' he said to the sentry who still stood at the door to Carlisle's apartments.

Chalmers came into Holbrooke's tiny cabin, looking tired himself. He'd assisted Carlton in dressing wounds and amputating limbs, work that was emotionally and physically draining. But there was one essential service that Holbrooke must ask of him.

'Take a seat, David, you look shattered,' said Holbrooke. The chaplain sat gratefully in the only chair while Holbrooke perched upon his sea-chest. 'Tomorrow we must bury our dead, and the Dutch pirates,' he said flatly.

Chalmers raised his head and looked quizzically at the young lieutenant. 'I'd assumed that you'd bury them at sea,' he replied, 'I thought that was the custom.'

'Not if we can bury them decently on land; the men don't like the thought of being slipped over the side. They accept it when there is no dry ground to hand, but they prefer a proper burial by a real parson.'

'Very well. There are six of them, I understand.'

'Yes. I've told the master-at-arms to take a party and dig six separate graves under that lone pine tree that you can see from the deck. They'll be ready by noon, so we'll take their mess-mates ashore in the cutter and lay them to rest at two bells in the afternoon. Chips is making the crosses, and he'll carve their names and the date on each. Young Angelini is quite an artist, and I've asked him to sketch the scene and colour it in at his leisure. Who knows? someone may be interested to see where they've been put to rest.'

'You think of everything George. Is there some way of marking the spot for future generations?'

'Good idea. I'll ask the armourer to inscribe something on a sheet of lead; I know he has some spare aprons for the nine-pounder touch-holes, which should be the right size. If he nails it firmly to that tree, it'll be there for our grandchildren to discover. Would you think of some words and tell the armourer?'

'I will, George, and if that's all, I'll leave you to get some rest and see you in the morning.' The chaplain pulled aside the canvas screen that served as a door, but he paused before leaving. 'What do you intend with the dead pirates?'

'I was hoping you wouldn't ask. You know that pirates aren't usually given a Christian burial?' Chalmers nodded cautiously. 'And in any case, I just can't spare the people to dig even a mass grave for that many bodies – there are over two hundred of them!' Chalmers hadn't moved a muscle, he was waiting to hear what the younger man intended and was ready to disagree. 'Well, I'm minded to bury them at sea on Saturday morning as soon as we're in deep water,' Chalmers waited, 'and as they aren't yet convicted of piracy, and they're from a Christian nation, I hope that you'll agree to conduct a burial service, just one for all of them. We don't know their names, so it'll be short,' he looked almost pleadingly at Chalmers. He knew very well that the chaplain could refuse, citing the long-held belief that pirates had by their actions put themselves beyond any hope of redemption.

'Of course, George, that's an excellent suggestion. If I sail in *Torenvalk*, perhaps you'll send a boat for me after the burial is complete?'

Both knew that most men in their positions wouldn't have given a thought to the dead pirates but would have heaved them over the side without any ceremony. However, neither man cared to be known for a tender heart, and no further words were spoken on the matter.

The gap between *Medina* and *Torenvalk* slowly grew as the frigate hardened her tacks and sheets and turned southeast towards Cape François. Holbrooke waved one last time to Wishart, the proud commander of this, his most significant command yet. The Dutch ship was patched and mended so that at a distance she looked untouched, but a closer inspection would reveal the deep gouges in her deck, the bulwarks and railing that had been beaten down and the scars around her gun ports. However, her rigging and sails were sound, as well set-up as the bosun and his crew could achieve in a day of furious activity. It was a matter of vital interest to all on board that this ship should reach Port Royal because, regardless of Holbrooke's caution, they were thoroughly convinced that she represented a substantial sum in prize money. Holbrooke had seen her safely past Great Inagua Island and from there it was just a matter of running through the Windward Passage, past the easternmost point of Jamaica, and home.

They'd buried the British dead under the lone pine tree overlooking the anchorage on West Caicos, and they'd slipped the dead pirates over the side with a brief service of committal. The people of *Medina* had done all that friendship and the customs of the sea dictated. Each of the Medinas had an inscribed wooden cross at his head, and there was a lead plaque nailed to the tree stating the bare facts of their burial with a passage of scripture. The tree looked as though it had stood there for centuries;

presumably, it and the low point of land on which it stood were proof against hurricanes. Now they were looking forward to an uneventful passage home to Port Royal after a quick look at the French at Cape François.

Holbrooke had considered sailing directly for Port Royal and missing Cape François entirely. He knew that he was justified in doing that with a wounded captain and a valuable prize to protect. Two considerations had ruled out that course of action. First, he was confident that Carlisle would have ordered him to complete his mission, had he been able. Second, although his captain was in the grip of the fever that the surgeon had predicted, Carlton had stated most decisively that he'd do better at sea than he would in the hospital at Port Royal, even if *Medina* could reach there before the fever broke. Those considerations alone would have kept him firmly to the fulfilment of Admiral Cotes' orders. However, there was a third consideration.

He, Holbrooke, was now *de facto* captain of this fine frigate, at least until he had to report to the admiral when he'd inevitably be superseded by a jobbing captain. For an ambitious officer – and Holbrooke had become that, after an inauspicious start to his career – this was the most golden of all opportunities to prove his fitness for command. So, it was with a clear conscious that Holbrooke waved farewell to *Torenvalk* with its cargo of apprehensive former pirates being guarded by the implacable Sergeant Wilson.

'How is the captain, ma'am,' asked Holbrooke.

'As you see him, George. The fever has him in its grip, and he's raving. I suppose it's a mercy that I can't catch most of what he says,' she gave George a wan smile. 'Mister Carlton tells me that it'll pass in forty-eight hours and that I'm not to worry,' she passed a hand over her brow, she was perspiring herself, 'but it's dreadful to see my husband like this.'

'Would a little more air help? I can get the sailmaker to rig a scoop through the gun port and force a breeze across the cabin.'

'Oh, would you do so, George? I'm sure that he'd be less restless if he were cooler.'

Carlisle turned to give the orders and then paused. 'When we clear for action tomorrow morning, I'll give orders that the cabin shouldn't be touched. We'll only lose two guns on each side, and I have no intention of fighting anyone. Just a quick look and we'll be on our way. I expect we'll reach Port Royal on Monday evening, or Tuesday morning if the current in the Windward Passage turns against us.

CHAPTER EIGHTEEN

Cape François

Sunday, twenty-first of August 1757
Medina, at Sea. Off Cape François, Saint Domingue

Medina was two miles north of Cape François as the sun showed itself over the eastern horizon.

'A superb piece of navigation,' Holbrooke said to Hosking. It was clear that they'd be able to see the French fleet anchorage just as the light became sufficient to make out the number and type of the ships. He regretted the remark immediately. Hosking wasn't the sort of man to accept compliments from a junior – a very junior – lieutenant, even if he was temporarily the captain of the ship.

Hosking sniffed disdainfully. 'A simple piece of reckoning such as this should be the least that we aspire to, but they don't teach the young gentlemen the skills of navigation like they used to,' and he turned away with an assumed business to berate the quartermaster.

Holbrooke smiled. He could take that kind of behaviour from the master if he knew his trade, and Hosking certainly did.

It was surprising how the sea, so empty only a hundred miles north, was dotted with vessels, mostly small country ships trading along the north coast of Hispaniola or local fishermen, each one of them a potential fair prize. It was tempting, but Holbrooke knew that he must concentrate on his mission and then get back to Port Royal; and anyway, they were poor prizes, worth little after the admiral and the agents had taken their shares, and their loss wouldn't be felt by the French war effort. He stared into the bay as the roadstead opened up past the cape, where he could see a few merchant ships at anchor. No, *many* merchant ships, but that wasn't unusual as Cape François was the rendezvous for all the French trade from the western Caribbean waiting to be convoyed across the Atlantic to France. They'd be waiting for the worst of the hurricane season to pass. Then in about two months, they'd take the Caicos Passage that *Medina* had recently passed through and beat northwards until they should meet the westerlies and the North Atlantic current.

Although Cape François was the principal base for the French Navy in the Western Caribbean, it was still a wild, isolated place. The harbour, however, was excellent. It was a deep bay guarded by a long, submerged bank, and even the channels around the bank were dissected by further reefs. The town and naval base were located on the western shore of the bay, with means of entry and exit in all winds except for a northeaster, and here the locally produced winds – the land and sea breezes – displaced the trade wind.

Medina moved across the bay, gradually opening a view right into the harbour. Holbrooke studied the anchored vessels; there must be about thirty large merchantmen, and now that the view was expanding he could see the men-of-war. There were two ships-of-the-line and three or four frigates. They'd need that number to see the convoy clear of the islands if Admiral Cotes was to send a squadron to prevent them leaving.

'Deck ho! there's a flag run up on the headland to starboard.'

That was the battery on the cape, kindly reminding Holbrooke of its presence. The enemy guns were two miles distant, and Holbrooke had no intention of coming any closer.

'They're firing, sir,' called Whittle from the masthead. Sure enough, the position of the battery was marked by three puffs of smoke. The shot fell well short. 'Twenty-four pounders, Mister Hosking? They can't be any more than that.'

'Eighteen, I believe, sir,' replied the master. Holbrooke nodded, Hosking was probably correct. It wouldn't need anything more substantial than eighteen pounders to dominate the passage between the cape and the submerged bank, it was merely three cables wide.

The town was now clearly visible, nestled in a plain between the encroaching green-clad hills. There were no more men-of-war visible. Those that he could see all had their masts and yards in place and looked ready for sea, but Holbrooke was sure that they wouldn't venture out with such a valuable convoy before the threat of hurricanes was reduced.

There was a light breeze from the north, not yet a sea breeze – it was too early – but it would probably get stronger as the sun rose higher.

'We've seen all we need to see, Mister Hosking. Put the ship about – I'd rather not get any closer to that battery – and take us home if you please.'

'Aye, aye, sir,' replied the master, privately in full agreement about the battery. It would have been easier to veer ship, but that would have taken them a cable closer to danger for no discernible advantage. 'North of Tortuga?'

'Yes, we'll save hardly any time going through the Tortuga Passage, and I'd feel vulnerable that close to land. Twenty miles with hostile shores two miles on either side and the chance of being becalmed? No, we'll go around, Master.' Holbrooke looked wistfully, 'but I shall regret missing the pirate's lair on the south coast.'

'There's nothing to see. The fort's overgrown, and the town and anchorage are abandoned. It was raised up and, in its wickedness, was cast down,' said Hosking in his best old testament voice, looking pointedly at Eli. 'Like Sodom and Gomorrah,' he added, in case anyone had missed the reference.

Medina turned her stern to Cape François and settled

on a north-westerly course to round Tortuga. The wind had shifted into the north-northeast and was two points forward of the beam. If it didn't back at all, they'd comfortably weather the island and then be able to turn into the Windward Passage, where the prevailing wind and current would sweep them back towards Jamaica. They should have the eastern point of Tortuga abeam at noon.

'Pass the word for the doctor, Mister Wishart. I'll see him on deck.'

Carlton was a busy man; he still had a full sickbay and a wounded captain in the grip of a fever. He'd usually have been a little peevish at being thus summoned by Holbrooke, who was much younger than he was. However, like everyone in the ship, the surgeon had noticed the change in the first lieutenant. Despite his youth, he'd quickly grown into his responsible position as second-in-command of a King's ship, and when Carlisle was wounded, Holbrook had matured at a frantic rate. His self-confidence had increased in a few hours to a level that would have taken years in the peacetime navy. The young man who only a year ago was considered hardly fit for the service, was now a figure of firm authority, to be deferred to and obeyed. Only Hosking was unimpressed, but then Hosking had known Holbrooke's father, and he'd met the infant George once at their cottage outside Wickham. But he kept that knowledge a secret, ready to use it when it should be of the greatest advantage to him.

'Mister Carlton, do you have any news of Captain Carlisle?'

Carlton's manner was deferential. 'I've just come from the cabin, sir,' he said. 'The captain's still feverish, but I believe the worst is past. His wounds are healing well, although he's not yet lucid. I believe he'll be fit for conversation tomorrow afternoon.'

Both men remembered Captain Jermy of *Wessex* and the delicate situation of a squadron whose commodore was, by his condition, unable to command. Thankfully there were no such tensions in *Medina*, and Holbrooke knew his captain's mind well enough to be confident that when he was fit again, Carlisle would regain command without any recriminations.

'Is there anything that can be done to make him more comfortable?'

'Nothing, sir. The sailmaker shifts the wind-scoops at every change of course, and the ship's motion is easy. I could almost wish for a few more days before we reach Port Royal; he'll do no better in the hospital than he does here at sea.'

Holbrooke nodded. He was quite prepared to linger at sea if it would help Carlisle's recovery, but he recognised the surgeon's statement as a rhetorical device to demonstrate how well he was caring for his patient. If he'd really wanted *Medina* to stay at sea, he'd have said so.

'And Lady Chiara, how does she do?'

'She's tired and not eating well, but she'll recover quickly when the captain's fever breaks.'

'I imagine she's hardly left his side,' said Holbrooke in admiration. 'The remainder of your patients, how do they do?'

'All the flesh wounds are doing well, and I expect them to be clear of the sickbay in a day or two. I'm worried about Williams with the head wound. It may need trepanning, but I'd like a second opinion and the surgeon in Port Royal is something of an expert. He's comfortable now, but he won't be leaving the sickbay except in a boat to the hospital.'

'And the amputees?'

'Well, sir, as you know, it's a race between healing and mortification, and I won't know which is winning for a day or two. I have high hopes, but their conditions could turn in twenty-four hours. I'll keep you informed.'

'Thank you, Mister Carlton. May I visit the sickbay at two bells in the forenoon?'

As Holbrooke returned from a visit to the cabin and the sickbay, he heard a hail from the masthead. 'Land Ho! Land two points on the larboard bow!'

That could only be the high land above the eastern point of Tortuga. It was well-named by Christopher Columbus who was the first European to visit in 1492. As the island appeared in the morning mist to the west, it had the shape of a tortoise or a turtle and thus was given the Spanish name *Tortuga*. Now Holbrooke was seeing it for the first time from the east, but it retained its distinctive form from whichever direction it was viewed.

'I'll take us three miles clear, sir,' said Hosking. 'There's deep water right up to the shore, and with the island's shape we can hardly become embayed.'

'Very well, Mister Hosking,' and the two men naturally fell into step as they walked the weather side of the quarterdeck.

'I've been thinking about that day when we went to Captain's Carlisle's house in Kingston, do you remember?'

'I remember it well,' replied Hosking. 'We had trouble finding it. We discussed the voyage before Don Alonso arrived.'

'We did,' said Holbrooke. 'We discussed the voyage to St. Augustine, our orders to look into Cape François and the route that we'd take.' He looked significantly at Hosking, who returned a blank stare.

'Those Dutchmen,' said Holbrooke, to Hosking's confusion, rapidly changing the subject, 'knew where to find us, both in the Yucatan Channel and the Caicos Passage. They lay in wait for us at the two places that were both choke-points and remote from civilisation. If you look at our route of the past month, you could hardly find two better ambush points.'

'They're clever devils – were clever devils, mostly,' Hosking corrected himself. 'But you're right, those are known choke-points.'

'But how did they know our route? They weren't

waiting for stray merchantmen, we weren't just a good opportunity for them, they were waiting for us at specific places, but more than that they were there at the right time to fall upon us.'

Light dawned on Hosking. He thought that he saw why Holbrooke had started by reminding him about that day in Kingston, two months ago. 'Then you think Don Alonso was playing us false? That he informed the Dutch pirates so that they could lie in wait for us?'

Holbrooke stopped at the taffrail, well out of earshot of the people whose duties caused them to gather around the wheel.

'That was my initial thought, I must admit. But we'd finished our discussions long before Don Alonso entered the room, and as far as I'm aware he knew nothing of our route from St. Augustine back to Port Royal. He may have guessed that the admiral would send us to Cape François, but he couldn't have been certain.' Holbrooke looked thoughtfully at the frigate's wake, a ruler-straight line stretching away behind them. 'I can't believe it was Don Alonso. He nearly lost his life and certainly endangered the lives of his family. If we'd only met the Dutchmen after St. Augustine, then I'd suspect Don Alonso, but the first meeting can't have been arranged by him.'

'Then who …?' Hosking's head came up with a jerk from his contemplation of the wake. 'That servant of Lady Chiara's,' he said, snapping his fingers. 'I should have known. I didn't like him from the start. Too much of the foreigner in him, too high and mighty,' said Hosking, evidently pleased to be accusing Black Rod.

'Perhaps,' said Holbrooke, 'he certainly heard the conversation. Of course, it could be anyone on the admiral's staff and nothing to do with that day at all. But the timings work well. There was a whole month between that meeting and our sailing, and it would take time to get information to the Dutchmen.'

'Yes,' said Hosking. 'The Dutchmen could have been

waiting in any of the ports or anchorages on the Jamaican coast. They'd have passed without any notice with Britain and Holland at peace. If they knew our route, they could have waited for word of our departure date and sailed ahead to meet us.'

'Not a word to anyone, master, not even Lady Chiara. I'm glad I spoke to you about this, it's cleared my mind. Whether it was Black Rod or someone else, I'm sure that we were betrayed. And I'm determined to discover the traitor's identity.'

'Sail ho! Sail right ahead.'

'What is she, Whittle?' shouted Holbrooke.

'I can't quite see yet, sir. She's ship-rigged, I believe.'

'This could be our fat French West Indiaman,' said Holbrooke to Hosking, as they walked forward. 'In any case, as we're cleared for action, the hands can remain in their watches until we see who it is.'

Two minutes went by, then three. Holbrooke was just about to hail the masthead when Whittle beat him to it. 'Deck there, she's a man-of-war, a two-decker I think.'

That cut through the complacency of a quiet forenoon watch. A small ship-of-the-line in these waters could hardly be anything other than French, although there was an outside chance that it was Spanish and an even lesser chance that it was British. However, Holbrooke knew that the admiral wouldn't have sent another ship to Cape François when he'd already sent *Medina*, not when he was so short of cruisers.

'Beat to quarters,' he shouted.

With the frigate already cleared for action, it was a matter of minutes for the hands to reach their appointed quarters and for the final preparations to be made. Holbrooke could see the topsails in his telescope from the deck.

'He must have seen us by now and will be wondering whether we're French or British,' said Holbrooke.

'In any case, he knows by now that we're smaller,' replied Hosking. 'They must have missed *Torenvalk* by a hair's-breadth. If that ship is heading for Cape François, she probably didn't care to chase what would have looked like a privateer into the Windward Passage, with a long beat back again.'

'Well, she's firmly in our path now,' said, Holbrooke, as he studied the topsails and coarses that were now visible above the horizon. 'She's French!' he said, snapping his telescope closed. 'She can't be anything else.'

'Deck there!' shouted Whittle from on high, 'she's one of our old fifties.'

It was curious the way everyone on the quarterdeck looked sideways at Holbrooke. He was supposed to be infallible but had been found wanting. They were disappointed.

'Whittle! could she be the *Greenwich*?' he shouted back.

There was a pause, while the quarterdeck digested this question. Everyone knew that *Greenwich* had been taken by the French in March off Cape Cabron on the eastern end of Santo Domingo, but none of them had thought to place that information alongside Whittle's report.

'She could be, sir, I'm sure she's one of our fifties – or was,' he added in a lower voice.

'Then she's *Greenwich*. The only other fifty in these waters is *Wessex*, and she's still with the Leeward Islands Squadron,' said Holbrooke, firmly. 'At least we know what we're up against.'

'In this chop, she's as fast as us,' said Hosking, gloomily, 'or faster if she's been careened recently and the French have given her a new suit of sails. Like they do.'

'Very well, Mister Hosking,' said Holbrooke, feeling the frustration that Carlisle felt when his otherwise excellent sailing master was involved in tactical discussions. His mind worked in straight lines and could never see a way to even out the odds.

Holbrooke decided then that he wouldn't discuss his

plans with Hosking. Let him stew in his ignorance.

'I'll handle the ship, Mister Hosking, you'll give the sail orders.'

The sailing master opened his mouth as if to argue but seeing Holbrooke's determination he swallowed his angry retort and moved to windward without a word, where he could better observe the tacks and sheets. Captains generally gave orders about where they wanted the ship to be placed and left the handling to the master. But Holbrooke had become irritated with Hosking and was quite deliberately punishing him. But also, Holbrooke didn't really have a plan, yet. Just a certainty that trying to outrun *Greenwich* in the open sea could only end one way. The quartermaster – old Eli as they were at quarters – and the steersmen exchanged wordless looks; they were old hands at interpreting the officers' moods.

'Mister Smith. My compliments to Lady Chiara and we're about to go into action. The captain must be taken below to the orlop. Make them comfortable and then return to your station. You may take whatever hands you need.' It would be a difficult task, moving the dead weight of the captain below.

'Two points to starboard quartermaster, I want you as hard on the wind as you can be, then ease her off a point. *Greenwich* must see our bows as though we plan to engage her.'

'Aye, aye, sir,' replied Eli and nudged his steersmen until *Medina* was pointing as high as she could, then indicated that he should take her back. He could hear Hosking giving the orders for the sheets to be hauled aft to flatten the sails as much as possible. He sounded strange, his voice toneless, probably brooding on Holbrooke's implied rebuke.

Holbrooke's mind was working fast – his plan was forming even as the two ships were closing at a combined speed of thirteen or fourteen knots – there wasn't much time.

'Mister Hosking,' he called over his shoulder. The older man had suffered enough and would be careful to be more positive on the quarterdeck in future, 'I'm going to take the Tortuga Passage, where the sea will be calm, and we've a chance of out-sailing her.'

'Then your course is west-by-south, sir,' replied Hosking. Holbrooke could see Eli ready to relay a course change to the steersmen.

'No, if we go directly to the channel,' he shouted back against the strengthening breeze, '*Greenwich* will just cut us off. We need to make him believe that we're trying to escape to seaward.'

Hosking nodded, he was beginning to see what Holbrooke intended.

'Mister Smith. Stand by the starboard battery, and we'll give him a broadside at least.'

Holbrooke recognised the madness in his action: he was taking a frigate within range of a fourth-rate's guns in defiance of all naval logic. *Medina* had neither the weight of broadside nor the strength in her scantlings to resist even the smallest ship-of-the-line, but nevertheless, he knew this was their best chance.

The two ships hurtled towards each other. With a mile to go Holbrooke ordered *Medina* hard onto the wind so that *Greenwich* would just see her larboard bow. Sure enough, *Greenwich* followed, coming two points to larboard so that the two ships, if they held their courses, must inevitably meet.

Holbrooke studied the relative positions. With five cables to go, he turned to Eli.

'Bear away, your course is west-southwest, keep that point of land fine on your starboard bow.' He pointed to the eastern tip of Tortuga, now only four miles away. 'Starboard battery, fire as you bear.'

The two ships passed three cables apart; it would have been easy gunnery except that they were hurrying past each other on opposite tacks. The French at least had an excuse because they'd been expecting to engage with their starboard battery. They managed a few shots with the larboard guns, but none hit *Medina*. Holbrooke's starboard battery also fired at the fast crossing target and achieved no hits or at least none that could be seen from the frigate's deck.

'Now then,' said Holbrooke, 'let's see how fast this frigate will sail. Set the stuns'ls. Mister Hosking, you have the ship.'

'Aye, aye, sir,' replied the sailing master, his earlier resentment forgotten in the exhilaration of out-running the stronger ship.

Medina piled on sail and headed for the southern side of the Tortuga Passage, where there were no shallow patches and where they'd be least affected by the wind shadow. Once in the lee of the island, the choppy sea diminished until eventually they were flying along with the wind abaft the beam on a sea only slightly bothered by a few ruffles. *Greenwich* was visibly slipping astern, and by the time they emerged from the western end of the channel she was five miles behind the frigate. *Medina* followed the land around to the south, and as the sun set she was passing Point de Jean-Rabel, and the Windward Passage was starting to open ahead of them. Their last sight of *Greenwich* was as she hauled her wind to beat back eastwards towards Cape François.

CHAPTER NINETEEN

Rear Admiral Cotes

Tuesday, twenty-third of August 1757
Medina, at Anchor. Port Royal, Jamaica

The squadron anchorage at Port Royal was bathed in early morning light that reflected off the rippled surface of the sea, making it painful to look over the side. Holbrooke sat under an awning on the quarterdeck beside Carlisle who was reclining in a chair. The captain's fever had declined rapidly after *Medina* had sailed through the Windward Passage and over the last twenty-four hours his recovery had been dramatic. He was in some pain from the wounds, but his head was clear, and he was pressing Holbrooke for the details of the fight with the Dutch pirates, the reconnaissance of Cape François and the escape from the French fourth-rate in the Tortuga Passage.

'So, you managed to keep them off our deck,' said Carlisle, looking at his first lieutenant with admiration. 'My opium-induced dreams were haunted by visions of a hundred fighting-mad Dutchmen pouring over the frigate's gunwales,' he patted the thick oak cap of the quarterdeck rail. 'I'll attach your report to mine when I'm allowed to finish it,' he cast a glance at Chiara, sitting protectively on his other side.

'You won't work on any report for at least a week, Edward, and when you do, it will be by dictation to Simmonds.' She looked sternly at her husband, an expression that her face wasn't ideally suited for. However, she was right. Carlisle's recovery was too soon and too fragile to withstand any sort of work. If he wanted to take *Medina* to sea again before the new year, he needed rest and nursing.

197

'Well, my report is written up to the day that we sailed from St. Augustine, so perhaps you'd be good enough to complete it to our arrival at Port Royal. There's no harm in having two authors for one report. I find Chalmers has a way with words, and you may want to use him as an editor.' Carlisle looked affectionately at his first lieutenant. 'It'll bring you to the attention of Admiral Cotes, and that may well be to your advantage,' he said with a significant gaze.

Holbrooke could only agree, if privately. He knew that he was very young to be looking for promotion to commander, he wasn't yet twenty, although as far as the navy was concerned, he must be over twenty because he'd passed for lieutenant a year ago. Others had achieved promotion at a similar age. Hervey, whom he had known quite well in the Mediterranean, had been made a commander at twenty-two and had been posted before he was twenty-three, and that at the tail end of the previous war, when promotions were slowing down. The Jamaica Station was an excellent place to be at this, the start of a war, as prizes came in thick and fast to feed the admiral's need for small cruisers. Each of those ships, if it were to be commissioned as a sloop-of-war, would need a commander to walk its quarterdeck, and the admiral had no spare commanders. He'd have to promote some lucky lieutenants, and he had every incentive to do so before the Admiralty imposed its own nominees upon him. Holbrooke had no illusions, however. The flagship was filled with lieutenants of greater seniority than himself, each of whom was known to the admiral and many of whom had influential friends and relatives. Perhaps some would have been followers of the admiral in previous commissions. Holbrooke knew that he'd probably have a long wait for his first command.

'The surveyors are looking over the *Torenvalk*, sir,' said Holbrooke, pointing over towards the yard where the little ship lay. Coated figures – who were clearly not *Medina's* prize crew – could be seen systematically examining her topsides and masts. 'There's talk of arming her with six-pounders instead of the Dutch eights and increasing the number of swivels. That'll make her lighter and allow her to be stored for a three-month cruise. They're even considering giving her a sixth rate's topmasts, her lower masts being so short and no replacements to be had in Jamaica. That'll give her a good turn of speed, although she may be a little crank.'

'That makes sense,' said Carlisle who was deeply interested in this kind of technical discussion, 'she's too slow for a little ship like that, and the ordnance board is emphatic about standardising armament, but she'll miss her eight-pounders. Are the six-pounders available in the yard, I wonder?'

Holbrooke nodded. 'She must have had a lucky passage to come in a full day before us. Wishart said that they saw a topsail to the northwest as they entered the Windward Passage. That must have been *Greenwich*, but she didn't alter course.'

'As you'd expect. If *Greenwich* chased *Torenvalk* south, she'd have had a hell of a job beating back to Cape François.'

'The cutter's returned, sir,' said Midshipman Smith, not knowing whether he should be addressing Carlisle or Holbrooke. 'I'll have her fitted out to take you ashore, sir,' he said, addressing Carlisle now.

'Jackson is back from *Torenvalk* and will take you as far as your home, with a few stout lads to see you safely indoors,' added Holbrooke, 'and Mister Carlton will see that you're made comfortable. He'll come to you every day and see to the dressings.'

Chiara had a self-satisfied look. She'd argued forcefully that Carlisle would do better at home than in the naval hospital.

'Very well,' said Carlisle, 'although I'm perfectly comfortable here.' He looked wistfully around the bay, knowing well that it would be late in the year before he was fit to take his own ship to sea again. 'I hope the admiral will let you have *Medina* in my absence, Holbrooke, I don't trust anyone else with her. I'll do anything in my power to influence him, but you know the pressures that he's under and the hordes of lieutenants just waiting for an opportunity such as this.'

'The admiral will see you now, Lieutenant Holbrooke,' said the flustered clerk. He had the look of a man whose morning had been less than satisfactory and was regretting his missed breakfast and the support of the admiral's secretary, who'd been sent away for the day.

Holbrooke knocked, waited for a second, and when there was no answer, opened the door and walked in. The admiral was reading at his desk and didn't immediately look up. Holbrooke stood stiffly in front of him awaiting recognition and wondering whether he should have paused for the admiral to call him in.

'Call that damned clerk back in, will you Holbrooke? He's never here when I need him.' He drew the ink-well towards the edge of the desk, carefully charged his pen and signed the document that lay in front of him with a flourish. The clerk had been listening and took the letter almost before the signature was finished. He carefully sanded it and carried it away to the outer office. Being the clerk to Admiral Cotes was evidently not an easy task, and there was little wonder that his secretary took every opportunity to leave the office. However, Holbrooke remembered the conversation with Hosking and Chalmers back in June when they had first heard of their mission to St. Augustine. A man who was responsible for the safety of two million in goods bound for England, as well as being accountable for preventing the French getting their own wealth home, should be allowed to be bad-tempered occasionally. The knowledge that it was upon his own judgement that the financial health of his country rested must lead to sleepless nights. And of course, the shadow of Byng loomed over all admirals since his execution less than six months ago. His ghost coloured their judgement and haunted their dreams.

'Now, Mister Holbrooke. I believe we met when the governor was bidding farewell to that Spanish fellow, eh?'

'Yes, sir,' replied Holbrooke, not knowing what else to say.

'Well, sit down man. *Medina* is back from her adventures, I see, and you've brought a prize,' he looked out of the window at *Torenvalk*, 'and a wounded captain. Whether she's a fair prize has yet to be determined, so don't get your hopes too high, but if she is, and if she's not too badly knocked about, I'll buy her into the service. I can always use an extra sloop, and she's damned-near frigate size. How badly damaged is she? But we're getting ahead of ourselves. You've given Captain Carlisle's report to the clerk?'

'Yes, sir. Captain Carlisle's report to the eighth of August then my report from the eighth to our arrival at Port Royal.'

'Good. I'll read it all later, Mister Holbrooke. But for now, if you please, give me an overview of *Medina's* proceedings since she left here two months ago. I have half an hour,' he said, looking meaningfully at the clerk who had no idea what appointment the admiral had in thirty minutes and wondered how on earth he could find out. His life was very hard with the secretary absent in Kingston.

Holbrooke told the story of the voyage: the fight with the pirates in the Yucatan Channel, Don Alonso's injury, the information about the Spaniard's earlier encounter with the Dutchmen, the welcome in St. Augustine and the indifferent reception in Savannah, which was where Carlisle's report ended.

'So those dogs in Georgia didn't see fit to welcome a King's ship? Thank you for that information, Mister

Holbrooke,' he said ominously as he made a note in the margin of the paper in front of him and looked significantly at his clerk, who merely looked confused.

Holbrooke recounted *Medina's* second meeting with the Dutchmen in the Caicos Passage, Carlisle's wound, the capture of *Torenvalk*, the fleeing westward of the second ship and the burial at West Caicos.

'He'll have nowhere to refit in that direction,' said Cotes. 'I'll send a message to Havana; perhaps they'll pick him up, but more likely he'll abandon the ship. I'll have to tell the governor at St. Eustatius of course, although whether he shares our views on what constitutes piracy is doubtful. In any event, humanity isn't likely to be bothered by that piratical crew any more.'

'His ship will need a regular yard to refit, sir. I doubt he can achieve much within his own resources, in my opinion ...' The look on the admiral's face made him end lamely.

'Just so. Proceed with your narrative, if you please.' Admiral Cotes evidently didn't like being given advice by lieutenants.

He reported the number and types of men-of-war and merchantmen at Cape François, which, at a nod from the admiral, the clerk recorded in a notebook. Finally, he told of the escape from *Greenwich*, and the progress of Captain Carlisle's recovery as *Medina* neared Port Royal. The admiral had started listening to Holbrooke with no more than mild interest, *just one more exaggerated report from my excitable frigates*, his expression said. But as the narrative continued, it started to dawn upon him that *Medina* had carried out an essential diplomatic and scouting mission with skill and courage, and that this young lieutenant, left in command at a critical moment, had been instrumental in its success. He looked afresh at the man sat in front of him, looking for some sign of greatness, something that set him apart from the rest. But Holbrooke was disappointingly ordinary, only his deeds spoke for him.

'Thank you, Mister Holbrooke,' the admiral said with a

cordial smile. 'Damn that Spaniard for not revealing the information on the Dutch ships, although whether it'd have changed anything, I don't know. Now, as I recall *Medina* had two objectives,' he said, holding out the first and second fingers on his right hand. 'First, to deliver Don Alonso and his family to St. Augustine, which you accomplished, albeit with some injury to the governor, and second, to carry out a reconnaissance of Cape François, which was successful, and I thank you for this most useful information,' he said indicating the clerk's notebook. 'I hadn't imagined that such a simple pair of tasks could become quite so dramatic. These Dutchmen – pirates perhaps, but that will be determined in court – how did they know to find you in the Yucatan Channel and again off the Caicos? It appears that they knew your plans.'

'I can only imagine that after they'd lost Don Alonso off the Windward Islands, they searched his probable track as far as Grand Cayman. Then when there was no word of them to the west, they turned back for Jamaica. They could have put an agent ashore and picked up the information in the taverns.' Holbrooke chose not to tell of his suspicions regarding Lady Chiara's household – not until he had some evidence.

'I suppose so,' said the admiral doubtfully. 'The information that *Medina* was taking the governor to St. Augustine would have been freely available. After all, Don Alonso and all his entourage knew of it, but the mission to Cape François was naturally kept secret.' He looked thoughtful, tapping his forefinger on the desk. 'I'll make some inquiries.'

'Thank you, sir,' said Holbrooke. He doubted whether the admiral's investigation would reveal anything this long after the event, but it was gratifying to be taken seriously.

'You've done well, young man,' said the admiral, 'but now I need *Medina* back at sea. When is Captain Carlisle expected to be fit for duty?'

'Our doctor believes it'll be two months at least. His

collar-bone must be healed,' Holbrooke knew better than to bandy technical medical terms with an admiral, 'and the wounds to his chest must be closed before ever he can think of setting foot onboard.'

'It's called a *clavicle*, Holbrooke. Don't they teach you youngsters anything nowadays?' replied the admiral looking distracted.

Holbrooke sighed internally. But he knew that this was a decisive moment. The admiral must appoint someone to command *Medina* and take her back to sea for the next two or three months; he couldn't afford to leave a frigate swinging around an anchor at Port Royal for want of a captain. Did he have a favourite? A senior lieutenant in the flagship perhaps? A spare post-captain waiting for his own ship to be repaired? Holbrooke knew that his report had made a good impression, but was it enough?

The admiral looked out of the window as if working through a delicate problem. His clerk sat expectantly, pen poised to record the great man's decision. After perhaps twenty seconds – a span of time in which Holbrooke's heart rate increased dramatically – he turned decisively, his mind made up. 'You shall have *Medina* until Captain Carlisle is fit, Mister Holbrooke. I can't offer you an acting rank, but you'll command in your present rank, as a lieutenant. I know that it's unusual, but there are precedents, and I have my own reasons. I'll have the orders drawn up today,' he said and pointed at the harassed clerk.

'Thank you, sir,' replied Holbrooke, unable to keep the grin from his face. What an opportunity! Command of a frigate even if for only a few months. He may take her into action and achieve fame. He may take prizes – two-eighths of the value of which would belong to him – a world of possibilities opened before him.

'You must be ready to sail in three weeks with a clean bottom and stored for three months,' he looked around suspiciously, but only the clerk was in the room. 'I need you off Cape François to watch the French. I'll send out a squadron of our own in October, when the hurricane season is past its worst, to prevent the convoy sailing. It'll probably be Captain Forrest flying a broad pennant.' The admiral looked suddenly grim, 'and you should think yourself lucky that you're not a post-captain, Mister Holbrooke, or you'd be called for the court martial on these Dutchmen. From what you've told me, it'll be a bloody business, and Port Royal will be hanging its first pirates for many a year.'

CHAPTER TWENTY

A Mystery Solved

Monday, twenty-ninth of August 1757
Kingston, Jamaica

Holbrooke had chosen an evening when he knew that Chiara would be away from home. She'd been bidden to supper with the governor's wife, and she'd certainly not return for an hour or so. Black Rod, as was his custom, had accompanied her in the hired carriage, and that was important because the Angelini head of household was at the heart of the discussion that Holbrooke planned. Chalmers was with Holbrooke; they had spent many hours in the intervals of refitting reviewing what they knew, and what they suspected, about the Dutchman's source of information. The captured crewmen hadn't been able to shed much light on the mystery. They confirmed that the two ships had lain at anchor off Port Maria in the north of the island through the period when *Medina* had been in Port Royal before sailing for St. Augustine, but they hadn't been allowed ashore and had no knowledge of any sources of information on *Medina's* movements. Even with their lives in the balance, they could provide no credible information that survived cross-examination. For six of the ten that had outlived their wounds to be brought to trial, it was now too late, their bodies were swinging from gallows point as a warning to all seafarers. The other four had been pardoned on the supposed grounds that they had been forced into piracy, but it was a safe bet that their lives had been spared to demonstrate the discrimination and justice of the court.

Captain Carlisle was looking much better than when they had last seen him, his face no longer showing lines of pain. His collarbone, though still tightly strapped, was evidently fusing into one in broadly its original alignment, and his wounds were healing. However, it was clear that the surgeon had made a fair prognosis of his recovery, and he wouldn't be fit to command a frigate off a hostile shore in two weeks.

'Well, Holbrooke, and how does command suit you?' asked Carlisle as he awkwardly settled himself in a chair, 'and Chalmers, you're very welcome. I regret that Chiara isn't here to greet you.' They all knew Chiara and each other so well that they had dispensed with any formality in names. 'But am I imagining it or are you here because you know that Chiara isn't?' he asked, with a knowing look.

Holbrooke looked around the room, noting the closed door to the hallway. He nodded briefly to Chalmers.

'You're correct, sir, but we mean no disrespect, of course, as you'll understand when we state our mission,' said Chalmers.

'Go on,' said Carlisle, 'I'm intrigued.' He looked earnestly at the two men.

'Well, first I must ask that we aren't interrupted, sir. It's of the greatest importance that no servant overhears our conversation, or even notices that we cease when they come in,' said Holbrooke, taking the lead in the discussion.

'I can set your mind at rest on that matter, George. The cook is off duty, and the only additional servant that we have other than Chiara's man, Black Rod, is visiting her friends. She won't be back for at least an hour. Is that sufficient time?'

'I hope so, sir,' replied Holbrooke, 'I do hope so.'

With some trepidation, Holbrooke laid out his hypothesis. He explained why he thought the Dutch pirate had foreknowledge of *Medina's* route and timings, he reminded Carlisle that although their voyage to St. Augustine was commonly known in Port Royal and Kingston, *Medina's* orders to investigate Cape François were not. There were only two likely sources of that information: the admiral's staff or Carlisle's own household. Holbrooke reminded Carlisle of the day that he'd told them the details of the forthcoming voyage, including the route through the Yucatan Channel and, crucially, the return from St. Augustine via Cape François. Then with a deep breath, Holbrooke outlined his suspicions.

'Only yourself, Lady Chiara, Hosking, Chalmers and I were involved in that discussion, and I believe we can rule out any of those as a potential informer.'

Carlisle inclined his head cautiously in agreement. His officers were neither traitors nor loose of tongue; they all understood the importance of operational security. He wished he could say the same of his wife. He didn't suspect her of being a willing informer, but perhaps she didn't understand the need for secrecy in ship's movements to the same extent that career sea officers did. And then, of course, she was a foreigner, so whatever he thought, there would naturally be a taint of suspicion hovering around Chiara. And she *was* very insistent that she should join the meeting. However, he said nothing to his two friends, but he noted that Holbrooke and Chalmers were watching him closely, trying to read his facial expressions; none of his thoughts would be a surprise to the two men.

Chalmers picked up the tale. 'But we weren't the only ones to be in the room that day,' he said. Carlisle looked at him quizzically. 'Lady Chiara's Head of Household was there – Black Rod as we know him, but it occurs to me now that I don't even know his name.'

Carlisle looked troubled. He privately resented the presence of Black Rod with its implication that Chiara's new husband couldn't adequately protect her. He knew that it was illogical, that he'd be many months at sea leaving his wife alone in God-knows-what ports and that a loyal servant such as Black Rod should make him feel easier when he was away. But still, there was that business with Hassan Ben Yunis in the Mediterranean last year. He was sure that this mysterious head of household was somehow involved in re-introducing the Tunisian trader to the Angelini family. He appeared to have loyalties that extended beyond the narrow confines of the household that he served.

'Black Rod was there but so also, briefly, was your servant-woman. She could have overheard the plan,' continued Chalmers. 'Of course, this is all speculation and the leak could have come from the admiral's office or someone in *Medina* who guessed our route.'

'The woman left without giving notice very soon after *Medina* sailed,' said Carlisle, his discomfort evident in his lack of eye-contact, 'and now that I remember, Black Rod told me that she was last seen riding out of Kingston, *riding* mark you, towards Spanish Town. That's the right direction for Port Maria, and she could have been there in six hours on a decent horse. If she was the source of the leak, she could have stayed in my employment until she was sure that there was no change in the plan, then rejoined her ship at Port Maria.'

'Whittle saw a ship's topsails, perhaps two, if you remember, before we stopped at Grand Cayman. That could have been the pirates overtaking us to be in place before we got to the Yucatan,' said Holbrooke. 'There was plenty of time for the servant to reach Port Maria, alert the Dutch captain and for them to sail to meet us. They probably coasted around the east of the island to follow us. When they saw that we were calling at Grand Cayman, they'd have hatched the plan to lie in wait past Cape Catoche. It's a good place for an ambush.'

'Then I believe our mystery is solved. However, I must speak to Black Rod about security, I haven't done so yet,' he looked pensively at the bandages that still covered his chest, 'that will be the easy part, but I must also speak to Chiara, that will be more, let's say, delicate.' He looked up at the two men and smiled. What he wanted to say was, 'Married life is hard. If you think you're the head of the household, then you can think again,' but he held his peace in front of the two bachelors. They could learn these eternal truths in their own time.

Holbrooke and Chalmers walked back to the harbour where the cutter was waiting to row them to Port Royal. The careening would be almost complete, and at the next tide *Medina* would float free, her bottom clean as a whistle, giving her at least an extra knot of speed. One of the glories of Port Royal was that the navy yard took care of all the dirty work – the burning, the scraping, the caulking and the paying – while the ship's company enjoyed the fruits of the land, spending in advance the prize money and head money from the capture of *Torenvalk*. The prize court had sat immediately after the court martial that had convicted the pirates and knowing the verdict and the sentences had found no difficulty in condemning the ship as a prize. If the Dutch governor at St. Eustatius should complain, then the grim evidence of the bodies swinging at Gallows Point would bear witness to the employment of *Torenvalk* and the justice of treating her as a fair prize. On the same afternoon, the admiral had bought the pirate's ship for the navy. After a few months refitting, she'd emerge as His Majesty's sixteen-gun, six-pounder sloop-of-war *Kestrel*, the first love of some favoured lieutenant, newly-promoted to the exalted rank of commander.

'Are you satisfied that the mystery is solved, Chalmers?' asked Holbrooke, in a non-committal tone.

Chalmers didn't immediately answer, and they walked on a few places in silence while he marshalled his thoughts. 'We know that the master of the *Torenvalk* had a score to settle with Don Alonso, a blood-feud perhaps,' he said. 'We created a hypothesis: that the woman who was engaged as a servant to Carlisle's household was deliberately implanted there as a spy. We believe that she gathered her intelligence, and when she was certain that our route wouldn't be changed, she stole a horse and galloped to Port Maria, where she rejoined her ship, which then sailed to confront us in the Yucatan Channel. When that failed they laid a second trap in the Caicos Passage where they were destroyed, and there the story ends.'

'Just so,' said Holbrooke. 'The facts fit the hypothesis, the mystery is solved.'

'And yet I'm uneasy,' replied Chalmers. 'There are other hypotheses that we could construct. Forgive me if some of what I'm about to say sounds disloyal but treat me in this case as the devil's advocate. I imagine you know where the term originates,' he looked at Holbrooke, who shook his head. He didn't know and had always thought it an empty expression, devoid of any real provenance. 'It's not just an idle motto,' continued Chalmers. 'In the Roman church, when the creation of a saint is proposed, or the declaration of a miracle is under consideration, a person of seniority is appointed to challenge it. He's known as the *Devil's Advocate*. The important fact is that he's appointed, he doesn't volunteer for the task. He may be personally in favour of creating this new saint, he may be convinced that a miracle has indeed occurred, but he must put forward the opposite view so that a thorough investigation may take place. By tradition and by canon law, the devil's advocate isn't held responsible for any opinions that he expresses.'

Holbrooke had long ago stopped pretending to knowledge that he didn't have when Chalmers was involved. The Chaplain, he knew, saw straight through him.

'For example, Black Rod could be an agent of the Dutch pirates.'

Holbrooke nodded, at one time he'd thought it quite likely.

'Lady Chiara, in all innocence, could have told all her friends the details of our voyage, or she could be an agent of the Dutch herself.'

Holbrooke didn't look at his friend. Devil's advocate

or no, this was almost seditious when speaking of his captain's wife.

'The admiral's clerk could be a drunkard and a gambler who trades information for rum and the relief of his debts,' said Chalmers. 'I raise these hypotheses, which I know you find offensive either to your friends or to the service, to illustrate that there is more than one possible answer to this mystery.'

'However,' said Holbrooke, 'the facts fit our first hypothesis so well that I'm inclined to leave it there.'

'Were there any women found among the crew of the *Torenvalk*?' asked Chalmers, challenging Holbrooke's certainty. 'Did anyone report seeing a woman fighting?'

'No,' replied Holbrooke, 'but that proves nothing. She could have fallen over the side during the attempted boarding – many of the crew did – or she could have been in the second ship, the one that escaped.'

'Does that sound likely? Would a woman be placed in the front rank of the boarders? Would the only person to have heard our plans be separated from the commander of the pirates?'

'Then perhaps she didn't sail with the ships. She could have been nothing more than a locally hired spy.'

'And yet we know that she spoke with a foreign accent that could very well have been Dutch,' countered Chalmers.

The two men walked on into the gathering dusk, lost in thought. Holbrooke was beginning to question his assumptions; perhaps they hadn't entirely solved the mystery. They followed a winding course along the narrow road that paralleled Harbour Street and would eventually take them to the eastern end of the town. There Jackson and the boat's crew would be waiting at a quiet quay where they wouldn't be bothered by the activity of the port and the men wouldn't be tempted by the taverns. They argued their theories back and forth as they walked, enjoying the mental stimulus of creating towers of supposition only to break them down.

Suddenly the darkness was shattered by the flash of a pistol, unnaturally red in the dark shadows beneath the derelict warehouse that loomed on their right. The sound of the shot echoed back from the walls of the narrow alley, and Holbrooke felt the wind of a ball passing close to his left ear. There was a wild shout, and three burly figures burst out of a darkened corner, yelling wildly and wielding cutlasses. Behind them was a fourth, a smaller person shrouded in a cloak, holding back from the fray and cocking a second pistol, the first lying discarded on the ground, still smoking.

Holbrooke drew his sword and moved to his left to cover Chalmers who he believed to be unarmed. The first man was upon him in an instant, slashing wildly. Whoever he was, he'd never learned his cutlass drill under the master-at-arms of *Medina*, and he utterly failed to defend his body while raising his weapons high for a killing slash at Holbrooke's head. But he stood no chance as Holbrooke's point caught him under the chin and cut deep into the lower part of his skull, severing arteries and nerves and thrusting into his brain. His cutlass dropped from nerveless fingers, and his legs gave way. He was dead before he hit the ground. The second and third hesitated and looked back at the fourth figure who appeared to be the leader. The leader raised the second pistol and Holbrooke could see that its aim would come to rest on him. He stood transfixed, off balance, unable to move after withdrawing his sword from his first assailant. There was another flash and a loud report. Holbrooke took a moment to realise that he hadn't been hit. He looked up to see the leader dropping to the ground, the second weapon spinning away into the blackness. He turned and saw Chalmers, standing motionless with a small pistol held steadily in his hand, smoke drifting from the muzzle.

More cautiously now, the remaining two closed upon

Holbrooke and Chalmers. They were aware that they were confronting a dangerous and determined foe and seemed to hesitate. The chaplain stooped and picked up the dead man's cutlass and stood beside Holbrooke, holding it ineffectually in front of him. It was better than nothing, but Holbrooke mentally resolved to arrange for him to have lessons in the small-sword as soon as they were at sea. They backed against the wall, but the odds were still stacked against them as their two assailants advanced, cutting off their escape. Holbrooke thrust at the nearest, but he skipped backwards out of range. If they rushed now, with their greater bulk and heftier weapons, it would be all over for Holbrooke and Chalmers. The two assailants looked sideways at each other, nodded and raised their cutlasses for the kill.

'*Medina, Medina*,' came a shout ringing along the alley. From their left, the direction of their boat, half a dozen men ran into the alley. It was the boat's crew, drawn by the sound of shots and shouts. Jackson wielded his own cutlass and carried a pistol, he never took charge of a boat without them. The remainder were armed with the boat's stretchers, the two-foot lengths of hard oak that they braced their feet against when rowing and which made formidable clubs. The two assailants turned to face this new threat. One reacted quickly and turned tail, disappearing into the darkness between the broken warehouses. The last turned too slowly and the point of Jackson's cutlass caught him under the ribs. He writhed desperately, trying to escape, but a rain of stretchers beat him to the ground, breaking his skull and pouring his life's blood onto the rough ground.

Holbrooke shakily thanked his saviour, 'It appears I owe you my life, Jackson,' he said as he wiped his sword on his first assailant's jacket, a sailor's jacket he noticed, but then every other man in Kingston was a sailor.

'Don't you think nothing of it, sir,' he said and leaned closer, 'just get me a bosun's warrant in your ship when you're promoted,' he whispered.

Chalmers walked over to the body of the leader, lying still and apparently dead. He kicked aside the pistol, the one that had been poorly aimed and had alerted them to the attack. The chaplain knelt to check for a pulse. He pressed his hand against the man's chest and recoiled in surprise. This was no man, it was unmistakably a woman! He rolled her onto her back; she was still breathing, but with a hole squarely in the middle of her chest and a pool of blood expanding from under her, it was clear that she'd only minutes to live. Holbrooke joined him, intrigued by the gender of their assailant and anxious for any clues as to why they'd been singled out for the attack. They weren't obviously wealthy, and this was too well organised for a random attack.

'This is the Captain's serving woman,' exclaimed Holbrooke, 'the one that ran away after *Medina* sailed.' She was trying to talk, but bubbles of blood were coming from her mouth with each attempt. The two men leaned closer.

'You protected my son's killer,' she coughed up a mass of thick blood – it looked black in the gloom of the alley – and sucked in an agonising breath. 'You killed my husband,' more blood, another breath. 'And now you have killed me.' She tried to spit, but the flow of blood and another involuntary cough prevented it. Her next breath just drew the blood deep into her lungs. Her head fell back, all strength gone. She glared furiously, speechlessly, at the two men, but then her eyes lost focus, she convulsed and died.

Holbrooke straightened himself. He noticed that his hand was shaking, and he tried to control it, but there was one thing that he had to say.

'Well, Chalmers, so much for your devil's advocacy.'

CHAPTER TWENTY-ONE

The Admiral's Strategy

Wednesday, seventh of September 1757
Marlborough, at Anchor. Port Royal, Jamaica

In the eighteenth-century naval strategy was both constrained and enabled by three factors that none of the protagonists had under their control: geography, the weather and the ocean currents. These three elements, along with an understanding of the enemy's likely actions and the limitations of the forces under the commander-in-chief's control, determined his dispositions.

On the Jamaica Station, Admiral Cotes had a relatively simple situation when he was only fighting the French. His priority was the security of the British trade with the plantations on Jamaica, and to achieve this, he needed to assemble large convoys twice a year and see them safely on their way back to Britain, as well as protecting the inbound convoys and the coastal traffic. With that trade protection task under control, his second concern was to destroy the French commerce which came in two defined areas: the trade with the northwest part of Hispaniola, and the lesser trade with Louisiana, deep in the Gulf of Mexico. When those essentially commerce-warfare missions were covered, his third commitment was to prevent the reinforcement of the French naval base at Cape François.

The geography of his station, the trade winds, the hurricane season and the currents left the admiral limited space for creativity. His smaller cruisers were dispersed around the island of Jamaica to protect the coasting trade from the ever-hungry and ever-present French privateers. Then he needed to dominate the maritime choke-points – the *defiles* in military parlance. So, a heavy cruiser – a fifty-gun fourth rate – and a larger frigate when one was available were stationed to the north of Hispaniola. That would block the three French routes: to their plantations in the French part of that island, to the growing colony in Louisiana and to the naval base at Cape François. In case any French convoy should avoid that first squadron, he set a further trap far to the west off Cape St. Antonio, to cover both the Yucatan Channel and the Florida Straits. His battle squadron, the second and third rates when he had any and the sixty-gun fourths, was held at Port Royal and deployed when he had information on a large convoy or a sortie by a French Squadron.

That was the ideal disposition, and it worked well when he had enough ships to fill all those stations and when the hurricane season wasn't at its height. However, August and September were the dangerous months for tropical storms, and Admiral Cotes was naturally anxious when his valuable ships were exposed far from their home port, though he was less concerned about his cheaper and more plentiful frigates. That's why *Medina* met no other British men-of-war in her long voyage in the Caribbean, the Gulf of Mexico and the waters off the Bahamas. The probability of destructive hurricanes would diminish with each day that passed as September gave way to October, and the Jamaica Station was about to burst back into life.

The great cabin of *Marlborough* was rapidly filling with uniforms, predominantly the blue and gold of sea-officers, but with an occasional red coat of a senior marine officer and the plain black or blue of the navy board, the ordnance board and the victualling office. There were far too many people for the usual invitation to dinner where the commander-in-chief would traditional reveal his strategy to his senior captains; that would take place later and Holbrooke, as the only lieutenant present, wasn't invited. Even Carlisle would have been squeezed out by the sheer number of post-captains of ships-of-the-line. However, Holbrooke was happy with the arrangement. He could sit inconspicuously at the back of the cabin and soak up this, his first opportunity to see the formation of naval strategy in action.

Holbrooke looked around the room. It was a large space because although *Marlborough* had been cut down to a third-rate of eighty guns, she'd been built as a second-rate of ninety guns and had the accommodation for a flag officer and his staff. Holbrooke recognised Robert Faulknor, Cotes' flag captain and the commander of *Marlborough*. In some ways, Faulknor had an unenviable position. Being a flagship, *Marlborough* had few opportunities to take prizes and, unlike the admiral, he didn't share in the prize money that was won by all the other ships on the station. He was one of the most junior post-captains on the list, yet he drew his pay as a captain of a third rate, and with the influence of a commander-in-chief behind him, he could expect to have a frigate next. *Marlborough* was due to be docked and would be unlikely to feature in Cotes' immediate strategy.

Sitting squarely in front of the admiral, Holbrooke saw Arthur Forrest of *Augusta*. He was a senior captain and evidently a confidant of the admiral. Holbrooke had met Forrest and shaken his hand, but he was still surprised when the captain made a point of walking over to greet him. *Augusta* was a sixty-gun fourth-rate, built to the 1733 establishment in Deptford. She was an old, tired ship.

Maurice Suckling also caught his eye. He had *Dreadnought*, another Deptford-built sixty-gun ship, but of a modified design and a generation newer than *Augusta*. Suckling had been posted less than two years before, and *Dreadnought* was his first ship as a post-captain. He was a Suffolk man, the son of a country rector and his patronage came from the politically Whig family of Robert Walpole, who was his mother's uncle. Suckling was in deep conversation with William Langdon who was an older man but had been made post only the previous year. He commanded another old ship, the Chatham-built sixty-four-gun *Edinburgh*, the smallest of the third-rates. Langdon had sailed around the world with Anson in *Centurion* and had received an acting lieutenant's commission after the taking of the Spanish treasure ship, *Nuestra Señora de Covadonga*. He had the best of all patrons in the First Lord, and Anson was known to look after the interests of the men who had survived his great adventure.

There were half a dozen other captains present, but no lieutenants. Holbrooke was the only one, and he felt conspicuous.

Some gifted artist had drawn on a large oblong of sailcloth a chart of the Jamaica and Leeward Islands stations, stretching from the southern border of Georgia to Spanish Guiana and from Barbados to Vera Cruz on the Mexican coast. The winds and currents were shown as broad arrows on the sea, and the ownership of the land had been coloured: red for Spain, green for France and yellow for Britain. Holbrooke was impressed, but it would have been better to unroll it after everyone was seated to heighten the dramatic effect and prevent speculation.

The admiral pushed back his chair and rose to his feet. He wasn't a tall man, but he dominated the cabin with his restless energy.

'Gentlemen. The hurricane season is waning, and Monsieur will soon be active again. I've invited you all here so that you can understand the dispositions that I intend. Please hold any comments until I've finished, and there's no need to take notes as you'll each receive my written orders in the next few days, telling you what part you'll play.' Cotes was an energetic man; he moved around twitchily as he described how he'd protect Britain's trade while harassing the French.

When that more-or-less routine distribution of forces came to an end, he turned to the more interesting issue of the French convoy that was being gathered at Cape François.

Chris Durbin

'Our main effort this autumn will be to prevent the French getting their convoy back to France. Now, we know that de Bauffremont's squadron has left the area. After taking our *Greenwich*, he sailed north, presumably for the St. Lawrence, so I have a little more freedom to manoeuvre. I've received timely information on the French force at Cape François as it stood eighteen days ago,' he caught Holbrooke's eye and nodded briefly. 'They have two ships-of-the-line, and three or four frigates. *Greenwich* was also seen on passage to the Cape and has probably joined them. At the last count, they'd gathered some forty ships so you can estimate the importance to France of this enterprise. Our intelligence suggests that they'll wait until late October or November before they risk sailing their most valuable convoy of the year. I understand that the French insurers are even more risk-averse than our own.' That was understood to be a joke as everyone present had taken their turn at convoy escort and every sea-officer knew that insurance rates were more important than operational issues in determining convoy movements.

'I intend to blockade Cape François.' That came as something of a surprise; the Jamaica Squadron had not been able to spare enough ships-of-the-line for a blockade since the war began. 'Captain Forrest will hoist his broad pennant in *Augusta* and will sail with *Dreadnought* and *Edinburgh* to be off the Cape in the middle of October.' There was a general swivelling of eyes towards Forrest; he was a lucky man to be made commodore and sent on such a mission. That was a most public mark of the commander-in-chief's approbation. 'We all know how hard it can be to beat through the Windward Passage,' he said to a sea of studiously blank faces. They did indeed know – it was the admiral's own flagship that had most recently failed to do so and been forced to return to Port Royal. 'Therefore, Captain ... excuse me, *Commodore* Forrest's squadron will sail before the end of the month to ensure that they're in position before the earliest date that the French can sail.'

Holbrooke heard a shuffling behind him. It was the commissioner of the victualling yard, hurrying away to alert his people to the urgent requests – each one backed up by the authority of the admiral – that he knew would be pouring in before the day was over. It required a significant logistical effort to put three ships-of-the-line to sea, and the responsibility was his. Admirals may play at strategy, but it was logistics that made their plans possible. Under Admiral Townshend, he'd have been informed in advance of the victualling requirements, but Cotes preferred to reveal his strategy at a single sitting, and it was generally understood that the commissioner's only reason for attending the meeting was to hear this one piece of information. The admiral noticed the departure and nodded his agreement. In a few minutes, they could all hear the commissioner's boat being hailed alongside and the noises of his hurried departure.

'Meanwhile, gentlemen, *Medina* will sail on the thirteenth to watch the Cape,' he looked squarely at Holbrooke. 'Now, Mister Holbrooke, you won't mind me mentioning that you're developing something of the reputation of a firebrand.' Holbrooke tried hard not to blush as laughter rippled around the room. In the navy of 1757, to be labelled a firebrand was the objective of all right-minded sea-officers. 'Your orders will state that you're to watch the Cape and to report to Commodore Forrest when he arrives. I regret that you're specifically forbidden the taking of prizes unless the convoy sails before the squadron arrives.'

There was a general wagging of heads around the room, the adults approving of measures to tame impetuous youth. It was sheer hypocrisy, of course. Every man there would rather lose an arm than let a prize get away, but they could harden their hearts to the constraints placed upon such a junior officer whose success was there for all to see, a fine sloop-of-war being fitted out in the navy yard – the *Torenvalk*.

'Yes, we can all understand the need to restrain one of our frigate captains when it's his duty to be our eyes and ears; we don't want him sailing off in pursuit of prizes and leaving us in the dark about the enemy's movements. However, I want to make this point to all of you,' he said fixing each captain in his turn with a fierce stare. 'When the French squadron has sailed with the convoy, they'll have no ships-of-the-line in these waters, none at all.' He paused to make the point. 'At that time, the priority of my command will be to safeguard our own trade. You know what that means, endless unprofitable skirmishes with French privateers. But it's vital to Britain's economy which in turn is vital to winning this war. Only after we've done our utmost to protect our own ships and clear our convoys, will we be free to make war on French trade. That will be made clear in my written orders, and I hope it's clearly understood.'

There was some uncomfortable shuffling among the gathered captains. Without exception, they had accepted the risks of the Jamaica Station – the diseases that could carry away half a ship's company in a week, the hurricanes that could cause a well-found ship to be lost with all hands – because the Jamaica Station offered the best chance of making a fortune in prize money. Each man, the admiral knew, would stretch his orders to the limit and in some cases beyond to capture anything more substantial than a fishing boat that appeared over their horizon.

The meeting broke up into small groups of sea-officers chewing over what the admiral had told them. The favoured few remained for dinner, but the others left one at a time, each in his own boat with his own crew. Holbrooke was last. He had nobody to talk to, he wasn't part of that select band – the post-captains – nor even a commander. He was politely ignored. The final humiliation came as he left the ship, the last to do so. He couldn't fail to notice that half the sideboys were dismissed after the last real captain had departed, and it was the least of all the flagship's lieutenants who saw him over the side.

CHAPTER TWENTY-TWO

Commodore Forrest

Friday, ninth of September 1757
Augusta, at Anchor. Port Royal, Jamaica

Holbrooke grasped the manropes and paused before climbing up to *Augusta's* entry port. Jackson had steered the longboat for the short pull across to the commodore's ship, and when hailed, 'boat ahoy!' from the flagship he'd replied '*Medina*,' the conventional response that declared that the captain of a King's ship was in the boat. Holbrooke knew it was going to happen, but the thrill was still intense, and now he had to brace himself for the next rite of passage. He ducked as he passed through the entry port to be met by the pipes of the bosun's mates and the doffed caps of the junior officers. It wasn't the scale of ceremonial that would have met Carlisle, and certainly not that of Commodore Forrest himself, who would have had all the officers of the ship meet him, but to a man who wasn't yet twenty, it was the sweetest of music. Holbrooke's commission, his authority to take temporary command of His Britannic Majesty's Frigate *Medina*, had only arrived that morning and until then, although he had effectively commanded *Medina* since the day of the fight in the Caicos Passage three weeks ago, he hadn't legally been her commanding officer. The simple piece of thick, cream-coloured paper that nestled now in his coat pocket had changed his status dramatically, albeit temporarily.

'Good afternoon, Captain,' said the commodore, the ghost of a smile turning the corners of his lips. Perhaps he remembered the first time that he'd been addressed by the courtesy title of Captain when he took command of the little eight-gun bomb-ketch *Alderney* sixteen years ago. For the navy didn't care what substantive rank you held, if you commanded a man-of-war you were entitled to be addressed as *Captain* and to be piped aboard every man-of-war, from a mighty first-rate to a tiny cutter.

Holbrooke could read the mixture of emotions on the faces of the officers that Forrest had mustered to meet him. He noticed that the first lieutenant was absent. It was a wise decision. The flagship's second-in-command was far senior to Holbrooke, and it would have been incongruous for him to be introduced to a man who, in a few months, would revert to his rightful position in the naval hierarchy. However, there was still quite a crowd waiting to be introduced. The second, third and fourth lieutenants, a pair of master's mates and six midshipmen, each of them masking their feelings, whether they were envy, admiration or sheer wonderment that such a young man could be commanding a frigate. He knew almost none of them, but the fourth lieutenant was a familiar face. Denham Farlowe was an old friend of Holbrooke's. They'd suffered together through the naval academy at Portsmouth, but Farlowe had been less lucky than Holbrooke. He'd passed for lieutenant but when Holbrooke had last spoken to him had not yet received a commission. But here he was, in a suspiciously ill-fitting coat.

'I see that you already know Lieutenant Farlowe,' said Forrest as he made the introduction.

'Good afternoon, sir,' said Farlowe, making his bow to his schoolfriend and trying to suppress a grin.

'Good afternoon Mister Farlowe,' replied Holbrooke, maintaining his dignity as best he could. It was hard to forget the day that they'd absconded from the academy and been found hours later in a sordid alley at the back of Portsmouth Point, dead drunk and stripped of everything of value. They'd been flogged for their transgression, side by side, bent over the master's table. Holbrooke chose not to tell Forrest where they had met. Many – no, most – sea officers of his generation thought the naval academy a dangerous waste of time and its output an unwanted imposition on the fleet. Holbrooke was always careful who he told about his early naval education. In this case, it was particularly important because Farlowe probably would rather that his captain didn't know that he'd been a King's Letter Boy until he had a chance to prove his worth.

'Then perhaps Mister Farlowe will take you to the cabin,' said Forrest. 'I see Langdon's boat is waiting to come alongside.' Forrest had *almost* orchestrated it correctly, but his first lieutenant appeared just before Holbrooke had been spirited below. It certainly wouldn't do for the second-in-command to be absent when a post-captain came on board, and the first lieutenant would be keen to be introduced to a man who may be able to influence his career in the future.

'Well, Denham, it's a surprise to see you here, and in the full glory of a commission, I see,' said Holbrooke, shaking his hand a second time. 'That comes of spending too much time on board; I miss the news of the station. The last that I heard you were in *Edinburgh*. In any case, my heartiest congratulations.'

'It's as much a surprise to me, sir,' replied Farlowe. 'I was resigned to a long wait for their Lordships to take notice of me, but I was helping with a new foretopsail in *Edinburgh* yesterday forenoon when I was summoned to the cabin. You can imagine my unease,' he said with a grin. Both men remembered how a summons to the master's office in the academy rarely turned out well. 'But Captain Langdon did it most handsomely. He shook my hand and told me how much he'd miss me; how sure he was that I'd rise in the service. He'd already asked the second lieutenant to lend me a uniform coat, it almost fits you see,' he said holding out his arms to show the sleeves only a few inches above their rightful position. 'Then I was in a boat bound for *Augusta* before the change of the watch. I haven't even wetted my good fortune.'

'But how does *Augusta* come to have four lieutenants?

These fourth rates are only established for three,' asked Holbrooke.

'It appears that the admiral decided that a commodore needs an extra lieutenant in his flagship, to help with the additional responsibilities that fall upon the commander of a squadron.' Holbrooke nodded. 'It seems that I was the only passed lieutenant on the station. Now I'll wear out my knees praying that their Lordships will be moved to confirm me.'

'I'm sure of it, Denham. This war has a very long way to go, and a lieutenant who already has a berth will be an easy promotion for them.' Privately, Holbrooke wasn't so sure. Anson was besieged by requests, nay demands, for preferment from officers with political and family interest. Farlowe would have to seize every opportunity to have his name mentioned favourably within the hallowed walls of the Admiralty.

'The prospect is pretty good, what with Swift, the first lieutenant, moving on. I'll move up to third, so even when Captain Forrest has to strike his pennant, I'll have a berth in *Augusta*,' said Farlowe, happily. 'I think I stand a good chance of being confirmed.'

'The premier is moving on, is he?' asked Holbrooke, 'where's he going?' It was always a matter of the utmost interest when officers were promoted in a remote station like Jamaica. Under normal circumstances, it created a series of vacancies as other officers moved up to fill the newly-available berths. In this case, as Holbrooke quickly realised, if Farlowe did stay in *Augusta* and if his commission was confirmed, there would be no further movement; it was a promotional *cul de sac*.

Farlowe gave Holbrooke a queer look, partly confusion, partly embarrassment. 'Didn't you know? I'm awfully sorry to be the one to break this news to you. He's being promoted into *Kestrel* – that's what the admiral has decided to call your *Torenvalk*.'

Holbrooke tried to hide his shock and disappointment.

He'd been telling himself that he was too junior to be given *Torenvalk*, or *Kestrel* as he should now call her. After all, it required a promotion to commander, and he'd barely been a year as a lieutenant. Nevertheless, whatever his rational mind told him, hope had been lurking close below the surface, and this news dashed that hope entirely.

'Well, I wish him the best of fortune. I didn't expect to be given her but, well, you know …,' he ended lamely. 'I imagine that's why Forrest dismissed him from the gangway when I came aboard.'

'Yes, I believe so,' said Farlowe, feeling wretched. 'Even post-captains have some finer feelings,' he said attempting to lighten the mood.

Holbrooke tried to cast this disappointment out of his mind. Here was his friend working hard to be confirmed as a lieutenant while he was moping about not being made commander. But it was a harder blow than he'd thought possible, and he hadn't been at all prepared for it. He couldn't shake off the conviction that if there were any justice in the world, *Kestrel* would be his. After his captain had been wounded, he'd out-fought the pirates at their favoured form of combat. He'd flung them back in bloody confusion from the boarding nets and had taken her!

With an effort, he stiffened himself. He was about to remind his friend of the need to distinguish himself in his new position when the door was flung open, and Forrest ushered in the two post-captains of his squadron. Farlowe made his excuses and left, casting a last, commiserating glance at his friend.

When captains dined together, it was generally a lengthy affair, but it had a serious purpose. By tradition, captains led a solitary life on board their ships. They weren't members of the wardroom or gunroom, where the other officers lived, and they were so shrouded in the awful majesty of command, that their conversation with their officers when they met on deck or when he invited them to their cabins, was almost inhuman in its lack of spontaneity or warmth. When captains met – and they invariably dined on those occasions – it was both an opportunity for them to exchange news and to relax among their peers. The three post-captains were very easy in each other's company, even now that Forrest had been given a broad pennant. They all knew that it was a temporary rank for this mission and it would be at least ten more years before he reached the top of the post-captains' list and could expect his flag. Forrest would undoubtedly have to revert to his substantive rank when it was over. One thing was sure, Forrest wouldn't quickly be moved from the Jamaica Station, where he successfully combined his naval duties with the ownership of several sugar plantations scattered around the island.

'Gentlemen, the King,' said Forrest, raising his glass of warm port to signify the end of the social event of dinner and the start of the business of the squadron.

'We may not get the opportunity to meet off Cape François,' Forrest said, as an introduction, 'so I want you to understand my thoughts before we sail.'

They all nodded in agreement. It was notoriously difficult to communicate at sea and signalling by flags was still in its infancy. The only way to understand each other thoroughly was to meet on board the flagship, and none of the captains relished the prospect of leaving his ship for any length of time within sight of an enemy port. This dinner in *Augusta*, safely at anchor at Port Royal, was by far the best way for Forrest to ensure that each of his ships understood their part in the hoped-for action.

'The ships you saw, Holbrooke,' he said with an acknowledgement to his most junior captain, 'have been sent here specifically to see this valuable convoy on its way. We know that there is a seventy-four, probably *Intrépide* with Monsieur de Kersaint in command of the ship and the squadron. There's a sixty-four, *Opiniâtre*, and of course *Greenwich*, one of our own fifties. We should be able to deal with them.' There was a general growl of agreement from around the table. 'De Kersaint also has three or four frigates, thirty-twos and forty-fours.'

'Is Holbrooke's the latest information?' asked Suckling. 'It's three weeks old by now. I'm sure the convoy won't have sailed, but de Kersaint may have been reinforced.'

'Or he may have lost part of his force,' said Forrest pointedly. 'But you're correct, Suckling, we don't know what's waiting for us, which is why *Medina* will sail as soon as possible to be our eyes and ears. When will you be ready for sea?' he asked, turning to Holbrooke.

'The admiral ordered me to be ready by Tuesday the thirteenth, sir,' he replied, 'but I can sail on Monday. I just need the last of my water and the powder and shot that *Medina* used up on the last cruise.'

'Very well, Holbrooke. My orders will be with you tomorrow at the latest. They'll send you to sea on Monday.'

Holbrooke almost replied with his usual 'aye, aye, sir,' but stopped himself just in time. That wasn't how the captains of King's ships spoke to each other. 'Very well, sir,' he replied.

'Now, the normal station for ships-of-the-line watching Cape François is to windward, here at Monte Christi,' said Forrest, leaning over a chart and pointing to a prominent headland some twelve leagues to the east of the Cape. It was a good place for a blockading force. From there a squadron could intercept anything that came to Cape François from across the Atlantic or from the French possessions in the Eastern Caribbean, and they could pounce on any convoy that left Cape François hoping to take the Caicos Passage. 'That's where we'll meet. The squadron will sail from Port Royal on the twenty-ninth. We all know how difficult the Windward Passage can be, but I'm confident we can be off Monte Christi by the sixth of October. I expect a report on the enemy's strength when I arrive, Mister Holbrooke.'

Holbrooke merely nodded. He had a hundred questions but was unsure how they'd sound in front of a trio of experienced sea-officers, so he confined himself to a single query. 'If I should find that anything substantial has changed, should I return towards Port Royal in the hope of finding you, or should I stay on station?' he asked.

'That's an excellent question,' replied Forrest. 'Ideally, I'd have two frigates or a frigate and a sloop, but the admiral can't spare me another. That being the case, if you see that anything has changed, you're to remain on station and wait for me. If you think it needs to be transmitted urgently, then you may wait for me off the Cape.' Forrest looked uncharacteristically stern. 'However, you must avoid being set to leeward of the Cape. Your station is between Monte Christi and Cape François; nothing is to draw you away from there.' Forrest knew only too well how the lure of fame and prizes could draw a frigate captain away from his duty. He smiled. 'You'll have plenty of opportunities to take prizes when us lumbering old ships-of-the-line have destroyed de Kersaint and the convoy is scattering in confusion with the Bahamas under its lee.'

'And if the French have been reinforced, sir, will you fight, or will you wait for the fourth ship when Admiral Cotes finds one?' asked Langdon.

Holbrooke studied Forrest as the commodore thought for a moment. He appeared to Holbrooke to be attempting to frame his words in the best way, to have the most impact.

'Gentlemen, please don't misconstrue my hesitation. I've given this a lot of thought, and I know very well what we must do. If we hold our position off Monte Christi, then however large the French squadron, they can't ensure the safety of the convoy. In fact, if they chase us, then they leave the convoy prey to all the British privateers in the Caribbean, and of course, we can beat to windward of the Caicos and take them before they're through the passage.

Mere tactics, then, would dictate that we should withdraw to windward if the French force is greater than ours.'

Langdon and Suckling looked blank. They could work out the tactics as well as their commodore, but a retreat in the face of the enemy, however tactically sound, was hardly what they needed to further their own careers.

Forrest saw the expressions on his captains' faces; he was expecting that reaction and had prepared a dramatic finish. 'However, gentlemen, neither our country nor our navy needs a tame withdrawal, not in the year after Minorca,' he nodded in Holbrooke's direction, acknowledging that the lieutenant had been at the Battle of Minorca, 'and not six months after Byng's execution. In this case, I judge that discretion is certainly not the better part of valour. Unless the French have double our force, I intend to stand my ground.'

Langdon and Suckling nodded silently in agreement. Byng's execution was too recent, and it had been too divisive within the navy, exposing the political rift that ran right through the service: this was no time for cheering a bold plan that used the disgrace of Minorca as its foundation. However, it was clear that each of the captains was privately delighted. There was little point in being promoted from a frigate into a ship-of-the-line unless there was the prospect of a fleet or squadron action. What Forrest had not said, the ghost that lurked in every sea-officers mind, was that Britain had taken the momentous step of judicially executing one of its admirals for what amounted to a lack of determination to obey his orders. If an admiral, the son of a peer and a man with political and family ties that ran right through the British establishment, could be executed, then no captain was safe unless he pursued the enemy aggressively, recklessly, even. The execution of Byng cast a long shadow over the navy.

Forrest went on to detail his own supplementary signals for controlling his squadron in battle. They were necessarily few as only a dozen flags were available to use.

He described how they would form line-of-battle, with *Medina* on the disengaged side to repeat signals so that they wouldn't be missed in the smoke of combat.

'Now, gentlemen,' he said with an air of finality, 'it's well known in Port Royal and Kingston, indeed throughout the whole island, that our squadron has a valuable chase in mind. You can expect every damned privateer in Jamaica to follow when we sail. They'll be useful in a way because if this convoy sails, even with its escort destroyed, there will be too many for us to hope to take them all. We can rely upon the privateers to sweep up most of them. You all recall the prize rules where privateers are operating within sight of King's ships?' Holbrooke certainly didn't, and neither did Langdon, but Suckling knew or was clever enough to make it appear that he knew. 'If a privateer takes a prize with a King's ship in sight, then the man-of-war shares in the usual way,' he said, and then added with significance, 'but the reverse isn't true, no privateer shares in our prizes!' Suckling and Langdon thumped the table in agreement, and Holbrooke felt that he must do so also. Forrest had been generous with his rum punch before dinner, with his claret during the meal and with his port after the table had been cleared. The effects were showing on the post-captains, and their hammering on the table would have wakened the dead. Holbrooke was no teetotaler himself, that would have been odd indeed in a sea-officer of the eighteenth century, or any century before or since, but he disliked being drunk. The memory of that interview in the naval academy still lingered.

'Then I believe we should wish success to the privateers,' said Langdon, with real enthusiasm. He'd used some prize money to buy a share in a sleek twelve-gun brig only a month before and sincerely hoped that his investment would pay dividends. So also had Forrest, his earlier condemnation of *damned privateers* was acknowledged as merely a matter of form.

'That being settled we'll meet off Monte Christi in the first week of October. Now, a toast.' He stood unsteadily and paused until his captains had followed him. 'To Monsieur de Kersaint, may he be inclined to come out and fight.'

CHAPTER TWENTY-THREE

Jacques

Monday, twelfth of September 1757
Medina, at Sea. Cape Tiburon, Saint Domingue east fourteen leagues

On Sunday afternoon Holbrooke signalled that he was ready to sail: wooded, watered, stored for three months and with the gunner's top tier of barrels touching the deckhead of the powder room. The commodore signalled affirmative, and *Medina* weighed anchor, hosing off the Port Royal ooze as the cable inched in through the hawse-hole. There was some grumbling among the hands when they realised that the frigate was voluntarily giving up another night at anchor, but it was soon forgotten as the land breeze wafted them down the South Channel and they were able to make an easy reach to the east. If they'd waited until the morning they'd have been forced to tow out of the harbour and down the channel, then the frigate would have faced contrary winds until they were clear of Point Morant at the eastern end of the island. By sailing early, they were clear of Jamaica by the time the easterly set in and could harden their tacks and sheets and make a bold beat into the Windward Passage.

'If this holds we'll be off Monte Christi on Wednesday,' said Holbrooke to Hosking as they passed to leeward of Cape Tiburon.

The master touched the weathered oak of the binnacle. 'Now, sir, let's not tempt fate,' he said and saw an answering grave nod from the quartermaster. Old Eli could tell tales of the malign effect of fate on sailing ships that would make your hair stand on end.

Hosking was having some trouble coming to terms

Chris Durbin

with Holbrooke as the legally appointed captain of *Medina*. It was all very well when Carlisle was onboard – even though sick, in the thralls of a fever, and incapable of commanding – he'd still been the captain, and young Holbrooke was only standing in for a few days. But now the frigate had stored for three months, and although Hosking hadn't seen their orders, he could guess their nature as well as anyone else in Jamaica, and he had to prepare himself to serve under this youngster until December. He had to admit that Holbrooke had done well, but it was unnatural that he should now be under the command of his old colleague's son.

As it happened, Hosking was proved right. The wind backed into the north-northeast, and *Medina* had a tough few days making her way up to Cape St. Nicholas at the northwestern end of Hispaniola. It was 'all hands,' at the turn of every watch to put the ship about and the watch on deck could look forward to an uncomfortable four hours tending the tacks, sheets and bowlines as though their lives depended upon it. By the time *Medina* rounded Cape St. Nicholas and started the hardly-less-difficult passage along the north coast the whole ship's company was tired and grumbling. They passed outside Tortuga – there was no sign of *Greenwich* this time – and made short tacks along the coast until Cape François came into sight, six whole God-forsaken days after they had won their anchor in Port Royal. The wisdom of Commodore Forrest's instruction to stay to windward of the Cape was evident. Any ship set to leeward could take days regaining her station, days in which a convoy could sail, kissing its hand to the blockading ships watching impotently from the leeward.

'We'll look into the anchorage while we're here, Mister Hosking,' said Holbrooke as the cliffs of Cape François loomed out of the morning mist. 'Mister Lynton,' he called to his acting first lieutenant, 'beat to quarters and clear for action.'

'Drummer!' bellowed Lynton, his voice cracking on the last syllable. The young marine hurried to the break of the quarterdeck, adjusting his cross-belts and dropping his sticks in his haste. Sergeant Wilson prided himself on being able to guess when his drummer would be called for, but like all the Medinas, seamen and marines, he was dog-tired and had missed the signals.

Holbrooke watched in a detached manner. Only a few weeks ago he'd been personally responsible for the speed at which the frigate's people went to their stations, and the decks were cleared. Now it was Lynton who strove to impress his new captain, a man with whom he'd shared a mess only fifteen months before. He looked as though the cares of the world were resting on his young shoulders. Holbrooke started to reflect on the harsh life to be expected in the navy and how it was good for young men to be harassed, but then he caught himself on the verge of pomposity – even if it was pomposity of thought.

The familiar headland became more visible as the mist was whisked away on the breeze. Holbrooke could see the battery that had tried its ranging shots against them four weeks before. The view into the bay opened up as the Cape moved to the right of their vision and with a changed perspective became less a prominent headland and more a part of the high bluffs and cliffs that girdled this coast. There was no need to go to the masthead; the anchorage could be plainly seen from the quarterdeck. Holbrooke trained his telescope at the mass of vessels crowding the holding ground in front of the town. Where there were thirty merchantmen a month ago, now there were forty or fifty. The wealth of the French West Indies was gathered in one place, waiting for the end of the hurricane season.

Further to the right, the man-of-war anchorage became visible. At first sight, it looked unchanged. Allowing for the addition of *Greenwich*, the ships appeared not to have moved since Holbrooke last saw them, but something was different. Holbrooke rubbed his eyes and counted again.

In this poor light, it was difficult to tell a ship-of-the-line from a large frigate, and a simple count didn't help because it was unclear whether there were three or four frigates at anchor a month ago. Nevertheless, it looked different. As Holbrooke was attempting to mentally catalogue the enemy ships, he was interrupted by Whittle at the masthead.

'Deck ho!' he called. 'There's an extra two-decker in the anchorage, the one nearest the town wasn't there last time.'

Now that he knew what to look for, it was obvious. Where there had been two ships-of-the-line and three or four frigates, there were now four of the line and three frigates. One of the additions was *Greenwich*, not much larger than a heavy French frigate, but the other was a newcomer.

'Well done, Whittle,' replied Holbrooke.

'Mister Hosking, no closer than two miles to that battery, if you please, then you may come about and take us out to sea. We must make some way to windward.'

'Aye, aye, sir,' replied the sailing master.

'Masthead!' called Holbrooke. 'Do you see anything to seaward?'

'Nothing but a local fisherman, sir, far off.'

'What does she bear?' replied Holbrooke.

'Three points abaft the larboard beam, dead to windward, sir.'

'Mister Hosking, belay my last order; I wish to speak with that fisherman, you may come about now and beat up towards her. I suspect she'll try to slip around us, she's probably not too concerned but not willing to take risks. Nevertheless, I want to catch her.'

It was indeed a long beat. The fisherman became alarmed when it was clear that this British frigate was chasing her. It wasn't usual to make war on fishermen, but the master of this boat was taking no chances, and he tried every trick to slip past the frigate and back towards land. Eventually, in the first dogwatch, the tiny vessel admitted defeat, let its sheets fly and lay wallowing in the swell, the three crewmen looking up in wonderment at the high sides and lofty masts of *Medina* looming above them.

'We're out of sight of watchers on the high land now,' said Holbrooke to a mystified quarterdeck. 'Mister Lynton. Send the cutter to bring the master on board. I'll see him in my cabin.'

Holbrooke paused at the quarterdeck rail. 'And pass the word for the chaplain, I'd be pleased if he could join me.'

Holbrooke tried to relax. This was a whole new adventure for him. He'd never interviewed a Frenchman before, at least he assumed that the man coming aboard would be French. There was a knock, and David Chalmers opened the door to the cabin.

'You passed the word for me, sir,' he said, waiting at the threshold.

'Please come in, Mister Chalmers and take a seat,' replied Holbrooke. It wasn't the challenges of commanding a King's ship that continually ambushed Holbrooke, it was the changed relationships with the officers and people of *Medina*. He and Chalmers had walked ashore together only a week ago and been very easy in each other's company, using each other's Christian names like old friends. But now it was 'sir,' and 'Mister Chalmers,' and would continue to be so until Holbrooke returned the frigate to Captain Carlisle's command.

'In a few minutes the master of the fishing vessel that's alongside us will be brought into the cabin,' said Holbrooke. He looked significantly at the chaplain but was rewarded with a blank face.

'I wasn't aware, I've been in my cabin working on my sermon for tomorrow, but if we're to be joined by a fisherman, then at least I have an excuse for addressing the question of the extraordinary haul of fish on the Sea of Galilee. It'll focus the crew's minds if we have an actual fisherman among us.' It was always tricky to know when the chaplain was joking, he had such a deadpan face.

'Sadly, he'll only be with us for a few hours, and he'll miss your sermon,' said Holbrooke with a grin. The thought of the master of a French fishing boat joining them for divine service amused him.

'An opportunity missed,' said Chalmers without any change of expression. 'In which case, how may I help you, sir?'

'With your command of French, if you please,' said Holbrooke. Chalmers bowed in response.

'I want to know the names of the French men-of-war at Cape François, and I'm hoping, with the aid of your excellent command of the language, that our friend in the boat will tell us.'

'What inducement do you propose?' asked Chalmers. 'I don't recommend coercion; apart from the moral issues, it'll probably lead him to tell you whatever he thinks you want to hear, rather than the truth.'

'Have no fear, Chalmers, I plan to offer gold or at least a moderate amount of silver. I have no *Louis d'or* nor do I have any *écus*, but I do have some Spanish coin that Don Alonso insisted on giving me for my expenses in St. Augustine.' He showed Chalmers a handful of assorted coins, some small gold ones and some silver coins the size of a half-crown. Chalmers gazed at them dubiously, attempting to determine their value, and more importantly what they would be worth to a French fisherman.

'English coin would be inadvisable, I imagine,' said Chalmers, fingering one of the silver pieces, 'although at least then we'd know the value of the bribe that we're offering. How much to betray your country?' he mused.

'Oh, of course, you weren't on deck. The fishermen look like they're freed slaves, at least they aren't native Frenchmen. The question is, how much loyalty does a sometime slave have to his erstwhile masters?'

They were interrupted by a knock on the door and

Lynton ushered in a most surprising figure. The man was clearly of African origin; he was tall, as tall as Holbrooke, and well-made. He wasn't above thirty years of age, and he carried himself with dignity, removing a straw hat as he stooped to enter the cabin and holding it casually by his side. He was dressed in old cotton clothes, patched but not ragged. The only jarring note was his bare feet which looked out of place in a man of such apparent consequence.

Holbrooke's first impression was that the person in front of him was wasted as a fisherman. His second thought was that he reminded Holbrooke of somebody that he knew. It was when the man bowed, that it came to him. The fisherman had the same grave, almost superior yet outwardly deferential demeanour as Black Rod. They could be twins, separated by race and nationality. If the man was concerned about being brought aboard an enemy frigate, it didn't show in either his face or his bearing.

Although Holbrooke could speak French reasonably well, he knew that his command of the language didn't match the chaplain's and that any nuances in the fisherman's replies would elude him. He addressed the man in English and then paused to allow Chalmers to translate into fluent French.

'Good evening, Captain,' he started. 'I regret that we may have startled you and apologise if you've been driven too far to windward. Please sit down.'

The fisherman waited for the translation, with no apparent understanding of Holbrooke's invitation, except for an intelligent return of Holbrooke's gaze. His stillness was almost pedantic, it must have been evident from Holbrooke's gestures that he was being offered a seat. If he knew any English, he was hiding it well. When Chalmers repeated Holbrooke's opening words in French, the fisherman made no reply, only responding with a short, non-committal bow. He sat in the chair that he was offered and looked directly at Holbrooke, his face impassive, waiting to hear why he'd been detained.

'I am Lieutenant Holbrooke of the British frigate *Medina*. May I ask your name?'

The fisherman paused for a moment after Chalmers had delivered the translated question as if he was deciding whether to reply, or perhaps he was composing an assumed name. Holbrooke was sure that he didn't want to give his real name, and he couldn't blame him for that. The fishing boat also had no name and probably no papers. There would be no trail of identity to be followed.

The fisherman still held Holbrooke's eyes, he'd hardly cast a glance at Chalmers. '*Jacques*,' he said. '*Je m'appelle Jacques*,' he repeated with a hint of finality, a decision made. He was testing the name, willing Holbrooke to challenge him, and he was fixing it in his own mind so that he shouldn't forget it.

'Would you care for some refreshment?' asked Holbrooke, 'rum or brandy, or perhaps you prefer beer or wine?'

'Brandy, if you please, sir,' he replied in French. Rum would be readily available to a freed slave in Saint Domingue, but Brandy was for Frenchmen. He wasn't about to pass up this opportunity.

Smart served the brandy. He was a good servant, as good as most and better than some who shipped as captain's stewards in frigates. But he lacked any real social grace and Holbrooke had the strange sensation that Jacques was assessing the standard of the Smart's service and not being wholly impressed.

Holbrooke started by asking about the fishing. Was it good? Had he made a satisfactory catch? The fisherman answered freely in between sips of his brandy. He appeared familiar with the spirit, familiar enough to know that it was best when warmed by the heat from his hand and savoured in small quantities. The conversation moved on to the weather, then what port did he sail from? Did he own the boat?

The man was apparently waiting for Holbrooke to reach the point of the conversation. He was no fool and knew that this majestic frigate wouldn't waste its time interviewing a poor fisherman without good reason.

His story came out piece by piece. His boat sailed out of a tiny fishing port, just a haul-out on a beach really, across the bay from the man-of-war anchorage at Cape François. He'd been born a slave on a plantation in the hills behind the town, but he'd never worked in the fields, having been taken as a household servant at an early age. He'd risen to the heights of major-domo in his master's household.

Holbrooke guessed that was why he so intently watched Smart serving the brandy; it was professional interest.

Jacques continued. When his master died, he was surprised to find that he'd been willed his freedom. But it was a dubious privilege, with no money and the enmity of his master's family, who weren't pleased to lose such a valuable slave. He'd fled the town and became a fisherman. With no family to support, he was able to accumulate a little money and had, after several years, bought this boat. But it was proving difficult to keep the vessel seaworthy. It needed new frames, and several of the planks were on the point of springing; it was a specialist job, and he didn't have the money to pay for it. Perhaps he'd soon have to find another employment.

'Is he softening me up before the negotiation?' wondered Holbrooke, 'has he guessed that he's about to be offered money for information?' Holbrooke found it challenging to reach the point where he asked the hard questions, and there was no doubt that this man knew they were coming. He'd probably even deduced what they were.

'We saw several fine French ships in the man-of-war anchorage, have they been there long?'

Jacques gave Holbrooke a half-smile; they both knew

that the crux of the conversation had been reached. The fisherman said nothing, he just turned down the corners of his mouth and rotated his hand about the wrist in a typically gallic equivocal response. The same motion that *Medina's* doctor used when discussing whether a leg would have to be amputated.

Holbrooke saw that subtlety would lead nowhere. 'Monsieur Jacques,' he said, leaning a little closer and looking directly at the fisherman, 'I would like information regarding those ships. I need to know their names, that is all, and I'm prepared to pay for the information.' He opened the desk drawer and withdrew seven small gold coins while Chalmers translated.

Holbrooke spread the coins in a neat row on the desk in front of himself. 'Here are seven gold pieces, one for each ship's name. Only the three of us need ever know that we've spoken. Now, can we do business?'

Jacques returned Holbrooke's gaze and paused for the span of half a dozen heartbeats, then slowly reached his hand across the table. He carefully, almost delicately, slid one piece of gold towards himself with his fingertip, testing Holbrooke's reaction. '*L'Intrépide,*' he said, enunciating the word carefully so that he was understood.

'A seventy-four,' said Holbrooke to Chalmers, nodding his encouragement.

Jacques also nodded, almost as though he understood what Holbrooke had said. '*Le vaisseau de pavillon,*' the fisherman added. The flagship. Jacques slid another piece over the desk towards himself, more confident now '*Le Sceptre.*' Another seventy-four of the same class as *L'Intrépide.*

He moved the third piece, '*L'Opiniâtre.*' Holbrooke wasn't sure, but he thought she was a sixty-four.

A fourth piece was moved halfway across the table, Jacques kept it under his finger as he continued, '*Le petit bateau anglais, je ne connais pas le nom.*' He watched Holbrooke with a strange intensity, as though testing him.

Holbrooke reached across and moved the gold piece to join the others in front of Jacques and nodded for him to continue.

'*L'Outarde, Le Sauvage, Le Licorne, toutes frégates,*' Jacques said positively, moving the remaining pieces towards himself. He explained that *Outarde* had been stripped of her cannon and used as a transport. '*Armée en flûte,*' he said, but they were re-arming her with guns taken from the merchantmen and making up her establishment with artillerymen from the forts.

Holbrooke knew that the French were running out of merchant ships to use as transports, and they had men-of-war lying idle for want of men. The logic of stripping their larger frigates was inescapable.

'*C'est tout,*' Jacques ended, and carefully stacked the seven coins, one on top of the other. That would be half a year's profit for a boat such as his; it would pay for a moderate refit and perhaps keep him at sea for another few years.

'Do you have a small bag that I could place the coins in, please,' asked Jacques, speaking in French.

'I should have thought of that,' said Holbrooke to Chalmers. 'I expect he'd rather hide the extent of his good fortune from his crew.' Both Holbrooke and Chalmers caught the flicker of intelligence on the fisherman's face as he heard this speech in English. Surely he knew at least something of the language, but in a split-second, his face returned to its closed imperturbable expression.

Holbrooke paused. He could easily ask the purser to bring him one of the many small canvas bags that he used for his money. However, on an impulse, Holbrooke opened the desk drawer and emptied the remaining coins from the draw-string purse that Don Alonso had given him and offered it to the fisherman. He wouldn't have been able to explain why he did that; the bag was of beautiful, made from soft leather dyed red with a design of laurel leaves embossed in gold around its lips. It had an intrinsic value and wasn't the sort of possession that a poor freed slave would typically own. Jacques received it with a lift of his eyebrow but without further comment. He slid six of the gold coins into the purse and then looped his belt through the drawstring and tucked it inside his loose trousers. The seventh gold coin he put carefully into his trouser pocket. It was a curious gesture of trust. Holbrooke had the information that he needed and could easily have let the fishing boat's crew know that there was not one, but seven gold pieces to be shared. For that matter, he could have recovered his money and sent the fisherman over the side empty-handed. He was touched. He'd made some sort of connection with this strange man, an odd meeting of minds between two people of such different backgrounds and with such a vast discrepancy in their likely futures. He'd have given another gold piece to know what Chalmers was thinking, but the chaplain's face was, as always, unreadable. Holbrooke briefly wondered whether he'd ever be able to claim his money back from the clerks at the Navy Board.

For five long weeks, *Medina* ploughed her lonely furrow between Monte Christi and Cape François. If she approached too near the battery on the Cape, she was warned off by a ranging shot. Once, she was forced to withdraw to windward when *Sauvage* and *Licorne* came out to chase him off, but they didn't pursue him far to windward.

Otherwise, the French admiral ignored the frigate's presence. It was the height of the hurricane season, so there was little shipping, just a few coasters that slipped into Cape François when *Medina* was well out to sea. No additional merchantmen joined the convoy that lay patiently at anchor behind the protective reefs and banks. The fishermen still put to sea, and they saw Jacques' boat once, beating back to the tiny port across the bay from the anchorage. The hurricane season created a curious interlude in the year's activity. For the merchantmen that plied between Europe and the West Indies, it was a time to swing at anchor, to fill up with the produce of the country that was brought in by the smaller local vessels, and to watch the weather signs. No owner would allow his ships to sail in August or September and the underwriters pushed up the premiums so high from late July to early October that only those with the most pressing financial incentive would stir from their safe harbours. Even then, a severe hurricane could clear an anchorage, dragging anchors to push even well-found ships onto the shore. Navies, too, observed the restrictions of the season and kept their battle squadrons in the safety of the established ports. But not so for the cruisers, the fourth, fifth and sixth rates and the sloops and cutters. They braved the elements and put to sea on their usual business.

In the last week of September Hosking reported the tell-tale signs of an approaching hurricane. *Medina* battened the hatches, sent down the upper yards and prepared as best she could to survive her second tropical storm in one year. They saw the high clouds massing in the east and felt the first hot gusts from the north. But the wind backed rapidly – it was evident that they were in the safe sector – and blew no more than a strong gale. Within twenty-four hours the hurricane had passed innocently to the north of the Caicos Islands and Bahamas and expended itself on the low-lying coasts of Florida and Georgia.

Chris Durbin

CHAPTER TWENTY-FOUR

Council of War

Friday, twenty-first of October 1757
Medina, at Sea. Off Cape François, Saint Domingue

Forrest's squadron caught the last of the westerly wind, the legacy of the second hurricane of the season, to round Cape St. Nicholas and run down to their station between Monte Christi and Cape François. They were patrolling now, in rigid line ahead: *Dreadnought* in the van, *Augusta* flying Forrest's pennant in the centre and *Edinburgh* in the rear. As usual, they'd moved closer to the Cape overnight and now lay just a few miles to windward of *Medina*. The frigate was in her customary position now that the squadron had arrived, patrolling off the bank that enclosed the bay and harbour of Cape François. Holbrooke had ordered his ship to clear for action an hour before twilight and now the hands were at their quarters, those with no immediate responsibilities dozing at their guns and sail handling stations. This had been *Medina's* morning watch routine since she arrived five weeks ago, and the hands were thoroughly used to it. The challenge for Holbrooke's officers was to ensure that the ship was ready for immediate action while letting her people get as much rest as possible. It was hard enough getting sufficient sleep in a watch-and-watch-about routine that was overlaid with the occasional 'all hands' for sail changing, without the need to spend an hour each day at quarters.

The rising sun was just starting to tinge the sky in the east. The land breeze had failed sometime in the middle watch, and now the familiar northeaster filled *Medina's* topsails and leaned her over a strake or two. The ships in the anchorage would soon be visible, and Holbrooke was

248

looking impatiently into the leeward darkness, hoping in vain to see what the masthead lookout couldn't.

'The wind will freshen, I believe, sir,' said Hosking, sniffing to windward. It was one of the sailing master's conceits, to set himself up as a wind seer. In fact, it was a near-certainty that the wind would increase as the sun rose. At this time of the year, nothing short of another tropical cyclone could disturb the trade wind, and with the land heating as the sun rose, the great rush of wind from the sea to the shore would reinforce it, and they'd be taking in a reef by noon.

'I think it may,' replied Holbrooke, hoping that Hosking wouldn't start one of his long homilies on wind forecasting. Holbrooke's only concern at the moment was to know whether today was to be the day that the French convoy sailed, or when de Kersaint's squadron chose to come out and offer battle. If he were the French commander, he told himself, he'd throw his four of the line and three frigates against Forrest's three of the line and *Medina* and clear the way for the convoy. The odds were clearly in de Kersaint's favour and with Forrest's squadron defeated or dispersed, the French merchantmen would only have to worry about the British privateers, three or four of which had been loitering to the east for the past few weeks. However, he wouldn't offer battle until the convoy was ready to sail so that the mass of merchantmen could escape through the Caicos Passage before the British squadron could recover from what would undoubtedly be a bruising encounter.

'Deck there!' shouted the lookout, 'I think I can see sails just becoming visible, more than one ship, sir.'

Holbrooke looked hard into the gloom. The speed with which sunrise in the tropics chased away the darkness was always a surprise, and it was only a moment before Holbrooke too could see movement in the harbour. Men-of-war or merchantmen, that was the question, but

Holbrooke was sure that he already knew the answer.

'Hoist '*Enemy in Sight*,' Mister Smith.' He watched as the flags ran swiftly up the halyard. The midshipman must have had them bent on and ready to go whenever they came close in at dawn. That was an intelligent move by the young man.

'Mister Lynton, two guns to windward.' Forrest wouldn't be able to see the flags yet, but he'd hear the two guns, and that was the poor-visibility signal that the enemy was coming out.

By the time the signal had been hoisted and the guns fired, the French ships were in plain sight. It was indeed the battle squadron. The two seventy-fours were followed by the sixty-four and *Greenwich*, then the three frigates. They were a brave sight, sailing close hauled to weather the Cape as they made for the Great Pass between the natural barrier of the banks and Cape François itself.

'Masthead, do you see any movement among the merchantmen?' Holbrooke called.

'No sir, they're all at anchor with their yards hoisted and their sails furled,' replied Whittle. 'They look the same as yesterday,' and in a lower voice, meant for his friends in the maintop, 'and the day before, and the day before that.'

'Set a course to beat up to windward of the flagship, Mister Hosking. Unless we get any further orders, we must take up our station for repeating signals.'

Medina swung to starboard, her bows as close to the wind as could be contrived. She heeled over another few strakes as the spray started to come in over the bow.

'T'gallants, Mister Hosking.'

The master frowned; the wind was just over his self-imposed limit for setting the topmost sails. The bosun, however, had anticipated his captain's next order and the topmen were poised to run out and cast off the gaskets.

'Close the larboard port-lids,' shouted Lynton down to the guns. He could see that the gun ports would be perilously close to the waves once all the sails started to draw. Frigates carried their main battery much higher than ships-of-the-line, but even for frigates there came a time when prudence dictated that they should be closed.

Medina heeled even further. The frigate's lee chains were touching the waves, and her stem was parting the water and throwing it out in a broad white swath.

Holbrooke looked over his shoulder, back towards the harbour. It was an imposing sight. The two big seventy-fours had just made the turn around the smaller of the inner banks, *Le Petit Mouton*, and were reaching towards the Cape past the larger bank, *Le Grande Mouton*. Each ship shook out its t'gallants in succession as it came off the wind. Holbrooke nodded in appreciation. 'De Kersaint must be sure of his squadron's seamanship to be crowding on sail in that fashion before he's through the Great Pass, those are damnably confined waters,' he said to Hosking and Lynton. There was something majestic about the *Intrépide* and *Sceptre*, some quality of form and function that British shipbuilders had failed to emulate. They weren't new ships, they'd been built as a class of three and were all launched at Brest back in '47 at the height of the last war. Only these two were left in French hands. The third, *Monarque*, had served only a few months before she was taken by Hawke off Finisterre and brought into British service as *Monarch*.

Holbrooke remembered that it was on the quarterdeck of *Monarch* in March of that year, just seven months ago, that Admiral Byng had been executed for *failing to do his utmost in the face of the enemy*. Holbrooke had been present at the Battle of Minorca as a master's mate in command of *Fury's Prize*, a small barca-longa, running errands between the ships-of-the-line and the frigates. He'd been privileged to have a grandstand view of the battle, and even now he couldn't say whether the British or the French had the best of the day. What he *did* know was that Byng's eventual fate had been determined at the council-of-war after the battle, where the assembled captains endorsed his decision to withdraw to Gibraltar for repairs. That left the French navy in command of the Western Mediterranean, free to protect the transports that resupplied de Richelieu's army at Fort St. Phillip. That decision sealed Minorca's fate and, eventually, Byng's.

When *Medina* had found her station on the windward side of Forrest's flagship, the squadron tacked to the northeast in line-of-battle, going about in succession so that each ship passed through the water that the one ahead had just vacated. It must have been evident to de Kersaint that the British commodore wasn't refusing battle, he was just choosing where he wished to fight. Forrest wanted to be well clear of Cape François with plenty of sea-room and no hostile harbour right under his lee.

'The commodore signals '*lie-to with heads to the west*' and '*all captains*,' sir,' reported midshipman Smith. That was a surprise. Forrest's conference in Port Royal and his written instructions seemed to cover all eventualities.

The bosun was already hauling the cutter alongside, and Jackson was hurrying the boat's crew over the side. Speed was necessary because Holbrooke should undoubtedly be the first captain on the deck of the flagship, being immeasurably junior to the other two. Naval protocol insisted that no senior officer should ever have to await the coming of a junior.

It was a short but choppy pull across to the flagship. *Edinburgh's* boat having less distance to row would have beaten them, but Holbrooke saw Langdon ordering his coxswain to pull slowly to let the frigate's boat hook onto the chains first.

Holbrooke waited for Suckling and Langdon at the entry port. He could see that de Kersaint had already rounded the Great Bank and was standing out to sea. Forrest had also noticed the French moves and had no time to waste; he chose not to leave his quarterdeck.

The three captains ascended the ladder to be met with a

brief handshake. It was a dramatic scene; Holbrooke was standing to one side with Forrest to his left and Suckling and Langdon to his right. Between them he could see the French line – four two-deckers butting into the sea, their gun ports already open and their yards chained and puddened. Two of them were superb seventy-fours, superior in firepower and sailing qualities to any of Forrest's squadron. Beyond them, he could see the three frigates, each one larger than *Medina*. It seemed ridiculous that Forrest should even consider engaging them. Surely he'd withdraw to windward, rather than accept a fight.

'Well, gentlemen, you see they're come out to engage us,' said Forrest without any sort of introduction. He looked eager, as though he just wanted a positive response from his captains.

'I think it'd be a pity to disappoint them,' replied Suckling, smiling broadly.

'Aye, that it would,' said Langdon in agreement.

Holbrooke felt that it wasn't his place to speak. *Medina* may have to fight the frigates, but that was an entirely different undertaking to the line of battle. Each of these captains was committing himself to take his ship into action with little opportunity for manoeuvre and with the unspoken contract that he personally would walk his quarterdeck with nothing between himself and the thirty-two-pound shot and canister that would sweep his deck.

'Very well,' replied Forrest, 'then I shall detain you no longer, go back to your ships.' He turned to Holbrooke, 'stay a few moments, if you please, Captain.'

Before Suckling and Langdon had left the quarterdeck, he called to the signal midshipman, 'make the signal for the line of battle and when that's been acknowledged, bend on another signal to bear away to engage the enemy.'

With a brief handshake, Suckling and Langdon returned to the entry port and to the wailing of the pipes, they dropped down into their boats. They'd been on the deck of the flagship for less than two minutes.

253

Holbrooke wasn't sure what he'd just witnessed. Was it a council-of-war? If so, it was the shortest that he'd ever heard of. Was it an exercise in sharing the blame if the day should turn out badly, a cynical yardarm-clearer? If so, then Forrest must know that the backing of a council-of-war hadn't swayed the members of Byng's court-martial board. They had correctly determined that the orders that sent Byng's fleet into the Mediterranean had been his own orders and that only the admiral was responsible for their fulfilment. Or perhaps Forrest quite genuinely wanted a final word with his captains before leading them into what he knew would be a hard fight with the odds against them. Maybe he wanted reassurance that their hearts were in it.

'Well, Mister Holbrooke,' said Forrest when the other captains had left, 'I just need a few words with you. It's easy for those fellows, they have only to obey my orders, stay in line and hammer the enemy. I need a little more from you.'

'Yes, sir,' Holbrooke could think of nothing more to add.

'The first point is that I need you to windward of me to relay signals. We have the weather gage, and I don't intend to give it up without a good reason. You must station yourself where you can best see my flags and where *Dreadnought* and *Edinburgh* can see yours. Be fast in relaying them and above all be accurate!'

That much didn't really need saying, every frigate captain knew his role in a squadron action. Forrest went on to talk about *Medina* being ready to embark the flag if *Augusta* should be severely damaged, to tow any ship out of the line if required, and to put a prize crew into a captured enemy. These again were quite ordinary tasks of a frigate.

'But last, Holbrooke, you must be ready to defend yourself against his frigates. If I were de Kersaint and had three frigates to hand, I'd place two for the normal frigate tasks, and I'd send the forty-four – *Outarde* – I believe?'

'Yes sir, *Outarde*. She's been armed *en flûte* as a transport, but de Kersaint has taken guns from an Indiaman that was in the harbour and from the forts to fill every gun port. He's also taken sailors from the merchantmen and soldiers from the garrison. I believe she now has a full complement of guns and men.'

'I'd send the forty-four to engage you. So, beware! Now I know that you're a bit of a spitfire but remember your primary tasks. I must have you in position to relay my signals, and I must have you ready to tow any of us out of action. Your own safety and any desire that you have to take on a heavy frigate, are secondary concerns.'

CHAPTER TWENTY-FIVE

The Battle

Friday, twenty-first of October 1757
Medina, at Sea. Off Cape François, Saint Domingue

Forrest's squadron bore away in line ahead and then tacked in succession so that the enemy was to leeward and on the squadron's starboard bow. *Dreadnought* was leading, *Augusta* with the pennant was in the centre, and *Edinburgh* brought up the rear. Holbrooke had a good view from his station to windward of the squadron where from the quarterdeck of *Medina* he could see all three of Forrest's squadron, and they could see his relayed flag signals. So far there was no smoke and no confusion to hide either the flags or their meanings, but it was important that the squadron should get used to looking at the frigate for their signals so that it would be natural to do so in the heat of battle.

The two squadrons moved closer together, each on the larboard tack. Simmonds noted that the course was east-southeast and that the British line was bearing down upon the enemy. At twenty minutes past three, the first shot was fired as *Intrépide* tried a ranging shot against *Dreadnought*. It fell short, and so did the next, the third pitched up well but was poorly pointed. The French admiral was satisfied that he was within range of his enemy and within fifteen minutes all the ships were engaged in a furious cannonade.

'Mister Simmonds!' shouted Holbrooke. The noise of the battle even at this range and in these first few minutes was loud enough to make normal conversation difficult on *Medina's* deck. 'Make a note that at twenty minutes past three the action commenced. The French line consists of *Intrépide* in the van, then *Greenwich* followed by *Opiniâtre* and *Sceptre* in the rear.'

Simmonds rested his notebook on the binnacle and scratched away, occasionally checking the time from his watch.

It was difficult to see what was happening, but Forrest's ships were all still in line. Although holes were appearing in their sails, they hadn't lost any masts or yards – yet.

'I'm surprised that de Kersaint even allows *Greenwich* into the line,' said Hosking. 'Her scantlings can't stand against any of our ships, and her fifty guns won't make much difference.'

'Yes,' replied Holbrooke, 'but she's protected by a seventy-four ahead and a sixty-four astern. She's as safe there as anywhere and that allows *Sceptre* to overlap *Edinburgh*. It'll be hard fighting in the rear.'

'Sir, I've noted the disposition of the frigates,' said Simmonds. '*Sauvage* is leading alongside the flag, *Licorne* in the centre and *Outarde* in the rear. Is that correct?'

'It is Mister Simmonds,' said Holbrooke trying to pierce the smoke that was now obscuring the frigates, 'or at least that was correct twenty minutes ago. Can you see them, Mister Hosking?'

'No, sir. The last glimpse that I had, they were in perfect order. Following along like lambs.'

'Who's at the masthead, Mister Lynton?' asked Holbrooke.

'It's Whittle, sir,' replied the first lieutenant, and under his breath, 'it's more than my life's worth to send someone else up there.'

'Masthead Ho!' shouted Holbrooke.

'Quarterdeck Ho!' replied Whittle, his voice easily piercing the din of the battle to leeward.

'Can you see the frigates?'

There was a slight pause as Whittle looked again over the smoke cloud. 'Not now sir. I have the occasional view of them when the smoke thins. They were still closed up in line ahead two minutes ago.'

'Let me know when you can see them again,' replied Holbrooke.

'I'd give a lot to know what orders that damned great forty-four has,' said Holbrooke to Lynton. 'Surely they have enough frigates without her? I wouldn't be surprised to see her tacking around the rear soon. Then we'll have our own battle.'

Lynton rubbed his hands. He'd become the sort of fighting sailor who enjoys combat for its own sake. A fight with a French frigate, even one mounting forty-four guns, was something to be eagerly anticipated. Holbrooke recognised the passions that moved his acting first lieutenant. He didn't share them, but he understood them.

'What on earth is *Greenwich* up to?' asked Hosking. 'Her bowsprit's almost over the flagship's taffrail.'

Holbrooke turned his telescope to the head of the line. He had a good view of *Dreadnought* and beyond as the smoke was being blown away from the British line onto the French. Through the murk, he could see *Intrépide* with the ex-British fifty-gun fourth-rate *Greenwich* very close astern and apparently running her bowsprit over the flagship's quarterdeck and into her mizzen rigging. De Kersaint's ship was yawing badly, trying to escape from *Greenwich*, but unsure which way to turn. Her gunnery had almost ceased in the confusion as the gun crews attempted to sort out the mess of yards, sails and rigging that encumbered her decks. Seeing his opportunity, Suckling's *Dreadnought* moved closer to *Intrépide*, concentrating her gunnery on de Kersaint's ship and completely ignoring *Greenwich*.

'That's right,' said Holbrooke, 'don't interfere with *Greenwich*, she appears to be on our side.'

Hosking gave a single bark of a laugh. 'Now look at *Intrépide*, she's falling out of her station; she can't take much more of that battering from *Dreadnought*.'

'And there's *Opiniâtre* moving up to the van to replace her,' said Lynton. 'Good God, *Greenwich* is having a go at her now!'

Sure enough, as *Intrépide* fell away to leeward, her rigging badly mauled, *Opiniâtre* could be seen through the smoke moving up to overtake *Greenwich* to windward. That was the correct move of course because *Sceptre* with her seventy-four guns was still at the rear of the French line and still substantially undamaged. However, *Opiniâtre's* shrewd move was frustrated when *Greenwich* luffed clumsily to get clear of *Intrépide* and came head-to-wind, the remains of her bowsprit raking along the sixty-four's side as she passed, damaging the lanyards for the shrouds and unhinging port-lids.

Dreadnought now moved ahead of the disabled group, pressed from astern by his commodore and their most powerful ship *Edinburgh*. These two took advantage of the confusion at the head of the French line and poured broadside after broadside into the tangled group. Through the smoke, it became evident that *Intrépide* was disabled and had nothing further to contribute to the battle.

'Deck Ho,' shouted Whittle from the masthead. 'One of the frigates is moving up to the head of the line. It looks like she's going to take the lead Frenchman in tow.'

'Very good,' replied Holbrooke, 'watch the other frigates.'

It looked like *Sceptre*, rather than holding her position, was intent upon joining the melée at the head of the line, firing to windward as she passed the other ships of her squadron. However, *Edinburgh* clung to her and matched the French ship gun for gun with such ferocity that *Sceptre* too was forced to leeward.

'Are they withdrawing?' asked Hosking in astonishment.

'It certainly looks that way,' replied Holbrooke. 'Damn this smoke, I can't see what they're doing.'

'Whittle! What can you see of the French line?' Holbrooke called up to the masthead.

'*Intrépide's* being towed to leeward, sir. *Opiniâtre's* being engaged by the commodore, and it looks like the second smaller frigate is moving up to take her in tow.' There was a short pause, then Whittle resumed. '*Greenwich* is in irons, and *Sceptre* and *Edinburgh* are still fighting in the rear.'

'Suckling's trying to double back to have another go at *Intrépide*,' said Hosking, 'but he's having difficulty bearing away with so much damage aloft.'

Before their eyes, the French line was dissolving into disorder. The flagship was being towed out of battle, *Greenwich* was in a sorry state with her bowsprit dragging over her bows, and the last two in the line were feeling the weight of Forrest's and Langdon's broadsides.

'Deck Ho! The big frigate has tacked and is trying to get around the rear of our line,' shouted Whittle. 'I can see her clearly now.'

Holbrooke could feel all the eyes of the quarterdeck upon him, willing him to order their course reversed to take on *Outarde*. There was a feeling of fighting madness around him, a sense that they had been cheated of a battle, that the ships-of-the-line were getting all the glory. The pressure was becoming intense, and it was Hosking who crumpled first.

'Shall I order the ship about, sir?'

Holbrooke punished him by pausing for a few seconds before answering and then doing so with a flat negative.

'No, Mister Hosking, hold your course,' he replied firmly.

Holbrooke could sense the disappointment as he stared to leeward towards the end of the line, hoping to see *Outarde* come out of the smoke. Whittle could see the French frigate from the masthead, but he had the advantage of looking over the bank of smoke.

Holbrooke considered whether he should explain his decision, but he knew the answer before the question was fully formed. He'd command *Medina* for at least a month more. So far, he'd avoided offering a running commentary on his decision, and he didn't want to start down that slippery path. In any case, his officers, if they let their blood cool a little, could see the reason. The battle wasn't yet over, *Medina* was Forrest's only frigate, and the commodore may call for him at any moment. *Outarde* couldn't possibly get around the line and beat up to *Medina* in less than half an hour, and there was plenty of time to worry about her should she do so.

The battle had turned decidedly in favour of the British squadron. The French were withdrawing towards Cape François, both *Intrépide* and *Opiniâtre* under tow by the two smaller frigates, while *Sceptre* covered their retreat. As Holbrooke watched, he saw *Outarde* haul her wind and follow; whether that was in response to a signal from de Kersaint or whether it was her own initiative, he couldn't tell. In any case, it was the right move because the ships-of-the-line were all leaving the battle and a forty-four-gun frigate would be horribly exposed against the four British ships.

Now was the time for Forrest to order a general chase and inflict a severe defeat on the French. Holbrooke could see that Smith had the repeat flags ready to be hoisted and was fingering them longingly. However, the next flag from the commodore was entirely different, and it ordered *Medina* to close *Dreadnought* and tow her out of the line. It wasn't only the French ships that had suffered, and with the smoke receding and chasing the French to leeward, Holbrooke could see the extent of the damage to Forrest's squadron. *Dreadnought* was in no fit state to pursue the French. Suckling had lost his mizzen topmast and his mizzen yard and as he watched the main topmast fell taking the maintop with it, the whole tangled mess dragging alongside and bringing her before the wind. Urgent action was required to prevent her being blown down towards Cape François, where the French army would make short work of her. *Augusta* was hardly in a better state. Although the flagship hadn't lost any significant masts or yards, every sail was shot through, and even from this range, Holbrooke could see the parted lines trailing in the breeze. *Edinburgh* appeared to have suffered the least and had tacked to chase *Outarde*, but there was little chance of the third-rate catching the smaller and faster frigate.

'Mister Hosking. Take us down to *Dreadnought*,' said Holbrooke in a conversational tone. It was necessary to re-establish a sense of calm before they embarked upon the difficult task of towing a two-decker off a lee shore.

'Mister Lynton prepare to tow aft.'

'Aye, aye, sir,' replied the master's mate sheepishly. At least he realised that he'd been guilty of letting the fighting madness carry him away; few others had yet regained their normal senses. Holbrooke could only hope that he'd learned his lesson.

Holbrooke understood them, all those men looking longingly at the French frigate sailing away unmolested. He empathised with them, and that was half the problem. Back in Port Royal, the people of the ships-of-the-line would show their scars and boast of their bravery, listing the dead and the terrible wounds as evidence that they had been in a fleet action. All that the Medinas would be able to offer was a lame story of scouting for the enemy and relaying signals. But that was the essential balance of life in the navy. The frigates had the day-to-day glory of single-ship actions and the hard cash from prizes taken, while the battle fleet swung at anchor losing men to the diseases that the shore wafted towards them. But when the fate of nations was decided in the clash of battle fleets, the frigates could only sit on the sidelines while the grown-ups traded savage blows that reverberated through the corridors of power in faraway Europe.

Holbrooke would take the frigates while he could, the line-of-battle could wait. He turned away to supervise *Medina* earning her keep. It was an interesting problem, manoeuvring a frigate of five hundred and eighty-seven tons to tow a fourth rate of nearly twice her weight off a lee shore. It took all the attention of Holbrooke, Hosking and Lynton to achieve it. By the time *Medina* and *Dreadnought* were making way to the north, Cape François was only a league to leeward and Forrest's remaining two ships were a mile to windward with the trade wind on their starboard bows.

Chris Durbin

CHAPTER TWENTY-SIX

Hope Frustrated

Saturday, twenty-second of October 1757
Medina, at Sea. Off Cape François, Saint Domingue

Holbrooke looked back at *Medina* from the stern of the cutter which Jackson was steering towards *Augusta*. His frigate looked perfect, under easy sail while the gentlest of breezes from the east gave her just enough steerage-way to straighten the tow and keep *Dreadnought's* head to the north. She could do with some paint on her topsides, and her canvas was worn and bleached by the tropical sun, but otherwise, she was in excellent condition, and she still had provisions for six weeks.

He turned away to look at the squadron, and the contrast was startling. Their people had laboured hard overnight, but the scars of battle were there to be seen. *Edinburgh* was the least damaged, but even her sails were pockmarked by shot holes, her shrouds showed visible new splices, and some of the yards had been fished. He could see where her starboard side had been badly mauled, but she still showed two long, even rows of gun ports. The sixty-four, the most powerful ship in the squadron, could fight another action at a few minutes notice. *Augusta* was in a worse state. She appeared unable to set any sail on her foremast, she desperately needed to bend on a new main topsail, and there were several great holes in her sides where the enemy shot had carried away the planking and timbers between adjacent gun ports, making huge, irregular holes where two neat gun ports had been before. She had no undamaged boats at all. In fact, she had no boats that could reasonably be repaired at sea. *Augusta* needed the services of a dockyard before she could be considered an

264

effective fighting unit, and that meant a return to Port Royal.

But neither *Augusta* nor *Edinburgh* had suffered as severely as *Dreadnought*. Holbrooke looked up at her sides towering above the cutter. Suckling's sixty-gun fourth-rate had been first into action and had soaked up the worst that *Intrépide* and *Greenwich* could throw at her. Holbrooke had seen her main-topmast and maintop fall towards the end of the battle, and at that point she'd already lost her mizzen topmast and mizzen yard. She hadn't yet managed to set any sail aft of the foremast, and even forward it had just been the forestaysail and jib to help keep her bows off the wind. He could see a hive of activity as the mizzen yard was being hoisted; that at least would give Suckling a balanced rig. If he could contrive to raise his main yard onto what was left of the mast and set up backstays on his foremast so that he could carry square sails for'ard, he'd have a reasonable chance of sailing unaided back to Port Royal. *Dreadnought* certainly couldn't stand in the line-of-battle without an extensive refit.

There was minimal ceremonial at *Augusta's* entry port, just his old friend Farlowe and two bosun's mates and a few sideboys. Even amongst the bustle and urgent activity of repairing the flagship after such a battle, the navy found time to pay at least this much respect to a visiting captain. Nevertheless, Holbrooke did wonder at the absence of both Forrest and his first lieutenant. He could understand the sensitivity when Swift's impending promotion into *Kestrel* had only recently been announced, but that was six weeks ago. The first lieutenant should undoubtedly have met him at the entry port; he felt slighted.

'Welcome, sir,' said Farlowe, shaking his hand.

'I'm pleased to see you in good health, Mister Farlowe,' replied Holbrooke. It seemed odd to have to speak so formally to his old friend, but here at the entry port, it wouldn't do at all to use Christian names. Even though they both held temporary appointments, there was still a great gulf between a lieutenant in temporary command of a sixth-rate and a master's mate temporarily filling the post of the fourth lieutenant in a ship-of-the-line.

'The Commodore will see you in his cabin, but he's asked that I spend a few moments showing you the damage, particularly the boats,' he said pointedly.

'Ah, I see.' Holbrooke did indeed see. Unless he was mistaken, he was about to be deprived of one of his boats, probably the longboat, the largest and heaviest of *Medina's* three. This was Forrest's way of softening him up before the inevitable demand, even though it would probably be disguised as a polite request.

They walked the few steps onto the waist, carefully avoiding the groups of men engaged in their specialist tasks. The sailmaker and his mates were patching the main topsail, working with a speed that would have rivalled the tailors of Piccadilly. The bosun was directing half a dozen different gangs in splicing and re-reeving the miles of cordage that made up the standing and running rigging. A carpenter's mate was swinging his adze rhythmically to-and-fro, fashioning a temporary knee to reinforce an upper deck gun port. In the middle of all this, the gunner had a nine-pounder dangling above its newly-trucked carriage, waiting for the moment when the ship's movement would allow him to lower it gently and accurately into place.

'Were your casualties terrible?' asked Holbrooke as he looked around at the scene of devastation.

'Not so dreadful,' replied Farlowe, with surprising brightness, 'nine dead, twenty-nine wounded. Of those, the sawbones believes that more than half will survive.' He looked around to make sure that they couldn't be overheard. 'Swift was killed,' he said, 'cut in half by a twenty-four pounder, right on the quarterdeck in front of the commodore.'

Holbrooke stopped in his tracks. If Swift was dead, then he couldn't command *Kestrel*. The admiral would have to find someone else to promote in his place. Of course, it was still unlikely that the admiral would select Holbrooke, but it was possible. Yes, it was indeed possible. He knew that he had to be back in Port Royal so that he was on the scene when the admiral was told the news. Surely the squadron would sail for the Windward Passage later today, once *Dreadnought* had her jury masts. He'd arrive at the same time as the news of Swift's death, and he believed that his conduct would be remarked upon with approval by Forrest. Suddenly Holbrooke was impatient to be away. But then another thought struck him, the reason for his friend's cheerfulness.

'Then there's an immediate vacancy in *Augusta*,' he remarked.

'Yes, and I've been made acting third lieutenant and lieutenant-at-arms,' said Farlowe, concealing his happiness under a stern countenance. 'With news of a successful action and, consequently, a vacancy opening, my chances of being confirmed have doubled – quadrupled!'

'I'm pleased for you,' said Holbrooke sincerely, returning the look. Neither man offered to shake hands, it would have been unseemly among all this frenetic activity, and it would be easy for any of the Augustas to guess why they were congratulating each other. Holbrooke had no idea whether Swift was loved or loathed by the men, but in either case, they wouldn't take kindly to a stranger and a newcomer apparently exulting over his death.

Holbrooke heard and saw little more as they picked their way slowly around the deck and so to the great cabin. His mind was full of the new possibilities for his future. If the squadron sailed directly back to Port Royal, then the news of Swift's death wouldn't precede it. With a successful action and a vacant post as master and commander of a newly-refitted sloop, a sloop which Holbrooke had captured, the admiral had an easy decision to make – and it would be even easier if Holbrooke were visible as one of the four victorious commanding officers.

Holbrooke stood back as a vaguely-recognised lieutenant hurried out of the cabin with a worried look on his face – a look that he knew well – a look that characterised a second-in-command with battle damage to be repaired and an impatient captain who wanted to be underway without delay. They briefly nodded at each other as Holbrooke walked into the cabin.

'Good morning to you, Captain Holbrooke,' said Forrest shaking his hand.

'My congratulations on your victory, sir,' replied Holbrooke, 'I hope *Augusta* hasn't suffered too badly.'

'Badly enough, I fear. What I've just heard has confirmed my first thoughts; the squadron must return to Port Royal to refit. I hope we can be back on station before de Kersaint is ready to sail, but I'm not very optimistic. The navy yard in Cape François has probably started work already, and it'll be perhaps a week before we can be brought in hand.'

Holbrooke nodded. It was unfortunate, but the French convoy would sail long before Forrest could return, and Holbrooke knew that Cotes had no additional squadron waiting for employment. Perhaps de Kersaint had a better day than it appeared at first sight.

'I hope you'll be released from your towing duties before the dog watches; I can see Suckling's mizzen being sheeted home now,' he said looking out of the stern windows. 'I intend to be on my way later today. However, you'll have seen the state of my boats; I haven't one that'll float and nor am I likely to have before Port Royal. I'm afraid I must take your longboat from you.'

Holbrooke was prepared for this demand and managed to look almost cheerful. It was a small price to pay, and the boat would be returned in a week. 'I'll have it rowed over as soon as I get back to *Medina*, sir,' he replied.

'You'll have heard that Swift was killed?'

'Yes, sir. I didn't know him except by reputation. The

service has lost a good man.'

'Indeed, he was a very good first lieutenant.'

Holbrooke was struck by the curiosity of the statement. Swift had been promised a sloop, and yet Forrest was commenting on his ability as a subordinate. Was the commodore implying that he had reservations about poor Swift's fitness to command? If so, it was an odd thing to say to another lieutenant.

'You know that he'd been promised *Kestrel* as soon as her refit is complete?'

'I heard it the day before we sailed, sir,' replied Holbrooke. There were many things that he could say to follow that flat statement – the sheer injustice of giving *his* prize to another was just the first of them, but they were best kept to himself.

'Then I want you to know, Holbrooke, that I'll be mentioning you particularly in my report to the admiral. I know that *Medina* wasn't engaged, but you carried out all the duties that I could require of a frigate and the information that you provided when I arrived on station was invaluable. I'll be recommending most strongly to the admiral that you're ready for command, at the same time as I report Swift's death. I hope that he'll see the connection and give you *Kestrel*.'

Holbrooke was speechless, this was a far, far greater endorsement than he'd expected from this man whom he'd served for such a short space of time.

'I'm telling you this now, Holbrooke,' he continued, 'because I've some bad news for you. I must leave *Medina* behind to watch Cape François.'

Holbrooke's disappointment must have shown momentarily, but he recovered quickly. If the commodore made the recommendation in the terms that he described, that would be better than Holbrooke being at hand when the admiral made his decision. He was being included in the victory; one of the four captains present at this first significant naval triumph of the war. Yes, it would do.

'What's the state of your stores?' asked Forrest.

'I've six weeks allowance of all stores, water and wood and the magazine is full, sir,' replied Holbrooke. That would mean he must return to Port Royal by mid-December and the last estimate for *Kestrel* was that she'd be complete by the end of the year. He could see that the commodore was making the same calculation.

'Very well. You're to remain on station until the thirtieth of November and then return to Port Royal. If the convoy sails, and I believe it will, you should do anything in your power to annoy it, and you may leave the station to do so. You can take prizes, and you can co-operate with any British privateers as you see fit. I'll send your orders when I return your longboat's crew.' He paused, thinking of all eventualities. 'In any case, if you have to leave the station, you're to be back in Port Royal by the sixth of December.'

'Thank you, sir. I very much appreciate your recommendation, and I wish you joy of this great victory.'

'A victory indeed, and the country needs it. However, I suspect if Monsieur de Kersaint can now clear his convoy without too much loss, he may see things differently. But I'm growing pessimistic. We can't count success merely by ships won and lost or by so much commerce destroyed or taken, but by the effect that they have back at home. The mob will go wild with joy. King George will hear the news and smile. Newcastle's government will have a few days, perhaps a week or two, of glory and Anson will find it easier to secure funds for his new ships. At this stage in the war, that's the true measure of our success.'

The squadron bore away for the Windward Passage, steering right into the track of the setting sun. *Augusta* led the line, with *Dreadnought* in the centre and *Edinburgh* bringing up the rear. It was fortunate that Jamaica was to leeward because Suckling's ship could hardly have sailed on the wind at all. In her present state, without the support of the other two third rates, she'd be easy prey for any stray French ship-of-the-line or even a bold frigate.

Holbrooke watched them go with very mixed feelings. His future, he knew, was in the hands of Commodore Forrest. The victorious squadron commander had promised to recommend him to the admiral, but would he keep that promise? Had he just used that as an easy consolation for the frigate that he was leaving behind for a long and lonely vigil? In his turmoil of mind, Holbrooke could easily conjure up any number of followers of Forrest who would be clamouring for his endorsement for command of *Kestrel*. That acting first lieutenant, for example. What was his relationship with the commodore? He'd be straining every sinew and sparing nobody in his zeal to repair *Augusta's* damage and present himself in the best possible light. There must be a dozen lieutenants in the squadron who were right now calculating their chances of preferment following the demise of Swift. If there were a dozen in the squadron, that number would treble once the news reached Port Royal. Each of them would be senior to Holbrooke, each of them would be visible to the admiral when he had to make his decision. With a pang of conscience, Holbrooke realised that his black mood was visible to the others on the quarterdeck. They'd wonder what the commodore had said to their captain to make him so glum after such a successful day. That wasn't the way to lead men.

'Take us to windward Mister Hosking,' he said in as natural a voice as he could muster. 'We'll spend the night five leagues to the west of Monte Christi. Call me if you sight a sail other than these fishing boats,' he swept his hand towards the two-or-three luggers lying close to the shore. 'I'll be in my cabin.'

As he walked down the ladder from the quarterdeck to the waist, Hosking and Lynton exchanged significant looks. They could guess to within a fraction of the truth what was eating at their captain. In Hosking's case, it was a detached interest, he wasn't subject to the same forces that governed promotion and appointments as Holbrooke was. In Lynton's case, it was closer to home. He desperately wanted to be in a position to be haunted by the ifs and maybes of life as a lieutenant. He was already planning when he could decently present himself for the lieutenant's examination and knew only too well that from the day that he passed for lieutenant to the day he died, his emotions would be governed by questions of preferment. He could hardly wait.

CHAPTER TWENTY-SEVEN

British Privateers

Friday, eleventh of November 1757
Medina, at Sea. Off Cape François, Saint Domingue

Holbrooke grew very familiar with the patch of sea between Monte Christi and Cape François. There was little for *Medina* to do. With no dock at Cape François, the French squadron could be seen through a good telescope unloading their stores to lighten their ships, then heeling them to get at the holes below the waterline. Later they started replacing masts and yards, rattling down the standing rigging and then re-embarking stores. *Medina* watched all this as she patrolled off the French harbour during the day and beat to windward to lie nearer Monte Christi at night. Each day, the master and one of the mates took the cutter away to run lines of soundings and to fix the position of the prominent features on the shore. Enrico's sketches became more and more exact, and Hosking ceased any pretence of making his own drawings of the shoreline.

They were alone, only fishing boats caring to set to sea when a British frigate was prowling off the harbour. Twice they'd seen Jacques' fishing boat and both times they'd exchanged friendly waves. Holbrooke had considered stopping the boat again to buy whatever information Jacques had, but they were too close to the land, and they'd have been seen with probably fatal consequences for the fisherman. Holbrooke was sure, in any case, that if Jacques knew anything useful, anything that could be traded for more gold, he'd have initiated a meeting further out to sea. But the unnamed fishing boat merely continued on its way, past the frigate and out to sea to the fishing grounds, returning in the evening as the light started to fade. *Medina* didn't even have the company of the fleet of British privateers that had followed Forrest out of Port Royal. Most of them had returned to Jamaica, disappointed that the convoy hadn't sailed. They had a limited endurance, and only a few of the larger ones remained at sea, scouring the coast for small prizes and every day or two returning to Cape François to check on the convoy's progress.

By the second week in November it was becoming clear that de Kersaint's squadron would soon be in a fit state to escort the convoy to sea. It seemed likely that the squadron would take the merchants all the way to France, as there was little apparent reason for the line-of-battle ships to remain in the West Indies. Their route would be directly north by way of the Caicos Passage. Then, lying as close to the trade wind as possible, they'd make their northing, right through the variables until they came to the region of the westerlies in about thirty or thirty-five degrees of latitude, the westerlies that would take them home to reach the coast of France perhaps as early as Christmas. But it was a perilous journey. They'd be hounded by British privateers until they were well out into the Atlantic, and any stragglers would be easy pickings for the motley selection of craft that would follow them. If they survived that first week or so, the Atlantic crossing would be reasonably routine until they approached the shores of France. With little real idea of their longitude, they'd be praying that the weather would allow them the leisure and daylight to determine their proximity to the coast before they were committed to a lee shore in a howling January gale. Holbrooke almost felt sorry for them, until he thought of the fabulous profits that they'd make with their valuable cargoes.

Holbrooke gave his octant to Midshipman Smith and took up his telescope. The master had just declared noon and the latitude to be nineteen degrees and fifty minutes north. Cape François was west-southwest at ten miles. Holbrooke didn't usually join the group that took the midday sun-sight, but he was starting to feel the tedium of blockade duty. He studied the land and then the northern horizon through his telescope. The sea was empty except for a pair of the larger sort of privateers a mile to leeward. They were lying-to and appeared to be conferring. 'Mister Hosking,' said Holbrooke, 'run down to those two privateers and request that their masters come aboard for dinner.'

'Aye, aye, sir,' replied the sailing master, a little surprised. Holbrooke had largely ignored the privateers for the past three weeks, and they'd made no attempt to communicate with *Medina*. It was quite normal for King's officers to take a superior attitude to these commercial men-of-war, and their masters were naturally unwilling to risk a snub if they made the first approach. Hosking, however, had served a year in a privateer in the last war when he didn't have a ship, and he had a different perspective to most sea-officers. If he'd thought about it, he wouldn't have imagined that Holbrooke was snobbish, rather that he was a little diffident. Anyway, the privateers had their duties and motivations, while a King's ship had its own; there was little useful to be said.

It took *Medina* only fifteen minutes to come within hailing range, and in a further thirty minutes, after the two masters had hurried into decent clothes, they came on board to be met politely by Lynton. It was by no means a naval ceremony; there were no pipes and no sideboys, those being reserved for officers holding the King's commission, but it was a more cordial greeting than they'd expected. Lynton showed the two men to the cabin where they made their own introductions.

Joshua Bates was the master of the *Two Brothers*, a ship-rigged privateer of ten guns that sailed out of Port Royal. He was a middle-aged, muscular, taciturn man, the very image of the hard-driving commander of a letter of marque. His handshake could crush a coconut and Holbrooke barely suppressed a grimace as his bones were pressed in that vice-like grip. Bates had made enough money in the last war for any careful man to lead a life of unassuming ease during the peace, but his habits were expensive, and his cash had run out just as war was declared in 1756. When he was offered the command of *Two Brothers*, he said farewell to his wife and family with barely a backward glance. Bates sailed the ship from Bristol to Jamaica and expected to spend the war away from home, replenishing his fortune.

John Carter was a wholly different sort and could readily have been taken for a King's officer had he been in uniform. Holbrooke wasn't surprised to hear that he was a passed lieutenant from the last war but had never been made, and after another year's frustrating service as a master's mate, he'd decided that he had neither the patronage nor the luck to achieve a commission. His sympathetic captain had released him, and Carter had sailed as mate on a privateer for the remainder of the war, then as master of West Indiamen in the peace and now as a privateer again. He could easily have resented Holbrooke, ten years younger and evidently successful, but if he did, he wasn't letting it show. Carter part-owned and commanded the snow *Blandford*, also out of Port Royal and mounting eight guns. Holbrooke wondered at the name; there'd been a sixth-rate *Blandford* at about the time when Carter was a passed lieutenant. Could he have named his privateer after his last man-of-war?

Lynton excused himself; he'd be taking the deck while Hosking joined them for dinner. There were places for five around the table and Holbrooke had invited Chalmers to make up the numbers.

Dinner was a cheerful affair. Even Bates mellowed after a few glasses of wine and soon found that he and Hosking had friends in common. Carter was a fascinating man, Holbrooke found. He had indeed named his snow *Blandford* in compliment to the captain of his last King's ship. Edward Dodd could legitimately have insisted that Carter continue to serve as his master's mate – he was evidently a good one – but had written an impassioned plea to their Lordships, who had agreed that Carter could be released.

Chalmers, always the great observer of humanity, enjoyed the dinner more than any he could remember. He followed with interest the tentative questions and cautious answers that elicited from Holbrooke and Carter their professional histories. Each man warily released an item of information, and carefully assessed how it was received before offering more. Bit-by-bit they came to know each other, and as they opened up, a trusting relationship developed. With Bates it was different. If he was aware of any constraint between King's officers and privateersmen, he didn't show it. His questions were blunt and delivered without any temporising, and his answers were equally forthright. Bates was happy with his lot, and it had apparently not occurred to him that anyone could feel in any way superior to him.

Smart cleared the table; the port was passed, and they each responded loudly when the loyal toast was proposed. Holbrooke eased back his chair. That inconsequential action caught the attention of his guests, the master and the chaplain; he looked around to find five pairs of eyes watching him expectantly.

'Gentlemen, you may have guessed that I've an ulterior motive in inviting you for dinner, in addition to a desire for the pleasure of your company.'

Bates nodded ponderously. He, perhaps alone among the company, had thought no further than the next remove and the next glass of wine.

'I believe the convoy will sail in the next few days,' he said, 'and I'm sure it won't surprise you to know that they'll undoubtedly sail for the Caicos Passage unless the wind shifts into the north when they may reach away for the Crooked Island Passage.'

'Back in '46 I saw a small French convoy take the Old Straits of Bahama, to try to outfox us,' said Bates, 'but they were a poor crowd, and lost one of their number near Green Island.'

'I think it's unlikely that de Kersaint will take a battle squadron and forty of the richest ships that the French have ever sailed through those dangerous waters,' replied Holbrooke.

'The Caicos is their best route, and the wind hasn't been north of east-northeast for two weeks,' said Carter. 'They'll be desperate to get out into the Atlantic. I'd put my money on the shortest route and anyway we can easily catch them as they clear Crooked Island – if they go that way.'

Bates nodded, satisfied that he had been taken seriously, that the option had been tested and eliminated.

'Well, I have a proposal, gentlemen,' said Holbrooke. 'If we act independently, we'll find it difficult to pick off any except stragglers – and those French merchantmen will have every incentive to stay with the convoy and the escort. That's a powerful squadron even if the two smaller frigates turn back for Cape François after they've seen the convoy into the Atlantic.'

'Excuse me, sir,' said Carter, 'but what makes you think the ships-of-the-line will sail home with them? I've enough stores to follow the convoy half way to France. If the battle squadron turns back for the Cape leaving only a frigate or two as an escort, it'd be unusual if I can't take at least one of them before they're too far into the ocean.'

'The French don't manage their affairs as we do; they deploy squadrons for stated purposes. This squadron, I'm sure, was sent to the West Indies with the sole purpose of bringing that convoy home. The two frigates will stay here, but de Kersaint and his four of the line will see the merchantmen safely to their berths in France.' He looked around the room, 'they may not be as manoeuvrable as frigates, but none of us can stand a single broadside from them. Once they get clear of the islands, we can kiss them all goodbye.'

The two privateer masters looked thoughtful while Holbrooke let the silence linger. It was Carter who spoke first.

'Then what do you propose, sir?'

'I propose that we co-operate, that we act together as a squadron.'

Bates looked immediately scornful. 'Aye, and you'll keep every penny of your captures while we have to share *ours* with you! Young Carter and I have already agreed that we'll share our prizes, what else can you offer?' He folded his arms and leaned back; he'd made his point. Carter looked more open, but even he evidently agreed with Bates.

'Very well,' said Holbrooke, 'you've thought about this already I gather, then let's hear no more of it. But as a matter of professional curiosity, I'd be interested to know how you'll cut out your prizes from a convoy that will have four ships-of-the-line and three frigates guarding them until they're clear of the passage.' He looked from Bates to Carter and back again. 'Well, gentlemen?'

Carter cleared his throat. 'Captain Holbrooke may have a point; don't you think Bates?' he said. 'We've been working on the assumption that either the battle squadron would stay at anchor or that it would turn back once it had seen them into the Atlantic. If that's not the case, then it'll be sheer luck if we take any prizes. That'll be a poor reward for two or three months away.'

Bates looked thoughtful. Evidently, the optimistic scenario that Carter had outlined then demolished was precisely the basis of his planning. He would only attack the convoy if it was guarded by a couple of frigates; a small battle squadron made that impossible. For all his gruff seamanlike bluster, Bates was a businessman at heart, and he was prepared to hear an alternative if his plan looked like it wasn't going to turn a profit.

'That being the case, Captain,' he said, 'and if that damned de Kersaint is intent on seeing the convoy home, I'm prepared to hear your proposal.'

Carter nodded in agreement. He was already half-way convinced that without the frigate's co-operation they were on a fool's errand.

'Thank you,' replied Holbrooke, nodding to each man in turn. 'The first thing to say is that I acknowledge the unfairness of the prize rules in this case,' he paused, 'but my proposal, I hope, will go some way to evening the rewards. We can talk tactics later, but the heart of my proposal is that *Medina* should provide the diversion by engaging the escort while *Two Brothers* and *Blandford* take the prizes.'

That had their attention. Every privateer dreamed that a convoy's escort should be so occupied as to be unable to protect the valuable and vulnerable merchant ships. The real charm of this idea was that they knew that no French national vessel would be able to resist being pulled away from the pedestrian duty of watching over its charges when there was a British frigate to be engaged. Captains of French men-of-war had the same incentives as their British counterparts and an even greater sense of the warrior code. Without a doubt, they'd prefer to fight a British ship of equal force than exchange blows in the air with privateers.

'Then do I take it, sir,' said Carter, 'that you won't take any prizes yourself?'

Hosking looked quizzically at Holbrooke. That would be a significant concession and one that would sound hollow if this affair should go wrong and end in a court martial. Admiral Cotes also had an interest in this deal and wouldn't take kindly to his share of prize money being given away.

'I think you know that I can't make such an absolute

undertaking,' said Holbrooke. 'What I can say, is that I'll do my utmost to create the conditions for you gentlemen to do your business. I can't commit to anything more definite than that. But remember, whether we have an agreement or not, if *Medina* is in sight when you take a prize, then my people share in that prize. I suggest to you that, knowing what we do know, if we don't co-operate there will be no prizes for you to share.'

Bates looked unsure, dissatisfied, but Carter was smiling.

'If I may offer my opinion,' said Hosking. 'I've been privateering as you know Bates, and I've come home empty-handed when the horizon has been full of the enemy's commerce, but it's been guarded by a strong escort. That's not a privateer's job, to take on frigates, much less ships-of-the-line. Sure, occasionally it comes off well, but mostly the result is good men spending the rest of the war in a French prison, and even if you get exchanged, the owners don't want to know you anymore. You both know that you're only as good as your last prize. If I were a privateer now, with this convoy and this escort waiting to sail, I'd jump at Captain Holbrooke's proposal.' It was Hosking's turn to fold his arms now, but he thought better of it; he had one last point to make. 'And I hadn't heard of this plan before you did,' he said, looking at the two privateer masters, before finally folding his arms and leaning back in his chair.

Bates scowled, he could feel the mood of the meeting going against him but didn't want to give way.

'May I make a few observations,' asked Chalmers, looking at the two privateersmen, and then towards Holbrooke.

'By all means Mister Chalmers, we'd be glad of your wise counsel as we appear to be at an impasse,' said Holbrooke.

'Well, it appears to me that we have a meeting here of two different breeds of man-of-war: the public and the private. Let's set aside any notions of honour, the bare facts are that each has its investors who demand – no deserve – a profit from their investment. In *Medina's* case the British public's return is measured in battles won and trade protected, only as a tertiary return do they expect *Medina* to destroy the enemy's shipping. However, in the case of you two gentlemen,' he acknowledged Bates and Carter who were already bemused at being reasoned with by a chaplain, 'your investors demand only one thing: a profit from the capture of enemy ships. Please stop me if anything I'm saying is at odds with your understanding of your purpose.' Chalmers paused for a few seconds. He could see that the two privateersmen were flattered that their motivations were being equated to those of King's officers.

'Captain Holbrooke's proposal – and like Mister Hosking, this is the first time that I've heard it – satisfies both of those groups of investors and incidentally provides that tertiary return to the public in the destruction of the enemy's trade. Here we have the opportunity for each party to concentrate on what it does best. Captain Holbrooke will have his fight with the frigates while you gentlemen will have your prizes. As for the question of shares, well, *Medina* is likely to be in sight when you make captures whether you have an agreement or not, but without the agreement, you run the real risk of having no prizes as well as the danger of having to fight a French frigate, or worse.'

Chalmers watched each man closely, looking for a reaction to his address. He could see that Carter was persuaded.

'Well, Bates,' said Carter, 'we hadn't concluded our agreement, and Captain Holbrooke's suggestion seems to offer a way for us to return to Port Royal with something to show for our cruise. I call it a handsome proposal that I'm happy to accept. I'm satisfied. What do you say?'

Bates still didn't look entirely happy, but the tide of

opinion was against him. He knew that he'd have no agreement with Carter now and if he didn't co-operate with the frigate, he'd probably return empty-handed, and he was only too aware of what the shareholders would say to that. He could be on the beach in a month. But still, it went against the grain to effectively put himself under the command of this very young man.

'I also accept,' he said. The privateer captain made a motion as though to spit on his hand, then thought better of it and settled for a dry shake. 'But commitment or no commitment, I expect you to play your part and hold those damned French frigates until young Carter and I have a fat West Indiaman each!'

CHAPTER TWENTY-EIGHT

The Volunteer

Friday, eleventh of November 1757
Medina, at Sea. Off Cape François, Saint Domingue

Hosking and Chalmers stood together on the quarterdeck, watching as the two privateersmen rowed back to their ships. It wasn't done quite navy-fashion, but both captains clearly had their crews under discipline. Carter's oarsmen had even dressed for the occasion, short blue jackets and red scarves announcing their status as the captain's own boat's crew.

'That was a most enjoyable dinner,' said Chalmers, 'and I found our guests very interesting. Clearly men who know their profession, not at all the wild sea-rovers that I had been led to expect. Will they keep to their bargain, do you think?'

'Aye, they'll stick to it,' replied Hosking, 'at least for as long as it's in their interest. If the French keep together, there is little that they can achieve alone, but if we can pin down an escort, they'll have a good chance of taking prizes.' The two men stood in silence for a moment. 'I often wonder at the reputation that privateers have among King's officers. If they were as wayward and undisciplined as the tales would suggest, half-pirates you'd think, then they'd never be trusted with the owners' investment. The cost of fitting out a Bristol privateer for Jamaica is staggering. The owners are quite rightly unwilling to entrust such an investment to wild sea-rovers.'

Chalmers nodded. 'Yes, I can see that it would take a man of quality and experience to command such a vessel. Tell me Mister Hosking, do their Lordships value the contribution that these privateers make to the annoyance of the enemy's trade?'

'Indeed, they do. The Admiralty lobbies for the granting of letters of marque right at the outset of each war. They know that the navy can't do it alone.'

'And yet it seems iniquitous that we'll share in their prizes, but they can't share in ours. Is there a reason for that?' asked Chalmers.

'Oh, there's a reason all right, and it makes perfect sense. The presence of a man-of-war is almost certain to influence an enemy merchantman's decision to strike, it'll make the contest shorter and less bloody, and the prize will be less damaged. Whereas the presence of a privateer when a King's ship is taking a prize is neither here-nor-there. Where it *is* unfair is when the man-of-war, say a small schooner or a cutter, is of less force than the privateer, but it'd be hard to design rules that allowed for all circumstances. Bates and Carter know very well that they have an advantageous agreement, even if Bates was reluctant at the start. They'll be happy men this evening, and not just because of the captain's wine!'

'Yes, I think Holbrooke struck a nerve when he pointed out the probability of returning to Port Royal empty-handed, particularly after they elected to stay on station when all the other privateers gave up,' said Chalmers. 'Theirs is, after all, a commercial concern and no prizes means no profit.'

'Mister Hosking sir,' said the quartermaster, 'there's that fishing boat again, and he's waving at us.'

Hosking took his telescope and trained it to leeward, where the familiar sight of Jacques' fishing boat was bobbing up and down in the moderate sea. Someone was undoubtedly signalling and as he watched the helm was put down and the boat came onto the wind. He'd fetch *Medina* in two short tacks, Hosking decided. There was no need to run down to him; he probably just wanted to sell some of his catch.

'Dash down to the cabin, Mister Smith and pass my

compliments to Captain Holbrooke. The fishing boat that we spoke to in September is beating up towards us and appears to want to talk.'

Smith was back before the fishing boat had made its first tack. 'Captain's compliments and would you please lie-to until the boat is alongside?' he said to the master. 'Captain's compliments to you also Mister Chalmers and would you care to join him in his cabin?'

Holbrooke and Chalmers waited as Jacques' boat hooked onto the main chains. 'Let's hope he has some news of the convoy's sailing date,' said Holbrooke by way of making conversation. 'I guess that it'll be in the next three days, but it would be good to have confirmation.'

'Do you have any more gold pieces?' asked Chalmers, 'I assume this will be a monetary transaction.'

'He may be disappointed,' replied Holbrooke. 'His information is less valuable now than it was before; I'll pay no more than two pieces for a firm sailing date and another for the route. To be honest, it makes little difference to us. We can see for ourselves that the convoy is ready to sail, but it'll increase our stock with the privateers if I can pass on reliable information.'

'I hope you'll remember my suspicion that he knows more English than he's admitting.'

'I will,' laughed Holbrooke, 'but if he does he's a better actor than I am!'

Chalmers kept his counsel and stifled an answering laugh. It wasn't the time or place to point out the impossibility of being a worse actor than the young lieutenant. Holbrooke wore his heart on his sleeve and deceived no-one; for him, dissembling was an impossibility.

A knock at the door brought Midshipman Smith ushering in the familiar, still imposing figure of Jacques, the freed African slave. Both men were again struck by his similarity to Black Rod; in all but their skin colour, they could be brothers.

'Mister Lynton's compliments sir, this man was alone in the boat. Mister Lynton has sent down a boat-keeper to save our paintwork.'

Holbrooke was curious. The man could hardly be fishing alone; he had two or three crew the last time they met.

Jacques bowed as he entered and waited to be invited to sit.

Chalmers was reminded how impressed he'd been by Jacques' impeccable manners. It was beyond the chaplain's understanding how he'd adapted to the life of a fisherman.

Holbrooke rose, and returning the bow, he gestured for Jacques to sit.

'What can I do for you Monsieur Jacques?' he asked, casting a glance sideways at Chalmers to start the translation. Chalmers was a quick translator, but he took a few moments to form the phrase and Jacques was quicker.

'I regret that I may have misled you, sir,' he said in passable English, fingering the brim of his straw hat, the first sign of nervousness that he'd yet displayed in Holbrooke's presence. 'As you can hear, I speak your language a little, enough for a conversation at least.'

Holbrooke frowned, ready to be angry. But he looked at Chalmers who gave him an I-told-you-so smile and the anger evaporated, to be replaced by curiosity.

'We suspected as much, or at least Mister Chalmers did,' he said, still frowning slightly, 'and of course, we took our own precautions. But it's hardly a way of recommending yourself to me. Why do you confess this now?' asked Holbrooke.

'If you will indulge me for a few minutes, Captain, my reason will become clear. But first, I have news of the convoy and the squadron. I can tell you when they will sail.'

'I think we know that within a day or two already, Jacques. We've seen the men-of-war being repaired and we've seen the merchantmen swaying up topmasts and yards. But if you have a firm date, I can offer you a single gold piece for the information.'

'That won't be necessary, sir,' replied Jacques.

Holbrooke and Chalmers exchanged puzzled looks, this was a very strange impoverished fisherman who didn't want to be paid in gold. If not hard cash, what did he want?

'This information is free, sir. The sailing date is set for early on the thirteenth of November, before the sea-breeze sets in,' he said. 'That's the day after tomorrow,' Jacques added.

Holbrooke nodded, that made sense. 'Is there any talk of which route they will take?'

Jacques considered for a moment. 'The talk – the rumour, it is nothing more – is that they will steer for the Caicos Passage and then north into the Atlantic.'

'And if the wind should head them?' asked Holbrooke, pushing for the best information that he could glean. But it wasn't necessary to put pressure on Jacques, he was eager to tell all he knew. It occurred to Holbrooke that he could have been sent by de Kersaint to spread disinformation, but it didn't seem likely, and it was hard to imagine what the French admiral would gain. Jacques clearly understood the navigation in these waters and even, to a lesser extent, the transatlantic trade routes. He spoke convincingly of how many points the wind would need to back before the convoy changed its plans and sailed via the Crooked Island Passage.

Chalmers, unconstrained by the need to translate, watched the two men with interest. Jacques was undoubtedly very free with his information, but Chalmers hadn't forgotten that the fisherman hadn't yet explained why he was offering this information without reward, and why he'd let his two inquisitors know that he spoke English. Without knowing that it was difficult to assess the man's honesty.

'And now, sir, may I come to the reason why I have sailed out to meet you, and why I am telling you all that I know?'

Holbrooke nodded with a reserved look on his face. *The man doesn't want gold, so what does he want?*

'You may remember something of my history, sir, how I was in service to an important family but am now a free man. I was born and raised a slave, but always worked in the master's household. Perhaps too much of my master's manners were ingrained in me; the life of a fisherman, I find, doesn't suit me. I understand that the British navy, like the French, is always short of men. I am here to ask if you could find employment for me in this ship.'

Holbrooke and Chalmers stared at each other in shock. Of all the reasons for this visit, some plausible, some less so, this one hadn't even crossed their minds.

'To be clear, sir,' Jacques continued, 'I wish to leave that island,' he gestured to leeward towards Saint Domingue, 'and take service in this ship, with the British navy.'

Holbrooke thought rapidly. It was possible, of course. The navy happily accepted volunteers from any nation and was often elastic in its definition of a *volunteer* if a ship was in dire need. *Medina* already had people from half a dozen different countries and a handful of skin colours, most of whom didn't speak English nearly as well as Jacques, and many of whom had no previous experience of the sea. But this needed further probing; what did this Frenchman expect of life in a British frigate? As he pondered, he could hear the everyday noises of the frigate about him, but there seemed to be some unusual activity in the waist. He briefly wondered at it and then decided that whatever it was, Lynton and Hosking would be able to deal with it.

'What would you do in this ship, Jacques? What skills could you bring?' asked Holbrooke, playing for time while regarding the man with new interest. It was hardly normal for the captain of a King's ship to personally quiz a volunteer's motives. In England, the press was out, and any man who used the sea as his profession was either being forced to serve in the navy or had made himself invisible. The thought of turning away a genuine volunteer was laughable.

'I have become a competent seaman,' he replied, 'and I can carry out all the normal tasks, although I have not been to sea in such a large ship.' He gave a curious sideways glance as though to confirm that there was nobody else in the cabin, 'however, my main skill is in managing a household, and I can easily adapt to serving the captain or officers of a man-of-war.'

Clearly, Jacques had been checking that Smart didn't overhear him. He'd seen the rough-and-ready standards of a naval servant and was less than impressed. Holbrooke thought for a moment, then addressed Jacques in slightly more formal tones. 'Well, I must inform you that I'm only a temporary captain, and the real captain will rejoin us in Port Royal. He already has a servant and is unlikely to want to change.'

Jacques was taken aback for a moment. He hadn't imagined that such a ship would be entrusted to a temporary captain, but he recovered quickly. 'Nevertheless, captain, I can serve as a seaman or in any capacity that you see fit; I will be content if you will have me.'

Holbrooke looked again at Chalmers who imperceptibly nodded his head.

'You have no ties to Saint Domingue, I gather, but what of your boat?'

'It wouldn't last another voyage, sir, and my crew have left me in terror of their lives, it leaks so badly. I chose not to invest in repairing it; that would be throwing good gold onto rotten timbers,' he said. 'I have no ties. All I have is a small bag in the boat.'

There was a knock at the door, and Midshipman Smith appeared, looking worried. 'Mister Lynton's compliments, sir, and the fishing boat is taking on water at an alarming rate. He's set six men to baling, but the carpenter says she'll be gunwales-under in half an hour and there's nothing he can do, the bottom's falling out of her.' Smith cast a wondering look at Jacques, who sat impassively while this information was conveyed.

Holbrooke associated the noise in the waist that he'd heard a few minutes ago with this new information. That would explain Jacques' eagerness to be taken in; he had no future in Saint Domingue and was looking for a fresh start. Holbrooke looked again at the fisherman and made a snap decision. 'Take this man to his boat Mister Smith, so that he can recover his possessions, then present him to Mister Lynton and ask that he be rated ordinary and entered into the ship's books. The carpenter may salvage whatever is useful of the boat, and he's to make an inventory and present it to the purser, then he may scuttle it.'

Smith looked from his captain to the fisherman, his mouth opened in amazement.

Holbrooke had put on his quarterdeck face, his look of command, because his relationship with Jacques had changed fundamentally in those few seconds. However, Jacques was smiling broadly. 'Your family name if you please?' asked Holbrooke.

'Serviteur,' Jacques replied. 'It is the name that was given by my owner to mark my profession.'

'Welcome to *Medina*, Jacques Serviteur.' He turned away and called through the door for the sentry, 'pass the word for Jackson.'

CHAPTER TWENTY-NINE

L'Outarde

Sunday, thirteenth of November 1757
Medina, at Sea. Off Cape François, Saint Domingue

Medina lay well to windward as the long line of ships filed out of the harbour through the Great Pass. It was a tricky channel with La Coquevieille – the rocky bank that guarded the harbour – to windward and Le Grand Mouton and Le Petit Mouton to leeward, with barely two cables of navigable water between them. De Kersaint's battle squadron led the way to ensure that *Medina* kept her distance, with all four of his two-deckers in line ahead and *Intrépide* in the van. His squadron was looking as good as new with never a fished spar or patched sail showing; the dockyard at Cape François had done a remarkable job in the few weeks since the battle with only the most rudimentary careening facilities and no dock at all. The battle squadron was followed by the merchantmen, forty or so in irregular groups but all crowding together for mutual support. Only one of them failed to make it through the channel. She was jostled by ships ahead, astern and to windward and ended up on the long line of rocks that skirted Le Grand Mouton, called The Sheep's Horns. It'd be a hard day's work to get her afloat and back to the dockyard and a long wait until another convoy could take her back to France. Her owner's profits would have to wait for another year.

If the merchantmen didn't know that the wolves were gathering, they had only to look to windward when they had cleared the channel where *Medina*, *Two Brothers* and *Blandford* rode to the breeze, watching the procession. Every French merchantman knew what a British frigate and British privateers looked like, many from bitter experience spanning two or even three wars. For the seamen in the convoy, the sight of those three competent-looking ships evoked vivid memories of miserable months and years spent in prison hulks in Portsmouth or on the Thames.

Finally, after the convoy had filed out past the Cape, the three frigates followed to bring up the rear. Holbrooke saw this as the moment when de Kersaint could change the dynamics of the encounter. If he were bold and sent those frigates to chase the British frigate and privateers away, he'd disrupt their carefully laid plans to coordinate their attack. But of course, he probably believed they'd act independently, as usual.

In a few hours, the battle squadron was nearly out of sight, beating north for the Caicos Passage with their bows as close to the wind as was possible. The convoy followed in its irregular groupings, the two light frigates disposed one on each beam while the forty-four-gun *Outarde* brought up the rear, a formidable counter to *Medina* and the privateers.

'They've been lucky,' said Hosking, 'the wind's veered, it's almost east now. It looks possible that they'll weather the Inaguas and Maguana Island on this tack.'

Holbrooke kept his own counsel; he'd learned that it wasn't always a good idea to let his officers know his plan until he was confident that it would work. He was counting on de Kersaint's lack of recent intelligence, his fear that a British squadron, perhaps even Forrest's, could be waiting for him to the north of the Caicos Islands, ready to fall upon the convoy as it emerged into the Atlantic in the early hours of tomorrow. If that were the case, the French commander would keep his battle squadron concentrated at the head of the convoy, ready to beat off a British force, and he'd have his frigates at the sides and the rear, just as he'd done. Once out into the Atlantic it would be difficult for de Kersaint to know what was happening behind him and he'd be reluctant to turn back. Holbrooke planned to follow the convoy closely, and when all but the last group and *Outarde* had passed West Caicos, he'd pounce. While he engaged the large frigate, the two privateers would take a prize each and flee for the Windward Passage before de Kersaint could react. At that point, he thought, the admiral would probably do nothing, thankful to have escaped through the islands with the loss of only a few of his charges.

'We'll follow *Outarde*, Mister Hosking. Keep close enough to make their captain nervous but not so close that he's tempted to turn and engage us. I want him to have a difficult day and a sleepless night. If we don't attack today,' Holbrooke mused, 'it'll reinforce de Kersaint's fears that there's a squadron waiting for him past the Caicos. He'll be focussed on his van rather than his rear.'

Medina followed the convoy, keeping the big French frigate two miles to leeward and occasionally closing to a mile, just to keep up the tension. *Two Brothers* and *Blandford* held station astern and to windward of *Medina*. Night fell as they were halfway to the pinch-point of the Caicos Passage. Holbrooke wondered how Bates and Carter were faring. Their natural instincts would be to close in at night and try to pick off a straggler, but in this case, in the open sea with three frigates guarding the centre and rear of the convoy, such a strategy carried a high risk of failure. Holbrooke just hoped that they'd have the sense to keep to the plan and wait until the French were constrained by the islands. They'd know when to attack – when *Medina* engaged *Outarde* – and then they must strike quickly and be away before the other frigates could intervene.

Lynton was exercising the gun crews, taking them through their drills before the expected engagement the next day. Holbrooke saw an unfamiliar figure at number nine gun, on the starboard side of the waist, just below the quarterdeck rail. It was Serviteur, learning how to throw his weight onto the tackles to run the heavy nine-pounders out in preparation for firing. He looked a natural, as far as Holbrooke could tell in the short time that he watched; at least he didn't make any of the usual first-timer's mistakes. He didn't haul on the tackle before the rammer was clear, nor did he apply more or less weight than his opposite number on the other side of the gun and cause it to run out crab-wise. Perhaps he'd make a seaman in King George's navy faster than Holbrooke had imagined.

Dawn revealed a promising scene. Predictably, the convoy had spaced out over the night. Few escort commanders could believe how slowly the most sluggish of his convoy could sail, and de Kersaint had fallen into exactly that trap. The battle squadron, despite its reduced sail, had drawn steadily ahead, pulling the fastest merchantmen behind them. Now the convoy was spread over nearly ten miles, and while the flagship was passing West Caicos, *Outarde* and the slowest merchants were still well to the south in the open sea. Fearing an encounter as they skirted the Caicos Islands, the two thirty-two-gun frigates had kept their stations half way along the convoy and consequently were out of touch with both the van and the rear.

To make matters worse, the wind had backed overnight, and while the battle squadron and the merchantmen at the head of the convoy could still weather the Inagua Islands and Maguana, those in the middle and the rear would have to put in a tack after they'd passed to windward of the Inaguas. That would space out the convoy even more. It appeared that de Kersaint, far away at the head of the convoy, was oblivious to the problems in the rear, or perhaps he was staking everything on gaining the open sea as fast as possible.

Holbrooke had harassed *Outarde* all through the morning watch and the first part of the forenoon. *Medina* had repeatedly born down on her as though to engage but hauled her wind just beyond the range of the larger frigate's guns. *Outarde* appeared to have grown bored of these antics and had hardly reacted at all to the last two feints. Then at six bells, Holbrooke hoisted the pre-arranged signal, a plain blue flag at the main masthead, the order for the privateers to move ahead to menace the windward rear flank of the convoy. With their superior speed they quickly moved up the line of ships, and in an hour, they were in position. At a command from Holbrooke, Smith hauled down the blue and hoisted a red flag in its place.

'Put me across that frigate's stern, Mister Hosking,' said Holbrooke, pointing to leeward. 'Pistol-shot range will be good.' He wasn't exactly dismissing *Outarde's* fighting capability, but a ship that had until recently been armed *en flûte* and had been reinforced by gun crews from the French Royal Artillery, rather than experienced seamen, would always be at a disadvantage.

'Aye, aye, sir,' replied the master, rubbing his hands at the prospect of some action after all these long days on the blockade. He turned to give the orders that would bring *Medina* swooping down on her opponent. 'She's only a mile off the island, we'll have to be sharpish after you've saluted her.'

'Yes, Mister Hosking, as soon as we've given her a broadside, veer ship and get us back to windward of her. I intend to pin her between the island and our guns.'

Holbrooke looked briefly ahead. The two privateers were in position, well behind the two lighter frigates but alongside a good number of helpless merchantmen, who had shied away to leeward in alarm. The whole mass of ships at the rear of the convoy would soon be squeezed against the lee shore of Great Inagua Island with the predators to windward. There was time for a quick look at the head of the convoy. Only the topsails of the battle squadron were visible, poking up above the horizon against a pure blue sky. De Kersaint would probably hear the gunfire, but would he do anything about it? His frigates were all to the south of him, and he had no scouts ahead. Would he leave the head of the convoy when he didn't yet know whether Forrest's ships lay in his path to the open sea? Holbrooke could see the thirty-two-gun frigate on the windward flank; it also was holding its position and was still four miles north of *Medina*.

Holbrooke asked himself what orders de Kersaint would have given to his frigates. Quite likely his priority was to protect the convoy against a hostile squadron, in which case he'd have insisted that the two light frigates continue to guard the flanks. He'd reason that the forty-four guns of the heavier frigate were more than a match for *Medina* and two privateers.

'Mister Lynton. Stand by the starboard battery.'

Outarde continued to placidly follow the tail-enders of the convoy, unaware that *Medina* this time was in earnest. She had little room to manoeuvre with Great Inagua under her lee and the gaggle of the slowest merchantmen ahead of her. Too late her captain realised his predicament as the British ship, with the wind behind her, came tearing down across her quarter. She tried to bear way, but to do that quickly she needed to brail her mizzen, and the afterguard fumbled it. *Medina* crossed her stern at twenty yards range.

'Fire!' shouted Lynton. At this range, every gun of the battery could train on the exposed stern simultaneously. *Medina* staggered at the recoil. That had been a double-shotted broadside delivered at point-blank range. Holbrooke had time to wonder what Serviteur thought of his first exposure to a battery of nine-pounders firing in unison.

Their adversary was much larger than *Medina* and much heavier-built, but even those sturdy frames and planks couldn't keep out that volume of nine-pound shot. It was difficult to see, but from the fleeting glimpses through the smoke it looked as though *Outarde* had taken some hard blows.

Hosking ordered the helm put up and at the shouted orders, the sail-trimmers ran to their tacks and sheets. *Medina* put her stern through the wind, further and further until she was close-hauled and moving fast away from her adversary. When Holbrooke next looked over his shoulder, the smoke had cleared, and he could see that *Outarde* was in a bad way. Her quarterdeck had been swept clear, her wheel was gone, and the foot of her mizzen yard had been shot away. That one broadside had destroyed both her ability to manoeuvre and her capacity for command. Holbrooke couldn't see any movement at all on the quarterdeck. It seemed likely that both her captain and sailing master were dead or wounded.

'Mister Hosking, as soon as you've enough way on her, bring her about and lay me alongside that frigate, as close as you can. I'm going to force her to leeward.'

Hosking nodded. 'Aye, aye, sir. She's already having trouble keeping her head to the wind, but she'll have her steering tackles manned soon.'

Holbrooke looked more closely. *Outarde* was unbalanced, her mizzen was spilling wind, and her head was tending to fall off. With no direction from the quarterdeck, the foremast hands hadn't yet realised that they must haul down the fore-staysail to balance the rig. Satisfied that she was no threat for the next few minutes, Holbrooke looked again at the privateers. They were moving fast now, like wolves in a sheep enclosure, and the merchantmen were starting to scatter. They all knew about the island under their lee, and some had tacked to give themselves sea-room, while others stood on. One, apparently not under command, was heading directly for the rocks, but somehow managed to veer and claw her way to windward moments before she destroyed herself. That put her further behind her fellows, and as the weaker member of a herd, she was vulnerable to predators. Bates in *Two Brothers*, with the instincts of a hunter, saw his opportunity and moved in for the kill.

'There goes her mizzen,' shouted Lynton, who'd been watching *Outarde* while the convoy's separate drama was played out ahead of them, 'the slings have parted.'

The heavy frigate was in a desperate situation. Even if her rudder tackles were manned – which they should surely have achieved by now – there would be a deadly confusion as the first lieutenant was brought up from the guns and had to rapidly assess his options. Now, with the mizzen gone, the bows paid off fast, and she swung away to the west until she was running directly before the wind, straight towards the island.

They watched in fascination as *Outarde* struck the rocks. It happened in silence. *Medina* was too far to windward for any sound to carry, but they saw her stagger as she hit Little Inagua Island's encircling reef, saw all three masts go by the board, snapped off clean near the partners, and watched her swing beam-on to the north-easterly wind, pinned against the cruel coral.

'Bilged, for sure,' said Hosking in satisfaction, rubbing his hands with glee.

'Deck there.' Shouted Whittle at the masthead. 'The windward frigate is coming about, sir.'

'Bring her hard on the wind, Mister Hosking,' said Holbrooke over his shoulder as he swung into the starboard mizzen shrouds, his telescope in his hand. He didn't have to climb far, nor did he need the telescope; it was all too clear what was happening. The thirty-two-gun frigate that had been stationed on the windward side of the convoy had seen the fate of *Outarde*, had realised that the rear of the convoy was now unprotected and had decided that, notwithstanding his orders, it was his duty to turn back and confront *Medina*.

Holbrooke looked to the northwest. *Two Brothers* was alongside the stray merchantman, her boarders were pouring over the gunwales, and as he watched, he saw her ensign hauled down. Bates had made his kill, and he'd be away to the south with a fair wind for Port Royal before the French frigate could interfere. That was *Sauvage*, decided Holbrooke. She was nominally the twin of her sister *Licorne*, but she'd been painted with a white stripe above her gun-ports, just visible through the telescope. She nominally out-gunned *Medina*, but she was armed with eight-pounders while *Medina* had nines. In fact, they were evenly matched. Carter, meanwhile, had chased his prey to leeward, and both the privateer snow and the much larger French West Indiaman had rounded Little Inagua Island and were running rapidly to the west, *Blandford* firing hard and fast. Unless *Licorne* chose to intervene, and that was unthinkable with one of the escorting frigates already wrecked and the second committed to a fight with *Medina*, Carter would have his prize. However, he'd have a long voyage home, having to pass to the west of the Inaguas before he could beat towards the Windward Passage.

'Well, I believe we've satisfied our contract with Bates and Carter,' said Holbrooke. 'They won't be bothered now, and we'll share in the value of those West Indiamen. Keep her hard on the wind, Mister Hosking, and let's see what *Sauvage* does now.'

The two frigates rushed towards each other; in ten minutes they'd be exchanging broadsides. Holbrooke could see the whole convoy now, and the lower sails of the battle squadron were clearly visible in the north. He looked closer; it appeared that they'd tacked. Either de Kersaint was waiting for the merchantmen to catch up or he was bearing away to intervene in the debacle that was unfolding at the rear of his convoy. As he watched, he saw a pair of flags run up the masthead of the flagship, but he couldn't make out their colours. He saw a puff of smoke, and a few seconds later he heard the low boom of a single gun. De Kersaint was signalling, probably to *Sauvage*, who was now level with the tail of the convoy. An answering flag run up the mainmast of the French frigate and she veered to put herself on the same course as the convoy, heading north, away from *Medina*.

'She's been recalled, damn her,' exclaimed Lynton in pure frustration. He looked pleadingly at Holbrooke, hoping that he'd hold his course and try for a few broadsides before the battle squadron came down to help. Holbrooke and Hosking exchanged glances. They'd both been making the same mental calculation; could they achieve anything before de Kersaint intervened? Hosking shook his head almost imperceptibly, but Holbrooke had already come to the same conclusion. They may have time to deliver a single broadside, but it would achieve nothing, and there was the danger of a lucky shot from *Sauvage* crippling *Medina* and leaving her at the mercy of the ships-of-the-line. It was a huge risk to take when there was no corresponding reward.

'Bear away, Mister Hosking. We'll keep *Blandford* in sight until the Frenchman strikes then we'll escort them home.' Hosking nodded his agreement. It was vital that they should be in sight when the privateer made its capture.

Holbrooke looked at Lynton. He could see that the younger man was still pumped up, still hoping for a fight. 'Your guns did well today,' he said, pointing at the dismasted wreck of *Outarde*, held fast in the iron grip of the coral reef.

'Thank you, sir,' he replied, removing his hat and bowing. Lynton looked with pride and fondness over his guns, each of which was ready for immediate action, loaded, primed, rammed and run out. The slow match was burning in the tubs, and the men looked keen, pleased with themselves.

'Keep the men closed up until we're sure that *Sauvage* doesn't turn back, but I think everyone can relax. It's good to see that there are no casualties.'

At that moment there was a dull bang, perhaps more of an explosion, like powder that is fired in an open dish. It came from under Holbrooke's feet and was followed by a howl of pain and a scuffling as men ran about.

'What the devil's going on? Mister Lynton, can you see what's happening?'

Lynton ran aft on the main deck, into what would have been Holbrooke's cabin if the partitions hadn't all been removed for action. After a few moments, he came back. 'It's Smart sir. He was using that new burner that the armourer knocked together, boiling water for the coffee, I believe, but it exploded. Anyhow, he's scalded all up his arm and the side of his face; he looks like par-boiled pork, sir.'

'Then I expect *Smart* will get his *smart* ticket,' muttered Hosking, referring to the certificate that could be traded for a pension or a place at Greenwich Hospital.

CHAPTER THIRTY

The Operational Art

Monday, fourteenth of November 1757
Medina, at Sea. Off Little Inagua Island, Bahamas

Medina rounded Little Inagua Island just after sunset and the small squadron, *Medina*, *Blandford* and the French prize, put the wind on their larboard quarter and ran down to pass Point Mornet at the western end of Great Inagua. They hoped for a quiet night in the lee of the island with every known French man-of-war occupied with the convoy, which was now starting to feel the Atlantic rollers as it thrust northwards into the dark ocean fifty miles to the northeast.

Carter looked a happy man as he waved cheerily at Holbrooke from his quarterdeck. His prize was one of the larger West Indiamen, loaded with sugar, and she'd been taken without any damage or casualties, the very dream of a capture and a sure way of pleasing the shareholders. *Medina* passed close, and Holbrooke could see that Carter's prize master was taking no chances; the hatches were battened down, and there were half a dozen armed men on the deck. The French crew would be uncomfortable for a few days, but that would be all. There were approving looks from the Medinas as they counted the guards and their weapons. There wasn't one of them who didn't know that half the value of the prize belonged to them.

Holbrooke stayed on the quarterdeck until the horizon to the northeast was clear of sails.

'Five cables to windward of the prize, Mister Lynton. Keep a close eye on her and let me know if anything changes or if you sight a sail – any sail. I'll be in my cabin.'

'Aye, aye, sir,' Lynton replied. 'Whittle. Run up to the main crosstrees and watch the deck of that Frenchman, if you value your share of her.'

Holbrooke and Chalmers were taking their ease in the cabin. It was the middle watch, but neither man felt like sleeping and instead they were enjoying a glass of Carlisle's Madeira wine. Serviteur stood in the background, balanced easily against the gentle pitch and roll as *Medina* responded to the quartering sea. The transition from Smart to Serviteur had been seamless. It was Jackson's idea. As soon as he saw the state of Smart, lying moaning in a sickbay cot, he sought out the newest member of the ship's company. 'I've never seen colours like those,' he said to his mates, 'his face looks like sunset over Molly's tavern with a storm brewing, all red and black and pink.'

'He'll have to watch his place, that Jacques looks like the real thing, a thorough gentleman's gentleman,' said Eli. 'Neither the captain nor young Mister Holbrooke will have Smart back after a few days of his service. You mark my words.'

Smart had never been a favourite with the Medinas, he was too puffed up with his own importance, but they'd already taken Serviteur to their hearts. He commanded friendship and respect by his sheer physical presence, by his competent demeanour and above all by his willingness to learn the sailor's arts. Smart would never have made a seaman.

Jackson took Serviteur to the pantry and showed him around. It had taken the freed slave only minutes to feel at home, and by the time Holbrooke returned to the cabin he had a new servant who looked as though he'd been there the whole commission. Serviteur had produced the Madeira after a brief search of the wine storage and was holding it now, in a napkin, waiting for an opportunity to refill the glasses. The very picture of a prosperous gentleman's butler.

'I'm sure the captain won't begrudge us this bottle after the day that we've had,' said Chalmers as he sipped and enjoyed the flavour of toasted sugar. He remembered when Carlisle had introduced him to this fine Madeira on the passage from Portsmouth to Grenada nearly a year ago. So much had happened in that time, not least that he, David Chalmers, who'd never had a spare penny to his name, was at last solvent. The prizes that *Medina* had taken since arriving in the West Indies and the share in these two latest French merchantmen, not to mention the head and gun money for *Outarde*, meant that such luxuries as a new suit of clothes and decent lodgings ashore were no longer out of his reach. He reflected on how it would affect Holbrooke. As he understood the situation, *Medina* would take a half share in these two prizes and Holbrooke, as the legal commanding officer, was entitled to two-eighths of *Medina's* share. That would be a staggering sum for a man who wasn't yet twenty, and it would dwarf his regular lieutenant's pay. It was easy to see how a few years on this station in command of a frigate could set up a man for life.

'I wonder, taking this campaign as a whole – I mean the blockade of Cape François, the action between the battle squadrons and this fight for the convoy – who won? Did we have the better of it or did the French?' asked Chalmers. He was genuinely interested to hear Holbrooke's view, although he was unlikely to take it as a definitive statement. Chalmers could see naval strategy from a unique, largely disinterested outsider's viewpoint, and he'd already seen what wheels there were within wheels, what different perspectives lay under each layer of reasoning that was revealed.

'That's a curious question, David,' said Holbrooke, using the chaplain's Christian name for the first time since he took command. Perhaps it revealed how relaxed he was now that they were on their way back to Port Royal with his mission accomplished. 'I have a view,' he said, 'but I'd be interested to hear yours first.'

Chalmers allowed Serviteur to pour him another glass of Madeira and swirled it against the candlelight. He appeared lost in meditation for perhaps half a minute.

'I remember what Captain Carlisle said about de la Galissonière after Minorca, how he thought that the French admiral understood his mission so much better than poor Mister Byng. De la Galissonière appeared unconcerned that he had to withdraw from the fight and in a British sea-officer that would have been singular in the extreme.' Chalmers took a sip from his glass; he wasn't going to be rushed into an opinion. 'He was unconcerned because his mission was to support de Richelieu's attack on Minorca, not to win a battle at sea. Carlisle's view was vindicated, I believe, when Byng withdrew to Gibraltar leaving the French fleet in command of the Western Mediterranean and in complete control of the re-supply route from Marseilles and Toulon. The battle wasn't important. What mattered was who controlled the sea, the lines of communication and supply. Carlisle's thesis is that while we're the masters of tactics, the French navy excels in that part of the naval art that lies somewhere below strategy but above tactics. Let's call it the *operational art*. I'm inclined to agree with him, and further, I'd say that the mastery of this operational art is dependent upon a complete understanding of the mission, and how that fits into the overall naval strategy. It's no good blindly obeying orders when the strategic situation is changing.'

Holbrooke nodded. He'd also heard Carlisle's views on the subject, but Chalmers was taking it a stage further. As a junior officer, it was uncomfortable to imagine *not* blindly obeying orders – wasn't that why Byng was executed? If the nation could do that to a senior admiral, how easy would it be to hand down a similar sentence to a lieutenant or a commander?

'De Kersaint's mission is to get the convoy safely home to France, where the economy badly needs this injection of wealth. I think we can assume that he wasn't sent across the Atlantic to destroy the Jamaica Squadron.'

'Certainly,' replied Holbrooke, 'it's a good example of a limited mission with clear boundaries. The French know it well; they have to with so many fewer ships than we have. They can't afford to keep ships on station without good cause.'

'To my understanding, all Commodore Forrest had to do was hold his position to the east of Cape François – to windward – and he could prevent the convoy from sailing indefinitely, isn't that so?'

'Yes, that's true,' replied Holbrooke cautiously, they were coming close to criticising the actions of a senior officer and even in the privacy of the cabin, they should be careful. 'Even a small squadron between Monte Christi and Cape François would hold the convoy indefinitely.'

'So, assuming the commodore's mission was to prevent the convoy sailing,' said Chalmers, 'while de Kersaint's was the opposite, it appears to me that the French are the outright winners of this campaign. The convoy has cleared through the islands with a strong escort for the ocean passage, and all for the loss of only two merchantmen and an old frigate.'

'Don't forget the one that ran aground on the Great Sheep,' said Holbrooke laughing. 'Would you accept a challenge to explain his failure to Commodore Forrest when we're back in Port Royal?'

'I would not, but my moral cowardice doesn't invalidate the thesis.'

Holbrooke smiled. 'Well, that's the clearest exposition of that view of naval operations that I've heard, and if you won't confide in the commodore, then at least you should commit it to paper for the education of all sea-officers,' he said, laughing again. 'And for what it's worth, I agree with you, in general.'

'In general, but not in particular, I take that to mean,' said Chalmers. 'If we agree on the principles, what's different in this case?'

'Forgive me if my thoughts aren't yet fully formed, and I'll try to make myself clear.' He was aware of Serviteur pouring him a second glass, but he was such a good servant that it didn't interrupt Holbrooke's thoughts. He took a few turns across the cabin, stooping under the low deckhead.

'What's different in this case?' he mused aloud. 'You said yourself that to understand one's mission one must understand the strategy. Well, let's look at the grandest of strategies. Britain has embarked upon a war for which the country in general and the navy, in particular, wasn't prepared. Anson needs money to build ships and to pay the people, and to get that money he needs political backing. Now, the war has started badly for the navy, and the tragic affair of Admiral Byng was the worst thing that could happen to us. It was the most public acknowledgement of our collective failure. Since then there have been no naval victories to redress the balance of public opinion. Convoys successfully cleared, and privateers captured just don't catch the public's imagination; they need a fleet action or at least a squadron action. If Forrest had blockaded that convoy, or even if he'd destroyed it, the public wouldn't have seen it as a victory, it's just business as usual. But a hard-won fight of three against four – no, four against seven if you count the frigates – where the French are forced to retire leaving ourselves in command of the sea outside one of their principal ports? That resonates throughout Whitehall and into the taverns and gin shops of London and the country. It may not have felt like a significant victory to those of us who fought it, but at this stage of the war, with what's gone before, Anson will certainly parade it as the greatest thing since Hawke's actions in the last war. It's no exaggeration to say that this sort of minor skirmish, if it captures the popular imagination, can rescue governments, loosen purse-strings and bring a smile to the King's face.'

'And the boost to the French war coffers when this convoy reaches port, is that not a consideration?'

'Sure,' replied Holbrooke, 'but in the great race to fund this war, it's nothing, a mere drop in the bucket, compared with the renewed confidence that the City of London will feel in sending its ships to gather in the wealth of the British sugar islands. The revenue from that convoy will disappear without a trace once the French army has been paid.'

Chalmers sat in silence, digesting what he'd heard, nodding gently to himself.

'Bravo,' he said at length. 'I'm convinced, and I see that I need to look beyond the operational to the strategic effect that it creates.'

'And there's one other consideration that must have been weighing on Forrest when he decided to accept battle,' said Holbrooke.

'Byng!' interjected Chalmers.

'Just so. The example that was set, for good or ill, will echo down the generations of sea-officers. Every admiral, commodore and captain will have to weigh his actions against that harsh yardstick. If we can shoot an admiral, the son of a famous naval father who was ennobled for his own victory at Cape Passaro, then nobody is safe.'

'You think that Forrest was influenced by fear of court-martial and death?' asked Chalmers. 'Surely that's a poor way to motivate the people who'll determine whether we win or lose this war.'

'Considered alongside the positive incentives for winning – prize money, promotions, knighthoods, parliamentary seats, peerages – the package works as a whole. It may seem harsh to execute a man merely for making a poor decision, but Byng was happy to accept the rewards of service. The navy made him a rich man, and if he'd succeeded at Minorca, he'd probably have had a baronetcy. Sea-officers have always known the positive side of the balance. Well, Byng's execution has highlighted the negative. Forrest cannot have missed the point.'

'Well,' said Chalmers, 'it appears that sea officers need something more tangible than the warm glow that comes from selflessly serving their country. But of course, I'm part of that system now, and I'll enjoy the fruits of our labours when the prize money is paid!'

CHAPTER THIRTY-ONE

A Sloop of War

Thursday, seventeenth of November 1757
Medina, at Anchor. Port Royal, Jamaica

Medina trailed her little squadron through the well-remembered East Passage. There were a few spectators on the ramparts of Charles Fort taking the evening air. Just a few, for frigates, privateers and prizes were hardly an unusual sight to the inhabitants of Port Royal. The land breeze hadn't yet started and after passing Gun Kay and Rackham's Kay the frigate kept enough way on her in the almost still air to come hard to starboard and ghost into her anchorage opposite the King's Yard. *Blandford* and her prize continued to their own anchorage off Kingston, with *Blandford's* boats towing both vessels.

Two Brothers had reached Port Royal the day before, so the news that the convoy had sailed had already reached the admiral. Bates had told all he knew, that *Outarde* was wrecked on Little Inagua and that all but three of the convoy had sailed clean away through the Caicos Passage and into the broad Atlantic Ocean. Their safe arrival on the western seaboard of France was all but assured; with that strong escort they'd hardly be bothered by British privateers, and the chances of encountering a squadron of men-of-war were slim.

Medina's topsails vanished from the yards as if by magic as the anchor was let go and the cable smoked out of the hawse. After all, this was Port Royal, home of the Jamaica Squadron, the most spit-and-polish of all the naval stations, and a thousand critical seamen in half a dozen men-of-war were watching them.

'There's a boat leaving the King's Yard,' said Midshipman Smith with his telescope to his eye. 'It could be Captain Carlisle,' he added, his face expressionless. They all knew that when Carlisle returned, Holbrooke would revert to first lieutenant, his God-like powers as the captain of a King's ship stripped from him in an instant. Holbrooke had already moved his possessions back into the tiny cabin off the gun deck that was the rightful place for a first lieutenant, and Lynton had moved back into the gunroom, a master's mate once more. There was little to do to complete the transition, just a private reading of Carlisle's commission before a witness and the deed would be done.

'Boat ahoy,' shouted the quartermaster. It was, of course, a formality. By now they could all see Carlisle sitting in the stern-sheets, his hand on the hilt of his sword and no sign of any bandages. He appeared to be fully recovered from his wounds.

The coxswain was about to reply when Carlisle said something to him. Whatever it was, the coxswain wasn't a man to hide his emotions, and his surprise showed.

'Aye, aye,' he replied in a loud voice to the quartermaster's hail. That was the conventional response that indicated a commission officer was in the boat, not the captain of a King's ship. In this case, it declared to all who were listening that the boat's passenger was a post-captain without a command.

Now it was the turn of the people on *Medina's* quarterdeck to show their consternation. They all understood that Carlisle wouldn't be the rightful captain of the frigate until his commission had been read, but it was customary for even a new captain to reply to the hail with the name of his ship. In Carlisle's case, as he was merely resuming an interrupted command, it was strange in the extreme that the answer to the hail was not '*Medina.*'

Holbrooke wasn't sure of his ground, but what he did know was that no sea-officer below the rank of admiral could be piped aboard unless he commanded a King's ship, and by his response to the hail, Carlisle had most emphatically stated that he was not in command.

'No pipes,' he ordered to the bosun's mates, who looked at him as though he'd gone mad, but nevertheless stowed their calls inside their shirts and assumed their best imitation of the attention position.

Carlisle came up the side quickly enough, perhaps he was favouring his shoulder a little, but he appeared to be more agile than half the men on the post-captain's list. Clearly, he was fit to resume command. He smiled at the assembled bosun's mates and sideboys; he knew just what confusion he'd caused and was enjoying it. Holbrooke found his hand being enthusiastically shaken by his captain. Carlisle looked around him at the familiar deck, the familiar faces and felt at home.

'Let's go down to your cabin, Captain Holbrooke,' he said.

Mystified, Holbrooke led the way and turned as though to descend the ladder to the gundeck.

Carlisle grinned, he was evidently relishing the disarray that he'd caused. 'No, you're still the captain until I'm read in,' he said. 'To the great cabin, if you please.'

Holbrooke recognised the scale of the compliment that Carlisle was showing him. Hosking, Lynton, the quartermaster, the bosun's mates, the sideboys and all the people within earshot had heard what Carlisle had said, and many heads nodded in appreciation. They welcomed Carlisle back as the rightful captain of *Medina*, but there wasn't a man who didn't acknowledge that Holbrooke had been an outstanding temporary captain, and they all felt his pain at having to revert to his old position.

'Well, I understand that you're to be congratulated,' said Carlisle. He saw Simmonds hovering at the cabin door, waiting to be called to record the change of command. 'I don't think you'll be needed today,' he said to the clerk.

Carlisle turned back to Holbrooke. 'The admiral will see you in an hour, and it would be fitting if you saw him as the captain of *Medina*, rather than as her first lieutenant. We can read me in tomorrow, and I'll sleep ashore tonight.'

'That's very generous of you, sir,' Holbrooke said with feeling, 'and I see you're fully recovered.' Holbrooke could tell that something was in the wind. His eye briefly caught a glimpse of *Kestrel* lying at anchor just a cable away as *Medina's* stern swung to the light wind. The sloop-of-war was enticingly close, but his rational mind knew that it couldn't be. While *Medina* had been keeping her lonely vigil off Cape François, the admiral would have appointed one of his own followers to command the sloop. This was just Carlisle's way of showing his appreciation for Holbrooke looking after his frigate.

'Yes, the doctor's declared that I'm fit for duty. Lady Chiara's been watching for your return this past month. Apparently I'm a much better husband when I only visit occasionally,' he grinned. 'Now, what of your adventures since I saw you? I have a glowing report of *Medina's* support for his squadron from Commodore Forrest and a somewhat gruff acknowledgement from Captain Bates of your worth in destroying *Outarde*, to allow the privateers to do their work.' He withdrew his pocket watch from his waistcoat, 'we've thirty minutes before you need to be moving,' he said.

Serviteur offered sherry – he'd been told Captain Carlisle's preference and was very keen to make an excellent first impression – it was the coldest sherry that could possibly be achieved between the tropic lines. Carlisle looked at the new servant quizzically.

'Serviteur, sir, your attendant until Smart has recovered from his injury, if you please,' said Jacques in a strong French accent, bowing low.

'Well, welcome aboard, Serviteur,' replied Carlisle, 'I see there is more to be told, Mister Holbrooke.'

Holbrooke related *Medina's* story from the day that they sailed from Port Royal two-and-a-half months before. It was a curious fact of life at sea in a King's ship, that what seemed at the time to be dull and monotonous, when related to those who weren't there, appeared full of action and drama. So, the tale of *Medina* under Holbrooke's command took on an heroic aspect. The long periods of patrolling between Monte Christi and Cape François were lost in the excitement of the battle, the sailing of the convoy and the destruction of *Outarde*.

'A squadron action – it's fast becoming famous, by the way, as *Forrest's Action* or some are rather grandly calling it the *Battle of Cape François* – a French frigate of twice *Medina's* force destroyed and a half share in two of the richest prizes to be brought to Port Royal this war. Your name is starting to be known, Mister Holbrooke, and you'll be able to afford a new coat,' he said, pointing at the sea-worn garment that was Holbrook's best. In truth, the coat would have looked far worse, but Serviteur had discovered it the previous day and laboured hard at cleaning away the salt and various stains.

Jackson steered *Medina's* cutter through the anchorage to Cotes' flagship. *Marlborough* had left the dock two days before and was already in the high state of polish that was expected of the flagship of the Jamaica Squadron. The two men left *Medina* bearing curious personas: Captain Carlisle without a ship and Lieutenant Holbrooke, commanding officer of His Majesty's Frigate *Medina*. It was a strange relationship and one that made Holbrooke uneasy. He felt that something was being kept from him.

'*Medina*!' replied Jackson with lungs of brass in response to the hail from *Marlborough*. He wasn't sure which of the two sea-officers he was referring to, but he was happy to let them sort it out among themselves. The naval protocol would have puzzled even Lord Anson himself. As the senior officer, Carlisle went first through the entry-port but received no pipe. There was then a decent pause until Holbrooke steeped through to the twitter of the salute that was reserved for officers in command. Holbrooke could feel himself blushing, and he feared that he'd stammered his reply to the greeting of the flag captain.

'Let's go straight to the admiral,' said Faulknor. 'Perhaps you'd join us, Carlisle. He's expecting you.'

Admiral Cotes was in good humour. The convoy may have slipped through his fingers but, like Holbrooke and all the sea-officers, he recognised a brave piece of work when he saw it. Forrest's action would be hailed as a great victory by the British people who were starved of good news and starting to doubt the ability of the navy to protect their interests. *Medina's* part was a footnote to history, nothing more than the sort of action that his cruisers were engaged in week-by-week. And yet, *Medina's* battle against the convoy had something a little extra. There was a single-ship fight to be celebrated, and they didn't come along every day, particularly when a twenty-eight-gun frigate utterly destroyed one of forty-four-guns. And of course, Cotes appreciated the one-eighth share of the frigate's half of the prizes that would come to him. He'd been visited by the owner of *Two Brothers*, a planter with political power in the island, who expressed his appreciation of *Medina's* co-operation with his privateer in the most handsome terms.

Holbrooke delivered his report and verbally related the happenings of the past few months. When he described the end of *Outarde*, the admiral nodded appreciatively.

'You say that the convoy and escorts held their course and didn't turn back to help? I expect the two frigates from Cape François will call at Little Inagua Island when they've seen the merchantmen on their way, but I'll send a sloop to look at the wreckage in any case.'

'May I bring to your notice, sir, the acting first lieutenant? Mister Lynton has performed to my greatest satisfaction.'

'You may, Mister Holbrooke,' he replied. 'Make a note, would you?' he said to his secretary. 'But what about you, Mister Holbrooke? What should be your reward?'

Holbrooke couldn't speak, he just stared stupidly at the admiral.

'You must have been disappointed when I gave *Kestrel* to Lieutenant Swift. He was a man with important friends and fully deserving of the step. But he's gone, and now I can more specifically reward merit.'

Time stood still while Holbrooke held his breath.

'I have the greatest pleasure in appointing you to command His Majesty's Sloop-of-War *Kestrel* in the rank of Master and Commander. You are to take command tomorrow and complete her establishment for a two-month cruise. Here's your commission, Captain Holbrooke,' he said handing over an envelope of stiff, cream-coloured paper, 'and given your conduct and the report that I shall make, I've every expectation that their Lordships will confirm by the first packet.'

Holbrooke was in a daze as he was rowed with Carlisle across to Kingston, where Chiara was waiting with a celebratory supper; it appeared that everyone had known except him. But he didn't care. He was a commander with a sleek, fast sixteen-gun ship-rigged sloop, and not yet twenty years of age! And with a sloop of this size, with at least a hundred men, he'd be entitled to a lieutenant and a sailing master, just like a frigate.

They passed *Medina*. The news must have reached Lynton only a few minutes before because he was furiously arranging the hands to cheer ship. It should have been an orderly affair, with every seaman appointed to a place on the masts, the yards or on deck, but the speed with which it had to be accomplished reduced it to a mad scramble as the hands ran up the masts to the first vantage point that they could find. But the cheer was heartfelt all the same.

Jackson brought the boat right into the heart of the busy Kingston commercial wharf and nosed into an improbable gap between two dirty local island boats, busy offloading their cargoes of sugar and indigo to the warehouses, ready for the next convoy. Carlisle stepped ashore first, and Holbrooke followed him but hesitated just a few yards from the boat.

'Excuse me, sir. I haven't given Jackson any instructions to pick me up, and I feel they're owed a few coins for refreshment.'

'Quite right, Holbrooke, you wouldn't want to ignore the traditions.'

Holbrooke turned back just in time to catch the boat before it shoved off.

'Jackson!' he called. 'Share this among the boat's crew, will you? Be back here at eight o'clock.'

'Aye. Aye, sir,' replied Jackson loudly, knuckling his forehead and grinning broadly. There was enough there for a famous run ashore tomorrow. He moved a step closer to Holbrooke. 'In that sloop of yours, sir,' he continued in a low voice, pointing at *Kestrel*, gleaming in the tropical sunshine, 'you'll be needing a good bosun, I expect.'

HISTORICAL EPILOGUES

Maurice Suckling's Nephew

Forty-eight years after the Battle of Cape François to the very day, on the morning of the twenty-first of October 1805, off Cape Trafalgar, the combined fleets of Spain and France were in sight. Vice Admiral Lord Nelson was heard by *Victory's* surgeon to remark that, 'the twenty-first of October was the happiest day in the year among his family,' and several times in the days before Trafalgar he said to Captain Hardy and Doctor Scott, 'the twenty-first of October will be our day.'

After Cape François on the twenty-first of October 1757, Maurice Suckling didn't take part in any more notable actions during his long naval career. If it weren't for his role in bringing his nephew, Horatio Nelson, to sea, his name would have sunk into obscurity long ago.

Nelson had no important naval connections other than his maternal uncle, of whom the whole family was immensely proud. His family annually feasted the anniversary of the Battle of Cape François, and it's entirely reasonable to imagine that it was the story of that action that led Nelson to choose the navy. For Nelson *chose* the navy, he wasn't pushed into it. More-or-less out of the blue he asked his father to write to Maurice Suckling asking if he would take young Horatio to sea. Suckling famously replied, 'What has poor Horace done, who is so weak, that he above all the rest should be sent to rough it at sea? But let him come, and the first time that we go into action, a cannon-ball may blow off his head, and provide for him at once.' Suckling took Nelson as a youngster into his ship *Raisonnable*, a sixty-four-gun third-rate ship-of-the-line.

Without the Battle of Cape François, Nelson may have chosen the church as a career. It would have been the obvious choice for the third son of a country parson, particularly so as neither of his elder brothers chose the cloth. Instead, he went to sea and achieved immortality at Cape St. Vincent, the Nile, Copenhagen and finally at Trafalgar where he lost his life giving his country its greatest naval victory.

De Kersaint's Convoy

Capitaine de Vaisseau Guy François de Coëtnempren, Comte de Kersaint, cleared his forty-one-ship convoy from Cape François in November 1757 and with his four ships-of-the-line, escorted it across the Atlantic without any notable incident. It was a great achievement in the face of the Jamaica Squadron and an excellent example of the maintenance of a naval objective. However, fate had a cruel surprise for him. As he approached the coast of Brittany in early January 1758, a winter storm scattered the merchantmen. By February only fifteen of them had reached their destinations, and it would be months before they were all safely in port.

His men-of-war fared even worse. The captain of the sixty-four-gun Opiniatre was wounded at the battle of Cape François and was put ashore as soon as his ship reached the roadstead at Brest. In his absence the weather worsened, the anchors dragged, and Opiniatre drifted onto the rocks and was destroyed. Meanwhile, the captured British fifty-gun ship *Greenwich* was lost when she ran aground on a small island off the entrance to the roadstead at Brest.

As Holbrooke forecast, the proceeds from the convoy were quickly swallowed by the insatiable French war machine. The naval treasury at Brest had run out of money in early 1758, and although the payment for the cargo in de Kersaint's convoy provided a brief respite, by August, it was again bare, with not an écu to be found.

De Kersaint went on to command the seventy-four-gun *Thésée*. In November 1759 at the Battle of Quiberon Bay, he rushed to the aid of the flagship *Soleil-Royal* as she was assailed by Hawke's *Royal George*. His crew omitted to close her lower deck gun-ports, the sea rushed in as the ship heeled and *Thésée* capsized, killing de Kersaint, two of his sons, and all but twenty-two of his six-hundred-man crew. The gallant De Kersaint deserved better.

The Seven Years War at the end of 1757

B y the end of 1757, Pitt was back in government after his three months in the wilderness following the trial and execution of Admiral Byng, and his grand maritime strategy was starting to take effect.

The French and Austrians were committed to an invasion of Germany where Frederick of Prussia, backed by vast British subsidies, was forcing them to spend huge sums of money for little gain. As a direct consequence, the French navy was starved of cash and men.

Meanwhile, Hawke's Western Squadron effectively prevented a French invasion of Britain while at the same time it complicated the French attempts to reinforce their naval deployments in North America. Although men-of-war occasionally escaped the blockade, merchant ships and navy transports found it increasingly difficult. New France starved, and its armies ran short of the necessities of war. This gave the British navy the freedom to reinforce North America, the West Indies and the East Indies.

As always, the key to the British way of making war was to safeguard its own trade while destroying the enemy's. A convoy system had been instituted early in the war which gave the City of London confidence to invest and kept insurance rates down. Sixth-rates and sloops escorted the merchant ships until they were out of danger, and when they had no convoy to protect, they occupied strategic stations, sometimes far into the Atlantic, where they aggressively suppressed French privateers. In 1757

France lost a total of three hundred and ninety merchant ships to a combination of British navy cruisers and privateers.

In the West Indies, the frigates and sloops of the Leeward Islands and Jamaica squadrons and the ever-present privateers played havoc with the French trade. By the end of 1757 exports to France were dropping towards a quarter of their peacetime volume, while insurance rates rose towards 50 per cent. This exacerbated an already dire situation in the French Royal treasury.

The Toulon squadron had been demobilised after the capture of Minorca and swung impotently at its moorings, leaving the Mediterranean as an operational backwater for the latter part of 1756 and all of 1757.

In the East Indies, where the British navy cooperated extensively with the Honourable East India Company the native Indian rulers were a more significant threat than the French. By early 1757 Calcutta and Fort William had been re-taken from the Nawab of Bengal and his French allies. This success was quickly followed by the taking of Chandernagore, and in June 1757 Clive won the battle of Plassey. All this was made possible by the absence of a significant French force in the East Indies, and by the end of the year, the French Admiral Comte d'Aché still hadn't arrived in the region.

However, the most important theatre of the war was North America, and here the British found it harder to make progress. The fortress at Louisbourg was the key to New France (Canada). It didn't block access to the St. Laurence, but if it remained in French hands, it was just too dangerous to commit a fleet to a passage towards Quebec and on to Upper Canada. The first assault on Louisbourg in 1757 was a failure, and the French positions in New France, the Great Lakes and the Ohio Valley remained as strong as they had been in 1755. However, the cabinet was working up a strategy for 1758 that exploited Britain's unique advantage – its sea-power.

As 1757 ended, Pitt and the navy were poised to turn the war in Britain's favour.

NAUTICAL TERMS

Throughout the centuries, sailors have created their own language to describe the highly technical equipment and processes that they use to live and work at sea. This holds true in the twenty-first century.

When counting the number of nautical terms that I've used in this series of novels, it became evident that a printed book wasn't the best place for them. I've therefore created a glossary of nautical terms on my website:

https://chris-durbin.com/glossary/

My glossary of nautical terms is limited to those that I've used in this series of novels, as they were used in the middle of the eighteenth century. It's intended as a work of reference to accompany the Carlisle and Holbrooke series of naval adventure novels.

Some of the usages of these terms have changed over the years, so this glossary should be used with caution when referring to periods before 1740 or after 1780.

My online glossary isn't exhaustive; a more comprehensive list can be found in Falconer's Universal Dictionary of the Marine, first published in 1769. I haven't counted the number of terms that Falconer has defined, but he fills 328 pages with English language terms, followed by a further eighty-three pages of French translations. It is a monumental work.

An online version of the 1780 edition of The Universal Dictionary (which unfortunately does not include all the excellent diagrams that are in the print version) can be found on this website:

https://archive.org/details/universaldiction00falc

BIBLIOGRAPHY

The following is a selection of the many books that I consulted in researching *The Jamaica Station*.

Sir Julian Corbett wrote the original, definitive text on the Seven Years War. Most later writers use his work as a stepping stone to launch their own.

Corbett, LLM., Sir Julian Stafford. *England in the Seven Years War – Vol. I: A Study in Combined Strategy*: Normandy Press. Kindle Edition.

Three very accessible modern books cover the strategic context and naval operations of the Seven Years War. Daniel Baugh addresses the whole war on land and sea, while Martin Robson concentrates on maritime activities. Jonathan Dull has produced a very readable account from the French perspective.

Baugh, Daniel. *The Global Seven Years War 1754-1763*. Pearson Education 2011. Print.

Robson, Martin. *A History of the Royal Navy, The Seven Years War*. I.B. Taurus, 2016. Print.

Dull, Jonathan, R. *The French Navy and the Seven Years' War*, University of Nebraska Press, 2005. Print

For an interesting perspective on the life of sea officers of the mid-eighteenth century, I'd read Augustus Hervey's Journal, with the cautionary note that while Hervey was by no means typical of the breed, he's very entertaining and devastatingly honest. For a more balanced view I'd read British Naval Captains of the Seven Years War:

Erskine, David (editor). *Augustus Hervey's Journal, The Adventures Afloat and Ashore of a Naval Casanova*: Chatham Publishing, 2002. Print.

McLeod, A.B. *British Naval Captains of the Seven Years War, A View for the Quarterdeck*. The Boydell Press, 2012. Print.

I recommend The Wooden World for an overview of shipboard life and administration during the Seven Years War:

N.A.M Rodger. *The Wooden World, An Anatomy of the Georgian Navy*. Fontana Press, 1986. Print.

THE AUTHOR

Chris Durbin grew up in the seaside town of Porthcawl in South Wales. As a sea cadet, he had his first experience of sailing in the treacherous tideway of the Bristol Channel. He was a crew member on the Porthcawl lifeboat before joining the navy.

Chris spent twenty-four years as a warfare officer in the Royal Navy, serving in all classes of ship from aircraft carriers through destroyers and frigates to the smallest minesweepers. He took part in operational campaigns in the Falkland Islands, the Middle East and the Adriatic. As a personnel exchange officer, he spent two years teaching tactics at a US Navy training centre in San Diego.

On his retirement from the Royal Navy, Chris joined a large American company and spent eighteen years in the aerospace, defence and security industry, including two years on the design team for the Queen Elizabeth class aircraft carriers.

Chris is a graduate of the Britannia Royal Naval College at Dartmouth, the British Army Command and Staff College, the United States Navy War College (where he gained a postgraduate diploma in national security decision-making) and Cambridge University (where he was awarded an MPhil in International Relations).

With a lifelong interest in naval history and a long-standing ambition to write historical fiction, Chris has completed the first three novels in the Carlisle & Holbrooke series, in which a colonial Virginian commands a British navy frigate during the middle years of the eighteenth century.

The series will follow its principal characters through the Seven Years War and into the period of turbulent relations between Britain and her American Colonies in the 1760s. They'll negotiate some thought-provoking loyalty issues when British policy and colonial restlessness lead inexorably to the American Revolution.

Chris lives on the south coast of England, surrounded by hundreds of years of naval history. His three children are all busy growing their own families and careers while Chris and his wife (US Navy, retired) of thirty-six years enjoy sailing their classic dayboat.

FEEDBACK

If you've enjoyed The Jamaica Station, please consider leaving a review on Amazon.

This is the third of a series of books that will follow Carlisle and Holbrooke through the Seven Years War and into the 1760s when relations between Britain and her restless American Colonies are tested to breaking point.

Look out for the fourth in the Carlisle Holbrooke series, coming soon.

You can follow my Blog at:

www.chris-durbin.com

Made in the USA
San Bernardino, CA
10 November 2018